P9-CAX-644

BY
EXECUTIVE
ARRANGEMENT

BY EXECUTIVE ARRANGEMENT

a novel by Taber McMordie

McGRAW-HILL BOOK COMPANY

New York   St. Louis   San Francisco

London   Toronto   Sydney   Mexico   Düsseldorf

1 2 3 4 5 6 7 8 9 BPBP 7 8 3 2 1 0 9

LIBRARY OF CONGRESS CATALOGING IN PUBLICATION DATA
McMordie, Taber L
    By executive arrangement.
    I. Title.
PZ4.M1676By   [PS3563.A3189]   813'.5'4   78-26047
ISBN 0-07-045490-6

For Arthur Nichols

A corporate executive, out of a job
and blacklisted as a result of company politics, finds himself president
of a dummy corporation that launders
illegal dollars.

PROLOGUE

Father Leonard Kody settled himself comfortably in the first-class cabin on the Boeing 747. Rome! Think of it! In a matter of hours now he would be in Rome. Since the day he decided upon the priesthood, he had longed to visit the womb of the Church. In his early years he had begun a campaign to have an official trip to Rome made part of ordination. But that effort had been no more successful than his rise within the clergy. At sixty-two he was still an ordinary parish priest serving a small middle-class church in suburban Chicago.

But Rome was at hand. It seemed like a miracle to Leonard Kody and, like most miracles, it had happened quite suddenly.

Averal Gregg had become a casual communicant of St. Vincent's Church during the spring months, rarely attending Mass more than once every other week. And a man like Averal Gregg was one of the advantages of the priesthood: that is to say, if one of limited means enjoyed personal relationships with people of wealth and intellect. Leonard Kody did.

Over the next few months he and Gregg became regular Friday-night chess champions. At least they did whenever Gregg was not traveling. And occasionally they dined together, at Gregg's expense, at some of the best restaurants in Chicago.

In one sense, there was something curious about his relationship with Gregg. Despite the closeness he felt to this man, he knew virtually nothing at all about him. Gregg had never volunteered any information about himself; career, family, politics, education, all remained his own business. He was particularly adroit at changing the subject inoffensively whenever the priest made oblique approaches to personal areas. The only things Father Kody knew about him were what he observed and felt. Gregg was obviously a very private person, and Father Kody's desire to retain the relationship overrode his otherwise inquisitive tongue. Most of the time.

One evening, the parish library had grown uncomfortably warm and his friend removed his coat. Play had continued for a few minutes when the priest noticed the small monogram on Gregg's left sleeve. Without thinking, he observed aloud that the initials were not those of Averal Gregg. His friend had merely responded with a lament about hotel laundries and their poor system of keeping track of guests' clothing. But even if the initials didn't fit the man, Father Kody observed, the shirt, of understated but obvious quality, most certainly did. As if it had been made for him.

Toward the end of summer, it was with some concern that Father Kody realized almost three weeks had passed with no word from Gregg. The priest telephoned several times, but all his friend's answering service would say was that he was out of town. Then Friday came, and with it a call from Gregg. He was in New York, he said, on his way back from Europe and hoped their chess game was still a possibility for that evening. It was.

Gregg arrived at the appointed time, apologized for his recent absence, and handed the priest a book-sized package, saying it was a simple remembrance, something he had picked up in Rome the week before. It was an exquisite leather-bound Bible.

There was no chess that night as Gregg, with glowing words

and over a hundred pictures, shared his trip to the Vatican with the priest. "How fortunate you are, Averal." Father Kody closed his eyes and there was a wishful, yet serene, smile on his face. "To have seen Rome. The Vatican. I'm afraid my greatest sin today is being extremely covetous of your means."

Gregg stared into the slowly dying fire for a few moments, then looked over and smiled at the priest.

"Do you have the freedom to travel, Leonard?"

"Yes, I have vacation time, if that's what you mean. But I don't understand . . ."

"Leonard, listen to me for a moment." Gregg paused, then continued. "I've done nothing all my life but work, and I've been very fortunate. At forty-six, I'm, well, shall we say very comfortable. A trip to Rome for you would mean nothing to me financially. On the other hand, it would mean a great deal to me personally."

"Dear Lord, I don't know what to say. I . . ."

"Leonard," Gregg interrupted gently, "simply say yes."

*   *   *

As the huge aircraft gathered momentum down the runway and rotated to its more natural airborne configuration, Father Kody said a silent prayer for aerodynamic success and included a special blessing for Averal Gregg.

*   *   *

Three glorious weeks later, at Leonardo da Vinci airport, Father Kody waited patiently for his return flight to be called. But suddenly a premonition swept over him: airplanes sometimes fall. And he did so want Averal Gregg to receive the gift he had bought for him. After a moment's thought, he hurried over to the ticket counter and explained his needs. Then he penned a short note to Gregg, folded it carefully around the gift, and entrusted the small package to the ticket agent to post for him. His flight was called, and Father Kody picked up his bag and walked slowly toward the boarding gate.

*   *   *

The return flight was uneventful except for some periodic turbulence that kept the apprehensive priest from any sustained amount of sleep. And by 11:00 P.M. Leonard Kody was back in his parish house.

He was extremely tired, but not in the least, it seemed, sleepy—a combination of jet lag and the lingering excitement of Rome, he told himself. The housekeeper had thoughtfully prepared some chicken which he retrieved from the refrigerator and, with two glasses of chilled white wine, managed to satisfy his confused stomach. Still wide awake, he decided he would unpack and arrange his things before trying to sleep. But for some reason he had trouble getting the keys for his bag to work.

When Averal Gregg had presented him with the fine, new bag on the eve of his departure, there had been two sets of keys. Maybe the other set would work—if he could remember where he put them. "Ah, yes, here they are," the priest mumbled as he dug them out of the cuff-link tray on his dresser. No. The spare set of keys would not turn the lock either.

He sat on the bed and looked about the small room, trying to imagine how to open the bag. It would be a shame to break the lock, but there seemed to be no alternative. He probed it gently with the small blade of his pocket knife. On the third try the lock yielded.

Fatigued as he was, it took Father Kody a few moments to realize the contents of the bag were not his. His clerical wardrobe was not nearly in such good condition. But it was what lay at the bottom of the bag that caused his sharp intake of breath. Slowly he removed one of the small, clear plastic envelopes and held it up to the light of the bedside lamp.

He stared at it, his time-confused brain struggling to comprehend, when suddenly he heard a sound. Instinctively he sought to hide the thing he held, slipping it quickly underneath the folded comforter at the foot of the bed. Then, turning toward the door, he watched, transfixed, as it opened and a stocky, balding man took one step inside, stopped, and smiled at the priest.

"I see I'm late, Father," he said in a soft, sorrowful voice, nodding at the opened bag on the bed. In his right hand he carried an identical piece of luggage.

Father Kody's eyes widened with fear. His heart pounded. "What are you doing here?" he stammered, dropping back on the bed. "Who are you? What do you mean coming in here?"

"I'm sorry, Father," the man said. "It wasn't planned this way, I assure you." He let the bag he was holding drop to the floor and moved toward the priest. "We simply wanted to exchange *unopened* luggage."

Paralyzed with terror, Father Kody tried to avoid the hands that were slipping quickly under his chin and behind his head. The last thing he saw on earth, before a savage motion suddenly broke his neck, was Averal Gregg's gift—the fine leather-bound Bible, lying on his nightstand.

Cursing softly, the man rolled the lifeless body of the priest off the contents of the bag that had spilled under his fall and began quickly repacking. Nothing appeared to be missing.

Minutes later, on his way out of the room, he paused and looked back at the grotesquely twisted head of the priest and thought how much easier old bones went than the young ones in Vietnam. Then, with a short, satisfied laugh, he hurried down the stairs, opened the back door of the rectory, and went out into the night.

Later that week the Diocesan newspaper reported with regret that Father Leonard Kody had been the unfortunate victim of the increasing violence of our society.

Father Leonard Kody, dutiful servant of God and journeyman cleric, who had returned from the Holy City the very day of his death.

Father Leonard Kody, unwitting accomplice to the most heinous of crimes.

CHAPTER 1

The atmosphere that was beginning to build in the office of Phillip Vanderlind, vice-president of acquisitions and mergers for the Apache Corporation, was, in a word, hostile.

"I'm not at all certain I'm hearing what you're saying," Vanderlind told his immediate superior, Samuel Rogers. "Are you trying to tell me that my promotion has been tabled because I used a club membership belonging to the company to entertain a personal friend? Hell, Sam, the only way you could know that I did was because I attached a personal check to my expense account in payment of the tab. I certainly had nothing to hide and I damn well resent any implication that I've done anything wrong."

Rogers shook his head. "Look, Phillip. Rules are rules. The thing that puzzles me—*and* the executive committee—is why you would deliberately flaunt a company policy. And, I might add, in the face of a direct order."

Vanderlind was stunned. "What do you mean, a direct order? What the hell is going on here, Sam?"

"Back in September you asked if it would be acceptable to use the Blackwatch Club to entertain personal friends. And I told you then what the new policy was. Are you denying that, Phillip?"

"No," admitted Vanderlind. "But that's not the real issue here and you know it, Sam."

"You're wrong, Phillip. It is."

"Look, Sam. What in Christ's name is happening here? Are you telling me my future at Apache has been affected by my—transgression?" He bit the last word off sarcastically.

"Well, yes. At least for a while, Phillip. Yes, it has."

Vanderlind sat perfectly still for a moment, a sort of twisted smile pulling at his mouth, his gray eyes blinking in disbelief. When he spoke it was more to himself than the man across from him. "I'll be goddamned. I'll just be goddamned. Nine years ago I *married* this company, Sam. And it's made a lot of money because of me. And now you're sitting there telling me that my career is in jeopardy because I . . . I can't even bring myself to repeat it, Sam. It's preposterous!"

"I'm sorry you feel that way, Phillip," Rogers said, rising to leave.

"Wait just one damn minute before you walk out that door, Sam." Vanderlind rose and faced his superior angrily. "I'm not totally stupid, my friend. I know what the hell's happening. You've just sold my ass down the river. You've sold out to that impotent bunch of nitwits we call an executive committee . . ."

"Now, just a minute, Phillip . . ."

"No, *you* wait, Sam. I'm going to say it and you're going to listen. Not one of those bastards has liked me since I went up against them on the Hughes acquisition five years ago. It didn't make a damn that I was right. It didn't matter a damn that we saved over a half a million dollars! All that mattered to them was that they were made to look like the half-assed clowns they are. They've been waiting for a shot at me ever since. And when this ridiculous club thing came up, they probably said to you, 'Sam, you're going to have to sit down on that man.' And, so help me God, Sam, I believe you're sacrificing me as your initiation dues to that inner circle of incompetence."

Vanderlind's face was flushed and his shoulders hunched in self-restraint as he glared at the now quite visibly shaken Sam Rogers. Rogers peered at him for a long second. Then, with neither affirmation nor denial, he walked hurriedly out of the office.

For several moments Vanderlind stood staring after Rogers, seemingly paralyzed by what had just occurred. Suddenly he shook himself and went over to the phone on his credenza. He dialed the extension of the chairman of the board and chief executive officer of Apache, David Marsh.

"I'm sorry, Mr. Vanderlind," said the secretary in a somewhat distant voice, "Mr. Marsh has already left for the day. Is there something I can do for you?"

"No, thanks. I just wanted to confirm our luncheon plans for tomorrow."

"Yes, sir. It's in his book. Noon at the yacht club."

For the briefest instant after hanging up, Vanderlind considered calling Marsh at his home. Why not settle this thing immediately? But then he changed his mind. Tomorrow would be soon enough, and he needed time to let the rage that engulfed him recede to a manageable level.

Just outside his office he heard Rogers saying goodbye to someone and turned to catch a glimpse of the older man as he strode out of the executive-office bay toward the elevators. It was absurd that his pending promotion to vice-president for administration of the overall Apache complex could be delayed even a day by the mediocrity that was Samuel Rogers. The nine companies that Vanderlind had searched out, negotiated for, and acquired produced almost 30 percent of Apache's bottom line. And everyone knew it, including David Marsh. It would be an easy matter to step around Sam Rogers.

Dismissing the situation with an absent wave of his hand, Vanderlind lit a cigarette and dug into the stack of papers on his desk. But twenty minutes later, suddenly realizing it was useless to try to concentrate on work, he banged his fist on the desk in exasperation, spoke briefly with his secretary on the intercom, and then left for the day. In less than an hour he was in his new high-rise apartment gazing moodily out across Houston's exclusive residential area of River Oaks, trying to decide how he would handle the situation with Marsh the next day at lunch.

Resignation was a possibility. Vanderlind knew Marsh liked him, thought of him as an outstanding executive. And Apache didn't like to lose good people. Tendering his resignation would be a good way of exposing cheap, political infighting; people would get very serious in a hurry. But maybe that wouldn't be the *smart* way. How could he be certain of Marsh? What if he merely accepted his resignation?

No. Don't be a fool, he told himself. Play the odds. If they wanted a fight, he'd give them one. He would not commit the cardinal career sin of looking for another position as an *unemployed* executive of forty-three. Besides, he needed a steady income. His financial responsibilities were awesome: a former, and very expensive, wife; his only child, a daughter, in college; and a newly emerging life-style as a single man left no margin for miscalculation. No, he thought, if the executive committee was after his hide they were going to have to work for it. And the most propitious course for him to follow at the moment, he decided, was just to lay back and see what the head of the shop had on *his* mind tomorrow at lunch.

Later that night, as he laid aside the book he was reading, switched off the light, and rolled over in his king-sized bed, Phillip Vanderlind was not overly concerned about his future with Apache.

*   *   *

The moment he saw Marsh enter the crowded dining room of the Houston Yacht Club, Phillip suddenly felt uncomfortable. Perhaps he should let the weekend pass before attempting to deal with this situation. But he discarded the idea. Now was the time, and as he rose to greet Marsh something told him that the chairman would bring the matter up if he didn't.

"Well, you couldn't have picked a better spot today, Phillip," Marsh said, shaking hands and nodding toward the bay. "Great weather, great weekend shaping up. You'll be sailing as usual, I suppose?"

"Not as usual, Dave," Phillip said. "I've agreed to crew for a friend in the Soling races rather than cruise my own boat. I just hope to hell the old body can handle it."

A round of drinks and luncheon were consumed over small talk that gradually became clumsy for both men. Finally Marsh leaned back, clasped his hands behind his balding head, and stared questioningly at Phillip for a moment. "Something tells me you're preoccupied with matters not of the sea or food," he said. "Want to tell me what's on your mind, Phillip?"

Relieved that the subject had come up, Phillip smiled. "Okay, Dave. I've got a problem. And I don't quite know how to begin, really, except to come directly to the point. I assume you're aware that my promotion has been tabled. I'd like to hear the reason from you."

"I'm aware, of course, of the action Sam took," said Marsh rather uncomfortably. "And I'll be candid with you, Phillip. It was an absurd action. The reason—that club thing—was preposterous. And I told him so. In fact, just so you understand, I asked for an open discussion and vote in executive committee. Frankly, I was shocked when the vote was unanimously against you. But that's exactly what happened."

"Dave, you have the power to override the committee on personnel matters," Phillip said. "I'm curious to know why you didn't in this case, since you apparently feel as you do."

Marsh looked closely at Phillip. "I think you already know the answer, Phillip. We've got three thousand employees at Apache. The company runs successfully, not because of a few super chiefs here and some misfits there. It's the mainstream that gets the job done. The executive committee is that mainstream. I want it that way. They represent the critical mass and I depend on them to function. Your situation was, unfortunately, something they felt most strongly about, Phillip, and I could not override them because I feel the unity and morale of the company are more important than any individual. In a way, I'm very sorry. In another way, I'm not. Do you understand?"

"I understand the rationale, Dave. But there are still a couple of things I *don't* understand." Phillip looked directly at the chairman. "The club thing was an excuse. Why do you think this thing *really* occurred?"

David Marsh nodded. "All right, Phillip. Let's walk down and take a look at your boat. I'll try and answer your question as we go along."

They left the clubhouse and walked across the lawn toward the bay. "As you know," Marsh began, "I'm somewhat detached from the day-to-day operations of the company. So some of what I am about to say is my own conjecture, the rest mostly hearsay. Not being a technical person, I imagine you had some doubts about what future an engineering company held for you when you came to Apache. But you made the most of your opportunities and you began to move. You're bright, Phillip, bright as hell, and you have an exceptionally analytical mind. But frankly, you're very naïve about human beings. You did your thing, as the kids say, at the expense of a lot of people in this company. Almost every time you looked good someone else looked bad. You ran roughshod through the company. You thought, I guess, that as long as what you did benefited the company, there were no other considerations. But that's where you made your mistake—and a host of envious enemies. And when they saw an opportunity to even the score, they took it."

Marsh paused, gazing out over the deserted bay. Phillip stood on the dock, his coat over his shoulder, looking intently at the older man.

"But all that is in the past, Phillip. Now let me lay it on the line about the future," Marsh continued, his voice taking on a sharper edge. "You have a future, and a good one, at Apache, *if* you want to make some changes. In fact, you'll have to make changes to have *any* future at all. I don't need or want any one-man shows at your level or above. So, as we used to say, either you get it on or get it off. It's just that simple."

A crooked grin crossed Phillip's face. "Another way to say it, Dave, is: don't make any more waves. Just go along to get along. Kiss the right ass at the right time and hope to God you make it to retirement."

"If that's how you wish to interpret it, fine," snapped Marsh.

"I'm not here to *discuss* how I run the company, I'm *telling* you how I run it. And that includes you. The long and the short of it is, if you want to keep your eighty-thousand-dollar-a-year job with all the fringes and options, get in line and stay there. And that means staying right where you are until such time as I'm satisfied you're senior management material, that you can sit in productive concert with your peers and take an even, realistic strain on the rope we all have to pull at Apache. Now, do I make myself clear?"

The two men had reached the slip where Phillip's sailboat was moored. Phillip pushed hard on the forestay and watched the small craft strain against her lines. Then he looked up at Marsh and smiled. "Good for you, Dave. I had that coming. I didn't like it, but I had it coming. The problem is I'm not really certain I know how to react at the moment."

"No reaction or decision is necessary at the moment, Phillip. I think we both understand the parameters of the problem, and that's the important thing." David Marsh's voice eased into a friendlier tone. "You know, Phillip, you haven't taken any time off, to speak of, for the past three years, if memory serves. You must be tired with all the work you've done, the divorce and now . . . Why don't you take a month? Go somewhere, get away, get in touch with yourself, think things through. Then let's talk again. How does that sound?"

Phillip laughed. He knew Marsh was right. God, he was weary. "Okay, Dave, you've got a deal." The two men, knowing the confrontation was over, turned and began walking back toward the clubhouse. "And, Dave, thanks for your candor. I appreciate it."

Marsh nodded and patted him on the back. "Forget it."

Neither man spoke again until they reached the parking lot. Then Marsh said, "Good luck this weekend, Phillip. But don't get so wrapped up in the races that you forget the company party Sunday night. Frances would raise hell with me if you weren't there."

Phillip smiled and waved as he watched Marsh's car pull slowly away. At least Frances Marsh likes me, he thought. But obviously there were a lot of other Apache people who did not.

*   *   *

Late Sunday afternoon, as the small boat approached the windward mark, Phillip wondered again if there was any way he could diplomatically avoid the company party that night.

"C'mon, Phillip, for Christ's sake!" the skipper yelled. "You're standing on the spinnaker halyard."

Phillip stumbled to the foredeck of the pitching boat and began wrestling with the unwieldy sail the crew was trying to strike for the windward leg. They were well back in the fleet and it was, in part, his fault. He knew he'd been a lousy crew the past two days. But he just couldn't keep his mind on the job. He had thanked David Marsh for his candor, but he had not yet been able to come to terms with the revelation that Phillip Vanderlind was far less than the fully adequate human being he'd always thought he was.

No one in his entire life, if he forgot his former wife Kate, had ever told him directly that he was unliked, didn't fit, or didn't have whatever it took to measure up. It seemed absolutely impossible that he could have fooled so many people for so long; everyone, he *thought*, had always marked him as a comer, a winner. And wasn't he? Or at least hadn't he been? But that Sunday afternoon it had suddenly occurred to him that maybe the only person he had ever really fooled was himself.

Three hours later, as he deftly eased his Porsche 911S into the northward stream of Houston-bound traffic on the crowded Gulf Freeway, Phillip sipped at a scotch roadie, then raised the plastic glass in silent tribute to Frances Marsh. The chairman's wife, believing that company parties were incestuous bores, always invited an equal number of non-staff people to the annual pre-Christmas Apache affair. It gave you the opportunity to avoid your associates gracefully if you so preferred. It was also the reason he had finally decided he could handle the party.

Arriving almost an hour late, Phillip virtually had to force his way through the crowd, and it was fully two or three minutes before he saw someone from Apache. He acknowledged the smile of a company wife, then turned in the opposite direction and began looking for a drink. Corporate politics were only part of his discomfort at being here. His divorce had been a hot item of company gossip, and this would be the first time he had been to a party without his popular wife. Christ, what a zoo, he mused, wedging his way in the direction of a small bar in the corner of the garden room. Then suddenly, unexpectedly, he was face to face with Sam Rogers.

"Hello, Phillip. Some crowd, isn't it?"

"Sam," he said, forcing a smile and accepting the hand Rogers offered.

"Dave tells me you two had a talk Friday. Glad everything got worked out. And you really should take that time off. Been intending to suggest it myself."

Despite the fact that Marsh had every right to talk with whomever he wished about a subordinate, Phillip was shocked and surprised; some sort of confidence, he felt, had been violated. Even so, he managed to chat pleasantly enough with Rogers until they got their drinks. What the hell, he thought, Sam only takes orders. But the edge of difference between them now was unmistakable.

When the bartender finally served them, Rogers nodded, smiled, and moved off into the crowd. Phillip shrugged, quickly downed his drink, and asked for another.

"A little hostility there?"

Phillip turned slightly to his left and looked down at an attractive woman in her middle thirties with a mischievous grin on her face, her almost-blond hair pulled tightly back in a bun. "Was that what it was?" he said with a self-conscious laugh.

"*That* was probably too much scotch," the woman said. "I'm sorry. My name is Jessica Westbrook."

"I'm Phillip Vanderlind."

"You're with the company, Phillip?"

"That, too, is obvious, I suppose."

"On the contrary. That's why I asked."

"I *think* that's a compliment. But before I claim it, I'd better ask if you're someone I've missed in the hallowed halls of Apache."

"No. Big Brother isn't watching," she said. "I live in Vail. I just came down to see friends who happen to be friends of the Marshes. I own a small shop there."

"That sounds a hell of a lot better than performing like a trained animal in a large corporation."

"Then why do you do it?"

For an instant Phillip was speechless, not because of the question but because the obvious answers were suddenly no answers at all. But before he could say anything, a tall, well-dressed man his age came up to Jessica and was introduced to him as her date. Then the couple with whom she was staying was there. And still another couple joined the group. Phillip observed them with a manufactured smile. But the more he looked at Jessica Westbrook the more attractive she became. There was breeding in her face: the large, wide-set intelligent eyes, the high cheekbones, the generous mouth gathered on either side by deep smile marks.

And then she was looking past the others and saying—to him, it seemed—"No, actually I'm leaving tomorrow afternoon. I have to go to New York on a buying trip."

Someone tapped him on the shoulder, and by the time Phillip had exchanged pleasantries with the Apache comptroller and turned back toward Jessica, she had disappeared in the crowd. He shrugged, got another drink, and began moving slowly from room to room, touching all the obligatory company bases. Occasionally, during the next hour and a half, he caught glimpses of Jessica, and each time she seemed to be smiling at him when their eyes met.

He spoke to the Marshes. And then, without knowing precisely when it happened, Phillip suddenly realized he had become completely detached from the humanity that swirled and babbled all around him. Like an unseen presence, he was watching, with a growing sense of repugnance, a heavily orchestrated opera of social and career prostitution. The characters were playing parts that seemed all too familiar to him. And, God help him, he was one of them. He wanted to leave. He *had* to leave—this plastic anthill was too much.

He met Jessica Westbrook again near the front door. "Leaving without saying goodbye?" she asked.

"I should have left a long time ago. Why don't you come with me?"

"If that were possible, I would probably have asked *you*," she said.

"Tomorrow then."

"I have to catch a plane at two o'clock."

"I'll take you to the airport. We can have brunch first."

She nodded.

"Meet me at a place in the Montrose area called 'Ruggles.' Ten o'clock?"

Before she could answer or he could ask her where she was staying, her date was back again and then she was gone.

*　　*　　*

He didn't expect she would come. But she did, breathless and embarrassed, at eleven o'clock, explaining that her watch was still set on Mountain time.

They ordered Bloody Marys. "Are you in the habit of meeting strange men in restaurants?" Phillip said with a smile.

"Oh, but I know you very well," Jessica said. "Phillip Vanderlind, native Texan, SMU in the fifties, married, recently divorced, a daughter in Wellesley, and a highly regarded executive in Frances Marsh's husband's company who's not certain he likes where he is."

Phillip felt his face grow warm. "Did Frances tell you that, too?"

"Goodness, no. She thinks of you as the heir apparent, I gather," Jessica said. "No, you just seemed so ill at ease at the party, as if you didn't belong—or *want* to belong. And I suppose, to me anyway, you seem very different from most corporate types I've known."

"And you're very different from anybody else I've ever met at a company party," Phillip said. He signaled their waiter. "I'm going to order us the best trout you've ever tasted. Then, since you seem to know so much about me, I intend to find out, in detail, who you are."

Phillip felt as if he were basking in a warm glow as Jessica told him about her life. She had been born in Massachusetts, where she and her sister grew up and went to school. A year after she graduated from college, she had met and married a young attorney in Boston. They had no children, and after several years of marriage a skiing vacation in Colorado had culminated in the decision to quit the city and stay in the mountains. They bought a small gift shop in Vail, but then her husband died of congenital heart disease and Jessica, with no reason to return to the East, stayed on. That had been two years ago and, while she was barely making it with the shop, she was determined to stick it out.

As he listened to her talk, Phillip suddenly realized how long it had been since *he* had opened himself up to anyone. After his divorce—when he discovered *their* friends had really been Kate's—his only acquaintances had been business-related. Damn, he thought—forty-three and ten years in this city and no friends. Maybe Kate had been right: maybe he *was* an antisocial workaholic.

Then, after the meal was over and coffee was served, it was his turn to talk. He lit a cigarette and smiled at Jessica. "You're right about my not liking where I am. I don't know, maybe I'm going through some sort of mid-life crisis, but I'd like very much to tell you about a couple of things that happened last week at the company. And, well, I guess I'd like an objective opinion from you. Okay?"

"Okay," Jessica said simply.

For the next two hours—until it was time to leave for Jessica's flight and halfway to the airport—Phillip talked about himself and his feelings about Apache. She listened without saying a word until he finally remarked with a grin, "Well, now you see what meeting strangers from company cocktail parties can get you into."

"Not at all," she said. "As a matter of fact, I'm flattered you feel comfortable enough with me to say the things you have."

Phillip laughed self-consciously. "Okay. Now how about that objective opinion?"

"You've told me a lot about the past, Phillip," she said. "And a little about the present. But nothing about the future. Isn't that your real concern?"

"Yes, I suppose it is."

"And you seem to have great contempt for the men who play the corporate game at Apache. If you stay, isn't there the danger of self-contempt?"

They were pulling into the parking area of the terminal then, and when they reached the ticket counter and checked in, Jessica's flight had already been announced. They hurried down the long concourse, and it was not until they reached the departure area that there was a moment to speak again.

Phillip suddenly felt a sense of panic. "Look, when can I see you again?"

"Vail is only two hours or so away," Jessica said. "I'll be back from New York in a few days." She found her checkbook in her handbag and tore out a check. "Here's my address."

"Thank you," he said. "For everything."

"And, Phillip, for what it may be worth, staying where you *know* you don't belong may only be wasting time. I think you can find whatever it is you want. And sooner or later a man like you will have to search anyway." She hesitated, then raised on her tiptoes, kissed him lightly on the cheek, and disappeared through the departure gate.

*   *   *

Phillip had made no plans for his vacation, and on an impulse he flew to Vail. He could think his problem through there, and the opportunity to ski for a few days, and to see Jessica Westbrook again, was too much to resist. But four days later, before Jessica returned from New York, he abruptly cut short his stay and caught the last flight to Denver as darkness and a new snow were beginning to fall. He had the answer he was looking for.

Even on the slopes, Marsh's sentence of conformity had continued to gnaw at Phillip. That, and Jessica's comment about wasting time—which intensified the startling discovery that he was now *middle-aged*—drove him into a deepening depression and concern about himself. Time, it seemed, was running out.

Then one evening, he sought refuge from himself with a young woman he met at the inn where he was staying. But the would-be respite backfired; still with him, apparently, was what his doctor had referred to as "a temporary impotence not uncommon among recently divorced men." Whatever it was, it only served to heighten his anxiety.

The following morning, fearing injury if he tried to push his strained and aching muscles through another day of skiing, Phillip browsed lazily through the village of Vail. He found Jessica's shop and went in but did not identify himself to the salesgirl. That evening something began working in his mind, and he never went back on the slopes.

Now, as the DC-10 climbed out of Stapleton Airport for the Denver-to-Houston flight, Phillip relaxed and thought again about the business people of the small ski resort. Totally absent was the frenzied, paranoid structure of the corporation; people did business on their own terms, there were no meetings to attend, no facades of dress or conduct, no politics or gamesmanship to practice or contend with, and there was no fear, it seemed, of tomorrow. And all of these people had two things in common: they were where they were by *choice*, and they were *happy*. His daughter's generation had a name for it: doing your own thing. Phillip had a name for it, too; he called it *freedom*.

Watching the lights of Denver disappear below him, he thought of someone else: a man he had met in Mexico two years before, a man who did beautiful things with a special kind of clay. Victor Mendoza was free, too.

Phillip knew that everyone had to pay a price for that kind of freedom. The people of the shops of Vail paid with a short selling season, the threat of not having snow, and probably limited incomes. Mendoza struggled with undercapitalization and a lack of management ability. And Phillips' price would be giving up his highly paid position with Apache and risking all the assets he owned.

He knew now what he wanted to do. The only thing left to determine was precisely *how* he was going to do it.

CHAPTER 2

Victor Mendoza leaned over the steering wheel of his jeep and listened for a moment to the wind in the tall grass beside the small mountain airstrip. Then he pulled a telegram from his shirt pocket and reread it. There could be no other conclusion: Phillip Vanderlind would not be flying in for a two-day visit unless there was serious interest on someone's part in Cocatlon, Ltd.

Almost nine months ago, he had casually asked his friend from Texas if perhaps he knew, or could find, someone who would consider investing in his company. At the time, Vanderlind had suggested it would be difficult: Cocatlon, Ltd., was too small and too far away to attract foreign capital. Mendoza knew that and had expected nothing. And so it was with great surprise that he received a call from his friend two weeks earlier asking if he still sought operating and expansion capital. Indeed he did. And, responding to Vanderlind's request, he had that very same day air-mailed a set of Cocatlon's financial statements to Houston.

To Victor Mendoza the function of business was as mystifying as it was distasteful. He was an artisan who survived financially only because, as his accountant told him, he was fortunate enough to take in as much each year as he spent. But that situation could not last much longer. The two power shovels that dug the clay for his ceramics were becoming all but irreparable. One day soon he would either have to buy new ones or become a simple potter in the markets of Mexico City.

Squinting against the glare of the afternoon sun, he saw the growing speck in the eastern sky long before he heard the sound of its engines. And, with a brief prayer that its passenger brought with him both business advice and the hope of a potential investor, Mendoza climbed from the jeep and began walking toward the ancient tin shed that served as a refueling station and passenger terminal.

*   *   *

As the twin Beech roared in low over the small field and pulled up sharply, banking into its downwind leg, Phillip shuddered, wondering if he would have been better off coming in by burro. Even so, he was looking forward to meeting Victor Mendoza again.

In the attaché case behind his seat there was a file over an inch thick with financial projections and marketing data based, to a large extent, on the information supplied him by Mendoza. On paper, at least, it flew: a cash injection of $100,000, plus trade credit of about $200,000, should permit plant and equipment improvement to an operating level capable of producing the quantity of goods needed to exploit profitably the projected market. But all that was blue-sky until Phillip could confirm the actual operation as it existed and determine whether he and Mendoza could work together. Even then, of course, figures would inevitably have to be revised, trade credit actively sought and commitments secured, test marketing conducted, and lines of working capital arranged before he would feel secure in submitting his resignation to Apache and investing the $100,000 or so he estimated his company profit-sharing plan to be worth.

So, as the pilot cut the switches and Phillip stepped out on the starboard wing and waved to the tall, aristocratic Mexican walking out to meet him, he was still not certain his plan would really work.

"*Con mucho gusto*, Victor!" he called.

"*Ah, el placer es mío, como siempre*, Phillip! Welcome to Cocatlon, my friend," Mendoza said, reaching up to help Phillip with his bags.

"Thank you. I hope my sudden decision to fly down hasn't interrupted your schedule."

"There are no schedules here in the mountains," Mendoza said. "Except today. Today, we open a magnificent new deposit of clay in celebration of your visit."

"You do me a great honor, Victor."

"Come then, they are waiting for us."

Less than an hour after the terrific explosion of dynamite that cleared the heavy slabs of rock from the site, two bulldozers had bladed away the debris to expose a section of the delicately veined blue-beige earth from which Victor Mendoza fashioned his uniquely beautiful pottery. In truth, Phillip could not see much difference between this and any other clay he had ever seen. But Mendoza had a monopoly on these deposits. That and Mendoza's skill as an artisan are what had fired his interest in Cocatlon, Ltd.

Digging the clay was, of course, only the first step, and for the rest of the day and into early evening Mendoza guided him through every facet of every operation in the production of his pottery. While it was fascinating, Phillip was dismayed by the obvious obsolescence of much of the equipment. And after dinner that night he voiced his concern.

"It is true," Mendoza agreed. "But then not so bad, I think, as even I had imagined. These," he said, handing some papers to Phillip, "are plans for a new firing system prepared just this week by engineers from the city. With such a system four kilns can do the work of eight. And the cost to make this conversion is less than it would be to repair the present kilns."

Phillip studied the plans and figures for several minutes.

"What could you do with *six* kilns on the new system, running three eight-hour shifts, seven days a week, Victor?"

Mendoza's quick and confident answer corresponded almost exactly with Phillip's own production estimate, but later that night, as he prepared for bed, he cautioned himself against the mounting enthusiasm he felt. He couldn't afford to have his objectivity shaded even the slightest. He still had to assess Cocatlon's books, and that would be the final determinant in the decision to proceed further with his plans.

The job took all of the next day, and just after six o'clock that evening Phillip sighed wearily, rubbed his aching eyes, and walked out of Mendoza's office into the falling dusk. He strode in the direction of the small house where Mendoza and his wife had invited him for dinner. He had made his decision. But what would his host's reaction be, he wondered, when he told him that *he* was the prospective investor?

"You, Phillip? You are interested in Cocatlon?" Mendoza said with surprise as the two men sat together after dinner, smoking and sipping coffee.

"Yes, Victor. I suppose I should have told you. But I was a coward. If I hadn't liked what I saw, I wouldn't have enjoyed saying no to a friend."

"And all the time I thought you looked for others," Mendoza said with a laugh. "Well, then, my friend, I am honored that you look. Do you find my efforts worthy of your interest?"

"Victor, I think you've got a hell of an operation here. In fact, with several ifs that need to be clarified, I think you might just be sitting on a *gold* mine. And, yes, to come to the point, I'm extremely interested—that is, if you would be interested in having me as a partner."

The older man's hand shook slightly as he relit a thin black cigar. "Yes, Phillip, I would like that very much."

What Phillip proposed over the next half hour was simple. Provided he was able to accomplish satisfactorily what he felt were the necessary financial and marketing arrangements, he would buy half of Cocatlon, Ltd., for $100,000 and would function as the chief executive officer responsible mainly for marketing and finance. Mendoza would run the production end of the business. He asked that Mendoza consider the proposition carefully and let him know within a week if he wished to go forward. In the meantime, Phillip would be gathering the data he needed. Assuming all went well, he felt he could give Mendoza a final answer within three weeks.

"Well, Victor, how does that sound? Is it fair, do you think? Are you still interested?"

Mendoza rose silently and gestured for Phillip to follow him. The two men left the house and walked slowly to the edge of the high rimrock overlooking the mining site. Slipping his arm around Phillip's shoulder, Mendoza gazed past him for a moment at the huge strip of barren earth far below them. Then he looked back, his face wreathed in a broad smile, and said, *"Nos haremos ricos y el mundo será nuestro, mi amigo!"*

"Hey, señor. *¿Qué diga, por favor?"* Phillip asked. "What the hell are you saying?"

The smile faded from Mendoza's face as he stepped back and extended his hand. "I say to you, we will make ourselves rich and the world will be ours!"

*　　　*　　　*

The morning after he returned from Mexico, Phillip made an appointment to see David Marsh that same day and had no difficulty arranging for additional time to "finish sorting things out," as he put it to Marsh. And for the next three weeks, his life revolved around airports, banks, heavy-equipment dealers, marketing research and advertising people, lawyers and accountants.

At the end of the second week, when Phillip was virtually certain it was a go-situation, Mendoza had flown up for a two-day series of meetings, and the lawyers, as usual, had a field day with their deal. But when he put his new partner on the plane that Friday night, there were only the formalities of completing the power-shovel deal with a heavy-equipment firm in San Antonio and analyzing the remainder of the marketing data with the research firm in Dallas. Now, it was simply a matter of submitting his resignation to Apache and having the bank that managed the company's profit-sharing funds disburse his pledged participation to the bank from which he had borrowed the $100,000 buy-in money a week earlier.

Looking out across the city from his high-rise apartment on the evening before the day he planned to resign, Phillip was elated by what he had done. All the clichés about the greatest rewards going to those who were gutty enough to take the risks were finally real to him. Yet, as he raised a glass of scotch and drank to himself, he remembered there was someone else to toast. Glancing at his watch, he finished his drink and went over to the phone. It was eight o'clock in Colorado.

"Hello."

"Just how in hell am I supposed to thank you?"

For a moment there was silence. Then Jessica Westbrook laughed. "Thank me for what?"

"I am referring to your supportiveness and insight which, to a large extent, are responsible for the resignation I am about to tender to the Apache Corporation."

"Oh, Phillip. Are you serious?"

He spent the next half hour telling her just how serious he was. And when he was through talking about Cocatlon, he thanked her again for having helped him gain the perspective he needed to accomplish the move.

"You did it, Phillip. I didn't," she said softly. "But if you *really* feel that way, why aren't you up here telling me in person? The skiing is simply fantastic now."

"I was there." Phillip said. "As a matter of fact, that's where I made my decision. I intended to wait for you to come back from New York. But once I made up my mind, I had to get started. Now there's nothing but coolie labor ahead of me for the next several months."

"Well, as one entrepreneur to another, I guess we'll have to settle for late spring after the lifts close and I can come to Houston again."

"I saw your shop," Phillip said. "It's beautiful."

"But still not very profitable," Jessica said sadly.

"How would you like to handle an exclusive line of Mexican pottery?" Phillip asked.

"I'd like nothing better."

"I'll be damned," Phillip said. "I just made my first sale."

Their conversation ended with laughter and promises to stay in touch, and when Phillip hung up he was disappointed that he would not be able to see her sometime soon. But then he refilled his glass, sat down at his desk, and began to type the final draft of his letter of resignation to Apache.

*   *   *

"Well, congratulations, Phillip," David Marsh said with a grin, leaning back in his chair and shaking his head. "You've really gone and done it." He held the dinner plate Phillip had given him up to the light. "Beautiful stuff. It almost looks like porcelain. How long do you think it'll take you to turn the operation around?"

"No more than four or five months, I hope, to retool, set the markets, get channels of distribution open—that sort of thing. But in terms of the bottom line, well, things are going to be very tight for the next eighteen months or so. The cash-flow situation is going to be especially critical. I have a feeling I'm going to miss that salary check I've been used to seeing for so long. But we're going to make it, Dave."

"I'm sure you will, Phillip. And I'm delighted for you, especially in view of the talk we had before Christmas. You had a good future here at Apache, and we hate like hell to lose you. But some men are born to do things their own way. And you're one of them. I think you've found your niche, Phillip." He paused and smiled. "Now, why don't we run up to the club, have a drink and talk about Apache. I know you're anxious to cut loose as soon as possible."

Two weeks later, Phillip took one last look around his now bare office, shrugged, and walked out to meet the chairman of the board for a farewell lunch in Apache's executive dining room. Later that afternoon, he would board a Pan Am flight to Mexico City, and the following day *he* would be the chief executive officer at a meeting of his own company.

* * *

As he watched Marsh and Vanderlind leave the executive dining room, conversing and joking in comfortable familiarity, Samuel Rogers again felt the pangs of jealousy and resentment. By all that was right, *he* should have the close relationship with Marsh, not Vanderlind. But Rogers didn't and knew he never would, even with Vanderlind leaving the company. All right, Vanderlind had been good—maybe, at times, even brilliant. Rogers had no trouble acknowledging that. In fact, he had used Vanderlind's abilities to enhance his own stature at Apache. But Vanderlind had risen too far, too fast, and once he had gained Marsh's confidence, Rogers realized that he had become a threat to his own ambitions to succeed to the presidency of the company. There were others at Apache who felt equally threatened, and when Vanderlind made one small slip, they had been quick and deadly.

Rogers had been secretly delighted when Vanderlind handed in his resignation. But his joy was short-lived. Just that morning David Marsh had announced a partial reorganization of Apache: Vanderlind's operation had been discontinued, and the president of one of the subsidiary companies had been named to replace him until June, when the man would become the new president of Apache. Samuel Rogers would remain exactly where he was in the organization. If he was lucky, he might even retire there. And all because of that cocky, manipulating bastard Vanderlind.

The irony of it all was that even in defeat, Vanderlind was victorious. Rogers had always played the game the company way, and now he was stuck with it. The whole thing was sickening. It was unfair. Life was unfair. He hoped Phillip Vanderlind would fall on his ass.

* * *

On the return flight from Mexico City, Phillip sipped at his second scotch and looked at the rough, chapped hand that held the glass; the other one was even worse. That damn Mendoza, he thought to himself. His partner had taken him literally when Phillip said he wanted to spend some time learning the operation from the ground up. For three solid weeks he had done just that: everything from running a power shovel to packing the product for shipment. And it had been an exhilarating experience. But now, as the 727 began its final descent into Houston, he couldn't think of anything more appealing than the comfort of an executive office once again. Which, he remembered, should be waiting for him in the Greenway Plaza complex, if the office-furniture people and the decorator had done their jobs.

It was just after nine o'clock in the evening when he landed, and five minutes later, as he was about to step onto the escalator to the baggage-claim area, he heard his name called.

"Phillip! Phillip Vanderlind!"

He turned, looking in the direction of the voice. It was a woman's voice, but he saw no one he recognized in the mass of people busily crossing the lobby of the terminal.

"Phillip?" It was a question this time. "Is it you?"

Then he saw her. She was standing a few steps directly behind him, a chic leather carry-on over one shoulder and a handbag over the other, staring at him with an uncertain look.

"Polly. Polly Savitch! I'll be damned," he said, walking over to her. "I didn't recognize you behind those sunglasses."

"I recognized *you* immediately," she said, taking his hand and kissing him lightly on the mouth. "How are you, darling? I hear you're making pots of money in Mexico these days."

"Well, pots at least," he said with a laugh. "We're going to get trampled here," he said, suddenly aware that they were standing too close to the busy escalator. He took her arm and guided her away from the crowd. "You coming or going? I thought I'd heard you'd moved to New York."

"A divine apartment on East Sixty-eighth. You must come see me. But I can't forget my old friends in Swamp City, can I? And to answer your question. I'm leaving. A marvelous party in Beverly Hills tomorrow night. But my flight has been delayed for some reason. Buy a lonely traveling girl a drink while she waits?"

"My pleasure."

Phillip had known Polly Savitch, in a passing sort of way, for at least five years. Apache had constructed some oil rigs for Charlie Savitch in earlier times. Savitch, more bravado than anything else, was heir to a family fortune that he had been trying to dissipate under the pretense of being an independent oil man. But Apache hadn't cared; Savitch had the money to pay for the work.

He and Kate, before their divorce, had entertained the Savitches on occasions, one of the unavoidable duties that befell high-level corporate officials. But it hadn't been totally unpleasant. Phillip thought that Polly Savitch was, out and out, the most sensual woman he had ever known. Just why, he was never quite certain. Efforts at describing her never seemed to get much past the vital statistics of medium height, dark hair, and a good figure. It was how she put everything together, he supposed: the manner of speech, the smile, the way she moved, her clothes, and the way she wore them. She had received a more than generous settlement when she divorced Charlie, and for a year or so she had cut a wide social swath in Houston until she moved to New York and, Phillip imagined, greener pastures.

Kate had always been amused by his attraction to Polly. And once when he was teasing her about Polly being so chic and sexy, she had put an end to the subject by observing that a woman like Polly would find nothing very interesting in a man like Phillip. Well, he had had to admit that Kate was probably right. He wasn't a high-roller or a partygoer; he had never had any interest in keeping up with, much less satisfying sexually, a woman like Polly. But now, as he laughed at something she said and watched her mouth caressing the rim of the martini glass she held, he thought it would be a hell of a kick to try.

"But, darling, you must come to Los Angeles. Here you are: attractive, divorced, president of your own company. What's the point of being independent if you won't even take time out for a little party?"

"Poor folks have poor ways, I guess," Phillip said. "Besides, as much as you get around, there's bound to be a party here in Houston some time soon. How about a rain check?"

"I'll hold you to that." She smiled coquettishly and, leaning toward him, let her wet mouth brush his in a teasing half kiss. Then, suddenly noticing the time, she pulled away and stood up. "Well, I suppose I'd better see what's happened to my flight. Sorry to run, darling. Thanks for the drink. See you soon."

He watched her as she hurried toward the concourse, stopping at the last moment to turn and blow him a kiss. He wished, in a way, that he could have gone with her. But then he shrugged, paid the check, and went down to claim his luggage.

When he reached his apartment an hour later, the phone was ringing. It was Polly Savitch; she had missed her flight and it was really too boring to go all the way back to the friends she had just left. Airport hotels were so depressing and would Phillip mind terribly? She arrived just after midnight, and the moment he opened the door he knew he had passed through his post-divorce sexual hangup.

In the dim light of the small entry, Polly dropped her carry-on and looked up at him from under a mass of dark hair. "You know, don't you, I never miss flights?" she said softly.

Phillip felt his pulse begin to pound as she leaned slowly into him, her legs straddling one of his. "What about the big party?" he breathed, pulling her slowly up his body.

"Flights all day tomorrow, darling. It's just that I had this fantastic urge—" her voice trailed off into his opening mouth, then seconds later she pulled slightly back—"to have you ball my brains out tonight."

*   *   *

For the next four months, Phillip never worked harder in his life—or enjoyed it more. He resented the ultimate fatigue that finally drove him to bed at night, and his sleep was less than sound with the anticipation of the next day. But he was alive and his own man at last.

And whenever he was in Houston for a week or more at a time, Polly Savitch flew down to join him. He considered it something of a blessing that his travel schedule was a heavy one; never before had a woman turned him on so completely, so consistently. He hadn't realized it was possible to party half the night, screw the other half, work twelve to fourteen hours, and then repeat the process. But Polly took him into the inner circle of the city's fast track where other men, rolling high like Phillip, played. Their life-style had always fascinated him, and he was privately pleased to discover he could run with the best of them. There was only one requirement—money.

He was still careful of the way he spent his, but his predictions for Cocatlon were fast becoming a reality. The new equipment was in place, and the kiln conversion had been completed. Thirty manufacturers' reps were selling the line, and orders were being shipped to major department stores across the country. By the end of the first week in May, phase one of the turn-around had been achieved: Cocatlon, like a finely tuned athlete at the point of competition, was poised and ready.

Phillip slumped back from his desk, pitched a pencil high in the air, and watched it land in the heap of files and boxes in the corner of his office. God, he was exhausted. Massaging his face for a moment with both hands, he heaved a long sigh, then reached for the phone.

"¿*Cómo está*, Phillip? I was waiting for your call."

"Well, Victor, we made it—four months, almost to the day. And I think you'll be impressed with the report I've prepared for you." He paused, dreading the thought of any more travel for a while. "Shall I come on down, or would you like to come to Houston?"

Mendoza was silent for a moment. When he finally spoke, his voice was weary but happy. "Phillip, four months we have worked like peons. It is time we rest. May I make a suggestion? Come to Acapulco. We can meet there. We will celebrate a little, lie in the sun, drink, make love to our women. Then we can talk of business. There is time. It will be my present to you, my friend."

*   *   *

On the afternoon of the fourth and last day of their meeting, clouds were beginning to build out to sea, but the sky over Acapulco was still a deep blue and the waters of the bay sparkled brilliantly in the hot sun.

Phillip pushed his dark glasses back over his eyes and

pretended to be napping. They were an incongruous group, he thought: he and Polly with the graying, dignified Mendoza and the small, dark woman who was his devoted wife. Señora Mendoza spoke very little English, and he wondered what she thought of the flamboyant Polly. She seemed to know someone wherever they went, and they went everywhere—restaurants, nightclubs, discos. The Mendozas always left them after dinner to retire early, while Polly and Phillip danced and drank and made love far into the night. And this was supposed to be a rest, Phillip thought with a smile.

He raised his glasses and saw Polly talking to a younger man at the pool's edge. Another friend, he supposed. A moment later she rose and started toward him. She was dressed in a minuscule red bikini, and everyone around the pool turned to stare. Phillip felt the pride of ownership. Polly was only one of the many luxuries he would soon be able to afford.

They dressed for dinner at the hotel with the Mendozas, but that night they all decided to go to bed early. And by ten o'clock he and Polly were snuggled on the sofa in their suite, watching a late-spring storm over the Pacific.

"What are you smiling at?" Polly said.

"I was just remembering the way you looked in that bikini," he said. "You probably have the sexiest legs in the country, my dear."

"Oh, well then . . ." She was lying stretched out, her legs crossed at the ankles. Slowly, she drew her left leg up and ran her hand provocatively under her calf, letting it slide to mid-thigh. She straightened her leg, holding it up for him to admire. "Is that better?"

"That's only part of the package," Phillip said, standing suddenly and holding out his hand. "Come on, the bed's better."

As they walked slowly into the next room, he began to unbutton the Mexican party shirt he was wearing. "Wait," she said softly, "let me do it." And when the last button was undone, she looked up at him with a playful but sensual expression. "Let me make love to you. Let it be my turn to do whatever I want, yours to take whatever I give. Okay?"

"Okay."

She undressed him quickly. They stood beside the bed, and Polly, still fully clothed, began at his lips and slowly traced a weaving line with her tongue down his body until his half-erection was only inches from her face. She pushed him gently onto the bed. "I love to feel it get big and hard in my mouth," she whispered softly as her lips closed over him.

Phillip's head spun and he felt himself go instantly hard. For what seemed an eternity, Polly sucked at him, letting her body move in all positions over and around him. As a stockinged leg brushed across his face and her skirt covered his chest, he made an effort to turn her around and pull her face to his mouth.

"Not now, darling. Remember it's my turn," Polly whispered.

She continued to caress him with her tongue. Then she moved abruptly away, positioning her body toward the side of the bed, one leg sliding up behind his head, the other across his chest. Then her hips began to move.

In the dim light of the bedside lamp, Phillip suddenly realized what was happening. She was beginning to masturbate. With her free hand, she unbuttoned her dress and began playing with her nipples. She raised her head slightly and smiled at him. "Like this, baby? Is it sexy for you?"

"Oh God, yes, it's fantastic! But what do I do? I mean . . ."

"Just lie still and enjoy it, darling." She slid a second finger into herself and then raised her head again. "Who do you do it with when I'm not around?"

"Does my making it with somebody else bother you?" he teased her.

"Of course not. It's very sexy to think about." She thrust her hips forward, taking three fingers deep inside her now. "It turns me on to think about you with another woman." She moaned. "Does it turn you on, too—me with another man?"

Phillip was startled at the suggestion. "I haven't really thought about it before," he said.

Polly continued the same provocative pace with her hand. "Maybe if I told you about the last man I was with, you could see?"

"Okay," he said huskily. Never in his life would he have

thought that the picture of another man with his woman could excite him. But what was happening tonight was different.

"His name was Jeff," Polly said. "He liked to call me his 'cunt.' He even gave me a ring with 'cunt' engraved on it. He had a massive cock, baby, and when he balled me, it was heaven. The last time we screwed . . ." She stopped talking and moved suddenly to a position on all fours across his body and took him in her mouth again. Her heels were on either side of his head, her skirt was up over her hips, and he watched her hand move with renewed intensity.

She let her mouth slide off him again and began stroking him with her other hand. "The last time he screwed me, I came so many times . . ." She reversed her position again suddenly, spinning on his body and shoving him deep into her for the first time. That was all it took. He came almost instantly. Thrusting violently upward in the orgasm, he rolled over on top of her and drove until he was completely spent.

*   *   *

It was a heavenly day, Polly thought as she emerged from the shower the following morning, slipped into a terry-cloth robe, and went out on the balcony of their suite. Phillip had taken Victor Mendoza and his wife to the airport for their flight to Mexico City, and she would be leaving that afternoon for Cuernavaca and a week with friends there before flying on to Houston to see him again.

Watching the mid-morning beach crowd below, she tingled warmly with the memory of the night before. Phillip was beginning to show the sexual potential she wanted in a man. Now, it should only be a matter of how fast she wanted him to progress. But not too fast, she warned herself; it would be senseless to risk turning him off when there were so many other ways to get what she wanted. Because she had already decided that what she wanted most from Phillip was his name. It was obvious she had picked a winner this time: looks, ambition, the ability to learn to enjoy her kind of life and—very soon now—the money to pay for it.

Suddenly her thoughts were interrupted by the phone. She ran back inside to answer it. It was a man's voice. "Still sound as interesting as it did by the pool yesterday afternoon, babe?"

"I thought you'd never call," Polly said. "Is your friend with you?"

"We're in 1209. Oh, and, Polly, if you've got some stuff, bring it along."

Slipping quickly into stockings and heels and a low-cut sun dress, she felt herself going wet with anticipation. She had made it with this young man before. And this time, the idea of two men sounded irresistible. She hoped she could take them both simultaneously—with a good jolt to help her relax.

From an overnight case she took a large antique brooch, clicked open the false back, and shook out three capsules of high-grade cocaine. Slipping them quickly into her bag, she paused for a moment in front of the full-length mirror, then smiled and went hurriedly out of the suite.

*   *   *

On Saturday morning, the third day back from Acapulco, Phillip powered his Pearson-30 out of the Houston Yacht Club and turned southward toward Galveston Island. It was the first time in four months he had been aboard his boat, but he had a sudden urge to be completely alone for a day or so, and sailing to Redfish Reef and anchoring for the night was an excellent solution.

The weather was perfect. In fact, life itself was almost perfect, he thought as he switched off the engine and quickly set a working jib and mainsail. Glancing at the time, he remembered that Mendoza would be leaving Mexico City for Cocatlon sometime that day. His partner had gone to the city for meetings with two representatives of South American companies interested in their line.

Tacking across the ship channel, he wished Polly had come back with him. And, for the next few minutes, he fantasized what marriage to her would be like. She was obviously interested. But he wasn't sure he was. Not enough money, at least not yet, he thought. And maybe never enough physical stamina. And marriage to anyone, anytime soon, was just simply out of the question.

Then, as the reef came up off the starboard bow, he busied himself with the approach and wondered if he had brought enough ice and beer to last through the next day.

*   *   *

The light, twin-engine Cessna broke ground at the Mexico City airport and began punching its way through the dark mass of clouds that had moved in over the city in the early-morning hours. In the right-hand seat, Victor Mendoza braced himself for the turbulence he knew would come. He hadn't liked the idea of flying in such bad weather, but he wanted to get back to Cocatlon. He had work to do.

Contrary to his expectations, the turbulence was very mild. Only a bump here and there. And all at once they broke through on top into dazzling sunlight. The young charter pilot turned and grinned at him. "That was not so bad, now was it, Señor Mendoza?"

"No. But still, I do not like weather like this." Mendoza stared out his window at the endless layer of billowy white below. Why should such soft beauty hold so much fear for him? he wondered. Suddenly his attention was diverted. A thin line of black smoke streamed from the starboard engine.

"There's smoke from the engine," he shouted.

The pilot looked quickly out the window, scanned the instrument panel, and immediately shut down the smoking engine. Mendoza's eyes grew wide with terror as he watched the propeller slow and stop, the blades themselves rotating to reduce the drag of the dead engine.

"Do not be overly alarmed, Señor Mendoza," the pilot said. "This airplane was designed to fly on only one engine if necessary." He switched on his radio and calmly advised the Mexico City airport of the emergency, requesting permission to return. But he was told the weather had worsened since their departure and the airport was now below minimums for the Cessna.

After reviewing his charts, the pilot reported his decision. "Mexico City, this is Cessna Twenty-four Delta. We are diverting to a small strip south of Morelia. Will advise on arrival. Twenty-four Delta out."

"Roger, Twenty-four Delta. We acknowledge your alternate. Weather appears acceptable in the area. Please notify upon arrival. Good luck, Twenty-four Delta. Mexico City out."

"Well, Señor Mendoza, we have only a short distance to go. We must begin letting down now for our landing. Please be sure your seat belt is tight. Once we are through the clouds, you will see our destination."

What both men saw as they came out of the clouds, at barely 500 feet, was a mountain directly in their flight path less than 200 yards away. For an instant, the pilot seemed to freeze; should he turn left or right? There was clearance either way, but he reacted to the right. Mendoza's breath sucked in suddenly as the aircraft, its left engine pulling against no resistance in the direction of the turn, whipped into a tight spin. At 500 feet of altitude, recovery was impossible.

There was no explosion. Only the splintering crash of 8,000 pounds of metal dropping out of the sky jarred the peace of the Mexican jungle. And within minutes of the impact, the jungle sounds began again: chattering monkeys, screeching birds, buzzing insects, dripping water. A small green monkey tugged at a glittering object, gently at first, then with a harder jerk. It came free, and the animal scurried off with its new possession. It hardly mattered. Victor Mendoza had no further need for his gold St. Christopher's medal.

*　　*　　*

The blue-hulled sloop rode easily to her anchor in the protected waters off Redfish Reef in Galveston Bay. But below, Phillip tossed relentlessly in his bunk. Finally, the noise and smell of a diesel-powered shrimp boat, in concert with several determined flies, drove him from the cabin out into the cockpit. He sat for a moment squinting in the early-morning sun. It would be a hot but beautiful day, he thought, which then made him wonder why he felt chilled and depressed.

CHAPTER 3

It was a handsome office, although its occupant had not had either the time or the inclination to decorate it personally. Instead, an interior-design firm responsible for something he had seen in *Architectural Digest* had been sought out and retained. Only a brief list of the owner's personal preferences had been provided, and no budget had been imposed. Averal Sutherland was pleased with the result. As chairman of the board of Kaufman Industries, the sprawling, international conglomerate, he was accustomed to the best. Of everything.

"Averal, the others are here," announced his executive assistant, Emile Novak, over the intercom.

"Thank you, Emile. If you'll just see them comfortably settled in the conference room, I'll be there in a moment."

Grudgingly, Sutherland pulled himself away from the view of the East River, walked to the spacious bath and dressing area at the far end of his office, and splashed his face with cold water. He smiled approvingly at his reflection in the mirrored wall: the almost unlined features of a patrician face, the full—if graying—head of carefully trimmed hair. At fifty-five, he was extraordinarily fit and, he was certain, the envy of most of his peers.

He selected a double-breasted Savile Row blazer to wear over his monogrammed shirt, and after adjusting a softly knotted burgundy tie, he left the office to preside over a special meeting of the board of directors. But it was *not* the board of Kaufman Industries. For, in addition to—and quite secretly apart from—running Kaufman, Averal Sutherland had his own private company: the Beta Group.

In some ways, Kaufman and Beta were alike. Both oversaw diverse operations in a number of areas, both were extremely well financed and managed, both produced above-average returns on invested capital. But there the similarity ended. For Kaufman was a venerable, immensely rich, publicly held company employing over 12,000 people worldwide, with interests in oil, shipping, defense-related electronics, steel, and a variety of smaller, less important operations.

Beta, by contrast, held title to nothing, had no assets and no employees—as such. In fact, Beta was not even a formal business entity. Its sole function was tracking and recording the operations and profitability of three small corporations located respectively in the cities of Los Angeles, St. Louis, and Chicago, from which each corporate president and Averal Sutherland made enormous sums of money.

Sutherland strode into the conference room and cordially greeted the three men who were waiting for him. Arthur Brenner, fifty-one, with a sharp and somewhat austere face, was president of Alliance Manufacturing. Located in St. Louis, Alliance produced unsophisticated yet highly profitable steel-wire products for the building industry. Before coming to Beta, Brenner had been a commodities trader in Chicago. Since the secret to high profit in his business was the ability to negotiate and buy raw materials in a highly volatile market, Brenner was well suited to his position.

Richard Manning headed Triangle Ventures in Los Angeles, a

commercial real-estate firm active in the areas of trading, investing, and developing. He was a tense and suspicious man, but at thirty-eight he was the youngest and perhaps the brightest of the three subsidiary presidents. Commercial banking had been Manning's field before real estate.

Paul Nichols Haverman, formerly in advertising, was the most relaxed and informal man of the entire group. His slightly shaggy hair and the studied casualness of his wardrobe made him look like a college professor. He was the president of the Rambo Corporation, which was engaged in franchising with headquarters in Chicago. Each of these three men were millionaires many times over from their respective operations. Each would grow much richer in the years ahead. It was simply a matter of time.

Sutherland called the meeting to order and began. "Thank you, gentlemen, for making the effort to get here this afternoon on such short notice. As I mentioned to each of you by phone last week, we have a problem. We must accelerate efforts to launch our leasing company. Investor funds are beginning to exert pressure. And, I don't have to tell you, we must be timely."

"How much lead time do you anticipate we have?" Arthur Brenner asked. "I mean before we actually run the risk of endangering our sources."

"We have four, perhaps six months to conclude the entire matter."

"Averal," Richard Manning said, "I assume the arrangement will be the same for the leasing operation as it is for each of us."

"Yes, certainly. Do you know of any reason why it shouldn't be, Richard?"

"No," Manning replied. "I suppose I just wanted clarification."

"Have you made any progress, Averal, in finding an owner for this?" Paul Haverman asked, casually patting the back of the elegant chair beside him.

There were a total of seven chairs around the conference table. Three of them were empty, but according to the plan, which had not changed since the inception of Beta three and a half years ago, a new chair was to be occupied every eighteen months. Eventually there would be six operating companies in the Beta Group.

"No, I haven't, frankly," Sutherland replied. "And I must say I am a bit concerned. Good people are very scarce. But you may rest assured that the selection will conform precisely to our standards. However, we do have a timing problem and we must begin without our new member. To that end, I've prepared a brief outline of interim procedures which you will find in the folders before you."

The three presidents scanned the outline. After a few moments, Richard Manning cleared his throat and looked apprehensively at Sutherland.

Cocking his head slightly toward the man, Sutherland asked, "Something disturbs you, Richard?"

"Yes, it does, Averal. I know, of course, how much confidence you place in Emile Novak. But I, for one, would not be too thrilled to find him as the executive vice-president of a company I'd just become president of. I'm thinking, of course, about our new partner."

"And I must consider the whole of the situation, Richard. Thank you for your thoughts, but we must begin *now*. So if there are no further comments, Novak will go to San Francisco to start up the leasing operation. We will leave all we possibly can for the new man, but work must commence immediately."

There were no further objections from Haverman and Brenner. They accepted Novak for what he was: Sutherland's right hand. To the extent that Sutherland's time for Beta was very limited by his responsibilities to Kaufman, no one quarreled with the necessity of someone being in day-to-day command of Beta. But that did not mean that they liked or even trusted Emile Novak.

Of all three presidents, however, it was Manning who had the most cause for his feelings, which, unlike the feelings of his colleagues, included fear. A year earlier, he and Novak had been attacked by a Doberman as they crossed a section of Central Park. Manning had frozen where he stood. But Novak had calmly crouched, caught the dog's lunge on his forearm, then, with a quick snapping motion of both arms, broke the animal's neck. Manning had served four years as an Army Ranger and he knew a trained killer when he saw one.

But the curious thing about Novak was that he didn't look the part. Slightly overweight and balding, he wore a perpetual sad smile that perfectly complemented a soft voice and almost hesitant manner. To complete the contradiction, the man held a degree in accounting, was an expert in the field of taxation, and had even represented Averal Sutherland before the IRS on several occasions.

Manning decided it was worth one last effort to try to keep Novak out of actual participation in the new leasing company. In his mind, it could set a precedent, and one day he might find Novak assigned to *his* operation. "Averal," he said, "before we get into the quarterly reports, I do have one last thought."

Sutherland nodded.

"Why wouldn't it be as well for one of us—and I would be happy to volunteer—to handle the leasing operation at first? We are all more experienced in such matters, and I'm sure it will be an inconvenience to you not to have Novak close at hand."

"*Greed*, Richard." Sutherland let the word register. "Greed must be managed—yours, mine, everyone's. Emile works for the Beta Group, not for himself. Is that a satisfactory answer to your question?"

Manning only shrugged and began pulling papers from his briefcase. Sutherland's eyes narrowed almost imperceptibly for a split second, then he smiled. "All right, gentlemen, how have we done this last quarter?"

An hour and a half later, after each president's report had been thoroughly reviewed, Sutherland adjourned the meeting, chatted informally but briefly with everyone, then said goodbye. But as he accompanied the group to the elevators, he asked Manning, with a slight motion of his head, to stay.

After the others had gone, Sutherland put his hand on Manning's shoulder. "Richard, come in for a moment," he said, gesturing toward his office, "and let's find out what you really have on your mind."

"First of all," Manning said when the two men were seated in Sutherland's office, "I don't appreciate the implication that my offer to start up the leasing operation was motivated by greed. But since you raised the subject of money, Averal, I've got to say that for the risks we take, I think we should have a greater share."

Sutherland nodded and was silent for a moment. "Is it just possible, Richard, that you feel unrewarded financially, not because your rewards fall short of your risks but because you resent the share that comes to me?"

"Is there any doubt that *my* risks are greater than yours?"

"Your greatest risk is Richard Manning," Sutherland replied easily, but his voice was cool and flat. "You have a binding contract to perform, the terms of which are eminently fair as well as irrevocable under any circumstances. And I would suggest that the risks you take in questioning our agreement are *infinitely* more dangerous than the ones which you take in the routine performance of your job."

Manning blanched. He got up and walked to the windows overlooking the river, and when he turned around to face Sutherland again there was a nervous smile on his face. "All right, Averal, my perspective got a little fuzzy. What the hell am I complaining about? I'm a rich man. You don't have to worry about a thing. Here's my hand on it."

After Manning left his office, Sutherland sat behind his desk for a long moment, lost in thought. Then he shook his head and went into the office across from his.

"Emile, we may have a problem developing with Manning. I want you to alert the Essex unit assigned to him."

Novak swiveled his chair and rose. "Of course, Averal. But I've just finished looking over his quarterly statement. There's nothing wrong from that end."

"That's not the problem," Sutherland said, shaking his head. "Greed, Emile, greed. The most creative as well as the most destructive of our emotions. I want Manning watched closely."

The smile faded from Novak's face. "Consider the matter taken care of, Averal."

There was one last item of business to take care of before

Sutherland could leave for the evening. Returning to his own offices, he noted the time, then picked up the phone and dialed a direct line to the offices of the firm of Chase and Connolly.

"Brock Chase here."

"Well," Sutherland said, "I am impressed to find the senior partner of the country's leading executive search firm steadfastly tending to business at this hour."

"Always on call to the captains of industry," Chase replied with a laugh. "Good evening, Averal. How may I serve you?"

"Would you do me a favor, Brock? You remember, of course, that I spoke to you a few weeks ago of the two key positions at Kaufman that were opening up. Frankly, we thought then we could fill them from inside the company. That now appears to be impossible, and we would like you to step up your search. I will handle the matter personally at this end and I would like you to do the same."

"Of course, Averal. I'll begin immediately. And I appreciate the opportunity and privilege of working directly with you. Not many men in your position would take the time."

"Perhaps more should. What could be of higher priority to any company than the right men? Good evening, Brock, and thank you."

*   *   *

Averal Sutherland enjoyed the ready subservience of men like Brock Chase. It was one of the fringe benefits of his position.

He was often called a self-made man. But he was not. And he, better than anyone, knew it. A man could climb only so far without power and money. Oh, he had done well enough at first for someone with nothing. But a time had come when he realized what he had was just that—*nothing*. And the reality of nothing- ness had transformed Averal Sutherland.

That day of reality was seared forever in his brain. After six years of fourteen-hour days, no vacation, and a dormant marriage, he had risen to the upper-middle-management level of a small corporation. He not only hoped for the vacant position of vice-president of operations; he expected it. And when it went, instead, to a man whose only advantage, in Sutherland's opinion, was a financially and socially prominent wife, something happened deep inside him. He left the company six weeks later, divorced his wife, and drifted out of sight. Some said he had gone to work for a shipowner in Southeast Asia. And he had, as operations manager for Monarch Lines.

At that time the conflict in Vietnam was accelerating rapidly, and the personal fortunes of those in business grew as fast as the stockpiles of war. However, had it not been for an American Green Beret officer, Averal Sutherland would not have prospered at all. Indeed, he would not even have been alive.

He would wonder later whatever had possessed him to go aboard one of his river freighters that night at the mouth of the Mekong River. In the early-morning hours, a small band of Vietcong somehow boarded the craft and slaughtered the six-man crew; only he and the captain were left alive. Taken ashore at dawn, they were force-marched inland for two days and one night before reaching a small, deserted village. Just before they arrived, Sutherland fainted from hunger and exhaustion and was dragged the rest of the way. When he finally regained consciousness, he was staring at the headless body of the ship's captain. Terror-stricken, he watched as his captors prepared to break camp, certain that his death would be included in their work.

Abruptly, all but two of the black-pajamaed Communists melted away into the night. Then, as if by prearranged signal, the two remaining men began to walk directly toward him. But as the one on the right turned to speak to his companion, something strange happened to his left ear; half of it jumped from his head. The man took another step and fell. Befuddled, the other man stared stupidly at his friend. And then he seemed suddenly engrossed with something about his own body. His face. His hands clawed at it, came away covered with blood, and were lifeless before his body struck the ground.

Sutherland lay frozen and speechless. Then he saw someone emerge from the underbrush and stand beside the bodies, his arms hanging loosely by his sides, a long-barreled pistol in his left hand. One of the forms on the ground moaned. The gun raised slightly and jerked twice. There was no report, just two muted, spitting sounds. Brains spattered the leaves close to Sutherland's face. He cringed in horror.

The man slid the strange-looking weapon into his belt, walked slowly over to Sutherland, and held out his hand. "I'm Captain Novak, sir. If you can still walk, it's time we left."

In the year and a half that followed, two events occurred that forged the bond that now existed between the two men. Accused of trafficking in drugs and facing a general court-martial and a long prison term, Novak appealed to Sutherland for help. In less than a month—through Sutherland's legal connections in the States and his highly placed friends in the military—he walked out of the stockade a free man. A life for a life, Novak had said.

Then several months later, the owner of Monarch Lines suddenly died and it was Sutherland who needed help: a $30,000 loan to buy a ninety-day option to purchase control of the company from the widow. The banks were not interested, and, strangely, it was Emile Novak who came to his rescue again. He made the loan to Sutherland from what he termed "family sources." It was not until much later that Sutherland discovered just what those sources were.

Finally in control of Monarch, Sutherland wasted little time in selling the company. Hostilities in Vietnam were winding down, and he could see no long-range promise in Southeast Asia. Kaufman Industries wanted a maritime capability and was willing to pay quite handsomely to get it in cash, stock, and other benefits—principally, a five-year management contract for Sutherland.

Once he understood the internal politics of Kaufman—a perpetual struggle for control between the Kaufman Family Foundation and a consortium of two large banks and a prominent law firm—Sutherland's rise in the company was swift. Once he had obliged himself with the legal and financial faction, it took him exactly five years to power his way to the chairmanship.

One year later, he almost lost it.

Too busy with his career to oversee personal investments,

Sutherland had turned his securities over to one of the bank trust departments to handle, and almost before he knew it the ineptness of the bankers in the collapsing bull markets of the late Sixties reduced the value of his portfolio to less than half the original $600,000. Two days after discovering the loss, he made a fateful decision for recoupment. Using the prestige and trust of his position, together with inside information about various companies, he embarked on a scheme of kiting securities: paying for stocks with worthless checks, reselling quickly, and then depositing the proceeds before the purchase check to the broker hit the bank for payment. Neither in his mind nor his heart was there an intent to defraud. Like someone who writes a check for groceries, then hurries to the bank on payday to cover it, what Sutherland was engaged in—as far as he was concerned—was nothing more than a convenient form of short-term borrowing.

But kiting is a criminal offense, carrying harsh penalties of fines and imprisonment—if one is caught and prosecuted. Seven weeks after he began kiting, a junior officer at the bank inadvertently failed to approve an overdraft check to the broker, and Averal Sutherland was caught. And while—through the influence of his friends among the attorneys and bankers on Kaufman's board—he was able to avoid formal indictment and borrow the $150,000 his account was short, the Kaufman Family Foundation had had no intention of overlooking the indiscretion. The day he sat before the president of the foundation was the only day in his life that Averal Sutherland could remember feeling like a child.

After enduring a two-hour lecture on morals and ethics, common sense, financial management, and responsibility to one's company, Sutherland was told the price he was expected to pay. In addition to requiring that he fully liquidate his loan within six months, the foundation demanded he sign what they termed "an instrument of prudence"—an *undated* letter of resignation. At any time during the next year, the directors who represented the foundation could dismiss him by simply dating the letter, which also contained a formal admission of his financial impropriety.

Sutherland's instinct for survival overrode his humiliation. He signed the letter. And if the conditions under which he lived the following year were calculated to impose an exquisite form of punishment for his sins, his tormentors were notably successful. But for every nightmare he suffered, for all the indignations he bore, for every quickened pulse of daily anxiety, Averal Sutherland grew. If they taught him servitude, they also taught him how to withstand pressure. If they teased him with loss of position, he discovered the value of it. If they made him grovel for money to pay his debt, they taught him how to make it. If he suffered from their power, he learned how to use his own. And if they proved Kaufman Industries belonged to them, they were the seed from which the Beta Group sprang.

Sutherland reached the 365th day of his sentence still in the chair. But not through benevolence: Kaufman had the best profit year in the history of the company. Averal Sutherland had survived. But it was not a docile, grateful employee who destroyed the insidious letter of resignation. Instead, his enemies had created the most formidable opponent they could have had. Yet they had also created their own reprieve, for by that time Sutherland was far too busy with Beta to bother with a straight-laced family foundation.

A month after Beta was conceived, Emile Novak resigned his position with a construction company in Saigon and went to work as Sutherland's executive assistant and personal accountant. Together—Sutherland the architect and Novak the implementer—they amassed the capital and cemented the connections that made Beta a reality. And three years later, according to the financial statements Novak prepared, Averal Sutherland's net worth was approaching twenty million dollars.

Kaufman stock accounted for only one fourth of his assets. So volatile was the stock in the market, so restricted was his ability to buy and sell because of his position in the company, that Sutherland considered this portion of his wealth the least stable. He would acquire no more Kaufman stock. The remainder of his net worth had come from Beta: huge sums of cash that flowed discreetly into banks, real estate, and blind trusts throughout the world.

The element, of course, that made it unnecessary for him to

touch the great wealth that Beta brought—and thus give rise to questions from taxing authorities—was his remuneration from Kaufman Industries. Sutherland's annual salary and bonuses amounted to nearly a half million dollars. He also enjoyed numerous fringe benefits from the company. There were, of course, the usual automobiles, club memberships, and travel. On a more lavish scale, he had the full use of a Lear jet, an expensive yacht in San Francisco, and leisure homes in Aspen and Martha's Vineyard. Together with the two homes he owned personally—a beautiful home in San Francisco and a townhouse in New York—these fringe benefits made his life-style as elegant as any man's.

He did not, however, resort to tax shelters as most men in his position did. He *wanted* to pay taxes. His tax returns, while not simple, were clean; he wanted no probing problems with the Internal Revenue Service. Yet, at Novak's urging, his returns always contained small, deliberate errors. Better to give the IRS something to find, something to bitch about. It stroked their egos. And Novak made it his business to know what the IRS investigators liked and didn't like. Sutherland's returns had never been subjected to anything more than a routine audit.

If there was a single, nagging frustration in Averal Sutherland's life, it was that he couldn't share with his teachers at Kaufman the dichotomy of their lesson. If he had suffered from their power, he had learned how to acquire power of his own. If they had taught him he couldn't prosper without their blessing, he had learned that he could. Within the next five years, according to his plan, he would be worth almost fifty million dollars. He would be sixty years old. He was in superb health. Years of splendor lay before him.

Averal Sutherland had only three problems at the moment. First, the enormous flow of cash into Beta had to be quickly and properly ingested. Second, qualified men must continually be found to increase the original dollar flow and, simultaneously, manage astutely the new member companies either purchased or created to invest these funds.

But it was the third problem that bothered Sutherland the most. It was a personal problem, not a business one. But it had the potential to impair seriously, if not totally destroy, everything. Yet he simply refused to eliminate it from his life. The public in general had perhaps become more tolerant. But not boards of directors nor shareholders. No, not even himself. Not really.

The door to his office partially opened and Novak leaned in. "Miss Parrish called about ten minutes ago, Averal. Your extension was busy. She's on her way. I'll go down and meet her and bring her up."

"Thank you, Emile. And if you would, plan to stay until we leave." He glanced at his watch. "We shan't be long. Ten or fifteen minutes for one drink before we have to meet a friend of hers."

When Novak had gone, Sutherland made a brief phone call to his townhouse and told his butler when to expect him. Moments later, the door of his office opened and Leslie Parrish came in. She smiled at him as she closed the door and walked to the small bar at the far end of the room. He watched her with amusement but said nothing.

She was dressed in a soft flannel skirt and jacket over a white blouse that contrasted perfectly with her carefully streaked dark hair. She wore simple gold bracelets that jangled as she mixed two drinks at the bar. She carried the drinks to a glass coffee table and smiled again at Sutherland as she seated herself on an immense sofa, one smooth, nylon-clad leg tucked under her, the other extended and moving in a slow arc as if beckoning him to her.

He returned her smile, rose, and walked slowly toward her. Incredible, he thought. Absolutely incredible.

And she was.

Leslie Parrish was twenty-five and very beautiful.

Leslie Parrish was also male.

CHAPTER 4

Phillip flew to Cocatlon early Monday. Victor Mendoza was buried Tuesday. The next day, Bustamonte Nacional, the powerful Mexican industrial firm, filed an injunction in the local courts. On Thursday, Phillip's law firm dispatched their foreign-business specialist to Mexico City. The future of Cocatlon, Ltd., suddenly hung in the balance.

Friday afternoon, Phillip sat in the bar of the Maria Isabelle Hotel waiting for his lawyer to return from a meeting with the court. Sipping a scotch, which he didn't really want but felt obliged to order, he wondered what else could happen. One minute he had owned half a smoothly running company about to burst forth into prosperity. Now, the whole thing seemed ready to collapse about his head.

He and Mendoza had done the best they could to plan for the possibility of death. But there was always a maze of legal and financial problems that accompanied the passing of a business partner—especially one of foreign nationality. That was hard luck.

The other problem—Bustamonte Nacional—was piracy. Roaring in before anyone knew what was happening, the company was claiming some vague title to the land that held the deposits of clay. And on top of that, they had petitioned to impound Cocatlon's equipment until such time as the court saw fit to rule.

Glancing again at the time, Phillip wondered what was keeping the lawyer. He had never had much patience with the legal profession; more than anything, he thought lawyers tended to complicate matters. Yet, the man who had come down the day before appeared to know what he was doing.

When he finally arrived an hour later, the lawyer slumped into the chair across from Phillip, ordered a large margarita, and launched into a twenty-minute account of his day in court.

"Okay, Counselor," Phillip said. "Tell me in a few simple sentences that I can understand what all of that means to me."

"Well, it means there's a chance the court will rule in our favor next Friday," the lawyer said. "And if not then, they will eventually. It's simply a matter of time."

"For God's sake, time is the one thing I don't have!" Phillip exploded.

"How long *can* you hold out?"

"A month, six weeks at the outside. That's when the money runs out. After that, no money for payroll means no workers, no product, no sales. And that's it. Do you think we really have a chance in a Mexican court against somebody like Bustamonte? I'm no lawyer, but the odds look pretty bad to me. Isn't there some other way to deal with those bastards?"

The lawyer was silent for a moment. "I suppose you would consider selling Bustamonte Mendoza's half of the company?"

"Sell? Christ, I'd *give* it to them in a second. But no, Counselor, they don't want fifty percent. They want *all* of it. And for nothing, if they can get it. It's a squeeze play."

"If we just had some time, the hearing next Friday wouldn't be so critical."

"Well, I'm going back to Houston tonight to try to find some money to buy us that time," Phillip said. He caught the waiter's eye and motioned for the check. "And while I'm doing that, I want you to concentrate on the equipment. I'm on the hook personally for eighty percent of the purchase price. One way or the other, don't let me get stuck for that."

Sitting alone on the late Pan Am flight, Phillip ordered a second drink and wracked his brain for potential investors. Even if the Mexican court ruled in his favor next week, he still had to find money; he couldn't afford to buy Mendoza's stock, and trying to operate a company with the man's relatives would never work. But he knew the chances of finding an investor who would put money into a foreign company whose operations had all but ceased because of the death of a fifty-percent owner—and a national at that—were, at best, slim.

His frenzied search for an investor came to an abrupt end six days after his return to Houston. Bustamonte had won. Persuading the court in its favor, the Mexican firm had bought enough time with its ploy to insure that Cocatlon, Ltd., choked to death financially. It would be a minimum of six months before Phillip could battle back and hope to resume operations. Now it became a question of how badly he could keep from getting hurt.

After nearly a week of conferences, he agreed to terms with Bustamonte: his stock in Cocatlon in return for Bustamonte's assuming his personal liability for the heavy-equipment indebtedness. It was better than nothing—so he took it.

*   *   *

On the last day of May, Phillip stayed late in his Houston office with nothing better to do than watch as various purchasers of the furnishings and equipment came and went. At six o'clock, he locked the door for the final time, turned in the keys to the building manager, and drove home. In his attaché case was his accounting firm's preliminary recapitulation of the Cocatlon debacle.

Five months of the hardest work in his life had cost him his original investment of $100,000 and left him owing $75,000 of borrowed working capital to banks, plus another $26,000 of Cocatlon-related debts. In his personal checking account he had an even $3,000—almost to the penny the amount of his fixed monthly living expenses. And he had only a vague idea of how much he owed on open-charge accounts around the city and to various credit-card companies.

It was dark by the time he reached his apartment. Shrugging off his coat and tossing it across a chair, he unbuttoned his collar, poured scotch in a glass, and slumped on the couch. When he heard the phone a few minutes later, it rang almost a dozen times before he finally blinked his eyes and decided to answer it.

"How can you expect to have a successful business if you sell to customers at cost?" It was Jessica.

"That," Phillip said quietly, "is something I no longer have to worry about." Then, catching the sound of self-pity in his voice, he laughed. "Isn't it great to call somebody and get a whine instead of a hello? How are you, Jessica?"

"I'm fine," she said. "But I don't understand. Has something happened to your company?"

As briefly and lightly as he could, he told her about Cocatlon.

"Oh, Phillip, I'm so sorry," she said. "I know you must feel terrible."

"I don't know what I feel," he said. "The loss of the money—well, since it represented my share of Apache profits and I never *had* it, as such, it's hard to feel a loss. And then, the debt's so damn big, I can't relate to that either." He paused, then sighed. "Maybe I just feel . . . lost."

"I know you must. And I'm dreadfully embarrassed about all those things I said back in December. I shouldn't have encouraged you. I mean . . ." Her voice trailed off.

"That's about the silliest thing I've ever heard," he said, half angrily. "I knew what I was doing—*exactly* what I was doing. Given the chance, I'd do it again. What happened wasn't my fault. It was just rotten luck. Anyway, to hell with all that. Tell me what's been happening to you?"

"Well," Jessica said, "the winter season is over and I'm just slightly in the black, but I don't know about next fall. We're quite a pair, aren't we?" She hesitated. "Phillip, why don't you take a few days off and come to Vail? We could cheer each other up."

For a moment, Phillip thought he might accept. Then he remembered he couldn't afford the airfare, much less the time. "God, Jessica, I'd like nothing better. And you're sweet to ask. But I just can't, not now. Besides, I'd be rotten company anyway."

"Do you have any idea what you're going to do now?" Jessica asked.

He knew. He had known all along. Yet somehow, until that very instant, the real tragedy for him of Cocatlon hadn't fully registered. Now it knotted in his gut. "What else?" he said grimly. "Go back to corporate life."

*   *   *

It was a gloomy weekend. Gray and still, the weather matched the two-day ordeal of replanning his life.

Late Sunday afternoon, he sat at his desk staring at two piles of neatly stacked papers: financial figures on the left, career strategy on the right. "It could be worse," he muttered as he stretched and went to the kitchen to fix an early supper.

The solution to his immediate financial crisis was as severe as the crisis itself, but with no borrowing power left, Phillip had no alternative. By selling the boat and the Porsche and moving to a much cheaper apartment, he could reduce his expenses and generate enough cash to get him through the next ninety days—the time he knew it would take to find an acceptable corporate job.

The most perplexing decision of the past two days, however, had been the bittersweet struggle with himself over his financial commitments to Kate and his daughter Carol. While he didn't relish the temporary reduction in his own standard of living, it seemed absurd to punish others for his bad luck. But in the end it was mostly pride that would not let him reduce his alimony payments to Kate and love for Carol that made him write the $1,600 check for the trip to Spain he had promised her months before. What the hell, he thought. I'll have enough to live on, and by August, at least, I'll be back at work.

There was nothing novel about his plans for the job search. The résumé came first. Irrelevant and immaterial things, résumés. But necessary. Then letters would go out to perhaps a hundred and fifty presidents of companies he thought might be interested. He also decided on an ad in the *Wall Street Journal* to run twice a week for four weeks. And of course he would read and answer ads run by employers.

Next on his list was registration with executive search firms—the headhunters. And the final avenue, the one that might hold the greatest promise but the one he found most distasteful—approaching friends.

If he had it to do over, Phillip would have been far less vocal about how great it was to break free of corporate life. He was just beginning to realize how his superior attitude and contemptuous remarks had probably been received by those to whom he would now be turning for help. And it wasn't hard to imagine what their reactions might be when they heard he wanted back in.

As he ate, Phillip scanned the employment section of the newspaper. Even though he knew before he looked that jobs at his level were rarely advertised, the fact that he saw nothing in over twenty pages of opportunities for which he felt qualified left him moody and depressed.

And there was another problem that seemed to make the walls of the apartment suddenly start to close in. Polly. This was to have been their first weekend together since Acapulco, but he had wired her to postpone it. Eventually he would have to tell her about Cocatlon, but he had no intention of telling her how deeply in debt he was. By putting their next meeting off for a few weeks, at least there might be time for something good to happen to go with the bad news.

All at once he had to get out of the apartment. Two days of nothing but the grim reality of his uncertain future were too much. Quickly throwing some things into his seabag, he scooped up the job-search file he had assembled and an hour later he was aboard the boat preparing his bunk for the night. He would spend the next few days working from the boat, putting his résumé together, launching the job-search, and listing the Pearson-30 with yacht brokers.

As he climbed into the small bunk that night, the thought of having to give up the boat made him madder than hell. But he quickly cooled. There was no other way—a necessary but, he hoped, a temporary situation. What he had to concentrate on now was finding a job. And who was to say he wouldn't get lucky and not have to sell everything after all? It was about time *some* luck came his way.

*   *   *

David Marsh spent the first hour of each morning in his office going over mail, phone messages, appointments, and meetings with his secretary. "These calls," she said, passing several pink slips across the desk to Marsh, "are all concerning Mr. Vanderlind. Calls for references, I believe."

Marsh thumbed quickly through the slips, thought for a moment, then handed them back to his secretary. "Let's just pass these, and any others we might receive, on down to Sam Rogers. He'll have to speak to the specifics anyway, and he'll do a better job for Vanderlind than I can."

"I wonder why Mr. Vanderlind doesn't give Mr. Rogers as the person to contact in the first place?"

"It's part of the corporate game," Marsh said, "pecking order, prestige and all that. Looks better on his résumé to give the chairman of the board as a reference. Anyway, ask Mr. Rogers to get on it, will you? It's very unfortunate that Vanderlind's business failed, and I expect he would like to get resituated as soon as possible."

*   *   *

On the last Friday in July, almost two months since he had launched his search for a job, Phillip stepped off the elevator into the reception area of the Anchor Life Insurance Company. He was fifteen minutes early for his second interview with the firm. Three days before, he had passed the obligatory half-hour screening session with the director of personnel with flying colors. And today, Phillip thought as he presented his card to the receptionist, was D-Day.

After checking her log, the receptionist acknowledged his ten-o'clock appointment with the vice-president of the company's venture-capital operation. "Now, if you'll just fill out this form," she said, "he'll be with you in a minute, sir."

Phillip glanced at the form, flushed slightly, and handed it back to the receptionist. "I don't believe this will be necessary," he said in a pleasant voice. "They already have this information."

"*Everybody* applying for a job at Anchor is required to fill out an employment application," the receptionist said sharply, then turned back to her typing.

Phillip picked up the form and walked slowly to a seat at the far end of the reception area. Three or four weeks earlier, he wouldn't have even considered working for Anchor Insurance, much less tolerating the rudeness of a receptionist. Now he had no choice: Anchor was the seventh and, from all indications, the last interview his two-month search was going to produce. The others had all ended in dismal failure.

Forcing back his pride, he began to fill in the form. A few moments later, he looked up to see a stocky young man with prematurely gray hair speaking to the receptionist. The girl pointed in Phillip's direction.

"Mr. Vanderlind?" the man said, coming over to Phillip. "I'm Robert Houghton. Please forgive our inefficiency here this morning. You were supposed to have been referred directly to my secretary. There's no need for you to fill out that form." He led Phillip down a long hallway, and when the two men were seated in his office, Houghton began. "Well, Mr. Vanderlind, this is quite a résumé you have here. I've never had much luck with executive search firms in the past."

"Thank you," Phillip said, trying to suppress the sudden elation welling up in him. "I do have a great deal of experience in a broad range of businesses."

"Yes, indeed you have," Houghton said. "There is one thing that puzzles me, however. The salary and fringe benefits we could offer you here are, I believe, less than half of what you received at Apache."

"I understand that," Phillip said. "But if we can, I'd like to relegate salary to a minor consideration for the moment. I'm sure we can get together on that. What interests me is the opportunity you have here."

Houghton shifted uneasily in his chair. "Well, it isn't just the salary, Mr. Vanderlind. What I'm trying to say is, a man with your credentials would seem to be grossly overqualified for this position."

Phillip's elation began to fade. How many times had he heard that sentence in the last two months? "Better overqualified than underqualified," he said, forcing a smile. "And I believe my experience in acquisitions would be a decided plus for Anchor, especially at a time when, I understand, you're interested in diversifying your portfolio."

"Yes, well . . . but you see, real estate is still our first line of investment. And frankly, Mr. Vanderlind, even if all other things were equal, I'm afraid you just don't have enough experience in that area."

Then and there, Phillip knew that the man across the desk had no intention of hiring him. First, he was overqualified for the job, and now he lacked the necessary experience. Obviously, there was some other reason Anchor wasn't interested. There was no point in continuing the interview.

"Well then, thank you anyway, Mr. Houghton," Phillip said, rising and extending his hand.

"Not at all, Mr. Vanderlind." The man got quickly to his feet. He seemed almost relieved that the interview was over.

Phillip was puzzled and now a little angry. "But I am curious about one thing," he said. "If you feel I'm so obviously unqualified, why did you bother to see me?"

Houghton stiffened slightly. "What can I say? Sometimes these things happen. I can only apologize and hope we haven't unnecessarily inconvenienced you, Mr. Vanderlind."

All the way back to the cheap one-bedroom apartment in Houston's old "Sin Alley" complex, where he had moved the month before, Phillip tried to figure out what in hell he was doing wrong. Seven straight times now the same thing had happened in the same way. Everyone seemed to love him the first time around, but on the second interview it all turned sour. Christ, he thought, it had to be his *personality*: all the objections that had been raised—salary, experience, age, and the half-dozen lesser excuses thrown at him—just didn't hold water.

Well, whatever it was, he thought grimly, he sure as hell had better get it worked out and soon. After selling the boat, trading cars, and moving, he had only enough money left in the bank for maybe thirty days of just *basic* survival. And he had long since ceased even opening the steadily growing stack of bills on his desk.

After a brief stop for milk and a carton of cigarettes, he was back at the apartment by noon, with a long, empty weekend stretching ahead of him. He clicked on his telephone answering device. There was only one message. Polly had arrived in Houston for the weekend. She was staying at a hotel and asked to be picked up at seven o'clock that evening.

"Damn it!" Phillip snarled, punching off the machine. The last time they met, he had told her about Cocatlon, passing it off as no big thing. And, he said, the lease had expired on his apartment and he would be living in an interim place until he could find something closer to town. But the thought of bringing her to this apartment was almost too much, and he had suggested they postpone their next meeting until he was resettled. But Polly was not easily put off. She was here, and he would have to see her.

Sometime during the weekend, Phillip decided, he would also have to tell her what was happening to him. He just couldn't go on pretending nothing was wrong. Besides, how long could he expect to fool her living in cheap apartments, having no money to spend, and driving secondhand cars? Then suddenly he remembered that she didn't even know he had sold the Porsche and bought a used Vega.

*   *   *

As she dressed for the evening, Polly was frankly puzzled. There were several things about Phillip that had seemed to change over the past three months. Ever since he lost the business in Mexico, he had been increasingly less interested in having fun and simply would not travel. Even their love-making had turned into quick, dull missionary affairs.

All at once, as she fiddled aimlessly with an expensive emerald ear-screw, she wondered if he was having financial problems. The thought had never really occurred to her before. But it made sense. It also made her suddenly nervous; a poor man was the last thing she needed—or wanted.

Phillip was waiting for her in the lobby. "Darling," she said, pressing her body into his and breathing a light, sensual kiss on his mouth. "I've missed you. Where are we going?"

"I made reservations at Rudi's."

"Marvelous," Polly said. "Everybody will be there."

She was chattering and laughing as they left the hotel. Her expression changed when she saw the car. "Where on earth did you get that ghastly thing?"

"That, my dear, is what's commonly called a 'loaner.' The Porsche is in the shop for a few days."

As they drove to the restaurant, Polly caught occasional glimpses of Phillip's face in the headlights of passing cars. He looked strained, she thought, older than she remembered. And when they stopped for a light, his hands seemed to shake as he lit a cigarette. Then he did an odd thing. He pulled to a stop short of the valet-parking zone in front of Rudi's. "Let's park this thing ourselves and walk," he said.

"All right, darling," she said with a wan smile, suddenly grateful for not having to be seen in whatever the funny little car was that kept on running even after Phillip had turned off the switch.

They had to wait for their table in the bar, and for a while Phillip was able to forget about the total failure of his job search and the fact that he was all but dead broke. It was like it used to be with Polly. But then she destroyed the mood with one impulsive wave of her hand that brought several of her friends from across the room to join them for a round of drinks. The waiter announced that their table was ready, but Polly refused to move. He had to order another round and the bar bill mounted. He endured the scene for another ten minutes, then said he wanted to eat.

"Damn good idea, sport," said one of the other men. He was a real-estate operator, and his conversation had been clearly aimed at impressing Polly. "But why don't you both come on over to the house for a nightcap later on?"

"Maybe some other time," Phillip said, ignoring Polly's expectant look. "But thanks anyway."

"Okay, I got a better idea," the man persisted. "We're all going to run up to my place on Lake Travis tomorrow for the weekend. Barbecue a goat, play some tennis and a little table-stakes poker, go water skiing if you want. Why don't you come along?"

"Darling, let's!" Polly exclaimed.

"Sounds like fun, but we've made other plans," Phillip said. He took Polly's arm and led her quickly into the dining room.

"What other plans?" Polly wanted to know when they were seated at their table.

"Spending the weekend with that crowd just doesn't appeal to me," Phillip said. "Now let's change the subject, shall we?"

She was silent for a moment. "Darling, have you found a job yet?"

"Getting nervous about me?" He laughed defensively.

"Of course not. But we never do anything or go anyplace anymore. Is it me, darling, or is it money?"

"Money has nothing to do with it," he lied. "And you *know* it's not you, Polly. It's just that I've got so many things on my mind now." Where in hell *was* his mind? he wondered. Why didn't he just tell her?

He got another jolt when the waiter presented him the bill. It was close to one hundred and fifty dollars. He handed the waiter a credit card.

"Where are we going now?" Polly said.

"How about back to your hotel?"

"Whatever," she said and sighed.

"Sir?" The waiter returned and bent over to whisper something in Phillip's ear.

Phillip drew back and shook his head. "I can't understand you."

"Do you have another credit card, sir?"

"What's wrong with that one?"

"I'm sorry, sir," the waiter mumbled, straining to keep his voice down, his eyes darting at Polly, then back to Phillip. "But your American Express card has been canceled."

"Well, what do you want me to do? I don't have any cash on me or any checks."

"I'm sure the maître d' can arrange something," the waiter said sympathetically.

Suddenly, Polly opened her purse and handed Phillip two one-hundred-dollar bills. "Will that take care of it?" she said dryly. "I'll meet you out front, Phillip." She got up from the wallside table and walked hurriedly toward the exit.

He caught up with her as she went out the front door. "What the hell was that all about?" he said angrily. They were standing under the entrance canopy of the restaurant. Rain was whipping in sheets across the parking lot.

"Would you please just call me a cab?"

"Where are you going?"

"Back to the hotel. Alone, if you don't mind."

"But I *do* mind, damn it."

A taxi was pulling up to the curb loaded with late-evening diners. Polly turned away from him and waited for the passengers to get out. "I'll call you," she said over her shoulder as she stepped into the cab, "from New York in a week or two. Goodbye, Phillip."

He watched her drive off, his mind numb with anger and rejection. Then, his shoulders hunched, he walked through the downpour toward the little car that looked as if it had been abandoned in the rainswept parking lot.

*   *   *

On Monday morning in New York, in the offices of the chairman of the board of Kaufman Industries, Brock Chase waited patiently, if somewhat nervously, for Averal Sutherland's reaction to the résumé and accompanying data sheets in the file folder on his desk. In Chase's judgment, there was only an even chance his client would consider the candidate he was presenting; the position of administrative vice-president was too important to misstaff.

"Interesting fellow, Brock," Sutherland said finally, "though obviously a maverick. Which, I suppose, accounts for the difficulty he appears to be having in finding a new position."

"That's part of it, Averal, yes. But there are two other factors. Time is one of them. He's only been on the market for two or three months, and at his level, as you know, it could take six or eight—possibly even a year. The second factor is his reference from Apache, his employer before he bought into the Mexican company. That's where he's having his *real* problem."

"Is Vanderlind aware of that?"

"I seriously doubt it. My guess is that he probably attributes his problem to the fact that he *is* a maverick; he knows that. And I'm sure he's aware of the career realities of being over forty and a generalist, and the taint of having once broken away from corporate life. Those things alone are enough to eliminate a man from top consideration in the open market. His best chance is if he knows somebody. Or—" Chase paused and smiled—"if someone like you, who has an instinct for sleepers, spots him and takes a chance."

Sutherland's eyes narrowed. "Is he a sleeper, Brock, or a loser? Specifically, what were Apache's comments?"

"Specifically," said Chase, shifting uneasily in his chair, "they confirmed Vanderlind's achievement record—in fact, even embellished it. But then they came down hard on the man's character. Supposedly, he is an unusually arrogant and ambitious man—and as such was a disruptive influence in the company. But most damaging, of course, was a veiled inference that Vanderlind may have taken *kickbacks* from companies he acquired for Apache."

"Well, I shouldn't wonder the man is having problems," Sutherland said, closing the file folder. "And since David Marsh, with whom I have a nodding acquaintance, by the way, gives such a poor recommendation, I would not be at all inclined to go any further with this man, Brock."

"But that's just it, Averal. I didn't talk with David Marsh. If *he* had given such a recommendation—which, in my view, is enough to destroy a man's career in the corporate world—I would have written off Vanderlind then and there. But when I called, Marsh was out of the country and his secretary referred me to a Samuel Rogers, Vanderlind's former, immediate superior at Apache. And, Averal, I swear to you, as I listened to Rogers talk, there was something in his voice, something in the way he said it, that gave me the distinct impression he had a hell of a personal ax to grind with Vanderlind."

"Come now, Brock," Sutherland said indulgently. "If *you* were able to perceive that, wouldn't others? And if the allegation is untrue, wouldn't that be easy enough for another prospective employer to establish?"

"A situation like that is too messy to fool with, Averal. There are plenty of unblemished, employed executives to be recruited, so why take the time and the risk? True or not, the taint is there and that's more than enough to cause people to back away."

"But not you."

Suddenly, Chase realized he was pressing too hard. The last thing he wanted to do was oversell a man like Vanderlind. His position was to remain neutral; the client had to be the advocate. "Well, Averal," he said as nonchalantly as he could, "I just felt a pretty good man might be getting a bum rap and be a real find for Kaufman. And you have asked me to be alert for just this kind of situation. But the more I think about it, you're probably right. Let's not bother with Vanderlind anymore."

"You give up too easily, Brock," Sutherland said. "If you believe he's a good man, go down and see him. If he still looks good to you, then I'll have a talk with David Marsh when he returns."

When he left the Kaufman Building a short time later, Chase felt good about his morning's work. Hell, he wished he had a dozen clients like Averal Sutherland who enjoyed shuffling around in the executive boneyard once in a while. He couldn't think of anyone else he could, or even would, have shown Vanderlind's résumé to. And now . . . well, perhaps there was a chance of turning a hog's ear into a silk purse. Or whatever it was they said in Texas.

*   *   *

At one that day, Averal Sutherland lunched quietly and alone in the small dining room that was part of the office-suite complex he occupied at Kaufman Industries. Of far greater interest than the Dover sole and green salad he picked at were the papers in the file folder to the left of his plate.

Finally, after coffee was served and he was alone again, he smiled, closed the file, lit a thin Cuban cigar, and reached for one of the three phones to his right. The instrument he selected was his private line, which was swept daily by electronics experts to insure the absence of taps. The purpose was to prevent industrial espionage, but there were, of course, other uses for such a line. Sutherland dialed.

"The Essex Group," answered a clipped, youthful voice.

"Novak, please."

"Sir, Mr. Novak is en route to Kennedy Airport. Shall I patch through?"

"If you please."

Seconds later, Novak's voice cut in over the hiss of a mobile phone connection. "Yes, Averal?"

"We have a possible candidate, Emile. Please instruct Essex to initiate a preliminary investigation before you board your flight this afternoon. I shall want a report within the week."

"You'll have it in the next seventy hours," Novak said. "I'm ready to copy."

Sutherland glanced down at the file he had reopened. "Phillip A. Vanderlind," he said, "6836 Idoux Circle, Number 308, Houston."

CHAPTER 5

Oushan Wou ground the gears of the army surplus lorry and jerked forward up the embankment. The fully loaded trailer lurched dangerously as he gained the top and descended to the overgrown goat trail that led to the paved one-lane highway five miles away. From there, it was another fifty miles to the small town of Dui Phong.

Wou had a nice crop this time—one that should bring him at least $500, if all went well. And it usually did. He grinned at the thought. It was so much easier to grow and sell the small plant that was illegal in Western countries than to make some of the legitimate handcrafts exported by his countrymen.

He arrived in Dui Phong just before dusk, spent the night with relatives, and early the next morning he was waiting when a decrepit DC-3 put down on the grass landing strip outside the town. There were the usual anxious moments when the buyer, a British ex-service man, inspected the goods and determined a price. But of the twenty or more farmers who were also sellers to the Englishman that morning, Wou had the finest merchandise and received, for all to see, a bonus of $50!

When the cargo was taken aboard and the DC-3 groaned its way airborne again, Wou and his fellow farmers gathered around their agent, a young man in stylish Western clothes, named Win Lei Ki, to receive their money. All agreed that they hated military men of every country. But without them, how could they have become so prosperous?

Three hours later, in a distant city to the west, workers began to unload the DC-3. What had been worth perhaps $12,000 that morning would be worth perhaps $75,000 that night. And the value had not yet even begun to build.

*   *   *

Phillip had been stunned by Polly's abrupt departure from his life. Like the apartment, his boat and the car, she symbolized another loss and an even more painful one because it was a personal rejection. But the trauma of Polly had a positive result, too. Stripped of the last vestiges of pretense about himself, Phillip at last had to meet reality head on. And it was simple, unconfused, and terrifying. His rapidly dwindling funds would be gone long before he could possibly expect to find the "right" job. To hell with his pride, he decided. Financial survival was the only thing that mattered now.

But with that decision he realized that he would probably have trouble finding even an hourly wage job. The only solution was some activity more directly related to his executive experience. If no one would hire him, he would have to work for himself. He wondered why it hadn't occurred to him sooner.

Shortly after lunch that day, he picked up the phone and called Lee Kelly, the president of a small steel-products firm he had tried to acquire for Apache a year earlier. At the time, the man had been more interested in going public with his stock than selling to Apache. But since then the market for new issues had almost ceased to exist.

"Phillip Vanderlind, I'll be damned!" Kelly said. "Been a long time. How's the old Apache raider?"

"Staying busy. How's the steel business?"

Kelly was even more talkative than Phillip remembered, which was good. Ten minutes later, he knew all he needed to know. "Sounds to me," he said, "as if you're still thinking about cashing in your chips and lying around in the sun for a while."

"You bet I am, if I find a buyer with the right bucks. But you know how it is. I just keep putting it off. Besides, I don't really know anybody offhand who wants to buy. Or is that the reason for this call?"

"I think I might know someone who's interested," Phillip said.

"Apache? I thought you people had written me off."

"I'm no longer with Apache, Lee. This is strictly for my own account."

Kelly was silent for a moment. Then he laughed. "Well, hell, why not? If you trade as hard *for* me as you did *against* me last year, you ought to be able to make a good deal. If you can find a buyer, that is. Okay, tell me what we need to do and how much this is going to cost me."

Phillip closed his eyes and squeezed the arm of his chair for luck. "I'll need three things from you, Lee: copies of your financials for the last five years, a letter from you stating that I'm authorized to act as your agent, and an afternoon of your time to get our signals straight. As far as the fee is concerned, it's pretty standard in the industry: five percent on the first million, four on the next, and so on. Like a real-estate deal, it's the seller's tab and we just tack it onto the sales price. And if I can't make a deal, I don't get paid. My services are strictly on a commission basis."

For a second there was no reply. Then there was a whistle. "Jesus," Kelly said, "no wonder you decided to start brokering on your own."

"What do you mean?" Phillip said a little nervously.

"Hell, do you realize how much you'll make if you pull this thing off for me? You know what my company's worth. I figure you'll pocket damn near a hundred and twenty-five grand!"

Phillip breathed a sigh of relief and grinned broadly into the receiver. "Damn near, Lee," he said.

*   *   *

It was funny how quickly things could turn around, Phillip thought as he walked up to the house phone in the Warwick Hotel and asked for the room of Mr. Brock Chase. Three and a half weeks ago, all he had going for him was the faint hope that he could put some sort of deal together for Lee Kelly. Now, it not only appeared that he had found a potential buyer for the steel company, but also the prestigious executive-recruiting firm of Chase and Connolly wanted to talk with him about a substantial opportunity—or so Mr. Chase had put it when he called from New York.

Chase answered his phone on the first ring.

"Phillip Vanderlind, Mr. Chase. I'm in the lobby."

"Fine, Mr. Vanderlind. I'll be right down."

Brock Chase was, more or less, what Phillip expected. Late forties, well-dressed, urbane. They went to the hotel restaurant for lunch, and Chase opened the subject of their meeting by generally describing the company he represented: a conglomerate, he said, listed on the New York Stock Exchange, with widely diverse interests. The job under consideration was upper-level management and the salary was an even $100,000 a year. "Of course," Chase said, "I can't divulge the name of the company until both sides have indicated an interest. Would you be interested, Mr. Vanderlind? "

"I'd like to explore the situation," Phillip said.

Chase smiled. "Good." Then the smile vanished and his eyes were riveted on Phillip's. "Cocatlon," he said. "What happened and what are you doing now?"

"My partner was killed in a plane crash," Phillip replied, catching and holding the man's stare. "We were undercapitalized and the competition took us apart. It was just that simple. Since then, I've been busy brokering a friend's company for him, waiting for the right corporate opportunity to come along."

"Putting deals together, especially here in Houston, must be quite lucrative," Chase said, lighting a cigarette. "Are you perhaps thinking of setting up your own shop and forgetting about a job as such?"

"I don't think so," Phillip said. "I really prefer working within the framework of a corporation." It was a lie, but he knew if he told the truth, the interview would be over.

For the next half hour, talk was mostly of Phillip's background—personal as well as business. Chase was a clever and thorough interrogator, and as the conversation progressed, Phillip became aware that Chase was trying to pinpoint something about his career at Apache. Then the question came.

"What is your opinion of Sam Rogers, Mr. Vanderlind?"

It was a loaded question, but he quickly decided to give Chase an honest answer. "Sam and I were friends for a long time," he said, "but I think I may have embarrassed him, at times, with his peers. Other than that . . ."

"Is Rogers a very competent man?"

"The chairman of the board thinks so," Phillip replied.

"What is *your* opinion?"

Suddenly, Phillip wanted to ask who Chase was interested in: him or Samuel Rogers? But he laughed and said, "Have you ever known a subordinate who didn't think he could probably do a better job than his boss?"

Chase looked at him almost quizzically for a moment, then, apparently satisfied, he grinned. "Rarely . . . if ever," he said.

From then on, until an hour later when Chase excused himself for another appointment, Phillip felt as if he were chatting with a friend rather than being interviewed. And as they left the hotel restaurant and walked out into the lobby, Chase asked him if he was free to come to New York in the near future for an interview with his client.

"Of course," Phillip said. "But just for scheduling purposes, do you have any idea when I might be expected to make the trip?"

"Perhaps as early as the end of this week, if the company accepts my recommendation."

Phillip nodded and smiled.

"In any event," Chase said, extending his hand, "you can expect to hear from me again in the next couple of days."

Phillip left the hotel feeling better than he had in months.

*   *   *

Looking across Lee Kelly's wide, ornate desk, Phillip wondered just how hard he could push. What he had just heard—and the fact that he hadn't heard at all from Brock Chase for over two weeks—made his temples pound with anxiety.

"Look, Lee," he said patiently, "the deal is tenuous enough as it is. In my judgment, if we go back to them and say you've changed your mind about personally carrying their note, they're going to want out."

"Well, fuck 'em," Kelly snorted. "I don't *have* to sell and I don't like the idea of being their goddamn banker."

"Now wait a minute," Phillip said. "The down payment is good, hard cash. Money is money, Lee. And the agreement I've worked out states that the note you hold will be secured by a like amount of General Electric stock in *addition* to all the stock of your company. You couldn't have a more gilt-edged credit."

"I want *cash* for my company, or to hell with it. They've got the money. You know it and I know it. What the hell's wrong with *cash?*"

Phillip once again started to explain the tax advantages of an installment sale to both Kelly and the men who were interested in buying his company. But Kelly spun around in his chair and reached for a golf putter lying on his credenza. "We're just leaving too much on the table for these guys, Phillip," he said, standing and stroking at an imaginary ball. "Too goddamn much on the table."

"Okay, let me ask you this," Phillip said, watching the man's face closely as he spoke. "If you walked off with another fifty thousand in cash, up front, would you go ahead with the deal?"

"What makes you think they'd go another fifty?"

"I don't think they would," Phillip said. "But *I* will. Just take it out of my fee."

Kelly straightened slightly from his putting stance and looked at Phillip. "Listen. I know you're anxious to make the deal. And if it goes through, I have no intention of cheating you out of your commission. I like you and you've been working hard. It's not just the money. I guess I just don't like the idea of those bastards running *my* company."

"I think," Phillip said evenly, "you've just told me what the problem *really* is. You don't want to sell, Lee, do you?"

Kelly stood staring out of the window of his office for a moment, then turned toward Phillip. "Well, I'll tell you. The wife and I are going to hop a plane tomorrow and run down to Puerto Vallarta and talk about just that for a couple of days."

"Okay," Phillip said, standing and snapping his attaché case shut. "I understand. I'll just say we'll get in touch with them later. When will you be back?"

"A week, ten days. I'll let you know," Kelly said. "But don't bother calling those bastards. I already told them I'd be out of town for a while."

"All right, Lee," Phillip said, trying to conceal his disappointment. "I'll wait to hear from you."

"Why don't *you* get out of town for a while, Phillip?" Kelly said. "Take a vacation. You look terrible."

Phillip left Kelly's office with no place to go but home. It had been foolish, he decided, to pin all his hopes on Kelly. He had been through the same thing before when Kelly was eager, and then had refused, to sell his company to Apache. And earlier that week he had been dealt another blow. His request for a small personal loan from the bank with which he had done business for years had been turned down flat. As for Brock Chase, that was clutching at straws.

What the hell was left?

*   *   *

At Kennedy Airport in New York, the black over dark-brown Rolls-Royce eased away from the International Arrivals building and moved into Manhattan-bound traffic. In the back seat, Averal Sutherland scanned the messages his young administrative assistant at Kaufman had selected for his immediate consideration upon his return from the Middle East. The assistant sat in the front seat with the driver. A soundproof glass separated the occupants of the car. Sutherland picked up the mobile phone, placed a call, and waited.

"Novak here."

"Good evening, Emile."

"Averal. You're a day early. Something go wrong?"

"Not at all. The trip was most rewarding. I'll share the details with you tomorrow afternoon when we meet. Now, if you will, may I have an update on events here during my absence?"

Settling back in the comfort of the Rolls, Sutherland listened intently to the voice on the other end of the phone. Only twice in the next twenty minutes did he interrupt. Once he asked Novak how much time he had been able to devote to Beta's new leasing operation in San Francisco. His second question concerned Essex operations in Houston. "One moment, Emile," he said. "Perhaps it would be well if I had the full particulars on Vanderlind this evening."

"He's close to rock bottom, Averal. Two weeks ago he got the word that a deal he's been working on will probably fall through. His only banking connection turned him down for a personal loan, and as of yesterday his bank account was less than three hundred dollars. He has debts of over one hundred thousand dollars, he has no personal property left to sell, and he's been to all his business friends for job leads and has come up empty-handed. No money, no friends, no prospects. That about says it all."

"Much worse than I anticipated," Sutherland said, more to himself than Novak. "And you are absolutely certain there is nothing to the charge that Vanderlind took kickbacks?"

"He's clean, Averal. He isn't even aware that such a charge is being circulated."

"I see. Please continue your surveillance, Emile, and I will pursue the matter from this end. Is there anything else?"

The car was passing through the Midtown Tunnel into Manhattan before Novak's report was completed. Sutherland replaced the receiver, then pushed a button on the console to his right and waited until the glass partition disappeared before he began issuing instructions to his aide. "Finally," he said as the car drew up in front of the man's upper East Side residence, "please call

Brock Chase at Chase and Connolly the first thing tomorrow morning and ask him to arrange a trip to New York for a Mr. Phillip Vanderlind at the earliest possible time. And offer my apologies to Mr. Chase for the belatedness of our request and suggest he convey the same to Mr. Vanderlind."

After saying good night to the young Kaufman executive, Sutherland glanced at a small gift-wrapped package on the seat beside him, thought for a moment, then asked to be driven to an address several blocks away.

"Shall I wait, sir?" the driver asked.

"Yes, I'll only be a few moments this evening."

Both the doorman and the elevator man recognized him when he entered the apartment building, and he rode up to the twentieth floor without the formality of identifying himself. He stood for a moment in front of the door of 20-E before he rang the bell. He heard the sounds of music. Leslie Parrish was home.

After a few moments he frowned and was about to ring again when a chain rattled, two dead-bolts turned, and the door swung open.

"Good evening, Leslie."

"Averal! I couldn't believe my eyes when I saw who it was through the peephole. I didn't expect you."

"That," Sutherland said, the smile on his face suddenly vanishing as he caught sight of a man rising slowly from a chair across the softly lit room, "would appear rather obvious. This, I suppose is your Mr. Cross."

"Averal, please. You agreed I could see Stewart occasionally."

"Need I remind you, Leslie," Sutherland said stiffly, "that whatever agreement I made I can also terminate."

Cross picked up a jacket that was lying across the arm of a chair. "Leslie could hardly have known you would be coming here tonight, Mr. Sutherland," he said. "Besides, you and I were bound to meet sooner or later."

"An occasion," Sutherland said, "that I fervently hope will not occur again." Then, as if Stewart Cross had suddenly ceased to exist, Sutherland turned to Leslie. "That's a very pretty gown, my dear. It's new, isn't it?'"

"I bought it for you, Averal."

"Of course you did. But I really must go now. This was my reason for stopping by." He handed Leslie the small package he was carrying.

"Oh, Averal, I am sorry."

"Let's hear no more about it. I'll call you in a day or so. Good evening, my dear."

"Goodbye, Mr. Sutherland," Stewart Cross said. He put down his jacket, obviously intending to stay.

"*Mister* Cross," Sutherland replied coldly, his eyes flashing with contempt.

An hour or so later, as he prepared for bed, Sutherland was still annoyed about finding Leslie with Stewart Cross. He was really not adverse to their relationship. It was necessary, he supposed. It was just that homosexuals like Cross, outwardly the epitome of masculinity, disgusted him. Leslie, at least, was honest with his perversion.

As far as his own arrangement with Leslie Parrish was concerned, Sutherland had never viewed it as anything more than a harmless fetish. Enjoying the company of a transvestite was hardly a perversion. But it *was* peculiar. And since he had no wish to defend his heterosexuality to the world, discovery was a matter of continuing concern. Then again, discovery seemed highly unlikely. For to all intents and purposes, Leslie Parrish was female, and no one with whom Sutherland was associated knew anything to the contrary. Not even Novak. And if you could deceive Emile Novak, you could deceive anyone.

Perhaps it was the element of not being in total control of the situation that prompted the vague uneasiness Sutherland felt as he drifted toward sleep. For now there was one person who had nothing to lose if his relationship with Leslie Parrish were exposed. On the other hand, Sutherland thought it shouldn't be too difficult to arrange something for Stewart Cross to lose—if that ever became necessary.

*   *   *

Brock Chase's office at One Rockefeller Plaza could have passed for a carriage-trade antique shop. He was sitting behind a large Chippendale desk and rose to greet Phillip enthusiastically.

"I want to tell you again how pleased we are you're still open to considering this opportunity with Kaufman Industries," he said. "When I was unable to get back to you as soon as promised . . . well, I was concerned you might have accepted something else or decided to hang out a broker's shingle."

The fact was that the steel-company deal was probably dead as hell, as was Phillip's job search. Everything now depended on what happened in the next few hours with Kaufman Industries. And Phillip supposed that knowing he had no choice but to succeed accounted for the supercharged confidence he felt as Brock Chase began briefing him on the company that was looking for an administrative vice-president at $100,000 a year.

After a thorough review of the company in general and as much as he knew about the specifics of the position itself, Chase turned to the politics of the interview. The men Phillip would see that day, he said, were Clarence Heath, vice-president of operations, and Clark Pendleton, vice-president of finance. Both men held positions equal to the one for which Phillip was being considered, and they would serve together on various staff committees. Chase explained that both the president and chairman preferred to have candidates acceptable to their peers before becoming involved themselves.

"Of the two," Chase continued, "I would say Heath is the more critical. He has Sutherland's ear and . . . well, he's somewhat of a bastard, if I may be abrupt. Pendleton is okay. You won't have any problems with him. He likes to talk. I suggest you let him." Chase glanced at his watch. "Well," he said, "shall we go meet some people?"

*　　　*　　　*

If Clarence Heath was the bastard, then Pendleton must be an absolute saint, Phillip thought as he was led down the hallway of Kaufman's executive floor for his second interview. Heath had chatted pleasantly about any number of subjects, and Phillip had the distinct impression that they were friends from the first moment. He couldn't have been more relaxed and confident as he shook hands with Clark Pendleton.

"Sit down, Mr. Vanderlind," Pendleton said pleasantly as he

settled into his imposing executive chair. Phillip took one of two rather uncomfortable-looking contemporary chairs immediately in front of Pendleton's paper-littered desk. He was right; it was uncomfortable. He was forced to sit almost at rigid attention to keep the back of the chair from cutting into his spine.

Pendleton seemed to sense—and enjoy—his discomfort, and Phillip suddenly smelled trouble. This man was an adversary. Just stay cool, he told himself. Wait him out. Let him make the first move.

"I understand you're looking for a job," Pendleton said finally, his voice flat and hostile.

I wouldn't touch that question in a million years, Phillip thought. He simply smiled and waited for Pendleton to continue.

"What is it you think you could bring to this company we don't already have?" Pendleton said.

For one thing, Phillip thought, a mature and sensible method of conducting interviews with prospective executives. But again he said nothing.

Pendleton began to lose his composure. "Well, Mr. Vanderlind, one thing we do require at Kaufman is the ability to communicate. Can you communicate?"

Now was the time. "What level of communication do you require, Mr. Pendleton?"

"Adult and mature communication, Mr. Vanderlind."

"Yes, I can participate at *that* level, Mr. Pendleton," Phillip said evenly.

The implication of the remark was quite clear, and Pendleton frowned. "What do you know about zero-based budgeting, management by grid, international logistics?" he asked quickly. "What do you know about the job you're applying for, Mr. Vanderlind?"

The question was condescending, sarcastic, and provocative. Something was wrong. This wasn't merely some interviewing technique designed to see how well he could withstand pressure. The man was genuinely hostile. Phillip's mind churned for a tactic. But he realized he could never win this game. To continue was suicide. Suddenly, it was quite simple—withdraw. Phillip rose from his chair. "You've been very kind to see me, Mr. Pendleton. Good morning, sir." He looked at the surprised Pendleton for a split second, then turned and left.

An hour later, at "21," Brock Chase drained the last of his second Manhattan and ordered another round. "Incredible," he said, shaking his head. "I can't make anything out of what you've just told me. The man must be crazy."

"No," Phillip said, "probably just scared. There's one in every corporation. I'm afraid we've both wasted our time."

Before Chase could respond, a man passing behind him stopped, touched his shoulder, and spoke.

Chase glanced up. "Well, I'll be damned!" he exclaimed, rising to shake hands. "I thought you were out of the country."

"Tomorrow," the man said simply. He turned his eyes to look at Phillip.

"Oh, I beg your pardon," Chase said. "Phillip Vanderlind, Averal Sutherland, the chairman of the board of Kaufman Industries. This is quite a coincidence, Averal. Phillip's here from Houston to talk about the administrative slot. He's been with your people all morning. Can you join us for lunch or at least a drink?"

"I wish I could, Brock, thank you. Unfortunately I have another engagement. But if Mr. Vanderlind would be so kind, I will take a moment to ask him something about Houston."

"Of course," Phillip said.

"Kaufman has no fixed operations in the Gulf Coast area at the moment," Sutherland said, "but it's a place we might want to be. In your opinion, Mr. Vanderlind, would moving a medium-sized aluminum extruding operation from the East favor us in any particular way?"

Phillip smiled inwardly. Sutherland was after an impression of him, not business information. "Generally, Mr. Sutherland," he replied easily, "I'd say yes. Lower tax rates, cheaper labor and plant-site locations, probably good local demand for the product as well as excellent transportation facilities would all make the Gulf Coast an excellent location. As for Houston itself and its satellite communities, they have a very aggressive program to encourage light industry."

"You make it sound very interesting indeed, Mr. Vanderlind," Sutherland said. "But now, if you'll excuse me, I really must go. Brock, nice to see you. And I enjoyed meeting you, Mr. Vanderlind. Have a pleasant stay in our city."

When he had disappeared across the crowded room, Phillip looked inquisitively at Chase.

"If you're thinking a chance encounter with the chairman of the board gives us a leg up, forget it, Phillip. Sutherland wouldn't hire Jesus Christ himself if his staff didn't like him."

"That's it then," Phillip said.

"Not necessarily. I'm going to try and talk some sense into Pendleton."

"What do you want me to do?" Phillip asked, feeling totally helpless.

"Just go back to the hotel and relax. I'll call you as soon as I can."

*   *   *

It was almost four-thirty before the phone rang in Phillip's room. It snapped him rudely back to consciousness, and he realized he had dozed off. He picked up the phone quickly.

"Brock here, Phillip."

"I was beginning to wonder."

"I know. I'm sorry, but I wanted to be certain." There was a pause. "It's bad news, Phillip. Pendleton was adamant. He won't recommend you. He doesn't consider you Kaufman's kind of man."

Phillip's heart pounded and his face seemed to go numb as if from intense cold.

"Are you there, Phillip?"

"Yes, I'm here."

"Well, that's it. We both lose. A nice opportunity for you, a nice fee for me. And," Chase added, "I think Kaufman loses, too."

"Well, hell, we tried." Phillip laughed to hide his crushing disappointment. "Brock, I don't know what a 'Kaufman man' is, and I don't give a damn now. But I'd be very interested to know how *you* rate me. In your opinion, how desirable am I as a management-level executive?"

"All right, Phillip, I'll be frank. For large companies, fellows like you—free thinkers, wave-making generalists who choose to ignore the realities of corporate politics—are too controversial, too threatening. And as far as smaller companies are concerned, the senior management there, as you know, is usually synonymous with ownership. I suppose what I mean is, you don't fit the corporate mold, Phillip. In harsher terms, you're a maverick, a renegade."

"In short, you're saying the job market is virtually nonexistent for me."

"I'm saying that it's tough. It's going to take time. You've got impressive credentials. I wouldn't have recommended you to Kaufman if I hadn't thought that. I'm going to keep your file active, Phillip. I'll get in touch with you if anything turns up. And I'd appreciate it if you'd keep in touch with me, too."

"Thanks, Brock," Phillip said. "I'll do that."

He hung up the receiver and sat on the edge of the bed. Who was Brock kidding? It was time he stopped kidding himself. He lay back on the bed and stared blankly at the growing shadows on the ceiling of his room.

*   *   *

That poor bastard, Chase thought. Kaufman was Vanderlind's last hope as far as he was concerned. With that scurrilous reference from Apache, there was nothing more Chase could do for him. He picked up the folder marked "Vanderlind—Private & Confidential," wrote "Return to General File" across the cover, and dropped it in his Out basket. Then he reached for the phone and dialed the offices of Kaufman Industries.

"Good afternoon, Brock."

"Averal, thanks for taking my call. I know you're busy, but I just wanted to apologize for Vanderlind and tell you the other two candidates you liked are already scheduled for later in the week."

"I appreciate your industry, Brock. We are beginning to feel the vacancy of that position. But as far as Vanderlind is concerned, you needn't apologize. *I* liked the man. In fact, I may want to talk with him at some later date about another opportunity."

Chase suddenly brightened. All at once two fees were a possibility, and he retrieved Vanderlind's folder from his basket. "That's encouraging, Averal. I liked the man, too. Would it be helpful if Vanderlind knew that? I wouldn't want to see him go elsewhere if you're still interested."

"No, Brock," Sutherland said casually. "It would be unfair to Vanderlind, and perhaps embarrassing to us, to say anything just now. When and if something concrete develops, I'll ask you to call him."

"Just as you say, Averal."

"And, Brock, it was good of you to arrange for me to meet Vanderlind in such an uncomplicated way today. After the fiasco with Pendleton this morning, anything other than a coincidental meeting would have been rather awkward. And it was important, because of his conflicting references, that I at least met the man."

"I understand, Averal. I'm always glad to be of service."

*   *   *

Sutherland hung up, leaned back in his chair, and sighed. How delicate a man's corporate career really is, he reflected. References. How exquisitely critical is what one man says or implies, or even fails to say, about another. Sutherland had taken the trouble to check Vanderlind's references personally, and the result had been a study in extremes. No one could have spoken more highly of a man than David Marsh had of Phillip Vanderlind. And no one could have spoken more venomously of him than Samuel Rogers. Sutherland had listened to him, without interruption, waiting for some indication that what he said was born of envy or malice. There had been no such indication at first; Rogers spoke with sincerity and, according to him, deep regret. But when Sutherland asked him for the particulars of Vanderlind's alleged corporate malfeasance, the man became evasive. Sutherland then asked if David Marsh was aware of what Vanderlind had done and if the company had ever considered bringing charges against him. Only then did Rogers quite simply admit that he had never discussed the matter with David Marsh or any other company executive. It was merely his own personal opinion.

That was what Sutherland wanted to find out: Vanderlind had done nothing more than arouse the emnity of his superior. But Rogers had effectively poisoned the corporate job market for Phillip Vanderlind, and curiously enough Sutherland had made no attempt to rectify the injustice. In fact, he had done just the opposite. For that was the precise condition he wanted intact.

Turning in his chair, Sutherland picked up the phone and asked for Clark Pendleton. "Clark, this is Averal. I wanted to call and thank you for handling that little matter for us this morning."

"Not at all, sir. Although I'll admit if you hadn't warned me about his references, I would probably have encouraged Vanderlind to consider Kaufman rather than discouraging him. I don't think I've ever been quite so rude. Too bad. I rather liked the way the man handled himself. What was the problem?"

"I don't think it matters now, Clark," Sutherland said with a slight edge to his voice. "Phillip Vanderlind just was not for Kaufman. That, I believe, is the sum and substance of the matter."

* * *

One early afternoon, two weeks after returning from New York, Phillip walked into the luxurious bar-lounge of the Petroleum Club and looked for his host. Swallowing his pride, he had finally phoned Lee Kelly. He was not available at the moment, his secretary said, but could Mr. Vanderlind meet him at the Petroleum Club at 2:00 P.M. on Friday? Phillip saw Kelly sitting with three other men and when Kelly recognized him he raised his hand in greeting, rose quickly from the table, and came over. "Glad you got here before I had to leave, Phillip. I'm sorry, but my secretary forgot about our two-thirty tee-time at

River Oaks. But come on, let me buy you a drink." He flagged down a waiter.

"Look, Phillip," Kelly said when they had been served, "the wife and I talked about it, and we've decided to hang on for a while." He shrugged and grinned self-consciously. "Hell, I'd be lost without that company."

"Thanks for telling me in person, Lee. I appreciate that."

"You probably knew it all along," Kelly said. "And you worked your ass off all the same. I admire that. Well, it's going to happen some day, and when the wife and I change our minds, you'll be the first to know."

Kelly's friends caught his eye, and he shook Phillip's hand and rose to rejoin them. "Take it easy, Phillip. Stay in touch, now."

That's it, Phillip thought. The end of the road.

He sat there alone, nursing his drink for a moment. Then he glanced around the room. They were all there, the high-rollers in oil and land and business deals—men who had fought their way up, like Lee Kelly, men at the top of corporate hierarchies and men who just sat contentedly on piles of family money. He knew some of them as business acquaintances; others he had met through Polly. One or two of the younger men nodded to him when their eyes met. He wondered what they thought about him now. He could have been one of them, he thought, if he had stuck with Apache. Or if he had been able to save Cocatlon. Or if he had landed a job with Kaufman. If, always an if.

And where was he now? Lost, adrift on a sea of disbelief, in himself and life. It was no longer paranoia—real or imagined. It was the truth: no one wanted him. As incredible as it seemed, he simply could not find a job. When he had tried it on his own, he was struck down—ruthlessly by Bustamonte Nacional, gently by Lee Kelly. But it was all the same. As an outsider, he was fair game for corporations, large and small. When he tried to join them, always he was either over- or underqualified—a misfit, a maverick, a renegade. And now in his own mind a bum. Perhaps he didn't look like a bum, not yet, but a man with only seventy-five dollars to his name and no source of income could hardly be called anything else.

Picking up his drink, he walked slowly across the room to the wall of glass that reached from the floor to a thirty-foot ceiling. Forty-five stories below sprawled the city of Houston. As far as the eye could see, there was activity. Buildings of every description shot skyward in all stages of construction. The whole city was alive, churning, growing, booming, some people making fortunes, everybody earning a paycheck. And he couldn't even find a job. Seventy-five dollars. He was a bum.

Phillip stepped closer to the glass and looked straight down. Suddenly he thought of Russ Miller. A fortune lost when his real-estate empire collapsed a year before, the man had jumped from the top floor of a hotel just down the street.

What would it be like to fall from such a height? Phillip wondered. Would you pass out? Would you start to scream halfway down? Would you float or flail? Did Russ Miller wish he hadn't jumped just before he hit? What would you hear, what would you feel, would you bounce?

All at once the questions stopped, and Phillip's mind seemed to shut down. There was no longer any discord. Only a vacuum of thought remained. He stepped quickly away from the windows. Jesus Christ, he said to himself, Russ Miller must have been insane. There were answers to every problem. And Phillip had just found the answer to his.

Driving home in the early rush-hour traffic, he hardly felt the oppressive September heat. Standing at that window, a revelation had come to him. And from it a decision. A simple decision, really, and now he was examining it, projecting from it, already making plans.

*   *   *

It was almost seven in the evening twelve days later when Phillip climbed wearily from the tub where he had soaked for nearly an hour. After toweling dry, he sniffed suspiciously at his hands and arms, then shook his head with disgust. "I *still* smell like fish," he muttered. Then he laughed. After almost two weeks aboard a shrimp boat in the Gulf, he couldn't expect anything else. And if the gut-wrenching labor had been no picnic, at least it was a job, and the money he earned would see him through the beginning of what he had decided to do.

Just to have earned money again seemed to give him back some remnant of pride. It was cause for a celebration, which was, he supposed, the reason he had invited Jessica Westbrook to dinner. In town briefly to see friends, she had called to say hello, and his invitation was completely spontaneous. He couldn't afford to take her out. He had invited her here, and he was glad she was coming. She would understand what he wanted to tell her—what he had to tell someone.

He promised himself he wouldn't apologize for the apartment. But the minute she walked in the door, he did. And he did it again after they had dinner. "So . . . after that long, sad story of the past five months of my life, it isn't hard to see why I'm living in *this* place."

"There's nothing wrong with where you live," Jessica said. "And the steak I just ate couldn't have been cooked any better by the chef in Houston's most expensive restaurant. You've done what you had to do. And I know if you can hang on a few more weeks, something will turn up. You'll find exactly what you want. It just takes time."

Phillip shook his head. "I'm tired of waiting, Jessica. And I'm tired of being the perpetual victim. I've made a decision, an important decision. I don't need corporations anymore. They obviously don't want me and I don't want them. It's rather a blunt way to put it, Jessica, but fuck the corporation."

"Fuck the corporation," she repeated without embarrassment. "Is that a smart decision, Phillip?"

"It's the only decision. Don't you see, Jessica? I've finally discovered that there is no real security, no survival through the corporation. It's a trap, a Trojan horse, a tranquilizer. If a corporation takes you in, it owns everything you own. And then if it decides to reject you, you have nothing left. I've spent almost five months trying to use one corporation or another to survive. And I'll be dammed if I'm going to spend another minute of my life at the mercy of a bunch of dull-witted, so-called executives. I'm not going to run that race anymore. And even if I *wanted* to, the odds in a race like that get worse every year."

Phillip crossed the room and sat down beside Jessica on the couch. "Just look at the odds," he said. "The older you get, the more you need all the corporate balms: job security, freedom from decision, retirement benefits, and all the rest. But at the same time, your bargaining power to get a job and the staying power to keep it diminish. Age is against me now. Past thirty and you're going *downhill* in the corporate job market.

"But maybe," he continued, "maybe the *worst* thing about being suckled by the corporation is the final payoff. What the hell's the reward for submitting to the system? It's old age before you ought to be old. Why? Because the corporation says you're old. And you're *ready* to be old because that's just what you've been trained to be."

"I know it does no good to tell you I understand how you feel. Because I probably don't," Jessica said. "But I do know you sound very cynical, very bitter. I wish I could do something to help."

"You really care, don't you?" Phillip said. "But you see, that's the final curse of being an executive. The corporation *doesn't* care. Do you realize that the corporate executive is the only highly educated, highly paid individual in our society who's completely on his own? Everyone else has unions or personal managers or agents or strong professional organizations behind them. The executive has nobody. The corporation even forces a man to choose between his job and his family."

Jessica glanced up at him, then looked down at her hands.

"You think I'm full of self-pity, don't you?" he said. "All just sour grapes."

"A little, maybe. You don't have to be the president of something, Phillip. You could take a lesser job."

"There is nothing in this world," he replied tightly, "more disgusting than a broken-down, has-been executive trying to grovel his way back up. There's no dignity in that, Jessica. No future. That's going backward. I can't do that. I can't start over and work for something I don't really want, something I've already been. But I *can* start over and work for something I haven't been. I'm going to find a trade. Something I can do with my hands, something no man can take away from me, something I can do as long as I live."

"What kind of trade?" Jessica asked.

"I'm thinking about boats. I can build and repair boats."

"Where? Here in Houston?"

"No," Phillip said. "There's too much history here, too many memories. I'm going to California. You think I'm crazy, don't you? You think I'm looking for an easy way out?"

"No, Phillip, not crazy. You forget my husband and I did the same thing when we moved to Vail. And it wasn't easy. It never is, being completely on your own. It's funny, isn't it? We seem to have this same conversation every time we meet—what Phillip Vanderlind is going to do with his life."

"God, Jessica, I'm sorry. Why the hell should you care?"

"I don't know. But for some reason I do." She glanced down at her watch. "It's late. I have to go, Phillip."

"I wish you'd stay."

"Thank you," she said with a smile. "I thought you'd never ask. But not this time, Phillip. You already have too many loose ends in your life. I don't want to be another."

"I guess I deserved that," he said.

"Will you let me know where you are in California?"

"Of course."

He called a cab, and when it arrived she took his arm as they left the apartment. And she kissed him briefly but tenderly when she said good night. "Thanks for dinner. If you ever get to Vail, I owe you a home-cooked meal."

"I'll hold you to that."

"And, Phillip, I hope you find what you're looking for. I keep saying that, don't I?"

"And I keep looking," he said.

Walking back to his apartment, Phillip thought of what he had to do in the days ahead: get the car in shape for the trip to California, pack, sell the furniture he had left if he could find a buyer. He wouldn't have to worry about Carol. He had opened an account in her name with part of the money from the sale of his boat, and that would be enough to see her through college.

Kate had a job, and she would survive without alimony. There were still debts and legal entanglements related to Cocatlon, but somehow he would work those out, too. The important thing was to move, to get started, begin again.

He was still awake long after midnight, lying on the bed in his dark apartment. There was no anger now, no self-pity, no regrets. He wondered briefly what he would do if the phone rang tomorrow morning and it was Lee Kelly or Brock Chase or someone else offering him a job. "No, damn it," he said out loud, driving his fist into the pillow. "Fuck the corporation!" Jessica was right: it wouldn't be easy going it alone. But this time he wouldn't be chasing money or status or security—or whatever he once thought he needed to survive. This time he would be looking for himself.

CHAPTER 6

In the south of Scotland, twenty-one miles from the nearest town, a medium-sized truck was parked at the edge of a small field. The night was pitch-black, and the wind had all but died under the heavily overcast sky. The four occupants of the truck waited quietly, occasionally checking their watches and peering into the darkness around them.

A quarter of a mile behind the truck, a single-lane road ran north and south. A thousand yards in either direction, a man was stationed with an electric torch ready to signal the approach of an intruder. The man to the north had a bicycle which he would use to meet the truck as it left the field and turned south. The man to the south would simply be picked up.

At precisely eleven-thirty, a small but powerful transmitting device in the truck was switched on. Ten minutes later all heads turned to the east, eyes straining into the blackness. A distant sound grew steadily louder until suddenly an aircraft was directly overhead, its blue exhaust flames clearly visible. And then it was gone, the noise of its engines fading rapidly to the west.

Even as the stillness settled back over the field, the men were running toward its center and the four parachuted crates that struck the earth within seconds of each other. The crates were quickly loaded aboard the truck, the lookouts retrieved, and the journey to the south begun. Not more than fifteen minutes had passed since the transmitter had been activated.

This scene was repeated at regularly scheduled intervals throughout the year, always at a different field, always with the same unerring precision. And from the moment the truck left a field, those involved could relax in the certain knowledge that its cargo would enjoy an uneventful trip to the outskirts of London. Once it was there and broken down for further transport, the situation became more stressful and less certain. But the system had been virtually infallible; for almost four years, millions of dollars of uncut heroin had successfully been prepared in this way for export to the United States.

*   *   *

In London, Arthur Tilton Beddington received the news of another shipment safely in from the north the afternoon of its arrival. He immediately cabled the United States:

> INVENTORY IN PLACE. STOP. AWAIT YOUR
> CONFIRMATION OF PURCHASE AND SHIPPING. STOP.
> REGARDS BEDDINGTON.

The Beddington family had been in cutlery for over a century and a half, and business had never been better. Exports to the States continued to accelerate, and Arthur Beddington profited handsomely as president of Sovereign Metals: £75,000 in salary and bonuses a year, to be exact. However, his wealth increased annually by many times that amount. Exporting sharpened steel was profitable, but it was nothing compared to the tax-free income he derived each year from the sale of massive amounts of 95 percent pure heroin to various parties in the United States and Canada.

Occasionally, Beddington was assailed with pangs of conscience. But they were infrequent and always of short duration. He had only to remind himself of the share of his income he was forced to pay in taxes and the percentage of company profits that was divided each year among three greedy, worthless uncles and the one sister who never spoke to him except at Christmas time. Then, too, there was Margot—young, beautiful, and terribly expensive Margot. And the villa in the south of France and the cars and . . . well, after all, he *did* need the money. Conscience was a poor excuse, really, for being impoverished.

* * *

Phillip made one last round of the vacant apartment, picked up his small flight bag, and walked out the door for the last time. As he started the engine of the packed Vega, the row of mailboxes at the end of the apartment building caught his eye. He sighed, climbed out of the car, and collected his mail. For a brief moment he considered leaving a forwarding address, then laughed and shook his head. Hell, he thought, he didn't know where he was going.

At noon the next day, a truck stop shimmered into view over the dull, sun-baked sheen of the Vega's hood. In the distance lay the city of Amarillo. Glancing at the fuel gauge, he took the turnoff. As he waited patiently for the attendant to fill the tank, Phillip noticed the small pile of mail in the corner of the back seat. He hesitated, then leaned over and picked it up. He began to look through it. Bills, notices, flyers—junk mail mostly. Except one. It was a telegram dated two days ago.

UNABLE TO REACH YOU BY PHONE. IMPERATIVE YOU
CONTACT ME IMMEDIATELY. BROCK CHASE.

Phillip shrugged. He was through with Brock Chase's world. Fuck the corporation.

He paid the attendant, pulled the Vega to the truck-stop exit, and waited for traffic to clear. There was a phone booth on his right. Two trucks and three cars passed. He could go now.

The phone booth was still there.

Two more cars passed.

Still he waited.

The phone booth hadn't moved.

"Well, what the hell," he said aloud.

"Phillip!" Brock Chase said. "Where in God's name have you been? I've tried for days to locate you!" There was an edge of irritation, or reprimand, to his voice.

"I wasn't aware that I was accountable to you," Phillip said. His words were flat and cool.

"Easy, Phillip. You're misreading me, I assure you. If I've offended you, I apologize."

Phillip immediately regretted his sarcasm. Chase was the only one who had really made any effort on his behalf during the past weeks. "I'm sorry, Brock. I've been out of town and I just got your telegram. What can I do for you?"

"Last Thursday, Averal Sutherland asked me to bring your file to his office. He was impressed with you, Phillip, that day at lunch. Anyway, after he looked over your file and we talked, he called some of his contacts in Houston. He was even more impressed after the calls and asked me to find out if you would consider coming to New York to see him. Tomorrow."

Two semi-trucks roared by with a deafening noise that was heard by Chase on the other end of the line.

"You still there, Phillip? What in hell was that?"

"I'm still here, Brock. You were saying something about New York—tomorrow?"

"Right. Sutherland would like to see you. That is if you aren't committed to something else. What *is* your status now, Phillip?"

The question embarrassed and irritated him. Another truck roared out of the exit. "I'm probably going to decide to accept an offer from a transportation company in the next couple of days." He had to smile as he said it.

"Of course, I have no way of knowing how attractive the situation is, Phillip, but I'd like to take a minute to tell you what's going on here, if you'll let me."

What did he have to lose? "Go ahead, Brock. I'm listening."

Chase waited as two other trucks interrupted the conversation. Then he said, "In the strictest of confidence, Phillip, Sutherland is a very wealthy man. And like all wealthy men, he has his money in many different things. He has done very well outside Kaufman, I understand, and he wants to talk with you about the possibility of your undertaking a new venture for him. That's all I know. But it sounds like the opportunity of a lifetime."

Phillip found it hard to believe what he was hearing. Chase was selling him—a corporate maverick, a renegade. "I'm not sure I can make it to New York anytime soon," he said at last.

"Let me make a suggestion," Chase said. "There's a round-trip ticket and five hundred dollars in expense money waiting for you right now at the Delta ticket counter at Houston Intercontinental. You're booked on a flight that leaves Houston at noon tomorrow. Sutherland's private car will meet your flight. You have reservations at the Pierre. You're invited to have dinner with Sutherland tomorrow night. I'm holding a return reservation for you leaving New York at eight A.M., which will have you back at nine Houston time. That's less than a day, Phillip."

He was confused. Why was Sutherland suddenly so interested in him? More relevant, why should *he* spend a moment's time thinking about something he had vowed never to consider again? He didn't know. He needed time.

"Look, Brock," he said. "I've got some thinking to do. Give me an hour or so to sort some things out before I make a decision."

"Of course. Call me back as soon as you've made up your mind."

A huge open field adjoined the truck stop. Phillip pulled away from the exit, locked the Vega, and walked. He studied the endless jigsaw puzzle of the crazed, sun-baked earth, watched the tall, sparse weeds bending in the direction of the wind. He was also conscious of the steady and purposeful drone of the traffic on the highway. He had a choice to make. He could drive on, blowing whichever way the wind took him. Or he could rejoin the stream of men traveling in different directions.

Phillip stood for over an hour in the middle of the field, head down, hands in his pockets. Then he turned back toward the truck stop and the phone booth. When the Vega gained the highway again, it was headed east toward the Amarillo airport and a flight to Houston.

*   *   *

For the next twenty-four hours Phillip moved as if he were in a trance, his emotions locked in a vise of objectivity. Nothing gained entrance. Not the elaborate VIP treatment he received at the Houston airport, or the chauffeured Rolls-Royce waiting for him at Kennedy, or the flattering reception by the staff of the Pierre, or the luxurious suite which he was given. He merely observed, never judging, never thinking—just waiting. It was as if he didn't care one way or the other. And he didn't. He couldn't afford to.

The phone in his suite rang within minutes of his arrival.

"Yes?" he answered.

"Mr. Vanderlind, this is Averal Sutherland." The voice was personal and warm. "I'm very pleased you could come. Welcome back to New York."

"Thank you, Mr. Sutherland. It was good of you to ask me."

"Was your trip a pleasant one, your quarters comfortable?"

"Everything is most satisfactory, sir." The words were polite, friendly, but without emotion.

"Splendid. Now, about this evening. I have made reservations for dinner at eight-thirty. I will pick you up at the hotel at eight."

At precisely eight the phone rang. Averal Sutherland was waiting for him in the lobby. As he took a final glance in the mirror, Phillip began to feel a trace of emotion returning. He was back in his corporate uniform: pin-striped suit, white shirt, conservative tie, black shoes. Was he really more comfortable in these clothes?

Sutherland greeted him in the lobby and led him to the hotel entrance where the Rolls-Royce was waiting at the curb. The chauffeur held open the door.

They were driving south on Fifth Avenue when Sutherland opened the conversation. "May I call you Phillip?" he said.

"By all means."

"Fine. And I'm Averal. I hope you will accept my apologies, Phillip, for the reception you were given at Kaufman last month. It was inexcusable and indeed most regrettable."

"Not at all. Things like that happen. And I'm sure I was equally to blame for the misunderstanding. But you're kind to mention it, Averal."

"And I would like to thank you for coming to New York again on such short notice. Perhaps this time it will be a more pleasant experience."

Phillip was taken slightly aback by Sutherland's choice of restaurant. Bill's, a bar and grill near Gramercy Park, was an unlikely place for the chief executive of a major corporation to dine. But the food was, without a doubt, as good as Phillip had ever eaten.

For the next two hours he found himself doing virtually all of the talking. And when it was time to leave the restaurant he realized not a word had been said about the purpose of his trip to New York. Relating one's background, personally and professionally, is common both to interviewing for a job and simply becoming acquainted with another man. But there is a difference: one is an explanation, the other an exchange. Phillip had been *sharing* with Averal Sutherland.

The evening was not yet over. They left the restaurant at eleven and were driven to Sutherland's townhouse on East 77th Street. Only when they were comfortably settled in the richly paneled library with after-dinner drinks did Sutherland begin to talk about himself. He said essentially what Chase had already revealed. He was a rich man and his "hobby," as he called it, was starting new enterprises. In addition to funds of his own, he explained, he had access, through numerous other wealthy men, to substantial sums of money. And periodically he became interested in this or that type of business as a form of investment. Then, if careful planning and research showed a favorable profit picture, he simply started a company.

Leasing had intrigued him for quite some time, Sutherland said, particularly in the areas of private aviation, shipping, health-care equipment, and computers. In addition to corporate advantages with which he, of course, was most familiar through

Kaufman, the profit potential for individual investors was extremely inviting. Current tax law together with properly constructed leases and impeccable lessee credit combined to attract enormous sums of private investment capital. With a few tentative phone calls, he said, he had *pro forma* subscriptions of over $100,000,000. And he hadn't even tried.

Sutherland then spoke of the urgency involved in putting a leasing capability in operation immediately. In fact, so great was the investor demand, he already had people at work on the project. Specifically, he had employed an executive vice-president in order to get the basics underway. Now he was searching for the individual who would complete the organization of the company and manage it. And he thought he had found his president in Phillip Vanderlind. "Would you be at all interested in pursuing the matter, Phillip?"

Phillip did not reply. He stood and walked across the library to the crackling fire. He honestly didn't know if he was interested or not. Then why had he come to New York? Don't be absurd, he told himself. Of course he was interested. But why was Sutherland interested in *him?* "I'm very flattered that you'd consider me, Averal," he said finally. "But there must be literally thousands of men in the leasing business who would make better candidates. Why *me?*"

Sutherland nodded. "That's an honest question, Phillip, and it deserves an honest answer. First, I enjoy the success I do as a very direct result of my ability to judge and select people." It was a simple statement of fact, entirely devoid of ego.

"Second, the leasing industry is filled with people who know the business," Sutherland continued. "But as in my corporation, expertise at the lower levels isn't sufficient to set up and run a new venture. And at the highest levels, people who would appear to be logical candidates are not. Why? Because, if they had the vital spark it takes, they would already have their own operations. No, Phillip, I'm not interested in expertise or specific experience. I am interested in a particular *type* of man who has what it takes to do what I want done in this new venture."

As he spoke, Sutherland rose and removed his suit coat.

Phillip noticed the impeccable tailoring of his shirt and the almost invisible monogram on the sleeve.

"I want boldness—not rashness, but boldness," Sutherland said. "I want a man with an analytical mind and the guts to implement his decisions. I want dedication and I want industry. I want someone who will say 'why not' rather than 'why' or 'it isn't done that way' or 'we'd better not' or 'we can't.' I need someone with whom I feel a kinship. I need a man who can think both with me, for me, and—without me. I need a *winner*." He began to walk slowly toward Phillip. "There aren't many around. The corporation, sooner or later, will kill these attributes in a man. The corporation has become the womb of mediocrity. But somehow you have survived. Everything I've read about you, heard about you, heard *from* you, my perceptions when I first met you, and all my instincts now tell me you're different. You may be a maverick, Phillip, but you're not a mediocrity. You're a winner."

There was something almost evangelical in the way Sutherland spoke. Phillip fought against the hardening knot in his throat, unable to say a word. A police siren from the street suddenly shattered the stillness of the room. It broke the spell.

Sutherland spoke first. "I must apologize," he said. "It must seem strange to you that a corporate executive could speak so passionately *against* the corporation. I suspect that you feel the same way, Phillip, but perhaps enough has been said for one evening. May I suggest that we meet again tomorrow morning at ten o'clock? I've prepared a memorandum that sets forth all the particulars of the job I'm asking you to consider, and I'd like you to review it before we go any further."

"Of course."

"Here is my card," Sutherland said. "My secretary will be expecting you. Until ten o'clock, then."

By the time he reached the hotel, Phillip had regained his composure; his mind was running at open throttle. Did he have a job? Where would it be? Would he report only to Sutherland? How much would he be paid? He was flattered by Sutherland's evaluation of his personality and abilities. Could he live up to it? Did he even want to try?

He hated business. For the first time, Phillip made that admission to himself. He not only hated the corporation, he hated business. The deals, the taxes, the records, the numbers, profits, losses, buying, selling, scrambling for personal gain. Why did he do it? Expensive cars and apartments, clothes, women, children in college, his ego? Or was he incapable of doing anything else?

*   *   *

At ten-thirty the next morning Phillip was sitting in Averal Sutherland's office, still waiting for him to arrive. The day, which had begun with so much promise, was rapidly beginning to deteriorate. While he didn't know Sutherland's habits, he had the distinct impression that the man was not given to being late. Now, as he rose and walked uneasily over to the bookcases lining one entire wall of the office, Phillip was certain something had happened; another so-called opportunity was about to explode in his face.

Suddenly, the door to his right swung open and Averal Sutherland entered, an apologetic smile on his face. "Phillip, I'm so sorry to be late. Good morning and please let's sit down. I have only a few moments before I must leave for England. We have an emergency abroad."

Phillip's mind spun. It *was* going to happen again. "Perhaps it would be more convenient to continue our conversation another time." He did not sit down. He didn't think he could endure another rejection. He had to leave.

Sutherland stared at him quizzically. "Have you decided not to consider my offer further, Phillip?"

"No. But I believe you may have had second thoughts."

"Not at all," Sutherland said. "I am more convinced than ever that you are the man I'm looking for. I regret having to leave so abruptly, but I simply have no choice in the matter." He handed Phillip a file folder. "This is the memorandum I mentioned last night. I have a brief meeting to attend which shouldn't last more than thirty or forty minutes. I will have time then, before I have to leave, to answer any questions you might have. You will notice in the memorandum that I have asked you to take two weeks to look us over before you make a final decision. That will entail a bit of traveling. My secretary is typing an itinerary now and arrangements have been made for you to use a company plane. I hope your reactions to the memorandum will be favorable."

Sutherland got up from his desk and started walking toward the door. "Oh, one thing more. It will become very obvious as you read the memorandum that I know a great deal about you and your personal life. It was necessary, as I'm sure you can appreciate." He smiled and was gone.

Alone in Sutherland's office, Phillip opened the folder and began to read. It was an incredible document.

MEMORANDUM OF UNDERSTANDING

From: Averal T. Sutherland
To: Phillip A. Vanderlind
Sub: Employment as President and C.E.O. of Omni Leasing Corporation, San Francisco, California

1. Terms: Employment by contract for five (5) years. Employee to own 40% of stock of Omni Leasing via purchase, simultaneously with employment, financed by a noninterest-bearing note to ATS. Stock to be held free and clear by registered owner.

2. Responsibilities: To conclude organization of company and immediately embark upon an aggressive program of fund acquisition and lease negotiations.

3. Salary: $125,000 annually.

4. Bonus: $50,000 annually.

5. Expenses: A full, open-end expense account.

6. Fringe Benefits:
   a. Exclusive use of residence in Marin County, California, at no expense. Option to purchase granted.
   b. Exclusive use of Turbo-Commander aircraft.

    c. Exclusive use of Mercedes 450SL automobile, to be traded annually.

    d. Exclusive use of Bermuda 40 auxiliary sailboat berthed at St. Francis Yacht Club, San Francisco, California.

    e. Coordinated use with ATS of vacation home in Aspen, Colorado.

    f. Coordinated use of Lear jet aircraft.

    g. Membership in various social clubs, including St. Francis Yacht Club.

    h. Life insurance in the amount of $1,000,000 payable to beneficiary of insured's designation.

    i. Full, non-contributory hospitalization insurance.

    j. Eight weeks' vacation at own discretion.

7. Other:

Arrangements shall be made, simultaneously with employment, to liquidate all outstanding debts of PAV to various commercial lending institutions, said debts to be rearranged between PAV and ATS as suitable to both parties and at the convenience of PAV.

8. Conditions:

    a. There will be no other employment nor income-producing activity, other than attention to personal investments, during the period of employment.

    b. An agreement not to compete in the leasing field in the State of California for a period of ten years after termination of employment must be signed.

    c. Prospective employee-owner shall devote two weeks of investigation into prospective employer's operation, including inspection and utilization of all fringe benefits, before entering into employment contract.

    d. An advance of $25,000 against first year's salary shall be made to prospective employee upon acceptance of this Memorandum of Understanding, to be used for whatever needs may arise.

Should he decide to decline employment, the $25,000 advance shall become the property of the prospective employee in full payment of any and all inconveniences arising from these negotiations.

e. This Memorandum of Understanding shall become full and effective upon execution thereof by both prospective employer and employee.

CHAPTER 7

C yril Kennedy had been an investigator for the Drug Enforcement Agency for almost twelve years when it happened. As anyone in law enforcement does, he had thought about it often, but he never really expected it would happen to him. More than the sudden shouts or the deafening explosion or the streaking pain or the carnival of erupting lights or the terrible roar he rode into unconsciousness, what he would always remember was the sheer surprise of being shot.

There was a second surprise: the man who shot him. His assailant was neither a street-corner tough nor a member of one of the organized-crime families born to his calling. Instead, he was the product of an average, middle-income family, educated and articulate, in every sense a peer of Cyril Kennedy. They had even belonged to the same national college fraternity. And in addition to the man's background, it was the *way* he had become involved with crime that both intrigued and alarmed the agent.

Of the ninety days he had been allowed before returning to his job, Kennedy spent almost the entire time in the records and computer sections of both his agency and the FBI. And by the time he was pronounced fit for duty, a vague but definite pattern had emerged from his long hours of research. Now, the problem was to sell the theory to his immediate superior, Harold Kane.

"All you've brought me is a pile of statistics, Cyril," Kane snorted as he leafed disinterestedly through the reams of data Kennedy had piled on the conference-room table. "Christ, we've already got more bona-fide cases around here than we have time for. And now you want to go chasing off after some pie-in-the-sky theory."

"All I'm asking for is another sixty days, Harry."

"And in sixty days you'll be right back in here wanting another sixty days. Damn it, Cyril, we were understaffed *before* you got shot. I need you back on the regular case load now."

"Harry, I'm telling you," Kennedy persisted. "If I can substantiate my theory in just *one* instance, think of what we'd have."

"No, Cyril. I can't forget that last James Bond goose chase you led us on. Remember the priest thing in Chicago? You thought that just because a priest had a kilo of heroin in his room, there might be some kind of ecclesiastical conspiracy to smuggle dope."

"Goddamn it, Harry, that's *not* what I suggested and you know it. I thought, and I still do, that someone was using that priest, and maybe others, to bring junk in. But this is a different ball game. Junk is only part of it, Harry. Can't you see what the implications are if I'm right?"

"*If* you're right," Kane said.

"Well, how in hell are we going to know if you don't let me follow it through?"

"All right, Cyril. All right. Take sixty days. Personally, I think it's a waste of time. You're going to come up empty-handed, just like in that priest matter. Go ahead, but sixty days is absolutely the limit. I want to see *hard evidence* or that's it. Sixty days, Cyril."

"Sixty days, Harry."

Sixty days wasn't much time, Kennedy reflected when he left

the conference room and walked back to his office. But at least his theory had official life now. A lot could happen in sixty days. All he needed was one, just one, solid confirmation. If he was lucky, he'd get it. And he *was* lucky, Kennedy thought as he felt the still tender place under his right arm where he had been shot.

*   *   *

The sleek, white Lear jet with powder-blue markings hung effortlessly at its assigned altitude of 43,000 feet, its starboard wing tip slowly tracing the south shore of Lake Erie. Its heading, 270 degrees; its destination, Aspen, Colorado.

Phillip had read the Memorandum of Understanding at least a dozen times after he signed it that morning in Averal Sutherland's office. Now it was tucked with a sheaf of other papers in his attaché case, but he was somehow afraid to read it again. He was like the child who peeks at the one Christmas present he really wanted and then quickly closes the box for fear it might suddenly vanish.

He turned in his seat to stare at the cobalt sky. Everything he had ever wanted was in the palm of his hand. Money *and* freedom. It was hard to believe that it was happening to him.

Restless now, he left his seat and helped himself to some scotch at the small bar in the aft section of the plane. He took off his coat and tie, lit a cigarette, and went forward to chat with the crew. The two pilots were informative and friendly but very busy. After a few minutes of conversation he fixed another drink and returned to his seat.

His itinerary for the next two weeks was simple. After a three-day visit in Aspen as Sutherland's guest, he would fly on to San Francisco, where he would be met by the executive vice-president of Omni Leasing, Emile Novak. The Marin County residence, the car, and the boat would be available for his use, and at his convenience, later in the week, Novak would begin briefing him on the status of Omni to date. Sutherland himself would fly to San Francisco when he returned from England. And if everything had proved satisfactory, Phillip would sign the contract of employment when they met.

Still shaking his head in disbelief, Phillip finished the last of his scotch, ground out the cigarette he had just lit, settled back in his seat, and was immediately asleep.

"Excuse me, sir."

The young co-pilot was gently shaking his shoulder. Phillip stirred and opened his eyes. "We're beginning our let-down into Aspen now, sir. I thought you might like to see some of the scenery. And it probably wouldn't hurt to fasten your seat belt, sir. We may hit a few bumps on our approach."

The jagged peaks of the Rockies were silhouetted on the horizon, and there was just enough light to see the great, gold slashes of aspen, spreading like lava flows over the mountains below. Magnificent, Phillip thought.

*   *   *

Cleo Harris and his wife had been born and raised in Aspen, and ever since Averal Sutherland built the impressive cedar-and-glass house on Red Mountain they had been his caretakers. Harris met Phillip at the airport with a Blazer that would also be available for his use, and after a brief tour of the house he said, "Mrs. Harris and I are just down the mountain. Please call us if there's anything you need."

"Thanks, I will," Phillip said. "By the way, when does it start to snow up here? Maybe it's my thin Houston blood, but it's *cold* tonight."

"Yes, sir, it's pretty nippy. Could happen any day now." Harris lit a fire in the rustic fieldstone fireplace and then said good night at the front door. Phillip walked quickly back to the warmth of the fire. His light, tropical-weight suit was out of place in this weather. But until now he hadn't even thought about clothes. First thing in the morning I'll have to buy a few things or freeze, he thought. Besides, you can't run around a ski resort in a *suit*, for Christ's sake.

He found the bar, fixed himself a large drink, and proceeded to explore the house. He quickly realized that, like everything Averal Sutherland owned, it was perfection. From the dramatic living room with soaring walls of glass to the informal dining room and the elaborate kitchen, it was beautifully designed and decorated. He climbed the circular steel stairs to the second floor and opened the door to the master bedroom suite where Harris had told him he was expected to stay. "Jesus," he muttered.

It took him a full ten minutes to see everything: the separate double baths and dressing rooms, the sauna and exercise room, a small dining area, even a library situated in a loft overlooking the bedroom. It was from that vantage point that he noticed an envelope lying in the middle of the giant bed below. It was addressed to him and contained a note from Sutherland. He welcomed Phillip to the house and suggested that he check the closets in the dressing room off the brown-and-white bath before he did any shopping.

Phillip pulled back the sliding doors and there he found hiking boots, leisure boots, ski socks, jeans, shirts, turtle-neck sweaters, cardigans, a tweed jacket, a leather coat, even underwear—all in his exact size. Everything was brand new, obviously purchased for him. Apparently, Sutherland's careful investigation of his personal life had included his clothing sizes. A little dizzy, he made his way back down the stairs and went to the bar to freshen his drink, wondering which he was higher on, the scotch and altitude or the fairyland moment in time in which he found himself.

His eye caught the stereo equipment in the bookcases to his right. Music. He began to browse through Sutherland's collection of tapes and records and finally decided on Rachmaninoff. With the entire house suddenly bathed in sound, he strolled happily into the kitchen to find something to eat.

The refrigerator was full of fresh meat, vegetables, and fruit, and it seemed that Sutherland had even anticipated his taste in food. He selected one of the T-bone steaks, threw it on the built-in charcoal broiler, and fixed a green salad with rich Roquefort cheese.

When the steak was ready, he settled himself at the circular dining table by the great windows that looked out across the valley and the winking lights of Aspen below. The fire in the fireplace behind him cast shimmering shadows on the high glass as Rachmaninoff's Third built to its bombastic conclusion. He got up once or twice to refill his glass and change the tape, and by the time he had finished eating, he was ecstatically drunk. He was just sober enough to climb the circular staircase, open a window in the master bedroom, take two deep breaths of cold mountain air, and smile at the sound of the night wind in the trees before sleep claimed him.

He spent the next two days touring the mountain roads around Aspen and the next two nights touring the restaurants and bars of the town. He met a young woman who invited him to a small private party, and when he left to go home that night, something white and cold exploded on the doorjamb beside his head. It was a snowball. The first snow of the season had begun.

The Lear climbed out over cold mountains the next morning, the gold of the trees replaced by a scattered mantle of white. The seasons, like Phillip's life, were in demonstrable change.

*   *   *

Emile Novak met him at San Francisco airport and they began the drive to the house in Marin County. Phillip was rather puzzled by the man. His demeanor was that of a subordinate, and he barely said a word during the trip. But Phillip noticed that he drove the Cadillac Seville with a grim aggression, as if he were engaged in a small private war with every other car on the road.

There was little to be seen from the Golden Gate Bridge that afternoon. A fog bank enshrouded most of it, and Phillip contented himself with watching the massive orange steel towers soar out of sight into the mist. But a mile off the bridge, they were suddenly back in bright sunlight and blue sky, and only a few minutes passed before they were on a twisting, two-lane street, climbing steadily. Around the next curve, a sign marked PRIVATE ROAD appeared. Two blocks farther and around another curve, the pavement ended in a cul-de-sac. Novak slowed the car to a stop in an empty, three-car parking area.

"This is it," he said.

Off to the right and below the level of the parking area, the red tiles of a roof were barely visible. They got out and walked down winding steps that paralleled a narrow driveway. The door of the house was open, and when the two men entered and walked down the steps from the landing into the living area, they were greeted by a stunning view of Raccoon Pass, Angel Island, and, in the distance, the city of San Francisco. The front of the house, hanging on a hillside over the bay, was totally glass.

"This is absolutely beautiful, Novak," Phillip said.

"Yes, it is," Novak said without changing his expression. But then a startled look crossed his face, and he turned abruptly.

Phillip had not seen or heard the small middle-aged Chinese enter the room. Novak looked at the man angrily, but then quickly regained his composure. "This is Irving," he said. "He comes with the house."

"Mr. Vanderlind," Irving said, bowing from the waist. "Welcome. I try and make you happy here."

"Thank you, Irving," Phillip said. Irving smiled, bowed again, and retired noiselessly from the room.

"That man Irving is an unknown quantity," Novak said. "Sutherland's housekeeper recommended him. If he doesn't work out, let us know."

"I'm sure we'll get along fine," Phillip said, "but where did he get the name Irving?"

"I think a former employer gave it to him and it stuck."

Phillip accompanied Novak back to his car, and on the way they passed through the garage, where Novak handed him the keys to a sleek, obviously new brown-and-beige Mercedes 450SL. "They delivered it this morning," Novak said. "If the color doesn't suit you, here's the dealer's card. Call him and exchange it. He has three other colors, red, silver, and blue."

"It's perfect," Phillip said, running his hand over the smooth leather of the driver's seat.

"Before I forget it," Novak said, "here's a letter from Mr. Sutherland. And if it's convenient for you we can meet at the office at ten o'clock the day after tomorrow. Here's the address, and these are phone numbers you can use to reach me."

Irving was waiting for him with a drink and an invitation to inspect the house. It was a small house, designed for a bachelor or a couple, but it contained every conceivable amenity. Phillip followed the silent manservant through the master bedroom with a dressing room and large bath, the guest bedroom at the other end of the house, paneled den immediately off the living room, the dining room and, finally, the gleaming, stainless-steel kitchen. As an afterthought, Irving asked if he would like to see his own quarters. Totally apart from the main structure was a small but comfortable apartment. An intercom system which Irving begged Phillip to use at any hour of the day or night was the one link between the two.

Irving prepared his dinner that evening: a filet of sole in a delicate sauce served with a chilled California Chablis. Irving was a superb cook. He was also an efficient servant. He unpacked Phillip's suitcases and laid out his toilet articles in the bath. And when Phillip inspected the closet in the dressing room, again he found casual clothes of every description that fit him perfectly.

Sutherland's letter was the frosting on the cake. Again, he welcomed Phillip to the house and then listed several names and phone numbers that might prove useful: the address and the dockside phone number of the St. Francis Yacht Club, where the Bermuda 40 was berthed; the location of the airfield where the Turbo-Commander was kept, along with the name and number of the pilot; and, finally, the name and number of Sutherland's own tailor, who had already been instructed to provide Phillip with whatever additional clothing he might need. It was all becoming too much to believe.

*   *   *

It was lunchtime the following day when Phillip drove the Mercedes through the gates of the yacht club and, after checking with the harbor master, found the boat. The Bermuda 40, built on the East Coast, was as fine a boat, for her size, as money could buy. Fully equipped, it ran to well over $175,000. Forty feet of sheer class, she swung easily on her lines, white and gleaming, with the name *Spellbound* in black and gold lettering across her stern.

The mate, a cheerful young man in his twenties who introduced himself as Reg, had the boat ready to sail. Phillip went below, and for the third time in almost as many days he found his clothing needs had been fully anticipated. By the time he had changed into jeans, deck shoes, and a windbreaker, they were underway.

He came topside and took the wheel from the mate. Clear of the breakwater, Reg set a number-one genoa and the mainsail. A warm ten-knot breeze carried them easily for the first several hundred yards, and Phillip was just beginning to shed the windbreaker when the boat heeled sharply in an unexpected gust of cold air. But it wasn't just a gust. It was a steady and freshening wind from the west.

"That's out of the Pacific high offshore," Reg said. "Wind's moving to fill the vacuum created by a low over the desert."

Whatever it was, Phillip had his hands full for the next several minutes until he began to get the feel of the boat. They stayed out for only two hours, reaching across toward Sausalito, then turning to run through Raccoon Pass between the mainland and Angel Island. Back out into the main bay, he set a direct course for the club, pausing briefly halfway across to watch a dark-gray destroyer slide silently by on her way to the open sea.

Phillip declined Reg's offer to maneuver the boat into the slip and was secretly pleased by how well he managed an almost perfect landing.

"You're some sailor, Mr. Vanderlind," Reg said with admiration. "I always figure to have to help the turk—I mean the guests."

"You mean the turkeys," Phillip said, laughing. "I've done some sailing, Reg, but never in a boat like this. She's a beauty."

It was dark when he returned to the house in Marin County, and after another of Irving's excellent meals, this time beef tenderloin sautéed in butter with mushrooms, he sat with his coffee on the deck overlooking the bay and watched the night until the chill drove him back inside. He was thinking about the boat, the car, the house. Was all this what he really wanted? There was still one unknown ingredient—the job and what

Novak would have to tell him about it tomorrow morning. But Averal Sutherland was obviously making one hell of an effort to convince him to take it.

* * *

The Omni offices were located on the northwest corner of the top floor of a new twenty-story building just out of the downtown San Francisco area toward the bay. The view was striking.

Novak was waiting for him when he arrived, and without formality he took Phillip into the office suite he would occupy. Except for a table and a few chairs, it was empty. "Some people are coming in this afternoon to talk about how you want this place decorated," Novak said. He then proceeded to describe Omni's operations. The proposition thus far was simple, he said. The bulk of investor funds to date had come from one man, Harrison Crocker of Denver. Crocker had committed $25,000,000—not a large figure by leasing company standards but enough with which to start. For the last few months, Novak had busied himself with the basics of setting up the operation: the legalities involved, renting office space, hiring a small staff, systems and procedures and the like.

Then he had begun the spadework for acquiring clients. To date, he said, he had almost a dozen interested companies ranging from hospitals to a major airline. All he had done was to call on these concerns to let them know of Omni's existence and to determine what needs they might have. All negotiations, as such, would be conducted by the president of Omni.

Domestic leasing would be only part of the operation, Novak continued. Sutherland expected a substantial amount of business to come out of Europe, especially England. But as yet those contacts had not been made. They were being left as the exclusive province of the president. As the executive vice-president, as Phillip understood it, Novak himself would eventually be cast in the role of procuring funds and maintaining relations with domestic investors—including Harrison Crocker. It was Sutherland's wish, Novak said, that he alone have contact with this key man. In other words, Phillip was not to meet with or even talk to him. Crocker, it seemed, was something of a recluse and preferred to deal with people he already knew. And he had known Novak for some years.

Phillip was puzzled, and annoyed, by Novak's brusque explanation. He supposed the reason was valid. Still, if he became the president of Omni, he wouldn't like being isolated from such an important aspect of the overall operation. But he said nothing.

They had lunch together in the office, and the remainder of the afternoon was spent going over the client data Novak had collected. Then at four-thirty, Phillip met for an hour with the interior designer Sutherland had retained to complete the offices. It seemed premature to Phillip. After all, he had not yet decided to take the job. But the designer explained that he was there to discuss only preliminary ideas and preferences that would facilitate his firm's work when, and if, Phillip's contract with Omni became a fact.

At the end of the day, Phillip considered asking Novak back to the house for dinner that evening. He decided against it. They had a brief drink together at the Blue Fox, and try as he did, Phillip was unable to penetrate the shroud of personal privacy Novak maintained. As he drove home across the Golden Gate Bridge that evening, he realized he knew absolutely nothing about the man.

It was probably just as well, he thought. Novak's social liabilities were as obvious as his business acumen, and there was much to be said for separation of office and personal life. Besides, Sutherland had emphasized that Phillip would have the prerogative of selecting his own executive vice-president if, for any reason, Novak did not please him. He would certainly consider replacing Novak, he thought. And then he realized that again he was thinking as if he had already accepted the job.

He spent the next two days poring over everything he could find to read about leasing and talking with a tax attorney about that aspect of the industry. By late Thursday afternoon he was very certain of two things. It wouldn't take him any time to become fully functional in the leasing business, and, more important, he knew he could successfully perform as the president of Omni Leasing, Inc.

He dropped by the Omni offices early Friday morning for an hour to clarify some of Novak's data, and then he was through with the business end of his trip. The remainder of his time in San Francisco, until Sutherland arrived the following Friday, was his to do with as he pleased. And now that he knew that he could handle the job, would he accept it? He would have some questions for Sutherland, some reservations about the way he had instructed Novak to set up the operation, and the dream of doing something on his own, outside the restrictions of a corporation, still lingered. But hell, he didn't have to decide yet. He had a whole week to make up his mind.

* * *

Phillip spent most of Saturday going over his personal finances, calculating what a contract of employment with Sutherland would mean in terms of his own income and his outstanding obligations and debts. It was a bright picture on both counts.

Sunday, he sailed again, by himself. He tacked offshore two miles, timing his sail to return in midafternoon on a screaming run before thirty knots of ever-freshening wind off the Pacific. As exhilarating as it was, as complete and perfect as everything seemed, something was missing, he realized. There was no one to share it. But in time there would be someone to fill the physical void Polly Savitch had left and the intimacy of spirit he thought he had shared with Jessica Westbrook.

Never in his life had Phillip shopped for himself beyond his immediate needs. Monday and Tuesday he did, and it turned into a spree which began with his indecision over which pair of Gucci loafers to buy. The salesman solved the problem and created another. "Buy both of them," he suggested in a bored, disinterested voice. And Phillip did. Before leaving the elegant shop, he bought eight other pairs of shoes, two dozen ties, a gold chain, and an attaché case. The total bill was just under $2,000.

By late afternoon, the Mercedes was packed with jackets and coats of every description, sports shirts, jeans, belts, sweaters, pajamas, robes, underwear, socks. He lost track of the numbers—and the cost.

The buying orgy continued the following day. Sutherland's tailor measured him, and Phillip devoted the better part of the morning to designing and afterward selecting the material for a dozen suits, five topcoats, and twenty-five dress shirts. After lunch, he seemed to buy whatever got in his way, including a gold ship-link bracelet and a Rolex watch from a jewelry store and three boxes of expensive cigars, a gold cigarette case, and two gold lighters from an exclusive tobacconist's shop on Hyde Street. In an expensive sports shop, three tennis racquets caught his eye: one wood, one steel, and one graphite. He bought all three. Four pairs of tennis shoes, a dozen shirts, shorts, sweaters, and two sets of warm-ups were added to the tennis list, and he then proceeded to buy a comparable assortment of ski clothes and equipment. In the gun department he bought a 9-mm Walther P-38 just because it was a beautiful handgun. And a half-dozen boxes of shells.

When Phillip drove up to the house in Marin County for the second afternoon in a row with the car packed with his purchases, Irving could no longer contain his curiosity. But he dutifully helped Phillip unload the car and unwrap and arrange the clothing in the drawers and closets of the dressing room before he asked with a broad smile, "Mr. Vanderlind has decided to stay?"

"It sort of looks that way, doesn't it?" Phillip replied.

Later that evening, he spent almost an hour on the phone talking and joking with his daughter Carol. She told him that she wanted to go to Europe again next summer, and Phillip said he thought that could be arranged. He also suggested that it might be a good idea to increase her allowance now that she was a senior. After they said goodbye, he thought for a moment and then placed a call to Houston. Kate was not entirely pleased to hear his voice, but her mood improved when he told her that he was prepared to resume her alimony payments immediately, and to make up for any inconvenience he may have caused her, a check for $10,000 would be in the mail next week.

Phillip took a shower before he went to bed that night. And standing in the dressing room wrapped in a towel, he opened the closet doors. Everything he had been able to carry in the car was there. The rest, jackets and trousers that had to be altered and the custom-made clothing from Sutherland's tailor, would be picked up later or delivered to the house. It was quite a collection. He chose a pair of crisp cotton pajamas, put on a silk robe, and went to the windows of the bedroom to admire the view across the bay. It was only then he realized that Phillip Vanderlind, technically, was still unemployed.

*   *   *

That Friday morning he had no trouble finding Averal Sutherland's house. Sea Cliff was just west of the Presidio, situated on the northern side of the sea approach to San Francisco Bay, and the house itself was built on a high windswept bluff overlooking the sea, its backyard a small beach a hundred feet below.

"Come in, come in," Sutherland said as his housekeeper showed Phillip into the solarium, where a breakfast table had been set. "It's good to see you again, Phillip."

"It's good to see you, Averal. How was your trip?"

"Excellent, thank you. Things turned out well for us. But here—" Sutherland gestured to a chair at the table—"let's have some breakfast. I want to hear *your* impression of the past few days."

Phillip began immediately to talk about the business of Omni, and it was quickly apparent to Sutherland that he had become very knowledgeable in a very short time. Breakfast was served and removed as both men discussed timetables, investors, possible equipment deals, clients, strategy—virtually every detail was covered in some depth.

Their conversation continued through lunch when Sutherland spent considerable time discussing the importance of the European market. Most of the traveling Phillip had to do, he said, would be to London. That was where Sutherland's contacts were the strongest. In fact, it appeared at the moment that at least one trip every four to six weeks would be necessary, beginning sometime in late winter or early spring.

In the middle of a sentence, Sutherland stopped abruptly and looked across the table at Phillip. Then he began to laugh. "I'm being very presumptuous," he said. "We have all but figured out Omni's first year of operation and I haven't even been courteous enough to ask whether you've decided to accept my offer."

Suddenly, both men were laughing, and within the next hour Phillip Vanderlind had signed a five-year contract as president and chief executive officer of the Omni corporation.

As part of their final discussion that afternoon, Sutherland suggested that Phillip take the following week to fly back to Houston to wind up whatever personal affairs he had. At the same time, there were banking and leasing contracts to be made in that part of the country. A week from Monday would be his first day on the job.

"Phillip, I must apologize for this evening. I had hoped we could have dinner, but I am forced to entertain some of my associates at Kaufman. I hope you will forgive me. When we get together in New York toward the end of the month, there will be more time."

"Of course, Averal. I'll look forward to that."

"Well, Mr. President—" Sutherland smiled warmly as Phillip began gathering up his things to leave—"I'm glad you've decided to join me. I think it will be a good, and a profitable, association."

"Thank you, Averal. And may I say how pleased I am that you've given me this opportunity? I'm certain that neither of us will ever have cause to regret it." .

*   *   *

At five o'clock, an hour after Phillip left, Sutherland had his second and third visitors of the day. They were not Kaufman associates.

"Ah, here at last," he said, patting Leslie Parrish lightly on the cheek and nodding at Emile Novak. "You must be exhausted, my dear. Come, let's have a drink, both of you. The bags can wait, Emile."

Novak smiled and shook his head. "I'll just take these on up and run, Averal. Too much to do at the office. Thanks just the same."

"Have it your way then, Emile." Sutherland turned to Leslie. "It's terribly rude of us, I know, my dear. But would you mind if Mr. Novak and I had a moment alone?"

"Of course not, darling. I'll just wait for you in the library."

When Leslie had gone, his spike heels clicking across the tile entry, down the steps and into the library, Sutherland returned his attention to Novak. "I concluded the arrangement with Vanderlind this afternoon, Emile. And I am convinced he will be a most satisfactory associate. He fully understands the situation with Crocker in Denver as well as the rationale of confidentiality with regard to Kaufman. Of course he knows nothing yet of the other members of the Beta Group. But I think we should be ready to indoctrinate him within ninety days."

"What if the Crocker matter does arise?" Emile asked.

"Just see that it doesn't, Emile."

Sutherland had learned long ago that his friend and confidant was best dealt with, in some matters, without a great deal of conversation. Novak understood simple, direct orders. And obeyed them. "Good night, Emile, and thank you again."

After Novak had gone, the doors to the library opened and Leslie appeared in stockinged feet, a drink in one hand and pumps in the other. "I hope you don't mind," he said. "I've been in heels for the last twelve hours."

"Of course not, Leslie," Sutherland said. "Are you quite certain you feel up to our plans this evening?"

"I wouldn't miss showing you my new things for the world, Averal! And I haven't seen that darling Greer Becket in ages. We'll have a wonderful time."

"Well, in that case," Sutherland said, looking at his watch, "I'll have dinner sent up in about an hour and then you can rest. Your friend will be here at ten."

"And I'll be deliciously ready," Leslie said.

* * *

Greer Becket was one of the most beautiful women he had ever seen, thought Sutherland as he watched her walk slightly ahead of him up the long staircase to the master suite. A striking blonde and an occasional fashion model, she was often seen in the company of very rich men. And now that Sutherland had seen Leslie's friend, he knew she was well worth the thousand dollars she would earn that evening.

As they entered the large, elegant bedroom, Greer Becket turned and smiled at him. "Do you like the way I'm dressed? Leslie said you liked your women in black." She wore a somewhat severe black pants suit and a white blouse with a high, flowing collar. The only hint of femininity about her clothes was the pair of black patent-leather sandals just visible from under the flaring leg of her slacks.

"You look absolutely exquisite, Greer," Sutherland said. He walked slowly across the room to a small bar. "May I fix you a drink?"

"Cognac, please," she said. "What a lovely room." She pointed to a large, low bed piled with pillows. "That looks like a heavenly place for us. Shall we?"

"By all means." Moments later Sutherland handed her a small glass of brandy and sank down beside her on the bed.

At the other end of the bedroom there was a mirrored alcove. On one side was a completely equipped vanity; on the other, a gleaming chrome clothes rack full of women's clothes. The doorway in the center led to the bath, and it was through this doorway that Leslie appeared. He was naked and unmistakably male.

Smiling at his audience, he quickly stepped into a pair of black bikini panties, then chose one of several lacy black bras to cover his budding hormone-induced breasts. "They're growing, don't you think, Averal?" he asked, cupping one in each hand to show them off.

Sutherland smiled and nodded.

The hair was next. "I just can't seem to make up my mind," Leslie said, pouting in the mirror as he pushed his long curly hair first one way, then the other. "What do you think, Greer?"

"Why not part it in the middle?" she said.

"Of course. Why didn't I think of that?"

Once the hair was finished, Leslie turned his attention to his nails. Selecting a shell-pink lacquer, which he held up for approval, he quickly and expertly painted his fingers and toes, keeping up a constant stream of chatter with Greer about clothes and jewelry. Sutherland simply lounged on the pillows sipping his drink, observing intently.

It took almost thirty minutes for Leslie to put on his makeup, but when he was through and turned to smile at the others, he was exquisitely beautiful. Then he began to dress, first the stockings and shoes.

"Aren't these simply adorable, Greer?" He held up a pair of navy-blue pumps with capped and slightly pointed toes. "They're the newest thing from St. Laurent. See how the heels are shaped? And they're so high. I'm thrilled that high heels are coming back, aren't you?"

"Wearing heels is one of the nice things about being a girl, isn't it, Leslie?" Greer said.

Sutherland groaned slightly and began to run his hand up Greer's legs. She put down her drink and removed her jacket.

Leslie crossed his legs, arched his foot, and slipped on the first pump.

Greer unzipped her slacks and wriggled free of her blouse.

Leslie slipped on the other pump, stood, and walked over to the rack of clothes. He selected a flowing silk print from the rack, turned, and held it up to his body. "Oscar de la Renta. An original," he purred. "I just love his things."

As Leslie slipped into the dress and preened before the mirrors, Greer removed her bra and panties, kicked off her sandals, and reached beneath Sutherland's robe. "How, baby?"

Without saying a word, Sutherland moved the blonde to her hands and knees and took her from behind. She began to moan sensually, while on the other side of the room Leslie was fussing to himself about jewelry, removing a bracelet, and slowly pulling on a pair of navy kid gloves.

Sutherland was breathing hard now, pounding in and out of his paid lover, but his eyes were riveted on the fully dressed woman across the room.

Finally finished, Leslie picked up a handbag and twirled before the mirrors. "Am I pretty enough to go out now?" he said.

Sutherland rolled quickly off Greer and onto his back. "Do me, now!" he said hoarsely.

As she went down on Sutherland, Leslie began walking toward them. When the navy pumps were within inches of Sutherland's face, Leslie stopped and posed again, one pump canted to the inside. "Aren't they darling, Averal?"

Sutherland gasped and came, one hand driving Greer Becket's head down hard and the other playing softly over the instep of Leslie's right foot.

*   *   *

Two hours later, Sutherland sat alone in the darkness of his study overlooking the sea. Leslie Parrish and Greer Becket long since gone from his mind, he watched the silhouette of a giant carrier slip past the lighthouse abeam of Lincoln Park. He was thinking about Phillip Vanderlind.

The man had a spark that reminded Sutherland of himself ten years earlier, that indefinable something that set them both apart from other men. The question, in Sutherland's mind, was whether or not that quality could be harnessed to reality. Clearly Vanderlind wanted money—and the possessions and power that went with it. What man does not? But how many men were willing, like Sutherland, to risk everything to get it? He knew a lot about Vanderlind now, perhaps more than Vanderlind himself. Still, it was always difficult to predict what a man will do when confronted with the decision Vanderlind would be forced to make in three months' time. But whatever the case with Vanderlind, Sutherland knew, as in any difficult undertaking, thorough preparation is always the determinant of success or failure. And Phillip Vanderlind has been thoroughly prepared.

CHAPTER 8

A concerned Richard Manning, president of Triangle Ventures and a member of the Beta Group, kissed his wife goodbye, checked the traffic, and got out of his car at the Los Angeles International Airport. Sixty minutes later, he settled back in his seat for the five-hour flight to New York. In the morning he would fly on to London.

Manning was concerned because he *wasn't* concerned. The flight had nothing to do with his uneasiness. He thought of airplanes only the way he did cars: a place to sit to get somewhere. The fact that he was so unconcerned about the *purpose* of his trip was what bothered him. What was the old saying, "If you aren't nervous before an important event, you probably won't do well"? And Richard Manning could ill afford *not* to do well on *these* trips.

He remembered the first such trip, almost three years ago. Only the fact that he had then had no alternative was what motivated him to go. And if sustained sweating and rapid pulse could have killed him, he would have died that dreary January week in England. Looking back, he had to be amused with himself. Just as Sutherland had promised, there had been nothing to worry about.

He was in London for a week that first time. And after a sleepless last night in the city, he had checked out of the hotel, taken a cab to Heathrow Airport, and boarded a transatlantic flight. Upon arrival in New York, he was waved through customs, caught a cab into Manhattan, checked into a hotel, made a local call, then went out to dinner and a show. The next morning he flew back to Los Angeles and was home in time for an early dinner with his family.

It was only later that same night, as he lay soaking in a hot tub, that Manning fully realized what he had done. And gotten away with. Since that precise moment, he had worried steadily less with each trip. But now, as the jetliner cruised over the southern half of Colorado, he sought to work up some degree of concern as a hedge against carelessness.

*　　　*　　　*

Early Monday morning, Phillip breakfasted on Danish pastry, a rasher of bacon, and coffee in his suite at the Warwick Hotel in Houston. After his breakfast tray had been removed, he showered and shaved; and dressed comfortably in slacks, shirt, and a sweater, he sat down at the desk to make a series of telephone calls.

First, the banks to make appointments to conclude the matter of his personal indebtedness and, with the three largest banks in the city, to arrange stand-by lines of credit from Omni business that would originate in Houston.

A secretary answered his first call. "Oh yes, Mr. Vanderlind!" She sounded as if he were the bank's largest depositor. "That was certainly a very nice story about you in yesterday's paper. Let me tell Mr. Henry you're on the phone." Before he had a chance to say anything he was put on hold. What was that she said about a newspaper story?

"Hello, Phillip? Calvin Henry. I've been trying to reach you for a couple of weeks. Wondered where in hell you'd gone. How do you like the city by the bay?"

"Hello, Calvin," Phillip said coolly. "What do you mean, the city by the bay?"

"That's what the paper said. Congratulations on the new job. Fine thing. Your banker has to find out about it in the *Sunday Chronicle*," he said in mock admonition.

"You weren't my banker a few weeks ago, Calvin, when I needed money," Philip said. "And I'm unaware of any newspaper story. That's not why I called." He made an appointment for the next day and hung up.

He delayed any further calls, waiting for the bell captain to locate a copy of the Houston *Sunday Chronicle*. When it was delivered, he was completely taken aback by the half-page article about him in the business section. FORMER HOUSTONIAN TO HEAD NEW LEASING GIANT was the headline. Fragments of sentences leaped out at him as he quickly scanned the article: "as part owner of . . ." "already significant sums have positioned . . ." "including negotiations with Boeing, Exxon and others . . ." "a man of unusually keen foresight, Vanderlind seems . . ."

After he settled down and read through the article, he could find no fault with anything that was said. Sutherland must have given the paper the necessary information. The article may even have been written and ready to run before he had decided to head up Omni Leasing. Obviously Sutherland knew his man.

The remainder of the day was an orgy of ego-stroking. The bankers he called were eager to talk business. Friends and acquaintances rearranged their schedules to have lunch or an after-office-hours drink with him. And less than a month ago he had been an outcast. Or so he had thought. Could he have imagined the elusiveness and, at times, the outright rudeness and disdain with which he had been treated? No. Not hardly. But now it was different. Very different.

Tuesday may well have been one of the supreme days of his life. He met with all the banks he owed and wrote each a postdated check in complete liquidation of his indebtedness. Sutherland had arranged for him to borrow the aggregate

amount from his bank in San Francisco by personally guarantee-
ing his note. And that same day was filled with people, some of
whom he had known for years. He had debated about seeing
them. They had dropped him when he needed them the most.
Why spend time and energy with them now? It was really quite
simple: ego. He was still in that game.

Wednesday he met Lee Kelly at the Petroleum Club for lunch,
not just a passing drink. People he scarcely knew came over to
their table to say hello, and Kelly introduced him to several men
who wanted to talk about Omni Leasing. Looking out over the
city, Phillip recalled his circumstances the last time he had been
at the Petroleum Club. He shuddered at the memory. Times had
changed. He was once again acceptable, treated as an equal,
instantly a member of the inner circle that was success. That was
all that mattered—success. What he was, what he thought, how
he felt, how he was different didn't matter. The *person* simply
didn't count. What he did—and what he had—was always the
measure.

By late afternoon Phillip's appetite for vindication by his peers
had been satiated and he was on his way to pick up David Marsh
at his office for drinks and an early dinner. He wondered what it
would be like to see Marsh, as well as the Apache offices, again.
One thing was certain: he was glad now he had never gone to
Marsh in those dark days, whining and asking for help. Pride
had served him well in that instance at least.

And what about poor old Sam Rogers? Damn it, thought
Phillip, he really should go by and say hello to the man. As far as
he was concerned, that petty incident over the club thing had
long since been forgotten. Rogers had simply been playing the
corporate game the only way he knew how. And after all,
mediocrity was no sin.

*   *   *

The son of a bitch was back *again*! Samuel Rogers snorted and
slammed the receiver down on the hook. All that to-do around
the office about the piece in the papers and now Vanderlind
was outside and wanted to say hello. Rogers knew that he was

coming in that afternoon. On Monday Marsh's secretary had called to cancel the dinner plans he and Marsh had for this evening; "Mr. Vanderlind is in town and Mr. Marsh knew you would understand," Rogers mimicked the secretary's high squeaky voice. He had intended to leave early to avoid seeing Vanderlind, but it was too late now. The bastard was there and wanted to see him.

When the door opened and Phillip entered, Rogers rose awkwardly and accepted the outstretched hand of his visitor. "Why, Phillip, I had no idea," he said nervously. "I knew you were in town, but . . . well, how are you?"

Phillip wished immediately that he had not come. One look at Rogers told him he wasn't welcome. But he was here. "Sam, it's good to see you. Hope you don't mind me just barging in."

"Yes, well, that's all right, Phillip, of course."

"Family okay, Sam?"

"Family's fine."

"I'm glad to hear it," Phillip said. Rogers had not offered him a seat; both of them were still standing in front of the man's desk. "Well, I know you're busy, Sam, but, if you've got just a minute, there's something I'd like to tell you."

Rogers glanced at his watch and cleared his throat. "Yes, all right. Have a seat."

"No, thanks. I'm meeting Dave, and this'll only take a second." Phillip hesitated, then laughed good-naturedly. "Unfortunately, you probably remember the day, a couple of years ago, when I got pretty abusive over that club thing, Sam. I know *I* do. Anyway, I guess I just didn't want it between us anymore. I'll admit I was angry, but my remarks were unnecessary and uncalled for and—" Phillip extended his hand across the desk— "I want to apologize."

Rogers stared at him. "Do you actually think I'd shake your hand?"

The smile on Phillip's face froze momentarily, then gave way to a look of puzzled embarrassment as he slowly withdrew his hand.

"Do you *honestly* believe a simple gesture like that can atone for everything you've done to me, all the things I've had to endure because of you, the humiliation, the . . ."

"What in hell are you talking about, Sam?"

"You know what I'm talking about. It's because of you that I'm not president of Apache, and you know it."

"Sam, you're not making any sense."

"How in God's name could those people who just hired you be so blind?" Rogers sneered.

Phillip looked at the man for a brief moment, then, checking his anger, he raised his hands in a gesture of futility. "Okay, Sam. I thought we could be friends. But now I guess it really doesn't matter what you think of me."

He was turning to leave then when the crashing sound of Rogers's fist on the desk brought him up short. "But you're *wrong*, you smug, hot-shot bastard!" Rogers shouted. "Everyone who checked you out with us considered what *I* thought about you to be damned important!" He was on his feet now, leaning forward with his hands on the desk, his face livid with rage.

"Obviously," Phillip said calmly, "I was wise to give Dave as my reference."

"For your information, David Marsh didn't have time for such *trivial* matters," Rogers said. "So he kicked all those inquiries down to me, down to good old Sam, not much by the likes of Phillip Vanderlind, but good enough for *something*. 'He worked for you, Sam,' he said. 'You can tell them what they *really* want to know.' And, by God, I did!" Breathing heavily, Rogers collapsed in his chair. "Now . . . why don't you just get out of here? Get out of here and don't ever come back. Get out of my life, Vanderlind."

Suddenly Phillip understood. "My God," he said. "You . . . it was *you*. It wasn't *me* they didn't want, it was what you said about me. Is that it, Sam? You crucified me."

Rogers slowly shook his head. "I didn't crucify anybody. You crucified yourself. All I did was tell them what you are. They had a right to know the truth. Now please, just get out."

"Say the words to me, Sam. Tell me what you said to them."

Rogers was silent.

"Talk to me!" Phillip shouted. "What did you say?"

"I told them the truth, God damn you! I said you were an egotistical, disloyal, arrogant, scheming bastard. That you had been a highly disruptive factor in this company—and would be in any company fool enough to hire you!"

Phillip tensed, every muscle straining with a sudden urge to attack Sam Rogers. Then all at once he relaxed and with a short, cutting laugh simply turned away and walked quickly from the office.

Twenty minutes later, David Marsh sighed, shook his head, and stared apologetically across his desk. "What can I say, Phillip? I thought I was doing you a favor by letting Sam handle your references. I had no idea he felt that way about you."

Phillip smiled thinly. "Dave, it's more serious than that. Sam lied about me. I want the record set straight, and I'd like you, not Sam Rogers, to do it. A simple phone call—or a letter, if you prefer—to the companies Sam talked to would be fine."

Marsh rocked back in his chair and clasped his hands behind his head. "Well now, Phillip, it isn't at all clear to me that such action is called for. You've obviously managed, quite nicely it seems, to rise above the shots Sam took at you."

"But, Dave, that's just it. A man doesn't get blackballed because of the things Rogers *told* me he said. There *had* to be something else, something slanderous as hell."

"Slander is a strong word, Phillip."

"So are its effects. That's why there are laws against it."

"Are you suggesting litigation over this?" Marsh said, leaning forward and placing his elbows on the desk.

Phillip stared incredulously at the man. "Look, what the hell is this? All I want is what I'm entitled to. I *earned* a decent reputation in the nine years I spent at Apache. Sam Rogers stripped me of it. Now I'm simply asking you to restore what's rightfully mine, Dave. Why are you so opposed to doing that?"

"What I'm opposed to, Phillip, is holding this company—and one of its senior officers—up to unnecessary ridicule. You say you were wronged and I've apologized. If you were still being adversely affected by something Rogers said, I would step in.

But, under the circumstances, no one would gain anything by some insipid letter of apology I might write."

Phillip took a long moment to respond. "That's the priority, isn't it: the corporation, always the corporation. And to hell with the individual. That's what you told me that day at the yacht club, and that's what you're telling me now. Well, thank God, *this* individual is finally in a position to say to hell with your corporation."

"With that attitude," Marsh said stiffly, "I trust we won't be called upon in the future to give you a reference."

"Your trust," replied Phillip, rising slowly to his feet, "is exquisitely well placed. Goodbye, Dave."

When he left Apache, Phillip was churning inside. But by the time he reached the hotel he had calmed considerably. He had spent most of his wrath literally forcing his rental car through the rush-hour traffic that crawled down South Main Street to the Warwick. But as he undressed and mixed a scotch, he thought again of Apache and the price Rogers and Marsh had made him pay for his nonconformity. But so what? In the end, *he* had won. And he would never need those bastards again anyway. If he had any anger left, it was toward himself for wasting nine years of his life at Apache.

Under the sting of a hot shower, the last of the tension from the confrontation left his body, and Phillip thought of what a difference there was between Averal Sutherland and men like Rogers and Marsh. Sutherland valued nonconformity, and he had listened to what Phillip had to say for himself, not to the scurrilous words of Sam Rogers. Yet, as he emerged from the bathroom, the question of just what Rogers had said about him continued to gnaw at Phillip. It must have been devastating, whatever it was. And if it was, why in hell *had* Sutherland chosen to ignore it? Or had he simply failed to check with Apache? Surely not, not a man as thorough as Sutherland. Chase, what about Brock Chase? Phillip *knew* he had talked with Apache. Something wasn't computing. He checked the time— almost five o'clock in New York. Chase might still be in his office.

"Well, hello, Phillip. Good to hear your voice. Congratulations. I spoke to Averal earlier this week and he told me you'd signed on with Omni. Of course, I understand his connection with Omni is being kept quiet for the moment. But you'll never regret working for a man like Sutherland."

"I'm convinced of that already," Phillip said. "But there is something I'd like to run by you if you have a second."

"Sure," said Chase.

Phillip took several minutes to tell Chase what he had discovered about his reference from Apache, then concluded, "So naturally I'm curious, Brock. What did Sam Rogers say about me? And did Averal talk to him or Dave Marsh?"

There was a brief pause before Chase responded. "I can't answer those questions, Phillip. Look, by your own assessment, everything has worked out beautifully for you despite what you said. Nothing else really matters, does it?"

Phillip felt a sudden rush of irritation. "Damn it, I think I have a right to know what was said about me, Brock. And why in hell didn't you at least tell me in New York, weeks ago, that the reason I was having trouble finding a job was bad references? Christ, man, the pain and money you could have saved me."

"Just a minute, Phillip," Chase cut in sharply. "There are a couple of things you don't seem to understand. One is something called confidentiality, which I owe one hundred percent to the companies I work for. Despite what I may have felt about you, Phillip, your problem was *your* problem. The second thing is, I advocated you *despite* what was being said. I have no cause, professionally or personally, to feel my conduct left anything to be desired."

"Of course you're right, Brock," Phillip said. "I apologize. And I'm grateful for everything you did for me."

"Don't thank me," Chase said with a self-satisfied chuckle. "Averal Sutherland is the one who hired you."

After he hung up the phone and all through dinner later that evening, Phillip tried to piece the puzzle together: why had Sutherland chosen to ignore what he must have heard about him? Perhaps it was as simple as the things Sutherland had mentioned that night in New York when he told him why he wanted Phillip Vanderlind. That *had* to be it; nothing else made sense.

As he prepared for bed that night, Phillip pondered one last question: should he mention to Sutherland how much he appreciated his willingness to overlook whatever he had heard? His conclusion at the edge of sleep was no. The best way to thank Averal Sutherland was to make a roaring success of Omni Leasing. And he would.

*   *   *

An annoyed and slightly disturbed Brock Chase offered a chair to his tall, gaunt visitor: annoyed because he couldn't imagine why this man had insisted upon seeing him and disturbed because Cyril Kennedy was an agent of the federal government. Nevertheless he smiled pleasantly and said, "Well now, Mr. Kennedy, what can Chase and Connolly do for you?"

"I think you could be very helpful, sir, in one particular aspect of an investigation I'm conducting."

"I can't imagine how. But please, go on."

"Before I can continue, Mr. Chase, I'll need your word that you will not divulge what I'm about to say to anyone, regardless of whether or not you decide to assist the investigation."

"Not even my associates?"

"Especially your associates."

"My wife?"

"I'm sorry, sir, to sound so cloak-and-daggerish, but I assure you it's necessary. No, not even your wife. But I want to make it very clear that you're under no obligation to talk with me. You can decline right now and I'll be on my way. It's strictly voluntary."

"I see." Chase rose and walked toward his office windows and stood for a moment with his back to the agent. The clever bastard has me hooked, he thought. What the hell am I going to say? No? He turned. "All right, Mr. Kennedy. My curiosity has the better of me. I'll listen and agree to maintain the confidence. However, I reserve the option to decline whatever your proposition may be. Agreed?"

"Yes, of course."

"All right. Let's hear it."

Ten minutes later, though mildly entertained by the story Cyril Kennedy told of being wounded by an assailant who happened to belong to the same fraternity, Chase was as bewildered by the purpose of his visit as he had been at the start. "That's quite a story, Mr. Kennedy. But I'm not at all certain I understand just what your point is."

Kennedy smiled a bit sheepishly. "Yes, sir. I know you don't. And I'm afraid I'll have to plead guilty to a bit of melodrama. But I did want to make the point. You see, the man who shot me, a man who had been involved for over two years in the operation of a nationwide crime syndicate, was located, recruited, and hired through an executive placement firm."

Chase broke into laughter. "You can't be serious."

"Yes, sir, I'm quite serious."

"That's insane, man! No recruiting firm, no *reputable* firm, could even be *approached* with such a proposition. Someone, if I may say so, is pulling your leg."

"Forgive me, Mr. Chase, but I didn't say the recruiter was approached with the *ultimate* purpose for which the man was to be used. The syndicate came in the guise of a legitimate company that was looking for a comptroller. And, while I'm not able to divulge the name of the executive recruiter, I assure you the firm was one of the most respected in your business."

Chase shook his head incredulously. "Are you asking me to believe, Mr. Kennedy, that crime syndicates *recruit* their members?"

"I realize how bizarre that sounds, Mr. Chase. But in this case it was true. Crime, at the upper levels, has become a complex and sophisticated operation. And like every other business, crime syndicates need competent men. The question then is, are reputable, legitimate executive recruiting firms being employed surreptitiously to locate these men?"

"I can give you a dozen reasons why something like that wouldn't work," Chase said indignantly. "For one thing, we *know* all our clients—*well*."

"So did the other firm."

"Obviously not well enough."

"Perhaps you're right about that," Kennedy replied.

"Then, too, what about the candidates themselves? If someone hires a respectable man and then tells him his job is stealing or killing or whatever the hell the deal is, do you think he's going to accept such a job?"

"In this case, the man did."

"And that's the other end of the spectrum, Mr. Kennedy. We don't, the top-drawer firms don't, go around recruiting just anybody. Hell, we know a man's personal and business history inside out before he's even remotely considered."

Cyril Kennedy shrugged. "The firm involved had a dossier an inch and a half thick on the man who tried to blow me apart."

"But that's one isolated case, Mr. Kennedy," Chase argued heatedly. "And, in my view, the man was obviously a criminal to begin with."

"Not at all," Kennedy replied. "He was formerly employed as a top executive in a perfectly legitimate business. He was clean, Mr. Chase. But he was vulnerable."

"What do you mean, 'vulnerable'?"

"He was unemployed. He was heavily in debt. He was ripe," Kennedy said. "And at least one logical place a man in that situation might readily be found is in the files of an executive search firm. Let me ask you, Mr. Chase, do you not, on occasion, have executives down on their luck come to you for assistance?"

"Yes, certainly we do. But we work almost exclusively for client companies that are looking for people with specific abilities. And the best candidates for any job, usually, are those people who are already productively employed."

"Yes, I understand that. But are you ever able to match one of the down-and-out executives who register with you with a client? Or, have any of your clients ever indicated a specific interest in looking at someone who isn't currently employed?"

Chase felt a sudden tightening in his throat. What the hell was going on here? Did Kennedy know something more than he was telling? His first question almost perfectly described the situation with Averal Sutherland and Phillip Vanderlind. "Of course there are times when companies are very willing to consider an unemployed executive, Mr. Kennedy. It depends, as you might imagine, on the circumstances involved. But I can honestly say that I have no recollection of a company interested *only* in a man who is unemployed."

"Then maybe we can go about this thing another way," Kennedy said. "Would it be possible for you to find out just how many unemployed executives have found positions through your firm over the past year or so? If you could do that, we'd like to follow up in each instance with an investigation of the employer."

Chase frowned. "I'm not at all certain I want to be put in the position of being responsible for a client of ours coming under investigation by a federal agency just on the strength of your theory, Mr. Kennedy. That may be going a bit far on my part."

"It would be senseless for me to debate the pros and cons of invasion of privacy by the federal government, Mr. Chase. No one wins. Everyone loses in that one." Kennedy rose then and looked directly at Chase, his eyes nothing more than slits. "I need your help," he said simply.

"I'd like some time to think about it," Chase replied uneasily.

"Yes, certainly," Kennedy said.

Chase's mind was racing. What in hell should he do? If he refused to cooperate, would the government initiate some sort of proceedings to obtain access to all of the records of Chase and Connolly? That would be disastrous for the firm if it ever got out. And what about his legal rights? He wanted to talk with his attorney before agreeing to anything. And why had *he* been singled out? That question disturbed him more than anything. "Have you talked with any other firms about this, Mr. Kennedy?" he asked. "Why have you selected Chase and Connolly for this . . . investigation?"

"Mr. Chase, your firm is only one of over thirty on my list. To date I've talked with almost twenty. You just happened to be on this week's list."

Inwardly, Chase breathed a sigh of relief. "Well, that's gratifying to know. Have any of the other firms you've called on agreed to cooperate?"

"Some have agreed to consider it, others have flatly refused. And I have the distinct feeling those who *are* considering it will also refuse. But I don't give up easily, Mr. Chase. Sooner or later, the majority of executive recruiting firms in this country are going to be involved—if my theory is correct. And I know it is. So it's simply a matter of making the rounds until someone cares enough to step up and be counted. I'm hoping that someone will be you."

Chase flushed. "I didn't say I wouldn't help you, Mr. Kennedy. But I hardly feel it's asking too much for a few days to consider all the various ramifications."

"I understand completely. You'll call me, then?"

"I'll be in touch," replied Chase.

*   *   *

Late Thursday afternoon Phillip wound up his affairs in Houston, and when he returned to the hotel to pack for his flight back to San Francisco the message light on his phone was glowing.

"I have five calls for you, Mr. Vanderlind," the hotel operator said. "All from the same person, a Mrs. Savitch."

"Who?" Phillip said with surprise.

"Savitch, Mrs. Polly Savitch," repeated the operator. "She said it's very important that you call her. And I believe she's the one who brought an envelope by for you this morning. Shall I send it up?"

"Yes, all right," Phillip said.

In the envelope was the newspaper article about him. And scrawled across it, under his picture, in bright red lipstick was "Viva Vanderlind."

"You bitch," he mumbled, wadding up the paper and dropping it into the dresser. But as he packed, he found himself remembering the mouth that same lipstick covered.

Along with his bill, when he checked out twenty minutes

later, were the call slips from Polly. "Forget these," he said indifferently, pushing them back to the cashier.

"Are you Mr. Vanderlind?" asked the bell captain, coming up to him.

Phillip nodded.

"There's a call for you, sir. A Mrs. Savitch. You can take it over there," he said, pointing across the lobby.

Phillip thought for a second, then reached in his pocket and handed the man a small bill. "Do me a favor? Tell the lady my car is still in the shop."

Minutes later, he stood just inside the entrance of the hotel waiting for his car. A strong wind was lashing the trees surrounding the Museum of Fine Arts across the street.

"Gonna need a warm place tonight," the top-hatted doorman said, eying the dark blue of the northern sky. "Here's your car, sir."

Phillip looked at the car for a moment, then at the sky, then again at the car. A strange sense of pleasure mingled with disgust welled up in him.

"Put it back," he said.

CHAPTER 9

I n Boston, Augustus Berman was better known to the public as an industrious civic worker than the owner of a prospering chain of auto-parts houses. But within his own business, which was constantly plagued by massive inventory problems and cutthroat competition, Augie, as he was affectionately called, was considered something of a genius. Except for occasional minor problems, his chain of stores remained profitable while others, at least as well managed, struggled to survive. And many didn't.

"Luck, sharp pricing, volume buying—and generous bankers" was the simple but impossible-to-follow explanation he always gave for his success. It was impossible to follow because Augie was his *own* banker. And, as such, he had a *reverse* cash-flow problem: he couldn't expand fast enough to employ all his capital in the business. But as problems went, it was a nice one to have, and he dabbled in real-estate investments so balances in foreign bank accounts did not become excessive. But today, as he hurried back to his office from Rotary, his problem was being intensified. More cash was due in again.

"I'm certainly glad you're here, Mr. Berman," his secretary said when he returned twenty minutes later than he was expected. "New York has called twice since two o'clock."

He merely nodded and went straight into his office, closed the door behind him, and minutes later his phone rang.

The only word he spoke during the five-second connection was "Hello." But he wrote down two words and a four-digit number.

Next he placed a call of the same duration to the number of a telephone booth in Grand Central Station in Manhattan. "The Biltmore, 1801," he said to the man who answered. He repeated the information, then there was a click and the connection was broken.

Augie Berman's face was wreathed in a broad smile as he sighed and hung up the phone. It wasn't that he had any particular _affinity_ for dealing in heroin; he just had an overwhelming aversion to the middle-class struggle to make ends meet. And with his all-or-nothing philosophy of life, he was perfectly content to run whatever risks were necessary to stay ahead of the pack in that rat race.

*   *   *

Phillip turned off the hanging lamp over the large teak worktable in his office suite at Omni Leasing. The office design firm had done a remarkable job in transforming once empty rooms into a comfortable and efficient complex. In addition to the work area and his desk, there were an arrangement of tables and chairs at one end of the room for informal meetings and, at the other end, a dining area with a bar and, behind louvered doors, a small kitchen, a bath, and a bedroom. The formal conference room adjoined his offices, and his secretary, Anne Elkman, had an office of her own.

Phillip stretched and looked at the date that glowed on the transistorized communications panel along one wall of the office. It was the middle of January. Loosening his tie and collar, he walked to the windows that overlooked the bay. It had been a hell of a two months, he thought.

Four major leases were under negotiation, and one, a five-million-dollar package for Hospital Associates, would be closed in a few weeks. Harrison Crocker in Denver had already advanced those funds, and the remaining twenty million Crocker had pledged would be drawn down as other deals firmed up. Phillip was pleased with the job he was doing, and he knew that Sutherland was pleased, too. He had made four trips to New York for conferences with Sutherland, and on the last visit Sutherland had suggested that he take a permanent suite at the Pierre. He would be making his first trip to London soon, and once the foreign phase of the business got underway, he would be in and out of New York a great deal. Only the day before, Phillip had shipped some clothing to the hotel to minimize his luggage requirements for what promised to be a heavy travel schedule.

Omni was almost totally consuming him now. The one occasional exception was Polly Savitch. He had let her back into his life that fall night in Houston when he swallowed his pride and returned her calls. They had spent most of that weekend together. Since then he had seen her in New York, and she had come to San Francisco twice. He knew what she wanted—sex and whatever pleasures his money could buy. But what did *he* want? Polly was dropping hints about marriage, perhaps because she was not as rich as she pretended to be. But that was the last thing he had on his mind. The sex was still fantastic, but now that he could afford her he could see her on his own terms. He had nothing more to prove. Besides, he didn't have time for Polly! Like the house in Marin County, the boat, the Mercedes, she had become a luxurious convenience.

The closing darkness outside his windows reminded him of the time. Irving was expecting him home for dinner, but he had more work to do tonight and over the weekend to get ready for a trip to Seattle. He went to his desk and began to stuff his attaché case with papers. He picked up a check for $25,000. It had come that afternoon, enclosed in a letter from Lee Kelly. He and his wife, Kelly wrote, had finally decided to sell—to the group that Phillip had been negotiating with on his behalf. The terms of the sale had been substantially altered, other parties were involved, and Kelly could not persuade them to honor the commission agreement he had made with Phillip. But he was sending him the $25,000 out of his own pocket just by way of saying thanks.

The letter and the check were so ironic that Phillip didn't know whether to laugh or cry. He had had $75 in his pocket and had thought of suicide the day that Kelly told him the deal was off. And now that he had more money than he could spend, he suddenly had even more. Money. Possession of it, or access to it, was a strange phenomenon. Once it began to come it just seemed to multiply without much effort. It was true—money begets money. And Kelly's check seemed to be undeniable proof of that.

But he was working hard for his money from Omni. Fourteen-hour days were the rule, not the exception, and he was exhausted. Even Sutherland had commented during their last meeting that he looked tired. He urged him to take a vacation before he began his trips to England. He even suggested that he didn't want an associate who couldn't enjoy himself, and he chided Phillip for not having made use of the house in Aspen.

Why the hell not? Phillip thought. And why not this weekend? The skiing would be terrific, and he would have plenty of time to plan for his trip to Seattle next week. He picked up a piece of his personal stationery and jotted a note to Anne Elkman. He asked her to deposit Kelly's check and told her he could be reached over the weekend at Averal Sutherland's address in Aspen, Colorado.

*   *   *

Brad Coleman rocked the turbo-charged Aero Commander up on its left wing over Independence Pass and began the turn to run down the valley to Aspen. As they made their approach to Sandy Field, Phillip could see the slopes were alive with skiers. Cleo Harris's wife, Betty, walked out to meet him as Coleman cut the switches and Phillip clambered out into the surprisingly mild day. Betty Harris was obviously a very efficient woman. When Phillip's bag and new ski equipment were loaded in the back of her car, she drove him to Sutherland's house on Red Mountain, where she had prepared lunch. The Blazer was again available for his use, and Phillip drove to the Highlands. He was surprised at how well he skied that afternoon. Yet the sport was only a bonus to being in the crisp, quiet beauty of the mountains again. On the last run he stopped off-trail and just looked and listened for a while. And that was when he began thinking about Jessica Westbrook.

He had written her a short note after their meeting last September, apologizing for once again burdening her with his bad luck. And several times since, he had thought of calling or writing about his *good* fortune. But somehow with time, and the lingering embarrassment of last summer, he just hadn't. Jessica was right when she had said that she was a loose end in his life. And yet there *was* something that tied them together.

All at once Phillip shivered; the sun had dropped behind the mountains and suddenly it was cold. As he pushed back onto the trail, his thoughts of Jessica were lost in the difficulty of a high-speed run back to the lodge in the lengthening shadows.

He decided to ski Ajax the following day, and as he prepared for the first run of the morning he casually observed the other skiers around him, all expensively dressed and equipped, all obviously enjoying themselves. He was one of them. Pushing off through the light but driving snow that was beginning to fall from lead-colored clouds, he couldn't help laughing aloud. "Only by the grace of money, baby. Only by the grace of *money!*" he shouted into the wind.

They closed the lifts shortly after lunch because of the blowing snow, and Phillip spent the rest of the day bar-hopping through the streets of the small village and left the lounge of the venerable Jerome Hotel just after dark. Despite the slick, narrow road up Red Mountain he reached the house without incident, put the Blazer away, and stood for a while in the swirling snow. One day soon, he vowed, he would live somewhere in this magic country. What was it Averal Sutherland had said during one of their meetings about learning to enjoy his new affluence?

The phone was ringing when he entered the house. It was Brad Coleman calling from Denver. "We've got ourselves a real storm, sir," he said. "I won't be able to pick you up tomorrow unless this weather breaks."

"What do the weather people say there in Denver?" Phillip asked.

"Maybe tomorrow, maybe Monday," Coleman said.

"Okay, Brad. I guess there's nothing we can do. Call me tomorrow."

The weather broke in Aspen about eleven o'clock Sunday, but when Coleman called he had bad news. Another storm was building right in behind the last one and was forecast to reach Aspen just after dark.

"Brad, I'm going to get on out of here in the next thirty minutes and just drive to Denver. If we can get out by around noon or so tomorrow, we can fly on back to San Francisco. Otherwise, I'll hop a commercial flight. Try and get me on some bird leaving tomorrow afternoon just in case."

He packed his bag and called the Harrises to tell them he was leaving. "I've got to get back," he said. "And this looks like the only way. Can you make arrangements to pick up the Blazer?"

"No problem," Cleo Harris said. "Betty and I will be driving down later this week. We can bring it back. Just let us know where to find it. And we're sorry this storm spoiled your weekend."

Phillip was walking out the door when he suddenly thought again of Jessica; he would be driving right through Vail. In seconds he was on the phone again.

"Phillip. Of all people!" Jessica exclaimed. "I thought you'd just disappeared."

"I almost did," he said with a laugh.

"I answered your note last fall, but mine came back marked 'no forwarding address.' Where are you now?"

"I'm just across the mountains in Aspen, and I'm about to leave in a few minutes to drive to Denver. I know this is pretty sudden, but you still owe me a home-cooked meal."

"It's not sudden at all."

"Is that an invitation?"

"Of course."

"I'm on my way," Phillip said. "See you in a couple of hours. And, Jessica, no hard-luck stories this time. I promise."

*   *   *

The second storm screamed in three hours ahead of schedule, catching Phillip somewhere east of Eagle on U.S. 70. "Whoa, baby," he coaxed as the Blazer's rear end skidded dangerously close to the shoulder of the winding, snow-impacted road. Great God, he thought. I've made one big mistake. I'm in a fucking blizzard!

The Blazer was in four-wheel drive and moving at barely ten miles an hour as he struggled to see through the almost opaque windshield, fighting constantly to maintain control. The wind gusts booming down the mountains on either side of him threatened to lift the car right off the road.

He had filled the Blazer's tank in Glenwood Springs, thank God. And if he absolutely had to, he thought he could survive the night by pulling off the road and periodically running the engine and heater. But the prospect of such a night was not at all appealing. Every blizzard in these mountains counted among its victims those trapped and frozen to death in vehicles.

He couldn't do much except guess where he was, but it seemed he should be somewhere within striking distance of Vail. And he knew there were a lot of filling stations and cafés strung out for miles on either side of the resort area. He had long since given up much thought of reaching Jessica's. What he was looking for now was *anyplace* to pull off the road. It would be dark soon. He would drive for another thirty minutes and then begin looking for a place to park if he hadn't reached Vail.

Forty-five minutes later he was still driving. He thought he remembered that the highway straightened and became flatter as it neared Vail. But he couldn't be certain. At the moment, he was descending a rather steep incline, wishing he had stopped miles back. Then he saw it: a gas station off to the right, its sign trying to push its light through the snow and the onrushing darkness.

Where was the turn-off? There had to be a turn-off! Damn it, where was it? There! A curving roll of snow encouraged him to turn . . . *now!*

The snow and his judgment betrayed him. The Blazer mushed to a stop at the bottom of a ditch that paralleled the turn-off. Well, hell, he thought, at least I made it. The Blazer appeared all right, just wedged in the deep drift. Phillip pushed open the door, grabbed his bag, and trudged the remaining hundred yards to the station.

*   *   *

Jessica had no idea why she continued to sit up, waiting for Phillip. The phones in Vail had stopped working hours before, and nothing less than a polar bear could travel anywhere on a night like this, she wryly reflected. An hour after dark, she knew there was no chance she would see or even hear from him tonight. Still she waited, curled up in a large chair before the fire. It was almost midnight before she finally fell asleep.

Now, something was pushing Jessica toward consciousness. The phone was ringing. Barely awake, she stumbled across the room to answer it.

"Yes, hello?"

"Jesus, what kind of weather is *this*?"

"Phillip? Phillip, where are you? Are you all right?"

"I'm fine, Jessica. And I'm here in Vail. Or almost. Orman's Texaco on I-seventy."

"You're only a mile or so away, then."

"I'll be damned. I've been here all night. The phones were out and these good people gave me a cot for the night."

"Thank goodness. But why didn't you just come on here?"

"I buried my car in a snowbank."

"Well, I'm so relieved you're safe. But you can't possibly get to Denver today if this storm keeps up. Can someone at the station bring you down here? I'll substitute a nice hot breakfast for that dinner."

*　　*　　*

She was dressed in jeans and a sweater, with her hair in pigtails, when she greeted him at the front door of her condominium. He stamped the snow off his boots and quickly ducked in the door, turning to help her close it against a sudden gust of wind and snow. "Thought I might not make it." He laughed as she leaned back against the door and faced him.

"I'm glad you did. It's nice to see you again, Phillip. Lets go up. Breakfast's almost ready."

He kicked off his boots and followed her up a short flight of stairs to a living room with a lofted ceiling. She had set a small breakfast table in front of the fire.

They exhausted the topic of the weather over breakfast, and Jessica was pouring fresh coffee for them when she asked, "What are you doing now, Phillip? Anyone who can afford weekends in Aspen obviously isn't repairing boats for a living."

Phillip grinned sheepishly. "You're right. But, for once, let's not talk about me. I want to hear about *you*. What have you been up to?"

"Mostly trying to run a business that doesn't seem to understand it's supposed to make a profit."

"Well, if you don't count Mexican pottery, I do know a little bit about business. Want to try me?"

Jessica did. And the longer she talked the more convinced he became that her small gift shop was not a viable operation. Then, when she brought him the books, he knew he was right. "You know what's happening, don't you?"

"Yes," she said, turning to look out of the window at the driving snow, "I think so. But I suppose I'm going to have to hear someone else say it before I believe it."

"Okay," he said quietly. "It's an oversimplification, but your inventory just doesn't turn over fast enough and you're too undercapitalized to offset it."

Jessica nodded slowly, still watching the storm.

"But there's an alternative to heading down the road to oblivion, you know."

"Sell out?"

"That's the best solution. And now, before the season ends, if you possibly can."

"Then I get a job waiting tables, or something." She laughed humorlessly. "And eventually spend whatever I get from the shop making ends meet so I can stay here."

"You really love this place, these mountains, don't you?"

"Yes, I do," she said wistfully. "Almost irresponsibly at times, I suppose. But I know I'll stay here, whatever I have to do." She was quiet for a moment, then she brightened and laughed. "So that's my sad story. Tell me what *you're* doing. I'm dying to know."

He told her about Omni then. And when he was through, their conversation drifted into the smaller areas of each other's lives. And on through lunch into late afternoon they talked, stories running into stories generating stories, until the light began to fade and both became aware of time again.

"Can you believe it's almost five?" Phillip said, glancing at his watch.

Jessica smiled. "We've never really talked before, have we?" She was silent for a moment, then with an even voice she said, "I like you very much, Phillip."

He understood. It was the very thing he had been thinking about her. No pressure, no lust, no designs—he truly *liked* her, too. And when he said it, he thought it was the easiest thing he had ever said in his life.

"I have a proposition for you," Jessica said suddenly.

Phillip raised his eyebrows. "Well, I hope so, for my sake."

"It's not what you're thinking. But you are going to have to spend the night here, you know."

Phillip glanced outside. Even though the snow had lightened considerably since midafternoon, it still swirled ominously through the blaze of light falling from the living room across the small veranda outside.

"And that," she said, pointing toward the couch, "is a perfectly comfortable sofa-bed which I absolutely insist you use. Say yes and I'll cook you the best pot of chili you've ever tasted."

Phillip said yes, and it *was* the best chili he had ever tasted. "Want to get married?" he said.

"Not for my cooking."

"Well then, let's go outside and build an obscene snowman or something to work off our gluttony."

They lasted less than twenty minutes in the biting wind and cold before they tromped back inside, shaking the snow from their clothes. "You know, this is really a good-looking coat," Phillip said as he helped her out of the hip-length sheepskin jacket she was wearing.

"It is lovely, isn't it? And very light and comfortable. The small company in Montana that makes them found a way to thin or shave the skins before they're cured. It's really a unique coat. In fact, I liked them so much, I talked the company into letting me buy a half dozen to see if I'd be interested in a franchise for the shop. All six were gone in less than a week—not bad for a three-hundred-dollar item. But the franchise was just too expensive for me to handle." She laughed, dismissing the subject, and nodded toward the living room and the crackling fire. "Come on, let's go in and get warm."

They sat quietly for a time, watching the glowing logs and listening to the wind. Then Phillip suddenly rose, walked over to the fireplace, and stood staring at the yellow-blue flames, unconsciously rubbing the corners of his mouth in thought. Finally he turned and said, "How much were they asking for the franchise?"

"I'm not sure it really was a franchise. They were just looking for an established business in town to take on their line and guarantee to buy a minimum of fifty thousand dollars' worth of coats a year."

"You're right, that's not a franchise, as such. But it doesn't matter. The question is, do you think you could sell that many coats a year in a shop that sold only sheepskin coats?"

"Yes, easily. And maybe even twice that, if I had an exclusive in the county. But I'll never have a chance to prove it. You've seen my books, Phillip."

"Why don't I look at them again? Who knows, maybe I can

figure out something. And if I can, would you be interested?"

"Of course. But I suppose I should tell you I've already talked to my banker and he said no."

"Good," Phillip said. "The chance to prove a banker wrong gives me added incentive. But before I start on the numbers, you're going to have to educate me about a few things up here."

It was almost midnight before Jessica finally finished telling him what she knew of the local economy and of her own experience in retailing. Then, while she went upstairs to soak in a hot tub, Phillip re-examined her books and began running numbers and projections. He was so engrossed that he scarcely noticed her when she came downstairs again and quietly made up the sofa-bed.

An hour and a half later, Phillip leaned back and gazed pensively at his work. Unless he had missed something, it looked as if there *were* a possibility of converting her gift shop to a business that retailed only the elegant sheepskin coats. He started to call up to her, then hesitated. She had probably fallen asleep, he thought, and it seemed a bit ludicrous to wake her up just to talk about a possibility. And he was exhausted, too. The morning would be soon enough, he decided.

When he finally stretched out on the sofa-bed and pulled the covers over him, it was 2:00 A.M. The room was quiet except for the wind that moaned softly outside. The storm was blowing itself out, and he hoped that Vail Pass would be open by mid- or late afternoon. He had to get back to San Francisco.

When Phillip's thoughts returned to Omni, he found he was wide awake. He lit a cigarette, finished it, shifted positions two or three times, then sat up suddenly on the side of the bed. He couldn't sleep.

"Can't sleep?"

The voice startled him. Raising on his elbow, he saw Jessica, in an old-fashioned flannel nightgown, sitting on the top step looking down at him. Her legs were tucked up under her chin and her face glowed softly in the light of the dying fire.

"No."

"I can't either." She rose and came slowly down the stairs,

stopping on the bottom step. "I've been remembering, Phillip—and I want to say it from here—I've been remembering last September and that night I walked away from you when I think you needed me. I didn't realize it until I was on the plane back to Denver, and then I wanted to turn around and come back and hold you in my arms. I tried to call for days until one day your phone was disconnected. Then my letter came back and I thought you were gone forever. I'm sorry, Phillip. I know what it is to need and come away with nothing. I'm sorry I left you with nothing."

He put out his hand to her and started to speak.

"No, please, don't say anything. I just had to say what I did. Good night." She turned and ran back up the stairs.

He lay still for a long time, trying to decide what to do. Should he go upstairs? He couldn't deny the way he was beginning to feel about Jessica; but it was part instinct, part convention, and part something he didn't understand that made him believe that, at least for now, they should leave things as they were.

*　　*　　*

Jessica was still asleep when he woke up at seven o'clock. He put on a pot of coffee, showered quickly, and spent an hour going over his calculations. By the time Jessica came downstairs, he had already been on the phone to Montana.

"Why didn't you wake me up?" she said sleepily. "How long have you been awake?"

"Long enough to have taken the liberty of calling some people in Montana and trading a preliminary deal for you to become the sheepskin-coat magnate of the West."

"Phillip!"

"Well, according to their banker, the company is honest and they know their business. And they were definitely interested in what I had to say."

"So am I," Jessica said with a bewildered smile.

"Good. Let's get some coffee and see what you think of my presumptuous dealings this morning."

After explaining how he thought she could liquidate her inventory to raise capital and showing her the projections he had made based on her thoughts the night before, Phillip moved into the specifics of the tentative deal he had negotiated. "My principal concern with this company was that they might be operating on too much of a shoestring. In other words, if they went broke, they could take you down with them. So this is what I came up with."

Thirty minutes later, Jessica looked up from the mass of figures and plans and nodded slowly. "I *think* I understand. But let me be sure. I have to buy a minimum of fifty thousand dollars' worth of coats from them over the next twelve months. But instead of paying for them as they're shipped to me, I pay the full amount immediately."

"That's right."

"And in return for—what did you call it?—'bankrolling' them, I get twenty-five percent of their company and an option on every new retail outlet they want to establish?"

"Exactly. And if, as you seem to feel, these coats are a unique item and they really catch on, the option feature alone could be worth the price of admission."

"But, if I'm wrong, you feel I have some protection because of the note I'm getting which would be secured by liens against their equipment plus their seventy-five percent of the stock?"

Phillip laughed. "Damned if you don't sound like a Yankee trader instead of a beautiful woman. And don't forget: if something went wrong, you'd own, outright, the patented manufacturing process they have."

Jessica blinked her eyes and shook her head. "Why are they willing to do all these things, Phillip?"

"That's a damn smart question. And the answer is twofold. First, they think they've got a winner. And if they're right, they've given up nothing, except a piece of their company. The second reason is, they have no choice; they can't get expansion money anywhere else—at least not today."

"Which brings me to the one thing I *don't* understand about all this," Jessica said, shuffling through the papers in front of her until she found the one she wanted. Then, circling a figure at the bottom of the page and drawing a line up to another figure, she asked, "Have I forgotten how to add? I mean, if I'm able to raise fifty thousand dollars from liquidating my inventory and I have to pay fifty thousand dollars to get back in business, where does this *other* twenty-five come from? Without it, I don't see how all this would be possible."

They were sitting side by side on the couch, and Phillip reached over and took her hand. "I want to tell you a story. Several months ago I did a little favor for a man in Houston. I found him a buyer for his company, and last week he sent me a check for twenty-five thousand dollars. In business, we call it a finder's fee. It was the easiest money I ever made."

Suddenly, Jessica's eyes widened. "Oh, now wait a minute, Phillip. I . . ."

"Let me finish," he interrupted gently. "As I've told you, I make a great deal of money now. I don't *need* this twenty-five. So what am I going to do with it? I don't like banks or the stock market, and it's not enough to put into real estate. I'm not doing you a favor. It's the other way around." He handed her the check he had written earlier. "Please take it. If you decide not to try the deal, you can always tear it up."

Jessica sat staring at the check in her hand. There were no tears, no cries of joy, no mock refusals or gushes of gratitude. "Thank you," she said simply. "And you realize, of course, that business partners should see each other once in a while."

"I think it's imperative," Phillip said. Then all at once he felt uncomfortable, as if he had implied some sort of personal obligation with the money. He stood up abruptly and began straightening out the pile of papers on the table. "Well, now that all the scheming's done, I think you ought to call your lawyer and have him run up here if he can. In the meantime, I've got to figure out how in hell I can get to Denver." He started across the room toward the phone, but before he had gone two steps she was in his arms. And for a long time they stood there just holding each other.

An hour later Jessica's attorney came, and by late afternoon, after numerous phone calls to Montana, facts and figures of the manufacturer were confirmed and the deal refined and reduced to a short but effective letter agreement. The president of the company and his attorney would fly to Vail the next day for signing, bringing with them the stock of the company. A note would be executed, and Phillip's $25,000 would be used as a down payment until Jessica's liquidation of inventory made available the remaining funds. Final contracts were promised by the attorneys within two weeks, and Jessica's first shipment of coats was already being packed by the enthusiastic Montanans.

"Well, that was as quick a deal as I've ever seen," Jessica's lawyer said when he dropped Phillip off at the gas station to pick up the Blazer. "Anything else you can think of before I go?"

"I guess that's it. Just go over the deal again before she starts signing tomorrow. Make sure I didn't miss anything. We went awfully fast."

"Don't worry. I won't let her get hurt legally. And from everything I've seen, you traded a very tight deal for that lady. Besides, she knows the retail business and she's sold those coats before. She'll be okay. But are you sure you don't want any stock in her company, don't even want to be an officer?"

"No. Just have her execute a note to me for the twenty-five so I can write it off if the deal folds."

"Okay. I'll call you if anything comes up. And tell Jessica I'll call her later tonight." He held out his hand as Phillip opened the door to get out. "You got a fine woman there," he said.

Driving back to the condominium to pick up his things and say goodbye to Jessica, Phillip thought about what the lawyer had just said. She wasn't his "woman," but the suggestion didn't displease him. He tried to sort out his feelings for her and hers for him. It seemed almost as if both of them had repressed whatever natural tendencies they might have had until an emotional barrier of some sort had formed between them. Had they missed their moment? Maybe not. There is a right time and a right place for every relationship.

*   *   *

It was almost nine o'clock that night before he made it through Vail Pass and regained the four-lane highway into Denver. He would have to spend the night there before flying out tomorrow morning with Brad Coleman. Reaching the outskirts of the city, he avoided the temptation of convenient roadside motels and drove to the downtown area. He had made an impetuous but not illogical decision. As long as he found himself in Denver, he wanted to meet Harrison Crocker. The hotel he selected was right across the street from the building where Crocker had his offices.

Despite Sutherland's counsel about not visiting Crocker, Phillip had grown increasingly apprehensive about having no contact with the man who represented Omni's total investable funds to date. Hell, *he* was the president of Omni, not Emile Novak. And he reasoned if he were Crocker, he'd damn well want to know the man who was investing twenty-five million of *his* money. There was another thing too: Phillip had all but concluded that Novak would have to go. There was just something about the man he didn't like. And Sutherland undoubtedly had a place for him in his other operations. It was time for Phillip to take full control.

He had breakfast in his room the next morning and then called Brad Coleman at the airport. He was ready to take off whenever Phillip got there, he said. They should be able to make San Francisco by early afternoon.

Phillip dialed his office. "Anne, this is Phillip Vanderlind."

"Oh, Mr. Vanderlind, we've been worried about you. Are you all right?"

"I got caught in a blizzard, but I'm in Denver now and will be flying out later this morning. I'll see you this afternoon. Is Mr. Novak there?"

"He's not in yet, Mr. Vanderlind."

"It's not important. Just tell him I'm leaving Denver right after I see Harrison Crocker."

"Yes, sir."

Depressing the button, he waited for a second, then dialed Information. "May I have the number for Crocker Enterprises, please?"

There was a long pause before the operator spoke. "Sir, I show no listing for a Crocker Enterprises."

More amused than puzzled, Phillip thanked the operator and

hung up. Harrison Crocker really did have a passion for anonymity. What the hell, he thought finally; the man was just across the street. He rechecked the office suite number on a carbon copy of a letter Novak had written to Crocker some two weeks earlier: Number 2650.

Phillip walked through the lobby of the Scanlon Building and rode the elevator to the twenty-sixth floor. He followed the numbers on the doors, looking for 2650. Damn numbering systems, he thought as he circled the floor for the second time. There was no 2650 that he could find. He was about to go into one of the other offices to inquire when a building maintenance man stepped off the elevator.

"Excuse me, I'm trying to find 2650. Crocker Enterprises?"

"There isn't no 2650," the man replied without hesitation. "Never heard of—what did you say?"

"Crocker Enterprises. Harrison Crocker?"

"Nope, not on this floor, anyway. But we've had some move-ins the last couple of days in the building. Maybe you'd better check with the manager on the main floor."

The building manager had never heard of Crocker Enterprises either. Phillip pulled the copy of Novak's letter from his pocket and read the address out loud.

The manager nodded. "Yes, sir, this is the Scanlon Building," he said. "But I'm afraid we just don't have—and never have had, for that matter—anyone named Harrison Crocker."

CHAPTER 10

Anne Elkman thought her job as executive secretary of Omni Leasing was near perfection. The offices were beautiful and conveniently located, the work was demanding but not difficult, and she admired her employer, Phillip Vanderlind. It was, however, Emile Novak who had interviewed her for the job, and somehow he had made her very uneasy. Despite the generous salary, she had decided to look elsewhere until she met Mr. Vanderlind. Since then her apprehensions about Mr. Novak had proved totally groundless. He had no personal warmth, Anne Elkman thought, but he always behaved like a gentleman. She decided that he was shy and lonely.

That morning, after speaking with Mr. Vanderlind on the phone, Anne Elkman was busying herself with preparations for his return when Emile Novak entered the office.

"Good morning," he said, scarcely looking at her.

"Oh, Mr. Novak," she said. "I have a message from Mr. Vanderlind. He was caught in a blizzard in Colorado. But he's in

Denver now, and he'll be flying back this morning right after he sees Harrison Crocker."

Novak stopped abruptly in front of her desk. "What do you mean?" he said in a low voice.

"He just called from Denver," Anne Elkman replied, "and . . ."

"I heard what you said, you stupid bitch!" Novak suddenly shouted.

Anne Elkman recoiled.

"Call him back," Novak said, his eyes blazing with anger. "I want to talk to him." He leaned toward the startled secretary until their faces almost touched, his words cold and deadly. "Do it *now*, you idiot broad, or I'll break your goddamn neck!" Then he turned and stormed into his office, slamming the door behind him.

Anne Elkman was terrified. Never before had she seen the mixture of fear and violence that seemed to leap from Emile Novak's pale-green eyes. What should she do? Was she in danger? There were people in the other offices. Should she go to them? Should she try and find Mr. Vanderlind or just leave now while she still could? Her emotions surged from terror to anger and back again as she sat frozen behind her desk.

A light on her phone console blinked on. Mr. Novak's line. She stared transfixed until it went off a few minutes later. It came back on immediately, burned for less than a minute, then blinked off. Three more calls were made in the space of the next ten minutes.

Just as she was reaching for the phone to try to call Mr. Vanderlind's pilot in Denver, Emile Novak came out of his office carrying a large briefcase and walked directly up to her desk. Instinctively, she drew back, putting her hands to her throat.

"Mrs. Elkman, I'm terribly sorry for the way I just spoke to you. It was totally uncalled for and I hope you can forgive me." He smiled at her sadly. "I've had some rather upsetting personal news this morning and I'm just not myself." Then he dismissed the matter. "I find I have to fly to New York today and I've no idea when I might be back. Goodbye, Mrs. Elkman."

After he had gone, Anne Elkman began to cry softly. She had never been so frightened in her life. Why had Mr. Novak spoken to her like that? A blizzard, Denver, Harrison Crocker—it was a perfectly innocuous message. And yet he had threatened to kill her. It simply made no sense. She would tell Mr. Vanderlind what had happened when he returned and then resign. She could never again feel safe in the presence of Emile Novak.

* * *

Averal Sutherland had taken the call from Emile Novak, listened without interruption, then instantly made the decision. "Vacate the office immediately, Emile. Today. Now. Your effectiveness in Omni is ended. I will leave for San Francisco this afternoon."

Without waiting for a reply, he terminated the call and buzzed his secretary with instructions to phone Omni Leasing and leave a message for Phillip Vanderlind inviting him to dinner the following evening.

Later, as the Rolls-Royce purred toward La Guardia Airport, Sutherland pondered how he should deal with Emile Novak. Beta was a finely tuned, sophisticated operation, and the man simply had to understand that one did not bully and batter; one finessed. Had it been any other man, Sutherland would have terminated him on the spot. But to Emile Novak he owed his life and, to a substantial degree, his fortune. He also knew that without Novak's contacts, Beta would cease to exist. And yet, unless he could effectively control the man's violent temper and impetuous actions, Novak could cost him everything.

Perhaps the answer was specialization, that and isolation, Sutherland thought as the car pulled to a stop outside the private hangar at the airport. Novak would remain in command of Essex and Beta's marketing contacts where his straightforward way of doing business was a definite asset. But he would be divorced from virtually any contact with the presidents of Beta's operating companies. Thus the chances of traumatizing personality conflicts would be held at an absolute minimum.

As the Lear raced the sun westward, Sutherland's thoughts turned from Novak to Phillip Vanderlind. The situation in

Denver was indeed regrettable. But more than anything else, it was merely an inconvenience that would require an acceleration of timetables. Vanderlind was still viable. And, within the week, Sutherland was confident Omni Leasing would be fully on-stream in all its operations.

*   *   *

Phillip arrived in San Francisco shortly before 3:00 P.M., and in less than an hour he was in his offices listening patiently as Anne Elkman, still emotionally distraught, told her story. He consoled her as best he could and then suggested she take the next two days off; a four-day weekend was the least she deserved, he said.

"Mr. Vanderlind, are you positive Mr. Novak will not be back?"

"That is the one thing I *am* certain of, Anne. I'll see you Monday morning."

For over an hour after the secretary had gone, Phillip sat in his office going through the Crocker file. There were copies of more than twenty letters from Novak to Crocker, dated and addressed to the nonexistent office in Denver, letters that were written but obviously never mailed. They—and Harrison Crocker himself—were façades, of course. But why? The $5 million was real; it was in the bank. And if it belonged to Sutherland, which it apparently must, why hadn't he just said so? It was nothing new, and certainly acceptable, for a man to participate in a deal as a silent investor—but not from his own partner, for God's sake. Well, whatever the reason, he thought, he would hear it from Sutherland tomorrow evening at dinner. That was certainly his purpose in making an unscheduled trip to San Francisco. Phillip knew there would be a plausible explanation, and probably a very simple one, as far as the mechanics of the money were concerned; that wasn't what bothered him. It was the unnecessary and demeaning deceit that made him angry.

Then there was Novak, the son of a bitch! The Elkman incident clearly confirmed Phillip's instinct about the man, as well as his decision to replace him. How Sutherland could employ such a man in his organization puzzled Phillip. And he was looking forward to saying as much to Sutherland when he told him that Novak was through at Omni. The Crocker deception and Novak's behavior were perplexing and demanded satisfactory explanations. But aside from that, he thought, he was in business with a man of unquestioned integrity, and he had the job he had always dreamed of. Those were the two points he must keep in mind.

* * *

Averal Sutherland rose late the next morning. The fatigue from his unexpected trip from New York was gone, and he ate a leisurely breakfast, watching the activity on the bay below. He was also preparing himself mentally for the meeting that evening with Vanderlind.

His recruiting methods had been extremely successful three times in the past, and he fully expected them to be so again. It was, he thought, a variation on tactics to elicit cooperation as old as the Spanish Inquisition. First, you torture a man until he reaches the stage of hopelessness and resistance is the only defense he can muster. Then you tell him it is all a mistake; he is innocent. You clothe him and feed him and restore the hope you have taken from him. But then th orture begins all over again. It is too great a shock and the will to resist finally crumbles. You get what you want. Simple but extremely effective.

Of course, Averal Sutherland had nothing to do with a man's initial downfall. He only had to make certain that he had reached bottom. That was the essential ingredient: *all hope had to be gone.* Phillip Vanderlind had been absolutely flat on his back when Sutherland found him. Now he was on top of the world—and consummately vulnerable. It wasn't a process Averal Sutherland enjoyed, but it was necessary.

* * *

Normally, a man doesn't relish having serious problems descend on him the minute he reaches the office, but in this instance it was a blessing. Phillip was so immersed in getting the

Hospital Associates deal back on track that it was almost six o'clock before he had a chance to think about the bizarre events of the day before. And the dinner with Sutherland was only an hour away.

He went into the small bath, shaved, changed into a fresh shirt, and thirty minutes later he was on his way to Sutherland's house in Sea Cliff. It was raining a steady drizzle. Fog was moving in from the sea and swirling up over the bluffs. When he arrived at the house, it was barely visible in the blowing mist. He parked the car, locked it, and went up the walk. It was cold, and foghorns sounded off the bay.

Sutherland answered the door himself. He was dressed uncharacteristically in a gray herringbone jacket, dark slacks, and a heavy cable-knit turtle-neck sweater. It was the first time Phillip had seen him in other than business attire. Somehow, the man looked even more formidable in casual clothes.

"Hello, Phillip. Come in. My apologies for making you brave this unpleasant weather."

"Not at all," Phillip said cordially, shaking hands and shrugging out of his raincoat. "As a matter of fact, I'm damn glad you're here. When I was in Denver the day before yesterday . . ."

"You went to see Harrison Crocker and couldn't find him. Is that the problem, Phillip? Here, let me have your coat."

"Yes. I knew Crocker wanted to remain anonymous. But I discovered he didn't even exist. What's going on, Averal?"

"All in good time, Phillip. All in good time," Sutherland said lightly as he gestured toward the rear of the house. "First, let's go back to the library and see if we can find a drink. The cook is preparing dinner. Pleasure first and then business."

Conversation during dinner was mostly of sailing, and the longer the discussion continued, the more irritated Phillip became. Dammit, he thought, why is he avoiding the Crocker thing? Over coffee he finally asked the question point-blank. "Averal, what about Harrison Crocker?"

The other man nodded, replaced his napkin, and pushed back from the table. "All right, Phillip. I'm certain you're confused.

That's quite understandable. On the other hand, I did caution you to leave the Crocker matter to Novak. Shall we have some brandy in the library while we talk?"

Rain lashed the windows of the library as the two men sat across from each other before the warmth of the fire. "Why did you choose to disregard my wishes?" Sutherland began.

"Going to see Crocker was based on my decision early last week to replace Novak, Averal. With that in mind, and finding myself in Denver anyway, I felt it would expedite matters at least to introduce myself to Crocker, whoever he is—or was."

"Yes, I would say matters have been expedited. Now, as for Emile Novak, Phillip, I . . ."

"As far as I'm concerned," Phillip interrupted coldly, "I don't want to see that man again, Averal."

"I have already anticipated your wishes," said Sutherland, raising his hand to take a sip of brandy. "He was permanently reassigned to another operation yesterday morning."

"Averal, what *is* all this about a Harrison Crocker?" Phillip said. "Phony letters from Novak . . ."

"There is no Harrison Crocker, Phillip. But it was important that you believe, for a time, that such a person existed."

"Why? I don't understand."

"Of course you don't. That's why I came out here—to explain the situation to you. Actually, you would have been told in another thirty days or so. Your trip to Denver merely accelerated things. I apologize for the necessity of having to deceive you. And naturally you are concerned about the source of the money invested in Omni Leasing. When you discovered there was no Harrison Crocker, where did you think the first five million dollars came from?"

"From you—or one of your affluent friends."

"It came from me. And that's what all this is about, Phillip. Where the money does come from. But before I tell you that, let me ask you a question. Why do you think I selected you for this operation?"

"I remember asking you that same question, Averal. And you told me it was because I was a winner."

"I should have added a caveat to that. *Could* be a winner—that is what I should have said. No, the reason I selected you, Phillip, was because you and I are alike. We're *losers*. Both of us are corporate losers."

"But you . . ."

"Forgive me, I know what you're about to say. I am chairman of the board of a major corporation and so on. But it might interest you to know that one year after attaining that position, I was probationed, under the threat of involuntary resignation, for the succeeding twelve months."

"The chairman of the board probationed?" Phillip asked incredulously. "Why, for God's sake?"

"A political thing, of course," Sutherland replied, choosing to omit the particulars of his financial impropriety. "One of two controlling factions of Kaufman Industries—the ultraconservative family foundation—had been keenly opposed to my elevation to the chair from the beginning. It was a matter of personalities. I was just not their kind of man. I just did not fit. Well, to shorten a very unpleasant tale, I obviously survived. But I learned a most important lesson: I would always be extraordinarily vulnerable to the winds of corporate politics. I would always be under siege."

Sutherland rose, walked to the large windows overlooking the sea, and gazed silently for a moment into the swirling fog. "I was still a young man, Phillip. I knew it would merely be a matter of time until whatever career defenses I could erect at Kaufman would be fatally penetrated. In the end I would lose. I was unfit to survive in the corporate jungle, either by paranoid subservience or gamesmanship. One way or the other I would lose." Sutherland turned to face Phillip. "No!" he snapped, and the word seemed to echo through the room. "I refused to live that way, cowering and beholden to the corporation."

He returned to the chair in front of the fireplace, and when he resumed his voice was softer, the cadence of his words slower. "Money. The prime root. Fear of loss, hope for gain. Synonyms for it are limitless: freedom, power, time, security, ego, success, measure, life, happiness, achievement, contacts, friends, recognition, and on and on. What money can't provide directly, it at least provides an alternate or a substitute or a possibility. I decided that I must have money. But where does it come from? We all must have a *source*. For the reasons I've just explained, the corporation is, at best, an indefinite source for me. I needed, and I found, an unimpeachable source. That source has given me, and will continue to give me, vast sums of money. And because of that money my impregnability to the corporation is absolute."

Phillip was totally captivated by his words. The similarity of their experience was incredible. This immensely successful man had suffered much the same as he had, yet he had prevailed and prospered. Phillip was silent for a moment. Outside the sound of distant thunder mingled with the dreariness of foghorns. "May I ask what source of money you found?" he said at last.

"Of course. That is, after all, what this conversation is about. Money. The source of our funds—our Harrison Crockers, if you will—is heroin. I import heroin into the United States, Phillip. That is my source."

Humor was a side of Sutherland Phillip had not seen before. He waited for a following line, but none came. Sutherland simply sat smiling at him, and all at once he felt extremely foolish. It was really none of his damn business. "Serves me right," he said. "I apologize. The question was out of line."

"Your question was perfectly in order, Phillip. And my answer was quite serious." The smile was still there.

Phillip decided he could play the game, too. "Well, why don't we combine operations? My whorehouses would make terrific distribution centers for your heroin, Averal."

Sutherland leaned back and laughed good-naturedly. "You're a most difficult man to convince, Phillip. But let me tell you another story. Several years ago, something in the newspaper concerning the seizure of narcotic contraband caught my attention. The person apprehended with the drugs, valued at two million dollars on the street, was nothing more than a common laborer. Think about that for a moment, Phillip. A common laborer entrusted with two million dollars. Absolutely ludicrous, wouldn't you say?"

Phillip shrugged his shoulders and smiled halfheartedly. "It would seem so." He was becoming more confused by the minute.

"The longer I thought about it, the more intrigued I became. I did some research and found that every substantial seizure of heroin had two significant things in common. First, the time at which the seizure occurred was invariably during the act of smuggling itself—after the product left foreign hands and shores but before it reached its first owners and distributors on this side. The second commonality of fault was the courier. In every instance there were incompetents involved who were caught either by accident or because of their own stupidity. Unusually interesting, don't you think?"

Phillip did not reply. He had decided to remain silent until Sutherland either tired of his game or he could determine what the game was.

"The conclusion I drew from all of this was simple," Sutherland continued. "An *intelligent* courier following a *precise* plan could reduce the act of smuggling to an almost riskless and mundane affair. A far cry, I should add, from my first hastily conceived, inordinately complex and futureless—but successful—effort in the Midwest. Based on that conclusion, I imagined an elite organization comprised of well-educated men who had achieved success in business, seasoned executives who were self-assured, poised, exceptionally cool under pressure and, above all, had a burning desire for wealth. Each man would have his own company, a legitimate business operation that would serve the twofold purpose of providing a respectable front and a means through which portions of the profits would be channeled. For obvious reasons, each company would have legitimate and continuing business abroad."

Belief, oftentimes, is a process of exhausting every effort to disbelieve. Phillip had one last chance. "It seems to me there would be one small flaw in your scheme, Averal. Where would such men as you've described be found? And what in Christ's name would induce them to participate?"

"I have discovered," Sutherland said, "that men whose

business careers have been prematurely but permanently damaged make excellent candidates. And they are easily found through executive search firms such as Chase and Connolly."

Phillip gasped involuntarily as the truth spilled over him. He felt waves of alternating heat and cold, his pulse raced, and the veins corded in his neck. His voice, when he found it, was like a distant echo of someone he didn't know. "You're actually serious," he said in a slow, hoarse whisper. "God help you, you're totally serious!"

"I have never been more serious."

"There really is such an organization and you expect me to be a part of it."

"Yes. I do."

Instantly Phillip was on his feet. "You son of a bitch! What have you done to me? You must be mad if you think you're going to involve me in something like narcotics. You can take your—"

"Sit down, Phillip!" It was a command, softly spoken but a command. "You have a decision to make and you cannot do so intelligently without being in possession of the facts."

"I don't give a damn about facts. And I don't want any part of a drug operation for any reason."

"Do you believe you have a choice?" Sutherland said. There was a note of warning in his voice.

"Are you threatening me, Averal?"

"I am only attempting to reason with you, Phillip. At least be good enough to hear me out. You have in no way been harmed, nor will you be. Now please, come back and sit down."

For fully a minute, Phillip stood looking at Sutherland, weighing his position. Something told him he was—somehow—already involved; leaving now would not change that, and staying to listen to whatever else Sutherland had to say might clarify his situation. Sutherland was right; he *did* need facts, facts that would permit him to extricate himself safely from this bizarre predicament. Outwardly composed now, he sat down and slowly took a sip of brandy. "All right, Averal, I'll listen. But why all the time and subterfuge? Why didn't you just come right out with this scheme from the start?"

"If I had done that, what would your answer have been?"

"I would have said no."

"Of course. And I would have been a fool to broach such a subject to a stranger. Far better to get to know the man first and to protect myself by at least partially involving him before discussing the matter."

"And you believe I'm already involved?"

"In the sense that you are part owner and president of a corporate façade, the purpose of which is to obtain and utilize profits from illegal narcotics."

"So you've been setting me up for the express purpose of functioning as one of your couriers?"

"If you choose to put it in those terms, yes."

"What terms would you prefer?"

"Rather that you have been selected to become a very wealthy man, Phillip, should you choose to accept my offer."

"I do have an option, then?"

"Under certain conditions, of course you do."

"What are they?"

"Just two. First, you would resign immediately as president of Omni. Second, you would bind yourself never to speak to anyone of this conversation tonight. That's all."

"You mean I can resign and walk out? Just like that? With just a promise to keep my mouth shut? What makes you think I'd keep my word? How could you be certain I wouldn't go to the police?"

Sutherland's eyes narrowed slightly and his voice became flat and hard. "You force me to be abrupt, Phillip. I have done you no harm. Should you, for any reason, attempt to harm me, I would employ whatever means were necessary to stop you. In which case, you, not I, would be the aggressor. But why talk of such things? My real concern is that you will leave and not accept this opportunity."

"What in hell makes you think for one moment I'll accept it? You've persuaded me that I'm free to turn it down. You're the self-proclaimed judge of character. Tell me, is my character so weak that you think I'd be a part of what you have going on here?"

"There are many aspects to character, Phillip. To view character as an absolute is unrealistic. The character of a man depends upon his circumstances. It is not difficult to be brave when there is nothing to fear. Nor is it difficult to kill when one's own life is in danger."

"You're talking in circles, Averal. Answer my question. Why do you think I'd even consider your offer?"

"Frankly, it occurs to me that you might entertain the prospect of continuing our relationship because of money. You care as strongly about it as I do. And I assure you, the material luxuries afforded you the past two months are only the beginning. Somehow, I find it difficult to imagine your renouncing all of that."

"In other words you think I'm hooked—like one of those junkies you create and then profitably sustain? Well, you're right. I like the material things I've had the past two months. But that's *all* I'm hooked on—the things. You've succeeded in creating an appetite, but I don't like the way you're suggesting I feed it. There are a thousand ways that I can make money legitimately."

"Horseshit!"

Profanity was so totally out of character for Averal Sutherland that Phillip almost dropped the glass of brandy he held in his hand.

"That is utter nonsense, Phillip, and you know it. Do you imagine that you could work again for a corporation? Your career as a highly paid corporate executive is over, I assure you. Why do you think Kaufman and all the others who talked with Apache turned you away? Because, among other things, you were accused of having taken kickbacks from companies you acquired for Apache."

"What?" Phillip sagged in astonishment at the words, then felt the nausea of helplessness swarm in his stomach as he finally understood what Samuel Rogers had done to him. "But that's absurd. I never took a penny! Those bastards lied! The truth is . . ."

"It does not matter what the truth is. The only thing that is pertinent to reality is that people *think* you did. *That* is truth,

Phillip. What people *think* and *believe* is what they perceive as truth! And now there is nothing you can do about it. Even if you had the money and the time and the cooperation of others to prove your innocence; even if, through some miracle, the residual innuendo did not bar you for life from opportunity—what then? What would you have to offer, a middle-aged generalist whose distaste for and inability to play the corporate game is well documented—even self-professed? Who would be interested?" Sutherland raised his hands upward in a gesture of despair. "What is left open to you? A business of your own? You tried that and lost everything. A job as a commission salesman, a blue-collar worker? No, my friend, without Omni—without *me*—you are destitute. You have no capital, no friends who will back you or employ you. You have exactly and precisely nothing. Turning away from me will place you squarely back in the despicable circumstances from which I raised you. You may be able to survive, but you cannot *live* at this time in your life without an independent source of money."

Everything Sutherland said was true. The weight of it crushed down on Phillip as he rose and walked slowly to the windows overlooking the bay, his mind in turmoil. Everything computed but the means. And wasn't that the whole of anything—the means? "Okay, Averal, maybe you're right. I'm stripped naked. I can't make it in the corporation—or anywhere else. I agree with everything you've said. Your analysis is correct. I need money. I want it. But how can you justify smuggling narcotics? Is anything worth that?"

"Think about it, Phillip, and tell me. Tell me which is the greater of sins. You have some idea of the rape and pillage of the human spirit brought about by men who call themselves a corporation. Do you for one moment believe those who make vast sums of money in business do not, at some point in time, commit unlawful acts? That they do not conspire, defraud, lie, cheat, steal, misrepresent, cripple, bribe, sometimes even kill, and, by whatever means they can conceive, *take* what they want? If you think otherwise, you are very naïve. And if you believe, for even the briefest of moments, they consider themselves dishonorable, you badly deceive yourself. No, Phillip. To them, it's simply the old refrain—business is business. And under that category of philosophical rationalization, every act is justified and excused."

Sutherland rose and walked across the room toward Phillip; he wanted to see his eyes. "And what of the industrialists," he said, "who, in time of war, cut costs in the production of arms to increase their profit which, in turn, takes lives when the equipment malfunctions? Do you think it inconceivable that businessmen hope for war, scheme for war, and precipitate war? Look about you, my friend. Open your eyes. Tell me my sin is greater. Tell me the sins of the corporation are more desirable, more moral. Labels, Phillip, labels. That's the only difference. The result is the same."

They stood facing each other, eyes locked and searching. "There are just two choices in this world, Phillip—two. Either you aspire to wealth or you shun it. Whichever choice you make, you must be willing to live with the consequences. If you pursue wealth, the price is the means. If you spurn it, a life without money is the price. Either way can become bearable. But it is not bearable to be where you are, Phillip—*in between*."

The eyes. Sutherland saw it, an almost imperceptible change in Phillip's eyes. It went as quickly as it had come. But it was there. Contemplation. He was close.

Phillip turned away and moved wearily toward the fireplace. Putting both hands on the mantel, he leaned forward, head bowed, eyes searching the flames. "How does a man live with himself, Averal?" he said in a low voice.

Sutherland remained standing by the windows, staring out through the rain and fog. "By thinking of himself, Phillip. By thinking only of himself. Because one day he realizes no one else thinks about him, no one else really cares. Not his wife, not even his children. And when one becomes fully aware that his life is of only passing interest to others, it changes his perspective."

Sutherland's words were persuasive, hypnotic. "I grant that fear of what others think about you is exquisitely seductive, Phillip. But don't you see? That's precisely my point. They *don't* think about you. They simply do not care. It is nothing to them if you choose, for altruistic reasons, to starve to death. They will simply pity you and call you a failure. And if you choose to take what you want and feel yourself compromised by doing so, they will acknowledge only your success, not the means by which you achieved it. The world is unforgiving of failure and patient with success. Money, Phillip. No one will reach out and help you or give it to you, but they will despise your lack of it. Money is finally, ultimately, and irrevocably what the world is about. And in the end, Phillip, there is only you—just you."

Sutherland could see indecision reflected in Phillip's face. He was torn by confusion and conflict. And from this point on, Sutherland knew, Vanderlind would not initiate, he would only react. He had reached the maximum vulnerability. But Sutherland sensed it would not last long. The man would swing one way or the other within the next few minutes. Sutherland knew what he wanted to hear.

"Forgetting the other aspects for a moment, Phillip, there's one important factor I haven't discussed—the risk." He moved away from the windows and approached the fire. "Is there danger involved? Essentially, no. I assure you I would be the last to court either danger or violence. But to comprehend the absence of risk in our operation, it is important to understand this fact: the inherent danger in smuggling comes not from the authorities but rather from within the ranks of those engaging in such activity—greed and betrayal internally, stupidity and incompetence externally. Because you see, Phillip, smuggling, as it is conducted by others, is considered to be only a part of a fully integrated operation; all the buying, transportation, and selling are performed by the same people, and the risks are multiplied many times over. What I have done is simply isolate the one function of transportation. My organization serves as an *independent* middle man between a European seller and a domestic buyer. I alone know who the buyers and sellers are. And no one on either end of the transaction has even the remotest idea of who the couriers are. Nor is there any chance they could ever know. Thus, risk is virtually nonexistent."

Phillip's mind was adrift as he sat down again in front of the fire. He was listening attentively to Sutherland's words, yet he could not react. He felt numb.

"We have made our arrangements rather well, I think," Sutherland continued. "The exchange of money is conducted in a foreign bank through the debiting and crediting of private accounts that are untraceable both as to the source of funds as well as the owners of the accounts. Our method of handling the merchandise is almost as simple and has as its primary consideration total protection for the courier. We accomplish this through a system of closed-end 'drops' on both sides of the Atlantic. For the sake of brevity, at the moment, this is how it works. In Europe, the merchandise is transferred to the courier by one of our people who acts as an impenetrable buffer between the seller and the courier. Once back in this country, the courier simply leaves the merchandise in a hotel room of his own selection and relays the number of the room directly to me. I, in turn, effect final delivery by informing the buyer of the location."

Sutherland went to the bar and picked up the decanter of brandy. He refilled their glasses before he sat down again in front of the fire. "It is quite obvious to you, of course, that what I have just described is merely the framework, a support system, if you please, worth nothing to a buyer and seller. Anyone can arrange foreign bank accounts and devise a system of drops. The actual intromission of merchandise into the United States is where we derive our value. Safe and certain transport, the fact that we can and do deliver our product on a consistent and reliable basis, completely free of peril for all involved, is why we can so profitably exist. And as for the moment when the merchandise actually crosses our borders, that is perhaps the simplest and safest function of all, Phillip. Traveling with a special passport from the State Department which exempts the bearer from the usual examination, the courier merely picks up the luggage containing the merchandise and walks unmolested through customs and out of the airport. And that is, literally, all there is to it. It sounds simple and it is. But it is only possible because I am able to arrange for the special passports, and the couriers are men, such as yourself, who, otherwise, are totally legitimate businessmen."

Smiling now, Sutherland drove home the final rationalization. "But, of course, you could quite properly ask what would happen if the courier *were* stopped and his luggage examined. Well, if I may be permitted a common expression, so what? They open your bags, and to your utter amazement they contain heroin. But they are not *your* bags. I shall explain later how all of this is possible, but *your* luggage is still at the hotel in London and can easily be found. The fact that your luggage is identical to the bags in your possession is hardly your fault. Embarrassing? Of course. Incriminating? Hardly. After a thorough investigation reveals that you are the president of a legitimate corporation, a man with an unblemished background, the entire matter would be dropped immediately."

Sutherland took a sip of brandy and sat back in his chair. "Of course, there may be something I've overlooked, Phillip. One can never be too certain. But I have three couriers who have been operating just as I've described for almost three years. The most serious problem any one of them has had to face is occasional bouts with jet lag. And each is now a wealthy man. You see, Phillip, in addition to your regular salary, bonus, and share of the profits from the leasing business, you will receive a *minimum* of six hundred thousand dollars a year—tax free, of course—for simply walking through customs once every two months. Overall, then, I would estimate your annual income would very shortly begin to exceed one million dollars."

Sutherland's words startled Phillip into a reaction at last. Suddenly, as if the strain were more than he could bear, he got to his feet. "What am I expected to say?"

"You needn't say anything, Phillip, except to assure me that you'll give the matter careful thought and let me know of your decision before I leave for New York on Sunday. Of course, if you've already made your decision, I would be pleased to know now what it is."

Phillip rubbed his face with both hands and took a deep breath of air. The fog had thinned and a rotating beacon light from the sea approach to the bay flashed periodically across the windows of the room. Finally, he spoke. "One final question, Averal."

"Certainly."

"I understand your motivation, your philosophy, the mechanics of your operation, but I still cannot comprehend the rationale that permits you to deal in heroin."

"Phillip, drugs have been with mankind since the beginning. And man will continue to use them as long as he is on this earth. He will secure them despite all efforts to prevent it. If I ceased my operation today, there would not be one less addict, not one less ounce imported, not one less dollar profited. You speak of ruined lives? *Alcohol* destroys an infinitely greater number of people each year than the aggregate of all the drugs. And if I were to offer you a lucrative liquor distributorship, and they are indeed lucrative, you wouldn't think twice. Perhaps you would excuse your involvement by saying alcohol is legal. Or that people are going to drink, so I may as well sell it to them. Legalities, rationalizations—all excuses. You may be very certain the effect is the same."

Perhaps until that very moment, Phillip had not fully believed Sutherland was serious. Now he believed. It was true: Averal Sutherland *was* dealing in narcotics. He stood looking at the man for a moment, then made his decision. "Averal, I honestly don't know what to say. I don't really know how I feel. Can you understand that? My natural inclination is to run. To get as far away from you, from all of this, as possible. But somehow that isn't . . ." He hesitated. "I would like some time to think, Averal. As you say, neither of us has been harmed, neither has cause to harm the other."

Sutherland felt the tension in his own body subside. He had him. He had been right about Phillip Vanderlind after all. "I understand your feelings completely, Phillip," he said. "Of course, you need time to think."

The two men walked together to the front door and Sutherland switched on the lights that illuminated the porch and the walk. "Perhaps we could plan to have a lunch aboard the *Spellbound* the day after tomorrow, Phillip?"

"Yes. I'll call you. Good night, Averal."

"Good night, Phillip. Sleep well."

Sutherland stood framed in the light of the doorway, watching Phillip get into his car and drive away. A moment later the lights of another car parked across the street flicked on. Sutherland recalled his instructions to the two men watching in that car. If the porch lights were not switched on as Vanderlind left the house, they were to take him then. Otherwise they were simply to follow him, receiving further instructions by mobile phone. The two men who waited were veterans of Vietnam recruited by Novak to staff Essex, Sutherland's private investigation and security force.

Sutherland closed the door and turned off the lights. There would be no need for violence tonight, he thought. Nor any night with Phillip Vanderlind.

CHAPTER 11

O ne of the two men in the light-green Oldsmobile shifted nervously and reached into the back seat for a thermos of coffee. "If he doesn't do something soon, Al, we're gonna be out of coffee."

"Relax, Bobby. You drink too much of that stuff anyway."

They had been parked less than a hundred yards from Vanderlind's house since two that morning. The hood of the car was raised, signifying trouble, an excuse for being there if one was needed. Both men were dressed casually, and there were cameras on the back seat. A street map of San Francisco was on the dash. Only a thorough search of the car would reveal that the two men were not tourists.

In the trunk was an array of the finest mobile communications equipment available. In addition, there was a small arsenal of firearms: two 12-gauge shotguns, one .306 rifle with an infrared telescopic scope, and two .357-magnum revolvers. All were carefully concealed, but readily accessible, in a felt-lined box covered with regular trunk flooring.

Mounted under the dash, behind an unobtrusive piece of paneling that matched the interior decor, was the communications console. The panel was raised, and the man in the right-hand seat was staring at the console. "Al, are you sure the tap is in a go condition?"

"It's working, Bobby. Just stay cool. He'll be moving around soon."

"Christ, I hope so. This waiting's a pain in the ass."

"Well, that's the job we got this time, man. Besides, there'll be plenty going down if he makes a wrong move. You know our orders. If he tries to call the Feds, we jam the connection, walk up to the door, and take him. And if he tries to go to them, we follow him and pick him up before he gets there. In either case, Novak'll give the final word. So just cool it and monitor that tap."

* * *

The small hand hesitantly touched his shoulder. "Mr. Vanderlind, Mr. Vanderlind, you must wake up now."

Phillip came slowly through the layers of filmy sleep, clawing at consciousness.

"Irving," he groaned. "What time is it?"

"Ten o'clock, sir. You are late for the office."

"I don't think I'm going in today, Irving. May I have some coffee, please?"

"You feel all right, Mr. Vanderlind?"

"I'm fine. Just went to bed late."

When Irving left the room, Phillip rolled over in the bed and lay still. Seconds ticked by. His eyes closed and then suddenly opened again, wide and darting. He sat straight up in the bed, his heart pounding. "Oh, my God," he said aloud, slipping quickly off the bed and going over to the tape recorder on the small table by the window.

Irving brought coffee, and for the next hour Phillip sat with his head in his hands, listening to his own voice describing the insanity Averal Sutherland would have him embrace. It was a decision he had made last night as he drove back from

Sutherland's house, the only decision his confused mind was capable of making. He would record everything Sutherland had said to him while it was still fresh in his memory. But even now as he listened to the tapes, he was undecided about what to do with them. There had been no witnesses to their conversation. The tapes were not evidence. It would be Sutherland's word against his. Who could he take them to? Who would believe him?

When the last tape ended, he rang Irving for fresh coffee and went into the shower. He knew now *what* he was going to do; *how* he would do it was the question. There were too many gaps; he needed time to think it through. And a place.

He decided to spend the time he needed on board the boat, and while he dressed, Irving packed a small box of food. He was on his way to the kitchen when he had another thought. He returned to the bedroom, and from the bottom drawer of his dresser he took the Walther automatic and a box of shells. Damn, he thought as he slipped the gun into his seabag, I've never even fired this thing.

Backing his car onto the road, Phillip almost didn't see the light-green Oldsmobile a short distance away with its hood up. "Problems?" he said as he pulled up beside the car.

"Just some battery trouble," the man in the driver's seat said. "Somebody's on the way. Thanks for stopping, though."

"Okay, if everything's under control, I'll be on my way."

"Yeah, we're fine. Thanks again."

An hour later, Phillip was powering out of the St. Francis Yacht Club. The sky was still overcast, but the winds were light. He ghosted the *Spellbound* across the bay under main and a number-three genoa, looking for a spot to drop anchor. He found it on the leeward side of Angel Island in a small, calm, deserted cove. Once the hook was down and holding, he went below and fixed something to eat.

Throughout the afternoon he sat huddled in the cockpit, letting his mind range over the countless implications and possibilities of his predicament. The confusion and near panic of the night before were gone. His thoughts were cool and logical, and by early evening he had a plan, a simple plan by any standard, yet one that seemed to afford him the two most critical elements—time and flexibility.

Phillip did not believe for a moment that he could resign from Omni and simply walk away from Averal Sutherland. His plan turned on the single premise that he had to get further in before he could get out. He had to *know* how compromised he already was, or could be made to appear, and by whom; the authorities as well as Sutherland had to be reckoned with. He also needed evidence—at least circumstantial—of Sutherland's complicity. And obtaining evidence of any kind was only possible, he realized, if he were able to penetrate the specifics of the operation. There something was bound to exist that could be used to implicate Sutherland.

So Phillip decided he would pretend to accept Sutherland's offer, and he would carefully document, on tape, everything he heard or saw. Thus far the only crime he had committed was out of ignorance, and he realized that he would have to avoid, if' possible, active and knowing participation in the operation. If he could not, he would then be as guilty as Sutherland, and who would believe that he had joined the scheme merely to expose it? It would be a dangerous game, both men trying to implicate the other, Sutherland to insure Phillip's cooperation, and Phillip to prove his innocence. But it was as good a plan as he could devise. He thought it would work.

Shortly after dark, he was hungry and broiled a small steak, which he consumed with almost half a fifth of scotch. He was drunk when he fell into a deep sleep, and when he woke up again just before midnight, his head was throbbing as he stumbled uncertainly on deck to check the anchor and make the boat ready for the night.

The icy wind, which had freshened since dusk, revived him, and he once again began to think about his predicament. Jesus, how had he ever got involved in such a mess? Averal Sutherland. The man had played with him like a marionette. He had money, power, connections. What chance have I got, Phillip thought, to win some cat-and-mouse game with a man like that? Suddenly he realized the significance of the nonexistent Harrison Crocker.

Of course, now it all made sense. There was absolutely no evidence to prove that Sutherland had any more than a legitimate business interest in Omni Leasing. He had taken precautions to protect himself, and obviously he would continue to do so. And he had already made a vague threat, Phillip remembered. Even if he did succeed in finding evidence to use against Sutherland, it might buy him his freedom, but it also might cost him his life.

The boat, despite her lee position, was riding heavily now to her anchor, and Phillip began to feel increasingly nauseous. He went below and struggled to arrange some semblance of bedding on the port bunk, but a few moments later he lay half sprawled through the companionway, his face inches from the cockpit sole, vomiting as if his very stomach were coming up. "Oh God," he moaned aloud. And for almost half an hour he lay whimpering in the cockpit, mindless of the waves that broke repeatedly over the low coamings inundating him with numbing water. Finally he dragged himself below. And wrapped in three blankets and wedged in the bunk against the motion of the boat, he slept.

It was eight o'clock when he awakened. He lay quietly for a long time, huddled in the blankets, fearing another onslaught of nausea. The wind had veered in the early-morning hours, and the small cove was once again calm. Finally he eased himself from the bunk. His clothes were still damp and soiled. When he had changed them, he began boiling water for tea. He felt as if his entire body had been drained. He was in no condition to face Averal Sutherland today. He lit a cigarette and reached for the VHF radio.

* * *

Sutherland readily agreed to postpone the luncheon with Vanderlind until the next day, said goodbye, thanked the marine operator, and replaced the receiver. He was not alarmed by the change in plans; the man still needed time. And while he had sounded somewhat tense, there had been no hint of deception or panic in Vanderlind's voice.

So he was thinking it through at sea, mused Sutherland—on a

boat that he would very much like to keep. Which reminded him: had Essex intercepted the call from Vanderlind? He picked up the phone and called Novak. Yes, the call had been monitored. An Essex unit was parked inconspicuously near the St. Francis Yacht Club, awaiting Vanderlind's return. And the tap on the boat's communications gear was functioning perfectly.

*   *   *

It was almost noon when Phillip decided he was sufficiently recovered to return to the yacht club. With no wind and smooth water, the trip was simply a matter of powering across. The sunny morning had filled the bay with boats, and several made it a point to come within hailing distance to call or wave their admiration of the Bermuda 40. It *was* a hell of a boat, Phillip thought. And he felt a sense of pride until the reality of his situation resurfaced. He kept his eyes straight ahead then, as if he were hired crew—which is what he was. The price tag of the *Spellbound* was higher than he had expected to pay.

With the boat back on her lines in the slip, he proceeded to put her in some semblance of order. As he stood hosing down the topsides, he idly watched a small group of people board the yawl three slips away for what was obviously a catered, leisurely lunch in the boat's sprawling cockpit. He casually knew two of the men. About his age, they were partners in a thriving construction firm with several large projects in Hawaii. In March they would be cruising to the islands and were looking for another boat to accompany them. Phillip had been approached. And he had thought about it. But that had been when he was one of them, when he had belonged, when he had had something in common with these people. Abruptly he cut short his task, locked the boat, and walked quickly to the waiting Mercedes.

He spent the rest of the afternoon in his offices at Omni. He had a reason for going there. Although he didn't know what he might be looking for, he decided he should review all of Omni's records. After nearly two hours of searching, he found nothing that would in any way implicate Averal Sutherland in an illicit drug operation. Nor was there even evidence that the man had any connection with Omni Leasing, except, of course, his association with Emile Novak. But what was that worth? Obviously the two had worked together to involve him in this madness. And his naïve greed had made their task easy. Goddammit, he should have realized something was wrong!

He left the office just after dark and drove toward Marin County. Coming off the bridge, he suddenly decided to take the Sausalito exit, and ten minutes later he was being seated at a small table in a campy-chic disco jutting out over the bayshore. The place was crowded with fashionably dressed men and women. My God, the money. Where did they get it? *How* did they get it? Snatches of conversation here and there included St. Croix, Aspen, Cancun, St. Tropez. Holy Christ, where did it all come from? Did they think he was one of them? Everything about him said he had money, too. Where did it come from, how did he make it? No one asked. Sutherland was right: no one cared.

All at once he had to leave, and minutes later he was cruising effortlessly in light traffic going back across the bridge into the city. He had no plan, no destination. He just wanted to keep moving. Turning off through the Presidio, he drove slowly, lost in thought, when he suddenly realized he was driving past Sutherland's house. Somewhat shaken by his lapse of attention, he pulled into the public observation area a few hundred feet farther along the street. He sat there, looking at the house. There was nothing to see.

Getting out of the car, he walked toward the house, listening to the breakers wash ashore below and looking at the other palatial homes nestled in the surrounding cliffs. Sea Cliff. So much money. How do people get so much money? He knew now where Averal Sutherland's came from. But how in the hell was he going to prove it?

He lit a cigarette, smoked for a few moments, then abruptly tossed the butt away and went back to the car. When he drove off, he did not see the light-green Oldsmobile that followed him at a respectable distance. On the floor of the back seat lay a high-powered rifle through whose infrared sniper's scope Phillip Vanderlind's brief walk had been anxiously monitored.

*　　*　　*

There were two letters beside his plate when he sat down to the simple dinner Irving had prepared. One was from Carol, describing her plans for her trip to Europe this summer. He would have to tell her that he could no longer afford it. The second letter was from Jessica. She and her lawyer had reached an agreement with the Montana firm that manufactured the sheepskin coats, and she just wanted to thank him again. Jessica! Twenty-five thousand dollars! "Son of a bitch," Phillip exploded, china and silver jumping under the impact of his fists on the dining table. And for a few moments he just sat there, eyes closed, fists still tightly clinched. In a moment of stupid sentimentality he had given away the only money he had that was really his. Supposing he could get free of Sutherland, how would he survive financially now?

He left the table and went wearily up to the master suite. Looking through the expensive wardrobe he had accumulated during his brief stint as president of Omni Leasing, he shook his head sadly as he realized he had not yet worn even a third of what was there. And he never would. The clothes would go with everything else. And more than that, he realized that Sutherland's bank would undoubtedly call the master note that had enabled him to pay his debts.

Sleep. He was desperately tired now. But when his body should have welcomed sleep, it savagely fought it. As he twisted and turned in the giant bed, his mind filled with one surrealistic nightmare after another, and he finally gave up. Switching on the light, he sat up on the edge of the bed and held his head in his hands. His heart was pounding and his breath came in short, wracking gasps.

Again, he would have nothing! And even worse, he would *be* nothing—not according to the yardstick by which all men are ultimately measured.

And he could conceive no answers, no way to save himself. An overwhelming sense of hopelessness made him tremble, and his mind slipped back to the good years at Apache when he had had it all and thrown it away. Was that what life was about? Remembering what you once had with no hope of ever having it again? If it was, if life couldn't be upward, then he wondered about living.

Sutherland's arguments began to surge and thunder in his brain. No one cares . . . it only matters that you have it, not where it comes from . . . drugs will always be with us . . . what if it were liquor . . . there is no danger . . . everyone who makes money commits transgressions of some kind . . . labels, nothing more than labels.

Was Sutherland right? Was it all really a matter of money? Was the value of life itself intrinsically economic? Other men could view the world as it really is. Why couldn't he?

Phillip was shaking now, and he realized it was from fear; he was terrified of being poor. But what else was there? Even if he could, through some miracle, separate himself from Sutherland, his corporate career had been destroyed and there was nothing else he knew how to do—not really. What, then, was left? Could he push aside his repugnance and agree to cooperate? Would that truly be so bad?

He rose and walked slowly over to the windows and stared vacantly at the hills of winking, shimmering lights far across the bay. Somewhere amid the splendor of those lights was Averal Sutherland's house. How in God's name could he hope to avoid the man? He was too powerful, too clever. If he went to the police, no one would believe him. And if he simply fled, where could he go? He already knew too much, and Sutherland would have no choice but to eliminate him or, at the very least, in some way implicate him with drugs. What had Sutherland said about truth? Whatever people *believed* was true became truth.

Why not cooperate? Phillip thought. And for the first time he began to consider what it would be like to be involved in smuggling. All he had to do was carry some luggage through customs, leave it in a hotel room, make one phone call. What was so difficult about that? But what if he were caught? And yet Sutherland had survived—and profited. Why shouldn't he?

Phillip turned and gazed at the opulence of his surroundings.

If Averal Sutherland had lured him into this trap, he supposed he had been a willing victim. He didn't know whom he hated more—Sam Rogers for what he had done to him or Averal Sutherland for what he was trying to do. But at least Sutherland was presenting him with alternatives: success of the kind the whole world envied—or death.

CHAPTER 12

Now, Emile Novak rarely left his suite in the St. Francis Hotel. He had been relieved of his duties at Omni—an undisciplined menace, Sutherland had called him. But they had exchanged sharp words before, and Novak still had a job to do in San Francisco. It was he who coordinated the surveillance of Phillip Vanderlind during this critical period. He was in continual contact with the Essex team that tracked Vanderlind's every move, and he reported regularly to Sutherland. The other members of Beta had been watched just as closely when they were first informed of the real nature of their association with Sutherland, and in each case it had proved to be no more than a routine precaution. Sutherland's judgments about men were usually good. But Novak found himself hoping Sutherland was wrong this time. He had disliked Vanderlind from the start, and now the son of a bitch had disobeyed instructions and forced him into a bad light with Sutherland. Then, too, there was just something about the man that made Novak feel uneasy. He would welcome, he decided, an opportunity to waste Phillip Vanderlind, which was precisely what his Essex agents were trained to do.

Essex was an expensive operation to maintain but a small price to pay for the secure continuation of Beta. Like Novak, all Essex agents were former members of Army Special Forces with heavy combat experience in Vietnam. And they all had something else in common when Novak recruited them; they had been malcontents in the service, and none had been able to readjust successfully to civilian life. Essex agents were completely unaware that their services supported a heroin operation. The nice thing was that none of them expected explanations. They were well paid to follow whatever orders Emile Novak gave them.

The work of Essex began with the investigation and surveillance of each prospective member of Beta and intensified during the period when he was undecided about his participation in the operation. But it did not end when a man joined the group. Continual surveillance of a courier was necessary to insure against possible defection and betrayal as well as interdiction by a third party. Thus Essex's security functions were not limited to the courier. Since there was always the threat of accidental discovery by a member of the family, a friend or a mistress, surveillance of people close to a courier was also maintained through the use of telephone taps and other means. In Vanderlind's case, there had so far been a minimum concern in this area. He lived alone, and the only close liaison he had was with the woman in New York. Novak had seen Polly Savitch on two occasions, once in San Francisco and once in New York. The Essex people who had compiled the dossier on her were right: she was a sexy bitch. She also lived expensively—perhaps beyond her means—and ran with a fast, coke-snorting crowd. And to Novak's mind, that was a potentially dangerous combination. Another excellent reason, he decided, to keep the surveillance on both Vanderlind and the broad screwed down tight.

*   *   *

A feeling of calm resignation pervaded Phillip Vanderlind as he waited for Brad Coleman to start the engines of the Turbo Commander. This trip signaled his second beginning as president of Omni Leasing. But this time he had no illusions about himself or what had seemed to be his good fortune. He had accepted Averal Sutherland's proposal, and he knew the price he would have to pay.

"Okay," announced Coleman. "We're ready to go flying."

"Let's do it, then."

"We're estimating L.A. about three, and ground transportation will be waiting."

The air was smooth as they climbed out over the bay on a southerly heading. Phillip unfastened his seat belt and began to go through some papers in the attaché case on his lap. But he couldn't concentrate. His thoughts were filled with the conversation he had had with Sutherland aboard the *Spellbound* two days before. If anything, he had underestimated the ingenuity of the man. Once Phillip had indicated his willingness to join the conspiracy, Sutherland had begun systematically to eliminate every written trace of a connection between them. As Sutherland had requested, Phillip brought to the meeting his copy of his contract with Omni, together with the original Memorandum of Understanding. Sutherland destroyed both documents. And in their place he presented Phillip with a new set of corporate records showing that he was the sole shareholder of the company. Henceforth, for purposes of decentralization and security, he said, Omni would operate entirely apart from him. And Phillip quickly realized that if he were caught smuggling narcotics, he alone would be guilty. While Sutherland was a generous man, his primary motive was self-protection. But whatever resentment or concern he felt about that was quickly forgotten when Sutherland began to discuss the profitability of the operation.

Phillip had been skeptical of an operation that moved only a few suitcases of merchandise a year. But after Sutherland supplied the figures, he understood and was astonished. With four couriers operating now, each making six runs a year and delivering forty kilos of heroin per run, Beta would be importing 960 kilos annually. At the Beta selling price of $20,000 for *one* kilo of uncut heroin, Sutherland explained, the operation would gross nearly $20,000,000 a year and net well over half that amount. Each courier received a flat $100,000 a run, which was paid immediately upon its completion, and $1,000,000 a year was paid into each courier's company. The rest went to Sutherland.

From the arithmetic of Beta, Sutherland had then moved quickly on to re-emphasize how important it was for Phillip to keep the Omni operation going at full tilt, and together they had recharted the next six months of work. Establishing Phillip as a regular traveler to Europe and Omni as an international concern was, of course, imperative. And then Sutherland dropped the bomb: Phillip's first run would be in two weeks. Phillip protested that he should have more time to prepare, but in the end he could hardly argue Sutherland's point that preparations had already been made. All he had to do was follow the simple instructions he would be given in New York on his stop-over to London.

When the meeting was over, Phillip drove back to Marin County in a daze. If, when the meeting had begun, he had harbored even the slightest thought of still being able to walk away from Sutherland, that was all gone now. He had been inextricably drawn into the operation. Not only had Sutherland cleverly divorced himself entirely from Omni, leaving Phillip no chance to implicate him in that way, but he had also insisted that he commit the criminal act that would *enforce* his cooperation— and his silence. That was the one thing Phillip hadn't counted on. He had hoped he would at least have time to find a way to protect himself before making a run. But he had made his decision, and now he could see no way to renounce it. He was in. And now it was all his: the house, the company, the boat—and half a million tax-free dollars a year. Everything was his.

"Whoa, sorry," Brad Coleman said. "Bit of clear air turbulence there."

The sudden upward jar of the aircraft startled Phillip back to the present. "Where are we, Brad?"

"Just beginning our let-down for L.A."

Phillip had a busy week of travel ahead of him. And it was probably just as well. It helped keep his mind off the trip he would have to make in two weeks' time. He had dinner that evening with several officials from a computer manufacturer, and the next morning he jetted to Houston, had a conference at the airport with two bankers and was in St. Louis by nightfall. Wednesday he met with a barge-building company until late afternoon and then flew on to New Orleans to spend the night. Thursday it was barges again. But what he thought would take two days of talks was ground out in one twelve-hour marathon. He was a day ahead of schedule.

Back at the hotel, he showered and had dinner sent up to his room. He was exhausted from the trip, yet pleased. Things had gone extremely well. But now, still charged from the long, tense hours of negotiation, he found it difficult to sleep. Impulsively he reached for the phone beside his bed and placed a call to a number in New York.

"Darling!" Polly exclaimed. "You just caught me on the way out."

"What's his name?" Phillip asked.

"Well, what can you expect when I don't hear from you for weeks at a time? Where are you? Can I meet you somewhere? When are you coming to New York?"

"Next weekend, as a matter of fact. That's why I'm calling."

"Marvelous. I'm supposed to go to Connecticut, but I suddenly feel a terrible cold coming on. When will you be here?"

"I'm not sure," Phillip said. "I've got business and then I have to fly to London. But I'll be staying at the Pierre and I'll call you when I get in."

"I'll save the whole weekend just for you, darling," Polly said. "Now I really must fly. I can hardly wait to see you."

Phillip hung up, rolled over in bed and thought about Polly

Savitch. Recently there had been a pathetic urgency in her voice whenever they spoke on the phone and an almost frightening eagerness to please him whenever they were together and making love. He wondered if it was money—what he had and she might *not* have. And suddenly it occurred to him how little he actually knew about Polly or what her life was really like. But then he decided it didn't really matter. What the hell, he liked Polly and they still had a good time in bed. What difference did it make what she did or didn't do—or with whom? Besides, who was Phillip Vanderlind to find fault with Polly Savitch, or anyone else for that matter?

At noon the next day he was already seated on the airplane for his return trip to San Francisco when he realized that it was not a nonstop flight. There would be a brief layover in Denver. He had things to do in San Francisco, but all at once something else began turning over in his mind.

*　　*　　*

Brock Chase waited nervously in the bar of the Algonquin Hotel for Cyril Kennedy to arrive. The government agent had been easily persuaded to meet him in a public place. He understood Chase's reluctance to have federal authorities prowling around the offices of Chase and Connolly. And Chase had absolutely no interest in spending any time in the cold, dehumanizing cubicles in which Kennedy operated.

As he sipped at his second Manhattan, Chase fervently hoped he was doing the right thing. But did he have an alternative? Even the most cursory investigation of his files would reveal that Phillip Vanderlind and Averal Sutherland were archetypes of the individuals the agent was looking for. It was mere coincidence, Chase decided. Surely there were many other corporate heads who had hired floundering executives. And in Sutherland's case, the man had once told him that he was convinced a company could gain unparalleled loyalty and superior performance from people who were offered a second chance. Far more so than from men who were simply lured away from another company. It made sense to Chase, and he would tell Kennedy exactly that. And if both Sutherland and Vanderlind were found to have no involvement in any illegal scheme, where was the harm? Everything would be fine. Brock Chase would have done his duty.

Then there was his own reputation to consider. Absurd as it seemed, what if Sutherland and Vanderlind *were* discovered to be engaged in some criminal enterprise? Chase could be accused of trying to shield them. If, on the other hand, he did cooperate with Kennedy and something funny *was* going on, he could claim credit for his role in their exposure and reap a harvest of good will—in *and* out of the executive headhunting business.

He was about to order his third Manhattan when he looked up and saw Cyril Kennedy enter the room. There was something about the man's expression that made Chase realize it would be difficult, if not impossible, to lie to Kennedy. And at that moment he knew he had made the right decision. He had nothing to fear. Averal Sutherland was above reproach. And Phillip Vanderlind may have been down on his luck, but he was certainly not a criminal. Cyril Kennedy was obviously a bureaucratic idiot.

*   *   *

Just before the seat-belt sign went on for their approach into Denver, Phillip asked the hostess for an airline schedule. There was a ten-o'clock flight in the morning that would put him in San Francisco by noon. As soon as they landed, he went immediately to the connecting airline ticket counter and made a reservation. Then he crossed the lobby to a pay phone. Maybe he was crazy. He would know in a minute—provided Jessica was even at home.

He hung up after six rings and was about to return to the ticket counter when he remembered the shop.

On the sixth ring she answered with a simple "hello."

"This is the Marlboro Man calling. Would you have something in a forty-six long, ma'am?"

"Phillip! Where are you?"

"Just down the road a piece from you. Stapleton Airport, to be exact. What're you doing?"

"Just about to close up for the day. What are you doing in Denver?"

"I was on my way back to San Francisco when I had this wild notion I might just lay over for the evening—if you have no other plans. I could rent a car and drive over, but my flight leaves first thing tomorrow morning."

"I don't have any other plans, and why don't I come there? Where are you staying?"

"The Brown Palace, I hope."

"See if you can get me a room, too. I can be on the road by four at least. I'll meet you there about six. What should I wear?"

"What you have on."

"I will not!"

It was almost six o'clock when Phillip signed his check in the bar of the Brown Palace and walked into the lobby to wait for Jessica. Several minutes passed before he looked up from the newspaper he was reading and noticed a woman standing at the registration desk. She was dressed in flared leather pants and a matching jacket that clung smoothly to her body. Phillip stared at her and then glanced self-consciously in the direction of the hotel entrance. It would be a hell of a note, he thought, if Jessica walked in and saw him leering at another woman.

Jessica? Christ, that *was* Jessica.

He walked over to the desk. "Jessica."

She turned. "Hello," she said, kissing him affectionately on the cheek. "Thanks for the room."

"Have you any idea how great you look?" he asked, holding her at arm's length. "How do you ever get into anything that fits so well?"

"Over absolutely nothing."

"I believe you're absolutely serious."

"I absolutely am," she said, blushing now.

Phillip grinned, then noticed the expectant bellman with Jessica's bags. "Why don't we send your stuff on up and I'll buy you a drink?"

They left the bar at seven. Arms around each other's waists and smiling mischievously, they walked quickly across the lobby into a waiting elevator. Without a word being spoken, they went together to Phillip's room.

Forty-five minutes later, Jessica sat up on the edge of the bed and suggested they dress and go to dinner.

Phillip rolled over and lit a cigarette. He was mortified. "Christ, I'm sorry, Jessica. I don't know what the hell's wrong. I just can't . . . all of a sudden."

"All of a sudden is not forever," she said softly. "I . . . I know you want me." She was silent for a moment, then looked back over her shoulder at Phillip, a smile spreading across her face. "If you *really* want to know what I think, I think it's hilariously unimportant." She burst out laughing and rolled over on top of him.

"Goddamnit, that's because . . ."

She cut him off with a kiss. "I don't care and you do."

For a few seconds Phillip lay rigid and humiliated under the lithe, firm body that shook gently with muffled laughter. Then a grin began to crinkle the corners of his mouth. He reached for the phone. "Room Service? Eunuch, here. Would you send up an instant erection for two, please. I . . ."

Before he could finish, they both collapsed in hysterical laughter. And they couldn't stop. Finally exhausted, they lay quietly holding each other.

Then it was there.

"Would you care to explain just what that is in bed with us?" Jessica teased.

"I may be wrong," Phillip said, "but I believe we finally have ignition."

Something both wondrous and frightening happened to Phillip Vanderlind in that next hour. It was as if he were meeting Jessica for the first time: man and woman instead of friends. The complete giving of himself to and for another person was an utterly new experience in his life. And Jessica had given herself completely to him.

They began to laugh again when Jessica had to dress and leave for her own room to get ready for dinner. "I didn't realize you were such a gentleman," she said.

"I don't believe in taking anything for granted," he replied.

After she left, Phillip wondered at the euphoria of their moment together. There was a sense of wholeness, as if the scattered parts of a puzzle had come together. All at once his life seemed so complete, so unenhanceable. There was nothing he would change.

Nothing? He closed his eyes and leaned heavily against the dresser, breathing deeply. Yes, God, there was *one* thing he would change if he could. But the time for choosing was over. Now, every facet of his life must contend with the choice he had already made. But why should he let it spoil *this* moment? Wasn't life, after all, only a succession of moments? You took what you could from each, enjoying it while it lasted. Nothing was perfect, he reminded himself. Nothing lasted forever. But if that were true, why was he afraid he would never see Jessica Westbrook again?

He waited for her in the hotel dining room, and when she entered wearing a sheer black cocktail dress, her hair done up in a French twist, the smile on her face was radiant. Phillip was certain he had never seen anyone more lovely.

"You are exquisitely beautiful," he said.

"What you really mean is, with heels and dress on, I look like a girl."

"If that's the case, I wonder who the hell I thought I was making love to an hour ago."

They ordered dinner and lingered over coffee and brandy until they were the last ones left in the dining room and the waiters were growing impatient. Back in Phillip's room, they made love again, then talked and finally fell asleep in each other's arms just as the eastern sky grew pink.

Breakfast was sent up, and before they had a chance to question the equity of time, they were checking out and driving to the airport to catch Phillip's flight to San Francisco.

As Jessica deftly maneuvered her car through the heavy early-morning traffic, she was talking about her new business. But Phillip was so totally absorbed in his own thoughts that he found it difficult to pay attention. How unlike Polly she was, or any other woman with whom he had ever been involved. Instantly a sort of panic seized him. What in hell was he thinking about? *Involvement?* With Jessica? That was absurd. Not where *he* was going, not with what he *had* to do. Polly Savitch was one thing; Jessica could be hurt. Emotional entanglements: he couldn't afford them, didn't want them. And now the one thing that was missing from his life would always be missing. There were priorities. Grow up, you dumb bastard, he said to himself.

By the time they reached the airport, his panic had subsided. But there was a deep sadness tugging at him as they checked in for the flight and went into a small coffeeshop to wait.

"You're very quiet," Jessica said. "Business? You've scarcely said a word about what you're doing now."

"It's not very interesting, I guess."

She stirred her coffee and was silent for a moment. "You're not sorry we had this time together, are you, Phillip?"

"Of course I'm not sorry," he said, reaching over and taking her hand. "It's just that I'm sad to leave you."

"But we'll see each other again soon?"

"Nothing could keep me away from you now. Don't you know that?" But even as he spoke, the words sounded hollow to his own ears. "There are . . . well, so many things I have to do in the next few weeks. It may be pretty difficult to see you again as soon as I'd like."

Jessica smiled and said nothing.

Phillip glanced at his watch and squeezed her hand again. "It's almost time."

"Yes, I suppose it is. It's never been so hard to say goodbye to you before."

"I know," he said quietly. And then he was gone.

*   *   *

Driving back to town, Jessica was close to tears. Once again Phillip Vanderlind had appeared suddenly in her life and just as suddenly had disappeared. Hellos and goodbyes, but this time there had been something in between. What did he want from her? Was he still searching for something she could not give him? Was he still searching for himself?

There had been moments during their last few hours together when she thought that he was happy, that she had found him at last. But now she realized she had not found him at all. Because there was nothing to find. Phillip hadn't said it, but she knew. She was only of passing interest on his journey to somewhere else.

CHAPTER 13

O
n the eve of his first courier run, Phillip relaxed in the back seat of Averal Sutherland's Rolls and let the driver worry about the heavy press of New York traffic. He had been nervous about the late-Sunday-afternoon briefing conference with Sutherland, but as Sutherland described it, the run would be much less involved than he had anticipated.

Two sets of identical luggage would be utilized, each set consisting of two pieces of moderately traveled bags. One set bore the embossed initials P.A.V. and tags with Phillip's name and San Francisco address. The initials on the other set were P.V. and belonged, the tags said, to Paul Vermile of Paris.

On the night before his departure from London for the United States, the bags containing the heroin would be placed in Phillip's room while he was out for the evening and his fully packed bags removed. In the unlikely event of difficulties with customs the next day, his luggage would easily be traceable to a remote corner of the hotel's baggage area in the lobby. A regrettable but not too uncommon error. But if all went according to plan, his bags would simply be disposed of. New sets of luggage would be used for each run.

Phillip had made his own reservation at the Savoy. He would be in London two days and three nights, leaving the morning of the third day. And on the afternoon of the second day, at precisely three o'clock, he was to call the telephone number given to him by Sutherland. The call would be answered with the time of day, and he was merely to say the name of his hotel and the number of his room and hang up. The entire matter was as simple as Sutherland had promised—and totally devoid of personal contact with others.

"Here we are, sir. The Pierre."

"Fine. Eight-thirty in the morning, then?"

"Yes, sir, I'll be waiting."

Phillip picked up his calls from the desk, noting on the way to the elevator that Polly had called to confirm their date for dinner. It was seven o'clock, time enough for a drink and a shower before he picked her up.

*   *   *

"Darling!" She greeted him at the door of her apartment wearing a dressing gown. "Are you early or am I late? It's been the most awful day. Come in and make yourself a drink."

"Can I make you one?" Phillip asked.

"I've got one in the bedroom. I'll only be a few more minutes, darling."

Phillip watched her cross the room somewhat unsteadily and close the bedroom door behind her. She's been drinking, he thought. Her face was puffy and her eyes were glazed. Polly could usually hold her liquor better than that.

"Are you sure you're feeling all right?" he asked when she reappeared.

"I'm feeling absolutely marvelous," she said. "And you will, too, I promise. I've got a lovely surprise for you after dinner."

They went to an expensive French restaurant that Polly frequented. The maître d'hôtel greeted her by name, and they were seated at an excellent table. But Phillip was slightly embarrassed by Polly's behavior. She drank even more at dinner, and her voice was too loud, her gestures too animated. She was almost a caricature of herself.

She suggested a fashionable new disco after dinner. "I can't, Polly," Phillip said. "I've got a flight to London in the morning and a lot of other things on my mind."

"Well, there's only one thing on my mind," Polly said provocatively, leaning across the table to kiss him.

Phillip realized the waiters were beginning to stare. "Come on. I'll take you home."

She was all over him the moment they entered the apartment. He pulled away from her, disgusted. "Well, I'm just trying to please you, darling," she said.

"What the hell's the matter, Polly? I've never seen you like this."

"Nothing's the matter, goddamnit!" Polly cried shrilly. She crossed the room and sat down heavily in a chair. "I am a little short on cash at the moment, but that's not your problem."

"I can let you have some money."

"Well, you do owe me two hundred dollars from that dinner in Houston."

Phillip pulled his money clip from his pocket and began to count bills.

"I was only teasing, Phillip!" Polly cried.

"Will a thousand be enough?" He laid the money on a coffee table.

"Oh, God," Polly whispered and began to cry.

Phillip immediately regretted his cruelty. He went over to her chair and took her hands away from her face. She had smeared her makeup.

"I'll pay you back, darling. I promise. Every penny."

"You don't have to pay me back," Phillip said.

"Well, then, I think you should get your money's worth," Polly said, brightening suddenly. "Why don't you make us a drink and I'll go get your little surprise."

"No more surprises tonight, Polly."

"Please, Phillip. Please." She tried to hold him as he straightened up to leave. "Everything will be marvelous again between us, I promise."

"Good night, Polly. I'll call you when I get back from London."

"Please, Phillip. Oh, please."

He left her sitting in the chair, a lost expression in her eyes.

*   *   *

Leslie Parrish sighed contentedly in the opulence of the Rolls-Royce as Averal Sutherland's chauffeur made his last trip of an unusually long day.

It had been a wonderful evening. Dinner at a small, dimly lit restaurant, then on to Sutherland's townhouse for coffee and the presents. It was the first anniversary of their meeting. Leslie had given him a gold crest ring, and he had given Leslie the incredibly beautiful sable coat he now nestled to his face as he watched the lighted store windows flash by. A whole year had passed since Sutherland had found him in a female impersonators' club in San Francisco. It seemed impossible. But here he was, living exactly as his benefactor had promised: elegantly and completely as a woman.

In the beginning, Leslie had been apprehensive. Was it reasonable to expect someone to do what Sutherland said he would do in exchange for only a few hours each month of voyeuristic pleasure? Perhaps not. But Leslie had taken the chance and had never been sorry.

In all that time only one thing had clouded the relationship: Stewart Cross. But Sutherland had grudgingly accepted Leslie's on-and-off affair with Cross, and now he was only a problem to Leslie. He wanted Leslie to move back to San Francisco and live with him. But Leslie wasn't about to give up the fantastic arrangement with Sutherland. When that ended, and if Cross was still around . . . well, then he might think about it.

"Here we are, Miss Parrish. Your apartment."

"Oh, so it is."

As Leslie reached for the evening bag that had fallen to the floor, he saw a white card that lay beside it. He picked it up and tucked it in his bag. A little housekeeping to earn his keep, he thought whimsically.

The chauffeur helped Leslie from the car and saw him safely to the elevator, eying him approvingly as the doors closed. On the way up, Leslie laughed at the thought passing through his mind: what a kick it would be one day to pull up his skirt and show that chauffeur what he was *really* lusting after.

What *was* he? He reflected as he let himself in the apartment and began undressing for bed. Did he *really* want to be a woman? Transsexual surgery terrified him, and he still enjoyed balling Sutherland's whores occasionally. Well, what the hell difference did it make tonight? He sat down at the dressing table and removed his makeup. Then he emptied his evening bag and noticed the card he had picked up.

> PHILLIP A. VANDERLIND
> President
> OMNI LEASING INC.
> 1500 LAGUNA CENTER
> SAN FRANCISCO, CA 94120
> (415) 666-6536

Leslie shrugged his shoulders and tossed the card back on the dressing table. It fell face down. On the reverse side was a phone number.

*   *   *

London weather was dreary: cold and foggy with the promise of more in the forecast. But this was Phillip's first trip to the city and he was enjoying it immensely. Including the weather. Like the movies, he thought. Street lamps dimmed by swirling mist, near deserted streets, trenchcoats—all of that.

Since he wanted the second day to himself, he had arranged all his business appointments for the first day. And they were far more rewarding than he anticipated. It appeared that three of the five companies contacted were prime candidates for equipment leasing. This promised to be a very profitable trip, he reflected wryly, even without the run.

On the second day, Phillip spent most of the morning with a

Savile Row tailor. The dozen suits he ordered would be cut and basted and ready for final fittings on his next trip. Then he went to a premier bootmaker in Devonshire Street, where he had his last measured, and placed an order for five pairs of shoes. These would also be waiting for him when he returned. At two o'clock that afternoon he lunched at the Savoy and was back in his room at half past the hour.

Since leaving New York, Phillip had purposely tried to keep his mind totally occupied so as not to consider the real purpose of his trip. But he had to think about it now. And as he did so, he began looking through his pocket secretary for the card with the phone number he was to call. He was surprised at how tranquil he felt, almost as if he were about to make reservations at a restaurant. But within the next few moments his tranquility gave way to sheer panic. He couldn't find the goddamn card!

He searched frantically, then calmly, but it was useless. The card was gone. Even if he could get a transatlantic call to Sutherland through in the next few minutes, he might well not be in his office. And Phillip had no way of knowing whether whoever was now waiting for the three-o'clock call would wait past that hour. Christ, how could he make such a stupid fucking error! He *had* to try to reach Sutherland.

The overseas operator took his call and said she would ring him back when the connection was made.

Where had he last seen the card? He couldn't remember. Yes, he could: the Rolls, going back to the hotel. He had been staring at the number. Maybe, just maybe, he could remember it. He tried to think, then stopped himself. He was getting confused. There was a trick he often used to induce recall. He forced everything from his mind for a few moments, then walked to the dresser and wrote down a series of numbers. It was close, very close, maybe even correct. Except for the last two digits, he was certain of it. Was it 59 or 95? It was five minutes of three.

At exactly three o'clock he dialed the number ending in 59 and held his breath. In two rings the receiver clicked and a voice said, "The time is three o'clock."

Phillip was struck dumb. He couldn't remember his room

number! There was a pause and the receiver clicked dead in his ear.

He waited a moment, his heart pounding. Then he dialed again. "The time is three o'clock."

"Savoy, two-one-two-two," Phillip said slowly and distinctly. The phone went silent. It was done.

He canceled the call to Sutherland and went quickly down to the bar. Good God, he thought. If I'm that nervous about a telephone call, what's it going to be like when I go through customs?

*   *   *

What Phillip would really have liked that evening for dinner was a simple hamburger, not the overcooked and highly seasoned game hen his host's club served with pompous pride. But the man was a prime leasing prospect and he couldn't turn down the invitation.

They said good night shortly after ten-thirty, and Phillip set out for the hotel four blocks away. He walked slowly through the freezing drizzle, the heavy meal weighing unpleasantly on his stomach. A block from the Savoy he stopped beneath a lamppost and turned his face up to the cold wetness. He thought about the luggage that waited for him in his room, and the shiver that passed through his body had nothing to do with the weather.

He also thought about the house in Marin County, the car, the Bermuda 40, his job. And then he thought of the desperate months in Houston and the used Vega. And the corporation. The goddamn corporation. Fuck the corporation. If he really believed that, why should the two suitcases waiting in his room bother him?

As Sutherland had instructed, he did not open the bags. He merely took note that the initials and name tags were correct. Sutherland was right: there was great psychological value in *not* viewing the contents of the bags. On this first run it might be easier if he really didn't *know* what was in them.

Early the next morning, as he stood waiting to pay his bill, he caught himself glancing around the lobby as if expecting any moment to see the whole of Scotland Yard coming at him. But the sensation passed rapidly enough and he was able to act like any other traveling businessman. He took a cab to Heathrow, and as he approached the ticket counter the feeling of being watched returned. And this time it persisted. Damn! He had to control himself. That was how most people were caught at whatever they were trying to hide; they *looked* guilty.

He finally managed to pull himself into a visibly relaxed mood and was in control when his turn came with the ticket clerk. But this proved to be the most difficult moment so far. Watching the two bags being thrown on the baggage conveyor belt and disappearing behind the counter gave him a feeling of panic. What if . . . well, there was nothing he could do about it now. He smiled his thanks to the agent, turned and walked briskly to the waiting room at his boarding gate.

The next half hour was complete paranoia. Every time someone with any kind of official look came near him, he expected to be apprehended. It was only after he had boarded the aircraft and it began to taxi toward the runway that Phillip was able to relax. As the aircraft broke ground he sighed, and minutes later he was asleep, not from fatigue but from nervous exhaustion.

Two hours out from New York, Phillip had his first drink. But it wasn't courage he sought from the scotch. He was looking for that edge: not high, but just relaxed and open. He knew if he approached customs cold sober, he might well press too hard to appear straight. A drink and a half, maybe two, would be about right.

Nothing happened. The first drink had absolutely no effect. Maybe if he got up and moved around a bit. He walked back to the small first-class lounge and ordered a second scotch—on the rocks this time. Sipping his drink, he looked around at the other passengers in the lounge.

The man sitting just across from where he stood seemed somehow familiar. Where had he seen him before: San Francisco, New York, on the flight over? He couldn't remember. Their eyes met for a moment, but the man turned away abruptly and looked out the window.

Phillip shrugged his shoulders, took another sip of his drink and went back to his seat. He was right. Moving about helped. He was beginning to feel the glow of the scotch.

*   *   *

As the engines of the DC-10 shut down and the passengers began to leave the aircraft, the full realization of what he was about to do struck Phillip with almost paralyzing effect. He walked to the arrival area and stood there, uncertain for a moment. Then, closing his eyes, he gave himself up to the inevitability of his circumstances. He knew what to expect when he reached customs; Sutherland had briefed him thoroughly. Nevertheless, he could feel a flood of perspiration under his arms and a slight ringing sensation in his ears as he claimed the bags. He hoped to God his face wasn't bathed in sweat.

Approaching the rail-thin, beak-nosed customs official who would pass him through or stop him, he tried to suppress the noise that would surely give him away; the heavy, rhythmic pounding in his chest was so loud that he was certain every person in the immediate vicinity could hear it. And at the precise moment he set the bags down and proffered his passport, his mind went absolutely blank. He could no more think than he could speak.

For what seemed an eternity, the customs official stared at the small blue book with gold markings. Then he smiled and nodded, returning the passport to the outstretched hand Phillip saw in front of him. It was *his* hand.

"You must have had a good time in London, Mr. Vanderlind."

"I beg your pardon?" It was *his* voice.

"That smile on your face. You must have had a good trip. All right, sir, please make room for the other passengers. Thank you and have a good day."

Moments later, Phillip found himself following the sky-cap who was carrying his baggage. It was as if he had awakened from a dream in a strange place. It was done. He had done it. It had worked. It had worked!

As the cab pulled away from the terminal and picked up the expressway toward Manhattan, Phillip slumped in the back seat with a long sigh. He was not home free just yet—but he was almost there.

Now, it was simply a matter of checking into the Sherry-Netherland Hotel, where he had reservations for one night, taking the bags to the room, then leaving and walking over to the Pierre, only a few steps away, where he would call Sutherland. Phillip glanced at his watch; an hour and a half at the outside and it would be all over.

*   *   *

As his car moved into the flow of traffic behind the yellow cab Phillip Vanderlind had entered moments before, Cyril Kennedy sighed dejectedly and wondered if he was getting a bit scratchy. Routine, but thorough, checks had been run on Averal Sutherland and Phillip Vanderlind and had revealed nothing in either man's background that even vaguely hinted at impropriety. Sutherland, particularly, was absolutely above reproach. Under the circumstances, a younger, less experienced agent might have dropped the matter. And Cyril Kennedy was sorely tempted. But Kennedy was a hunter.

Everything fitted his theory too perfectly. An executive down on his luck recently employed by a new corporation with business abroad. And why would Vanderlind have any use for or be entitled to a para-diplomatic passport, Kennedy wondered, with no search by customs? It was conceivable the man might be bringing something in illegally. It was a long shot, Kennedy knew, but he had nothing else to go on. He wanted a look at the contents of those bags Vanderlind had with him. So he would just follow the man to his hotel and wait for him to leave his room.

He trailed Vanderlind's cab to the Sherry-Netherland. But what Kennedy had expected to be as much as a four- or five-hour wait in the lobby turned out to be hardly that many minutes. He barely had time to scan the front page of the paper he had sat down to read before Vanderlind was walking back through the lobby and out the front door.

Kennedy followed him, and a minute later he watched as Vanderlind walked up to the desk of the Pierre Hotel, said something to the clerk, was handed a key and went immediately to the elevators.

Puzzled, Kennedy waited for a few moments, then went over to the house phone. When he left the hotel minutes later, he was more puzzled than ever; Phillip Vanderlind had a permanent suite at the Pierre.

Back at the Sherry-Netherland, he asked a bellman for directions to the manager's office, and shortly thereafter Kennedy and the assistant manager on duty were entering the room Vanderlind had briefly occupied. Other than one cigarette butt, a slightly damp hand towel and the broken sanitary paper band on the toilet, the room was in perfect order.

Then Kennedy found two large suitcases in the closet. He cursed lightly under his breath as he went through the contents of the first bag. After inspecting the second bag, he slammed it shut, stood up, looked at the assistant manager and began to laugh.

*   *   *

As the door to his suite at the Pierre closed behind him, Phillip shot his fist ceilingward in victory, ripped off his tie and made a call to Averal Sutherland.

"The line is clear, Phillip."

"Room one-eight-three-two. The Sherry-Netherland."

"Excellent. Any difficulty?"

"No," Phillip said.

"That's fine. Now, I'm certain you'll want to rest a bit before dinner. I'll send the car for you at eight, if that's convenient."

Phillip lingered for a long time in the warm, steamy refuge of the shower, letting the remaining tension ooze from his body. He was suddenly drained and extremely weary.

He toweled himself dry and went into the bedroom, pulled

down the covers and checked the time. It was almost 3:00 P.M. He left a call for seven and sprawled naked across the cool, clean sheets.

*   *   *

"Averal, I think that has to be the finest meal I've had in years," Phillip said as he and Sutherland left the dining room and went into the library of the townhouse.

"Yes, my cook does an incredibly good Beef Wellington, I think. I'm glad you enjoyed it." Sutherland poured two snifters of brandy and handed one to Phillip. "Welcome to Beta."

"Beta?" Phillip said.

"Yes," Sutherland said, "that's the name of the rather informal organization to which you now belong. There are six of us now that you have joined. You'll learn more about the organization and meet the other members soon. I think you'll find us a very congenial group."

Both men smiled, their glasses touched and they drank.

"And now I have something for you, Phillip." Sutherland walked over to an ornately carved desk and took a large plain envelope from the middle drawer. "A bit more substantive than brandy," he said, handing the envelope to Phillip.

"What is this?"

"It's what you've just earned over the last twenty-four hours."

Phillip tore off the end of the envelope and withdrew a neatly bound packet of bills.

"One hundred thousand dollars, Phillip. Your personal share for this trip."

Phillip stared at the currency in his hand. When he spoke, his voice was filled with disbelief. "It was so simple, Averal. One hundred thousand dollars. Just like that. Absolutely incredible."

"And it's just the beginning, Phillip. Just the beginning." Sutherland sipped his brandy and nodded toward the fireplace. "Come, let's sit. I have one or two things I would like to discuss with you."

"What do I do with this?" Phillip said, holding up the bills.

Sutherland laughed. "I'm sure it would be reasonably safe right there on the desk."

Phillip grinned and felt his face grow warm. "What can you expect from a poor boy?" He put the packet on the desk and took a chair across from Sutherland. "Speaking of money, may I mention something so I don't forget it?"

"Of course."

"The equipment lease with Hospital Associates will be coming to fruition within two or three weeks. I'd like to go ahead and remove Novak from the bank account so that the five million can be disbursed without any delays or complications."

"Yes, certainly. If you'll prepare a corporate resolution to that effect and send it to me, I'll have Novak execute it as secretary."

"Fine. I'll get it off to you Monday."

"Now, I have a rather large favor to ask of you, Phillip," Sutherland said. "As you know, there are now four couriers, including yourself. Two are abroad at the moment, one in Singapore, the other in Australia. The third underwent an emergency appendectomy this afternoon. And therein lies the problem that gives rise to the needed favor." He took a long sip of his brandy. "It is absolutely essential that another run be made in two weeks. I have no alternative but to ask that you make it."

Phillip shifted uneasily in his chair. He had programmed himself to a run every two *months*. "Frankly, that comes as a bit of a shock, Averal. May I ask why another run is necessary?"

"You may indeed. First of all, demand has strengthened considerably on this end in the past two weeks. And, on the other end, our friends in Europe have an unexpected oversupply they wish to move immediately. I feel it essential to our operation that we accommodate both parties if we possibly can."

"I see." Phillip leaned back, lit a cigarette and stared into the snifter of brandy. "And I'm the only one available."

"I don't believe this sort of situation will ever arise again, Phillip. And all of us would be most grateful to you."

"All right, then. Of course I'll go." He drew on his cigarette deeply and exhaled. "Specifically when?"

"You're to leave on the twenty-second and return the twenty-seventh."

"Same procedure, I assume?"

˙ "The same. Except I'll have another telephone number for you by the time you're ready to leave."

Both men were silent for a few moments, then Phillip asked, "Averal, when do you anticipate I'll be able to meet the others?"

"That has already been scheduled. For the twenty-eighth, the day after you return, here in New York."

"That sounds fine. I'm anxious to meet them."

"And they you, Phillip."

"You know, I've never asked, but I am curious about who they are."

"No more so than they are about you, Phillip. Call it an idiosyncrasy, but I prefer that everyone meet personally at the same time."

"Of course. It really doesn't matter. But I do have one other question, Averal." Phillip cleared his throat; he wasn't sure how to ask it. "You said that Beta is an informal organization, but there must be records and books and names. I know my concerns are groundless, but . . ."

"But of legitimate concern nonetheless," Sutherland said with a smile. "Let me put your mind at ease, Phillip. There is absolutely no way you or any other member of the group could ever be identified with Beta. Yes, to be sure, we have records. But they're all coded. And without the code, everything is just a mass of figures, totally without meaning."

"But if the code . . ."

"The code—" Sutherland pointed to his temple—"is here. And, of course, Novak, who devised the entire system, has it committed to memory as well. I assure you, Phillip, there is no need to be concerned about incriminating documentation. It simply does not exist."

Phillip was relieved in one way. But on the other hand, he realized that there was no evidence that he could use to implicate Sutherland if the need should ever arise. It was, at the moment, a stand-off.

Phillip rose from his chair and stretched. "You know, I'm still drained from the trip, Averal. Emotions more than anything, I suppose. Maybe a bit of jet lag, too. Would you mind if we said good night?"

"Not at all. But aren't you forgetting something? One small little detail."

Phillip looked questioningly at his host for a long moment, then burst into laughter. "Great God! I'm about to walk out of here without my money." He started toward the desk, then stopped and turned back toward Sutherland. "What in the hell am I going to do with one hundred thousand dollars this time of night? I've got a better idea, Averal. Why don't I just give it back to you and let you pay off my note at your bank?"

"Well, certainly, if you wish, Phillip. However, I would be more than pleased to let the note . . ."

"No, thanks all the same. I'd really rather clear that thing up. Besides, in two weeks, I'll have another one of these packages anyway, won't I?"

*   *   *

Cyril Kennedy concluded his verbal report to his superior, Harry Kane, and waited for a response.

The senior agent merely sucked at the long-stemmed pipe in his mouth and gazed through slitted eyes at the picture of the President of the United States hanging on the far wall of his office.

"Well, Harry?"

"Well *what*, Cyril?"

"I'd like to know what you think."

"After what you found in Vanderlind's room, you're asking *me*?"

"Come on, Harry," Kennedy said. "The whole thing smells to high heaven. What about the name tags on the luggage—Paul Vermile, the same initials as Vanderlind's. And the fact he checks into one hotel when he has a permanent suite at another. And then *leaves* the bags. I know we're onto something here."

"Cyril, I think you're blowing smoke up a goose's ass. And the next time—if there is a next time—you go rummaging around in Vanderlind's luggage, you're going to find the same thing you found yesterday: nothing but expensive hand-tailored clothing."

CHAPTER 14

Phillip had never sailed northward out of San Francisco Bay. As the Bermuda 40 rolled lazily on a beam in the quartering sea, he lounged in the cockpit with a can of beer and a sandwich, steering with his foot. The sun was bright and hot and felt good after the cold beat out of the bay earlier that morning. It was just past noon and time to set a more westerly course. He wanted to be well off shore by nightfall.

He tossed the empty beer can and sandwich wrappings below, pointed the *Spellbound* closer to the wind, and sheeted in the sails. He was close-hauled now, beating out to sea on a rising wind. His sail plan was simple: seaward for a day and a half, then back. Three days of solitude. Nothing to consider but the sea. And himself.

He had been right about Averal Sutherland. Two runs in such quick succession were obviously intended as a test of his loyalty. And there was no way he could refuse. Nor, if money was the only consideration, did he want to.

Two hundred thousand dollars in two weeks. It was incredible! There was no danger; he had proved that to himself now. And the rewards were enormous. Why, then, the lingering sense of uneasiness? And why had he tape-recorded everything he could remember about the first run—the names, the numbers, times, places, everything? Fear? His conscience? Why couldn't he just relax with his decision?

He had plenty of time to think about it as he explored the waters of the Pacific—until he hit the fog. It caught him on the afternoon of the second day as he turned eastward to go back in. He had just enough time to prepare a jug of hot coffee and sandwiches before the bow all but disappeared from view in the yellow-white mist.

Other than the sound of the sea against the hull and the motion of the boat, there was no sensation of forward progress. It was eerie and frightening—and, since he was approaching the shipping lanes, dangerous as hell.

He sounded his foghorn at the prescribed intervals, watched the tiny radar screen forward in the cabin, and maintained the compass heading he had struck before entering the opaque wetness. Those things, together with the depth-sounder to give him an indication of where he was over the bottom and the radar reflector on his mast to alert other boats of his presence, should see him safely to port.

Five miles from land, his radar malfunctioned.

Thirty minutes later, Phillip almost jumped out of the cockpit when a foghorn suddenly erupted immediately aft of the *Spellbound*. He quickly broke away to starboard and reached off to safety, watching a seagoing tug with several barges in tow ghost into view over his shoulder.

In moments he was below, trying to establish radio contact with the vessel. On the third call the tug answered. They were bound for a port in the bay. Phillip started the engine, struck the sails, and fell in behind, steering on the running lights of the last barge.

It was two in the morning when he thanked the tug and bore off toward the yacht club. An hour later he slipped wearily into the starboard bunk and slept.

The next two days were consumed with the affairs of Omni:

mail, phone calls, contracts, and the board resolution on the bank account. But Averal Sutherland and the next run were never very far from his thoughts. And he thought of Polly Savitch, too. Her behavior that last evening they had spent together in New York puzzled and troubled him. He felt sorry for her, and if there was any way he could help her, he would. But he decided it was time to end their affair, and one evening before going to bed he wrote her a brief, gentle letter. It was a good letter, he thought. But in the end he tore it up. He would be in New York in less than two weeks. He would see her and would simply tell her then. She deserved at least that much.

And he thought of Jessica. One morning at the office he pushed back from the worktable and realized he was only going through the motions. There was no pressing business, not even any routine tasks that required his presence. Why not go to Sutherland's house in Aspen and ask her to join him there? All at once he wanted very much to see her again.

"Phillip! I'm so glad you called. Would you believe I've been thinking about calling you all morning?" There was a happy ring to her voice.

"I'm glad one of us acted on our feelings."

"You may not be. I think I'm getting cold feet on the deal."

"Everybody gets a few butterflies just before the plunge. It's a good sign, really."

"I'm not so sure. The deeper I get, the less I understand what it's all about."

"Well, let's talk about it, then."

"Do you mind?"

"Of course not. As a matter of fact, that's why I called. Look, I've got a lull in my business and the next three or four days are free. Would you like to get together and go back over this thing? I can leave here tomorrow morning in the company plane and be in Vail around noon or so. But I want you to be my guest this time. I'll pick you up and we can just hop on back to Aspen. Does that sound okay?"

"It sounds marvelous."

"Then it's done. Gather up all of your stuff and I'll call when we land."

"Phillip?"

"Yes?"

"I don't want you to think that I'm . . . I mean the last time we were together, you . . ."

"I don't think anything, Jessica—except that I really want to see you."

*   *   *

The house on Red Mountain was ready for them when they arrived, and by mid-afternoon they were engrossed in a total reassessment of Jessica's new business. When the high glass windows caught the flare of the sunset, they broke for a drink and silently watched the vast sweep of the Rockies slip away in the icy winter dusk. Then, while Jessica went to the kitchen to put steaks on the grill, Phillip settled down to a final run-through of the numbers, more pleased than ever with what he saw. Only briefly did he remember that it was his $25,000 that was making it all possible. He was glad now that he had given it to Jessica. And he quickly pushed from his mind the reason he would no longer need that money.

During dinner he explained to her the few problems that he could foresee and the changes in the original plan that would be necessary to resolve them. In the end he was astonished by how thoroughly she seemed to understand all the interrelationships involved. "You're a damn good businesswoman, Jessica. Forget the butterflies. If it can be done, you're the one who can do it."

"God, I hope you're right."

Dinner over, they sat quietly in front of the fire, sipping wine. Outside, it had begun to snow. It was Jessica who broke the silence; she reached out and lightly touched his arm. "Thank you, Phillip."

They looked at each other for a moment. Then Phillip rose and held out his hand. She took it and they walked slowly up the stairs to bed.

For the next three days there was nothing in the world for either of them except each other. They made love whenever it pleased them. They took long, slow walks to nowhere and marveled at the discovery that they had no recollection afterward of anything but each other's presence. The shops and restaurants of the town were snubbed by their intimacy and delight with each other. And they broke whatever records existed for slowness in getting down ski runs, stopping every hundred yards or so to tease and kiss and touch.

Neither spoke directly of what was happening to them. Somehow both sensed it was neither necessary nor the time. Facts were simply facts; they had fallen deeply in love. And on the day he said goodbye to her at the small airport in Vail, Phillip cupped her small cold face in his hands and whispered simply, "Okay?"

She had closed her eyes and answered, "Okay."

Now, as she watched the speck of his plane climbing westward over the mountains, Jessica wondered whether everything was real and whether she deserved to feel so consummately happy. And then, for some reason, she remembered the way she felt the last time they had said goodbye to each other at an airport. It wasn't that she doubted what they had between them now. It was just that she still sensed there was something else, something troubling Phillip, that was pulling them apart.

*   *   *

From the day he returned from Vail until the evening before he was to leave for London, Phillip circled despondently between the two worlds he had created for himself: Beta and Jessica Westbrook. Finally, so desperately did he want what each held out to him that the possibility of coexistence slowly became a viable possibility in his mind.

The two worlds were separate, after all. Why even consider them in terms of compatibility? Didn't life consist, more or less, of naturally opposed phenomena? And chaos occurred only when contact was made. He was the only point of contact between his two worlds, and he could keep them apart. Yes, why couldn't he have both?

Yet, by the time he checked into the Savoy in London for the second time in as many weeks, Phillip was aware of a nagging sense of apprehension. Something, it seemed, was trying to slip into his consciousness. Was it something he had forgotten to do?

He wondered. For the first three days of his stay in London he was able to repress that feeling in a busy round of appointments, sightseeing, and social engagements. But on the evening of the fourth day he returned to the Savoy in a state of mild anxiety. Even after two double scotches in the hotel bar, the gently tapping vagueness that demanded recognition was still there. Then suddenly a chilling thought struck him: was he having a premonition that something was going to go wrong with the run? Convinced that was it, he paid his check and went hurriedly up to his suite.

During the next half hour he pored over every detail of the run several times, but nothing—absolutely nothing—he could detect offered even the slightest complication. Sutherland had given him a number to call, and he had it committed to memory this time. The bags would be switched as before, and all he had to do was fly to New York, carry them through customs, and call Sutherland. What could go wrong? And yet whatever it was that was pulling at him pulled even more strongly now.

The next day was devoted to Omni business, and Phillip found that it was almost impossible to concentrate. His head throbbed, and his entire body seemed constricted with tension. He canceled his afternoon appointment and returned to the hotel. He spent the evening in his room, fighting the haunting, inexplicable anxiety. I've got to get my head straight, he thought. I've got a job to do tomorrow! He tried to sleep but was startled to consciousness in the middle of the night and found the sheets soaked with perspiration.

The following morning he found no pleasure in visiting his tailor for the final fittings on the suits he had ordered during his previous trip. And that afternoon, when he dialed the number Sutherland had given him and spoke the name of the hotel and the number of his room, his voice sounded hollow, as if he were in a trance. He left the hotel after he made the call and simply wandered the streets. He caught a reflection of himself in a shop window. He stopped and stared back at the image. It revealed an urbane man of obvious success, a man to be envied by other men. He turned away, repelled by his own reflection.

That evening in his suite he did what Sutherland had advised him not to do. He opened the luggage that had been substituted for his own. And there, under a thin layer of clothing, he saw the tightly packed plastic bags of heroin. He was fascinated at first and then disgusted. "Goddamnit, don't think!" he raged at himself. But he could not quiet his thoughts. What did he want? Where was he going? He no longer knew. Dear God, he only knew what he had to do to get there. And for the second night in a row he fell into a shallow and troubled sleep.

*   *   *

Emile Novak's attention wandered from the Beta financial data he was checking before he committed it to code. He was always apprehensive on the day of a delivery. And this time it was worse because it was Phillip Vanderlind who was making the run. He didn't trust that son of a bitch and had protested when Sutherland decided that it was not necessary to assign an Essex man to monitor Vanderlind's second run. But then maybe Sutherland was right. The first run had gone without a hitch.

The memory of that first run amused him. He wished he had been a fly on the wall and had watched Vanderlind sweat turds smuggling a couple of bags full of expensive clothes through customs. Sutherland's insistence on a dummy run by a new courier was sound, but it was funnier than hell, too, Novak thought. And then he had another thought. What if Vanderlind had looked into those bags? What if he knew he was being tested on that first run? And what if he had looked into the bags this time, too? It was the real stuff this time, and Novak felt his whole body tighten with a spasm of apprehension and fear.

*   *   *

As his cab sped toward Manhattan, Phillip knew he had been right: the ambiguous, intolerable anxiety of the past several days had nothing at all to do with the fear of being caught. He was safely through customs now, less than two hours away from another $100,000, no more than twelve from Jessica. Yes, he could have both. Why, then, was his mind still in turmoil?

Coming out of the Midtown Tunnel into the snarl of city traffic, Phillip felt his pulse quicken. He was running out of time, playing it too close. If he didn't look now at what was just beneath the surface of his consciousness, something told him he never would. He was scheduled to call Sutherland at two o'clock. But he had to stop the world, if only for a moment. He had to have time to think. Polly's place. It was the only refuge he could think of. It would be perfect—if she wasn't there. He had a key. And if she was, he would have to think of something else. He leaned forward to speak to the driver. "I've changed my mind," he said. "Take me to the corner of Sixty-eighth and Park."

By the time he reached Polly's apartment building it was beginning to rain. On the chance that she would be there and he would have to leave, Phillip handed the driver a twenty and asked him to wait. He would never catch another cab in this downpour. But he couldn't leave the bags. Nodding to the doorman, who recognized him, he carried them into the building, rode up in the elevator, and rang Polly's bell. There was no reply.

He was looking for the key when suddenly the door opened and Polly was standing there. She was dressed only in a thin robe, her hair disheveled, her face without makeup.

"Phillip, what in God's name are you doing here?" She caught sight of herself in a mirror hanging in the foyer. "Oh, Jesus," she said. "I must look awful." She started to comb her hair with her fingers. Her hands were shaking.

"I'm sorry I woke you," Phillip said.

"I wasn't asleep. No, not asleep." Her words were slurred, her voice hoarse and low.

"Can I come in? I just need a place to think for a while. Maybe a drink. Are you alone?"

Polly tried to pull herself together. "Of course I'm alone. Of course you can come in, darling."

Phillip picked up the bags, stepped inside the door, and closed it behind him. Polly lurched forward, her arms outstretched to embrace him. She stumbled and fell heavily against his chest.

"For God's sake, Polly," Phillip said. "What's the matter with you? You can't be drunk at one o'clock in the afternoon."

"No, darling, I'm just a little hung over. But why are you here at this hour? I didn't expect you until this evening." She pulled away from him and suddenly began to cry. "Oh God, Phillip, I've lost you, haven't I? You've come to tell me it's all over between us. I saw the way you looked at me that night we had dinner. But I can explain. It's so simple really. And it can be good again between us. I've got something that will make it good, I promise. Please, Phillip, you can't just walk out on me. Not now."

Phillip stared at her incredulously. "I don't understand. Are you in some kind of trouble, Polly? If I can help you, I will."

"Oh, Phillip. You really don't understand, do you? You really don't know." She was laughing now, a high, shrill laugh that sent a chill down his back. "I'm hooked, you stupid bastard, and now I'm coming down. Can't you see that?"

Phillip's head snapped back with the impact of her words. "What the hell are you talking about? You're not telling me you're an addict!"

"What else, darling?" She was coquettish now, pressing her body against him, lifting her knee into his crotch. "It's the most wonderful feeling in the world. I've never been really alive before. Come with me, darling. Let me take you with me. We're so good together. Come with me, darling. We can have it all."

Phillip pushed her away angrily. "What are you doing to yourself? How did this happen, for God's sake? When did it start?"

"I don't need any lectures from you," Polly cried, her body trembling. "If you don't like it, you can get out and leave me alone. Get out of my life!"

For a moment he just stood there, staring at her. Then he looked away. "I'm sorry, Polly. God, I'm sorry."

He opened the door, picked up the bags, and left.

Averal Sutherland listened with only a minute portion of his mind to the droning voice of the Kaufman legal counsel briefing him on some aspect of a contract with Boeing Aircraft. Where in hell was Vanderlind? It was three o'clock. He should have called in by now.

Finally, Sutherland dismissed the lawyer, and as soon as he

disappeared through the door he called the Pierre. No, Phillip Vanderlind was not currently registered. Yes, he was expected sometime this afternoon. Yes, they would give him the message to call Mr. Sutherland the moment he arrived.

Damn it, where was the man? What could have happened?

An hour later, at four o'clock, Sutherland knew that only one of three things could have happened: an accident, an interdiction—or defection. He picked up his private wire and dialed a number.

"Yes, Averal? I assume everything went as planned."

"Everything has not gone as planned, Emile. I have not yet heard from him."

"God damn it, Averal. I told you we should have kept him under surveillance. If that bastard has—"

"There is no reason to be alarmed yet, Emile. We can't be certain what might have happened. I want you to check the airlines to see if he arrived in this country as scheduled. If so, then I want you to check your sources to see if the merchandise had trouble clearing customs. And then I want you to check the police. There may have been an accident. Is all that clear? And I repeat, Emile, there is no need for alarm."

*   *   *

Cyril Kennedy had always believed that luck and coincidence were mostly the result of perseverance. And he had been convinced Phillip Vanderlind's special passport, another person's name tags on the luggage he carried, and double hotel accommodations added up to duplicity of some sort. At least one obvious conclusion was smuggling narcotics. And discovering nothing but clothing in the luggage had been a rude shock. But he was still convinced the man was involved in something illegal. As he viewed it then, Kennedy had had no choice but to play out the string with Vanderlind.

The agent-in-charge of the bureau's San Francisco office had easily ascertained Vanderlind's most recent travel plans to London, and Scotland Yard had been only too pleased to cooperate on their end with round-the-clock surveillance. Kennedy was informed that morning that Vanderlind had boarded a London-to-New York flight, checking through two large bags that he had brought to Heathrow Airport; and within the hour, two of Kennedy's subordinates were in place at the International Arrivals building at Kennedy Airport with instructions to follow Vanderlind wherever he went. They had no trouble trailing his cab into Manhattan, but there they lost it in a midtown traffic jam. When the driver was finally located later in the afternoon, he revealed that he had taken his fare to an apartment building in the East 60s, waited a few minutes while he went in, and then drove him to a charter flying service at La Guardia Airport. According to the driver, his fare was carrying two bags when he picked him up at Kennedy and never let them out of his sight all the way to La Guardia. He remembered because he had asked the man if he wanted to put his bags in the trunk, and he said no.

The people at the jet charter service were equally cooperative but of marginal help. By the time they were contacted, they could only report that their charter passenger had already landed at San Francisco International Airport. And yes, they said, his luggage consisted of two large suitcases.

Kennedy immediately alerted agents in the Bay Area to try to ascertain the whereabouts of Phillip Vanderlind, and now he was waiting impatiently for their report. But he was absolutely certain of one thing: New York, not San Francisco, had been Vanderlind's original destination on this day. And something had happened. A man just didn't take a cab into the city carrying two big bags and then turn around and drive out again, still carrying the same two bags. Or were they the same bags? Kennedy wondered. And what was in them? He was more convinced than ever that they contained narcotics—probably heroin. It was the only thing that made any sense.

*   *   *

Emile Novak felt his temples begin to throb. It was a feeling he remembered from his years in Vietnam when his life was continually in danger. And it was a feeling that had returned the night he stood in the doorway of a priest's bedroom in Chicago, moments before he snapped the old man's neck.

Phillip Vanderlind had disappeared. He had been listed among the first-class passengers on a London-to-New York flight that morning and had apparently cleared customs without difficulty. But after that Novak could find no trace of him. The son of a bitch had disappeared.

Sutherland had warned him again to stay calm. "There is nothing we can do, Emile, until he contacts us and we can discover where he is and just what had happened. If he contacts the police, we will, of course, deny everything. There is no evidence against us, Emile, no evidence whatsoever."

Maybe there was no evidence against Sutherland, Novak thought, but *he* had been arrested for trafficking in drugs in Vietnam. What if federal agents succeeded in tracking down his contacts there? What if they talked?

No, Sutherland might be safe, but Phillip Vanderlind had Novak's balls in a vice. Where the hell was the bastard? Where would he go? Who did he know in New York?

* * *

Polly Savitch watched the steam rising off the hot bath she had just drawn and tried to forget what had happened that afternoon. So Phillip knew at last. So what? He'd be back. They always came back. And what if he didn't? She could live without Phillip Vanderlind.

She took off her robe and eased her naked body into the hot tub. Oh God, that felt good. She ran her hands over her breasts and down her thighs. Yes, her body was still beautiful. There were plenty of men who wanted her. Men with money. Rich men who could feed her habit. Suddenly she began to laugh. She remembered the expression on Phillip's face when it had suddenly dawned on him that she was a junkie. It wasn't a very pretty word, she thought, but that's what she was. Poor Phillip. Poor, dumb Phillip. Still, they had had some good times together and maybe he would come back. They always came back.

All at once she stirred; the hot water had become oppressive rather than relaxing. Annoyed, she listlessly toed open the drain, got out of the tub, and tried to towel some energy back into her body. She looked at the clock. God, she had the whole evening ahead of her. She would call friends; she had plenty of friends.

She was in the bedroom putting on a new face when the house phone rang. She picked it up. "Yes?"

"There's a man here to see you, Mrs. Savitch."

"What man? I'm not expecting any man. What's his name?"

There was a pause at the other end of the line. "He says you don't know him, Mrs. Savitch. But he has a message from Mr. Vanderlind."

"All right. He can come up."

When the doorbell rang, Polly walked through the living room, pulling her robe around her and tying the sash. She glanced through the tiny inspection port, turned the locks, and opened the door. She saw a stocky, slightly balding man with glasses standing there. And instantly his right arm was flashing around her neck and slamming her face into his chest. In the suffocating blur of the commotion that followed, Polly was only vaguely aware that the man was closing and locking the door. And then she was being dragged toward her bedroom.

Lifting her easily onto her bed, Emile Novak slid his right thumb and fingers to a vital nerve in Polly's neck. "One sound out of you," he said, "just one and you're dead." He pressed the nerve slightly, and an excruciating pain shot through Polly's body. He released the pressure and saw her gasp for breath. "Understand?"

Polly's eyes were glazed with terror. "What do you want? God, don't hurt me. What do you want?"

"I want answers from you, bitch, and I want them quick and straight. Where's Vanderlind? I want to know where he is and I want to know now."

"I don't know. I don't understand what . . ." Suddenly her breath choked off and her eyes bulged as Novak reapplied the pressure on her neck.

"Don't understand, my ass!" He played the nerve again and Polly's body trembled on the edge of convulsion. "I know he's coming here. He always sees you when he's in New York. Now when's he coming?"

"He's *not* coming." Polly gasped.

"Get off that shit and listen to me, cunt. Your boy friend has two bags of heroin that belong to me. He's somewhere in this city and I think you know where. Now, the next words out of your mouth better be where he is or when he's coming here."

Novak pressed the nerve again and Polly groaned in agony. As the pressure eased, she thought she was going to be sick. Her mind, too crazed with fear to comprehend what the man was saying about Phillip, raced for survival. The truth, tell him the truth, she thought wildly. "He was here this afternoon. But he's not coming back. I swear to God, he's not coming back!"

"Then where did he go? Where is he?"

Polly's body writhed in his grip. "I don't know. You've got to believe me. He came here this afternoon when I wasn't expecting him. And he saw me like this. And he just walked out."

"Saw you like *what*?"

"Strung out," she choked. "He didn't know I was . . . I was a junkie. Look!"

Novak's eyes followed Polly's nod to the arm she was trying to raise. Carefully, he took it by the wrist, shook back the sleeve of her robe, and stared at her arm. "Holy shit, look at those tracks."

"I have a stash," Polly said. "It's in my dresser, if you don't believe me."

"I believe you," Novak said. Vanderlind had been here, seen her in this way, and gone. "Did he have a couple of bags with him?" His voice was gentle now, soothing.

"I think so," Polly said. "Yes, I remember now."

"What did he do with them?"

"He took them with him when he left."

Polly looked at him. He was sitting on the edge of the bed, his shoulders slumped. And at that moment she sensed a new danger. His face was contorted in a sad smile; his hands were twitching in his lap. The man had said too much.

She moved toward him on the bed. The fingers of her hand that lay in his lap suddenly twitched. "Now, aren't you sorry?" she pouted. She touched his chest with her hand. "I mean, if you had just asked me when you came in, I would have told you."

Her fingers curled lower, searching. "And then all that lipstick on your shirt could have been right here." She gently squeezed what her hand had found and Novak stirred slightly. "But I'm not mad or anything." She ran the tip of her tongue along the edge of her lips and pressed harder with her hand.

Novak felt his face grow hot and his body tense as Polly moved closer to him. She took his hand and placed it on her breast. His head began to spin and then he was on his feet tearing at his zipper. Polly squirmed to her hands and knees on the bed, her head poised expectantly, her mouth open, her tongue flicking and waiting.

"Take it, baby. Come on. Blow me quick!"

At the instant Polly's head moved sharply down, Novak sensed he had made a mistake. He jerked abruptly to one side, but even so her teeth caught the tip of his penis. He shrieked as the pain blazed through his body. "You pig!" he screamed, coming down with all his force on the back of her neck with the side of his right hand.

Polly grunted and crumpled off the bed to the floor.

"Goddamn lousy cunt!" Novak moaned as he stared at the wound in his flesh. "Dirty, stinking, rotten, junkie whore!" He drove his right foot viciously into Polly's stomach. Then, stepping over her, he stumbled toward the bathroom.

When he came back into the bedroom a few minutes later, Polly had not moved. Bending quickly down, Novak felt for a pulse and found it. Then he picked her up and dropped her onto the bed. He went over to her dressing table and found what he was looking for.

Within minutes, the milky substance in the spoon was ready. Loading the syringe, he walked over to the bed and stared down at Polly Savitch. She moaned, stirred slightly, and was still again. He grinned as he wrapped the elastic band around her forearm and pierced the bulging vein with the sharp needle. Polly moaned again. Emile Novak removed the elastic and tossed the empty syringe on the bed beside her. "Enjoy it, bitch," he muttered. "It's your last one."

CHAPTER 15

Phillip couldn't escape the obvious correlation between Polly's addiction and what he carried in the two bags. The shock of seeing her like that had unlocked his mind, and when he left her apartment he knew he couldn't go through with it. He couldn't make the delivery.

Somewhere on the flight between New York and California the shroud had lifted, and he prayed there was actually such a thing as temporary insanity. Money was not what he had been seeking when he left Apache or started Cocatlon or came to San Francisco; it was *himself* he sought. Money was a veneer, a tranquilizer masking the symptoms of something he either wouldn't or couldn't recognize.

The insight was not much. He didn't know what it meant in terms of his immediate future. But it was a beginning. And he clung to it now.

After the chartered Falcon-Jet had touched down at San Francisco International Airport, he picked up his car, loaded the suitcases, and drove straight to the St. Francis Yacht Club. He immediately stowed the bags in the forwardmost compartment of the *Spellbound*. And after changing into jeans and a heavy sweater, he sat down and began to dictate on the portable tape recorder. It took him little more than half an hour to update the tape with all the details he could remember of his second run. It would be his word against Averal Sutherland's. He knew that. But maybe somewhere there was some shred of information that would incriminate Sutherland. He had to believe that. What's more, he had to make Sutherland believe it, too. It was the only weapon he had.

An hour later, Phillip was in the safe-deposit vault of his bank. On the outside of the sealed manila envelope that held two tape cassettes, he printed: "In the event of my death, this envelope is to be delivered immediately and personally to the Attorney General of the United States."

*   *   *

Averal Sutherland tried again to reach Novak at the Beta offices, as well as his apartment, but failed. The digital clock on his desk read 7:00. His chauffeur would be waiting below, and there was nothing more he could do here, he decided. He might as well go home and wait. Vanderlind had the number of his townhouse.

Entering the Rolls-Royce, Sutherland experienced a mild shock. In the far corner, dressed for the evening, was Leslie Parrish.

"You look surprised, Averal. Had you forgotten our evening?"

"Yes, to be quite honest, Leslie, I had," he said. "But no matter. Except that I am afraid we must have dinner at my house rather than the restaurant. I must be available for a telephone call. Is that all right with you?"

"That would be lovely, Averal." Leslie opened the sable coat and recrossed his legs. "Do you like my new dress? The shoes are new, too."

"You look positively enchanting, Leslie," he said.

Driving across town, Sutherland realized he was glad Leslie

was with him. There was nothing to do now but wait, and Leslie would be good company.

They were having cocktails in the large, formal living room when the phone rang. Sutherland got up and went into the library. A moment later he reappeared in the doorway. "This is the call I've been waiting for, Leslie. Would you excuse me, please? I will rejoin you as soon as I can." He smiled, closed the doors between the two rooms, and picked up the receiver again.

"Phillip?"

"Hello, Averal."

"Where in heaven's name are you? Where have you been?"

"I want out, Averal." His voice was flat and sure.

"What did you say?"

"I want out. I'm through with this crap."

"Phillip, please, calm down and tell me what has happened. Where are you now? I assume the merchandise is safe? Why haven't you called?"

His questions were ignored. "Deal with the issue, Averal. I said I want out."

"The issue, Phillip, is that for some reason you have failed to perform this trip as expected. Why, I cannot imagine. But we obviously need to sit down together and discuss the matter intelligently. In the meantime, however, I cannot emphasize enough the urgency of positioning the merchandise for the buyer. Where is it, Phillip? Where are you?"

There was no answer, only the faint static of a long-distance connection. Sutherland's puzzlement and irritation turned to apprehension and rising anger. "Phillip? My patience with you is growing short."

"What will it take to convince you, Averal, that I mean what I say? I'm getting out."

"Now you listen to me, Phillip," Sutherland said, his voice hard with command. "There is no such thing as out. Once you're in, you're in to stay. Do you understand? I want no more games. I want that merchandise and I want it now!"

"You've got to come up with that merchandise, haven't you, Averal? Well, if you ever hope to see it, I suggest you listen to me. You're in no position to dictate to anyone. And we both know it."

Sutherland knew that it was imperative that he make good the delivery. "All right, Phillip," he said tersely, "I'm listening."

"It's very simple. I'll turn over the merchandise in exchange for your agreement that I'm no longer involved in this thing. You can have everything back, Averal, including the job. You won't lose a penny."

Sutherland sensed what had happened. Conscience. The naïve, altruistic fool! "You've decided, I gather, that what we're doing is morally wrong, is that it? Are you having an attack of conscience, Phillip? That is a luxury that none of us can afford. But you are, of course, free to leave our organization if that's what you wish. I ask only for your silence. And now, if you'll be good enough to tell me when and where the shipment will be available, I will see that it is picked up immediately."

"In a moment. First, I hope you'll understand that I'm unable to accept your word completely. I've had to protect myself, Averal. And to that end, I've placed some tape recordings in my safe-deposit box. They contain a full scenario of this whole scheme. Should anything happen to me, and I mean ever, those tapes will be delivered immediately to the Attorney General of the United States. Do I make myself clear, Averal?"

For a brief moment Sutherland was speechless with rage. But the priority was still possession of the heroin. He would have to strike a bargain, at least temporarily. "All right, Phillip. But you will forgive me if I doubt that you have any evidence against me that would stand up in a court of law."

"How can you be sure, Averal? You're the great exponent of truth being what people believe, rather than what it is."

"Very well, you need say nothing more. I'll admit that such tapes would be inconvenient to me. Possibly even embarrassing. But there is no need to threaten me, Phillip."

"Can you absolutely assure me, I mean *guarantee*, that I have nothing to fear from you—or anyone else? I don't think you can. I'm sorry, Averal, but I have no alternative."

"Surely something can be worked out that would be equitable

to both of us, Phillip. I can arrange to be wherever you are by morning and we can discuss the matter more thoroughly. Reasonable men can always find alternatives."

There was silence. Phillip would not budge.

"All right," Sutherland said. "You have something I want, and I'm willing to pay your price. When may I have the merchandise?"

"I want it out of my possession within twenty-four hours. No later."

"That may not be realistic."

"I want that goddamn stuff away from me, Averal," Phillip snapped.

Sutherland's knuckles turned white around the receiver of the phone. "Just as you say, Phillip. Tell me where and how it should be picked up and your schedule will be adhered to."

"The bags are aboard the *Spellbound*, locked in the forward compartment. As you know, there's a spare set of keys at the club."

"I see. Well, Phillip, I regret that our association is over. But wouldn't you agree that I am entitled to know why all of this has occurred? What made you change your mind?"

Phillip's voice was tired and barely audible when he spoke. "You wouldn't understand it if I talked for a thousand years."

The line went dead.

Sutherland stood there holding the receiver in his hand until he heard the dial tone and then slowly replaced it. The swine—he thought. It would be easy enough to obtain the tapes. Sutherland was not particularly concerned about that, except he would have to have them before Vanderlind was eliminated. And he would be eliminated. The man left him no alternative. But at the moment the shipment came first. Sutherland knew that if he did not make delivery as promised, his entire operation would be compromised. And as long as Vanderlind remained in possession of the merchandise, he could not be killed either. But the poor, dumb fool had told him exactly where it was. Thus the solution to his predicament was quite simple: obtain the merchandise and the tapes and then kill Vanderlind.

Sutherland picked up the receiver again, dialed a number and waited. It was answered on the third ring.

"Where have you been, Emile? I have been trying to reach you for the last two hours."

For a moment Emile Novak was at a loss for a reply. If Sutherland learned that he had seen Polly Savitch, there would be hell to pay. "I've been trying to run down Vanderlind," he said.

"You're wasting your time, Emile. Vanderlind has defected."

For the next ten minutes Sutherland went over the entire chain of events. Then he began issuing specific instructions. "The first thing you do, Emile, as soon as we are through here, is charter a private jet and leave immediately for San Francisco."

"Done."

"Now, under no circumstances are you to attempt to retrieve the bags until after dark tomorrow. Is that clear? You are to spend the day merely observing the boat. We cannot be absolutely certain Vanderlind hasn't already gone to the authorities. Do you follow me?"

"Yes, I follow you."

"Now, Emile, about the tapes. I am virtually certain that they contain nothing more than circumstantial evidence, and Vanderlind may even be bluffing about that. But I want them back. They could severely hamper our future operations. You know I have considerable influence in every banking house in San Francisco. It will be easy enough to locate the particular bank in which he has the box. Once that is accomplished, I am confident I will be able to make whatever financial arrangements are necessary to permit you to enter the box and remove the tapes. You are to call me here, at the residence, at two o'clock San Francisco time tomorrow for instructions. Is that clear?"

"I understand, Averal."

"Good. Now about the merchandise. You will go aboard just before dark, take the bags off, and return immediately to New York. If the merchandise is not there, you will notify me immediately."

"Yes, sir."

"If, on the other hand, you are successful in acquiring it, you are to eliminate Vanderlind. I will leave the details to you, Emile, except to say this. You must make absolutely certain that it either appears completely accidental or that he is never found. Do you understand?"

"Perfectly."

"Very well. It's up to you now, Emile. We must carry this off. I think you understand the consequences of failure to all of us."

After he hung up, he thought for a moment and reached for the phone again. As he dialed, he heard a slight noise behind him. He turned to see Leslie standing behind him in the open doorway.

"Leslie, what are you doing in here?" he said sharply, replacing the receiver.

"Nothing, Averal. Nothing," Leslie stammered. "I just wondered what was keeping you."

"How long have you been listening to my conversation, Leslie? Dammit, answer me!"

"Averal, please. I didn't hear anything. I just . . ."

"Then why be frightened? You are frightened, aren't you, Leslie?"

"No. Yes! Yes, I'm frightened, Averal. Frightened for you. Please don't have that man killed!"

Sutherland lashed out with the back of his hand. The blow caught Leslie on the side of his head. He stumbled slightly, tripped over his spike heels, and went down.

"You freak!" Sutherland snarled. "You perverted queer! How dare you eavesdrop on me? How dare you?"

Leslie screamed and covered his face with his hands. "Don't hit me again, Averal. For God's sake, don't hit me again!" Then he felt the blood; the blow had torn the small gold ring from his pierced ear.

Sutherland was livid with rage. "Get up, damn you! Get out of my sight!"

Leslie crawled away from him, panting, trying to speak.

"Clean yourself up and get out of here," Sutherland said. "You're disgusting. Look at you!"

He walked to the bar and threw a small towel in Leslie's direction. Then, abruptly, he regained control of himself. What was he thinking of? He couldn't just send Leslie away. He had overheard the conversation with Novak.

Leslie cringed as Sutherland walked toward him. "Please, Averal. I meant no harm. Please don't hurt me any more."

"Leslie, Leslie, Leslie," Sutherland said, smiling now. "What am I going to do with you? What am I going to do with this abominable temper of mine? Here, let me help you."

Leslie finally accepted his apologies as well as his explanation of the phone call. Sutherland convinced him that his words pertained to a man's career and not his life. And when he put Leslie in the Rolls-Royce later that evening, he was reasonably persuaded that all was well and that he had made the right decision. After all, he couldn't very well afford to hold Leslie captive. And the thought of *personally* taking another person's life was out of the question. Yes. Apology and appeasement had been the right course. This time. At least for the present.

But he would have to give a great deal of thought to Leslie Parrish and the events of the evening. And unless he could conceive complete safety for himself, Emile Novak would have further duties when he returned from California.

* * *

The phone at Harry Kane's bedside rang insistently. He groaned, rolled over, and picked it up. "Yes, what?"

"Harry." It was Cyril Kennedy.

"Jesus Christ, Cyril, do you know what time it is?"

"I know. It's four in the morning. But listen, the San Francisco office just called me. They've located Vanderlind at his residence out there."

"And you're waking me up to tell me *that*? For Christ's sake, Cyril!"

"I'm calling to tell you I'm on my way out there, Harry. That bastard has got two suitcases full of heroin with him. I know he has. And I'm going to sit on him until he makes his drop."

Kane slumped back on his pillow. "Okay, Cyril. Go make

your big California bust and let me know what happens—during working hours, if you can manage that."

"The *big* bust won't be in California, Harry."

"But you said . . ."

"I said Vanderlind is in California. Averal Sutherland is in New York."

CHAPTER 16

Phillip woke up with a start the morning after his break with
Sutherland. It was almost ten and he would have to hurry to
be gone before nightfall as he planned. He had finished
packing the clothes he wanted to take with him by late
afternoon. They were in the Mercedes. He would take that, too.
But that was all. Sutherland owed him at least that much.

Where he was going he wasn't sure. His first thoughts had
been of Colorado and Jessica. But if he was in danger from
Sutherland, he didn't want her involved too. And he wasn't at all
sure he was ready to deal with that part of his life just yet. He
knew he had weeks, even months, perhaps, of putting himself
back together before he would be capable of knowing how he felt
about many things. All that really mattered at the moment was
putting as many miles as possible between himself and San
Francisco. And just the relief of being free from Sutherland was
enough to compensate for the slight emptiness he felt at going
away from, rather than to, all the things he thought he had
always wanted.

He looked at his watch: nearly five o'clock. Outside it had begun to rain; a storm front moving in off the Pacific promised early darkness. He was waiting for the darkness. It was conceivable that he was being watched and would be followed when he left the house.

The phone rang for the second time that afternoon, and on the third ring Irving picked it up downstairs. The night before, Phillip had left instructions that he was neither in nor expected, regardless of who might call.

He would miss Irving, Phillip thought. He had told him that he was leaving, but all he had been able to suggest was that he should look for other work in the Bay Area.

Suddenly the door to the master suite burst open, and Irving, ashen-faced and shaking, was trying to say something to him in a mixture of English and Chinese.

Phillip held up his hands. "Hey, take it easy. Take your time. Tell me what's going on."

"Mr. Vanalind! A strange phone call. Some lady say she must talk with you, say your life in danger."

Phillip's heart jumped. He caught Irving by the shoulders and held him. "A woman? What woman?"

"No name. No name. She just say she want to talk with you."

"All right, Irving. Everything's all right. I'll talk to her. Now, you go back downstairs and hang up. I'll use the phone up here. Hurry now."

Phillip cursed the pulse hammering in his ears as he picked up the receiver. "Who *is* this?"

"Well, you needn't be so huffy about it. I *am* trying to do you a favor."

The woman's voice was soft and husky, her words almost lackadaisical. Phillip's nerves grated with impatience. "Look, if I was rude, I apologize. But I don't recognize your voice."

"My name doesn't matter in the least, Mr. Vanderlind. I am, or *was*, a close friend of Averal Sutherland's."

Phillip's mouth went dry. "Yes?"

"And you know a man named Novak?"

"Yes."

"Well, I suppose it's none of my business, but last night I overheard Averal telling him to kill you."

"*Kill* me?" Phillip's voice rasped. "Are you sure that's what he said?"

"Of course I'm sure. I was standing right there. Averal tried to tell me it was just a business call, that he sometimes says things like that when he's talking business."

Phillip's mind was clawing to find a reason for this call. "Who are you?" he said. "How did you get my number and why are you telling me this?"

"I found your card in Averal's car one night. And I'm certainly not inhuman, after all. But I will admit—" the woman's voice was now full of loathing—"after what he did to me, beating me up, hurting me like that, I simply *despise* Averal Sutherland. The man is absolutely insane."

Phillip pushed his mind hard. Was revenge this woman's reason for calling? Or was this part of some scheme? If he could just rattle her for a second without losing her. He grabbed at a name. "Marsha? Is this Marsha Baker?"

"Who's Marsha Baker?"

"Come on, Marsha. I know your voice. Averal put you up to this, didn't he?"

"I'm not Marsha, you idiot. I'm Leslie. Leslie Parrish. And Averal didn't . . ."

Just before the connection was broken, Phillip heard the garbled voice of a man in the background. He had obviously told her to hang up, and Phillip stared incomprehensibly at the silent instrument in his hand. He *had* to believe what the woman, what Leslie Parrish, had told him. Sutherland *had* sent Novak to kill him.

He slumped to a sitting position on the edge of the bed and closed his eyes. He couldn't think anymore. He didn't know what to do. He didn't dare go to the police; what would he say? And it was too late to appeal to Sutherland. Novak could be sitting outside the house at this very moment.

The tapes. Averal Sutherland had called his bluff. Either he didn't believe they existed, or he had refused to be intimidated by them. No, that didn't make any sense. Sutherland couldn't take that risk. Then, suddenly, he had the explanation. Somehow, someway, Sutherland had managed to get the tapes!

If Phillip had been frightened before, he was terrified now. Even if he could avoid a killer like Novak, where could he hide from a man of Sutherland's power and influence? From the very beginning that is what he had always feared. Sutherland had no intention of letting him get away alive.

Phillip almost gave up then. The only thing that saved him was his temper. Slowly, the terrible fear and frustration gave way to white, hot anger. "No, goddamnit!" he snarled, shoving himself violently off the bed. "If that cocksucker wants to kill me, he's going to have to find me first!"

Furiously, he began to look through the seabag that lay in one of the closets and found the Walther automatic. The clip was full. He rammed it back into place, levered a shell into the chamber, and clicked the safety. Shoving the weapon into his belt, he went quickly out of the bedroom and down the stairs.

"Irving!" he shouted as he reached the main floor. The man appeared instantly in the doorway of the kitchen.

"Listen to me now and don't argue. I don't have time for questions either. I want you to get out of this house. When you get to a phone, call a cab and go stay with your relatives." Phillip dug into his pocket and gave Irving a handful of hundred-dollar bills. "Here's some money. Now, I need your car. Where are the keys?"

"Mr. Vanalind, I don't understand what is happening."

"Goddamn it, Irving!" he roared. "Give me the keys, man!"

Irving reached into the pocket of his white jacket and held out a set of keys.

"Okay. Now get out of here. I said *now*, Irving!" Phillip grabbed his arm and pulled him through the short hall into the garage. He hit the electric garage door switch. "Run, goddamnit!" he snapped, propelling the frightened man toward the open door. And Irving ran.

Moments later the small red Volkswagen spun out of the garage, up the incline, and onto the winding road toward the Golden Gate Bridge.

The boat. On the face of it, his destination seemed insane. But

Phillip now realized his best chance of survival lay in regaining possession of the heroin. Then, too, the boat was the last place they would expect to find him. God, let me get there first, he prayed as he shifted to a higher gear and shot out onto the six-lane expressway.

*   *   *

Cyril Kennedy and the agent with him were startled as the Volkswagen careened down the hill past their car.

"Hell, that's Vanderlind, isn't it?"

"Right," Kennedy shouted, jumping from the car. "Stay with him. I'm going into that house. Have somebody pick me up."

Spinning gravel from the car hit Kennedy on the back of his legs as he broke into a run up the steep incline. He approached the house carefully down the winding driveway. No one had left or entered the place since Vanderlind had been located there. In that case, there should only be the Chinese servant to contend with, Kennedy thought as he rang the bell and stepped to one side.

After the fourth ring and no answer, he slipped the .38 Special from its holster and tried the door. It was locked. Moments later he entered the kitchen through the garage, locking the door behind him. Moving rapidly and quietly, he satisfied himself he was alone, then began a thorough search of the house.

Twenty minutes later he picked up the phone in the kitchen, advised operations of his failure to locate the two suitcases, and asked for a position update on Vanderlind. He was informed that the subject had just moved off the Golden Gate Bridge and was proceeding eastward toward the city on Marina Boulevard.

After confirming that another car had been dispatched for him, Kennedy left the house and walked slowly back up to the road to wait. On the way he reversed a decision he had made. _Now_ was the time to take Vanderlind. No more waiting and hoping to learn who else was involved; they would simply have to try and break Vanderlind down, once they had him and the two bags.

That was the priority now: stop the junk from hitting the

streets. Of course, Kennedy still didn't know—but under the circumstances he had to believe—that Vanderlind still had the bags and they did contain heroin. Otherwise, he might as well pack it in, he thought grimly.

The car arrived within minutes of his reaching the road. And even as it swung the arc of the cul-de-sac to race toward the bridge, Cyril Kennedy was on the radio issuing intercept and arrest orders for Phillip Vanderlind.

*   *   *

Emile Novak leaned against the starboard bulkhead of the *Spellbound* and breathed a sigh of relief. The bags were there, just as Vanderlind had said they were. And in another twenty minutes or so it would be dark enough to remove them from the boat and take them to his car.

Then it would be time for Vanderlind. He patted the tape cassettes in his coat pocket and smiled. It had been simple. Averal Sutherland *was* a powerful man.

This was a job that Novak wanted to do himself. But as a back-up, in the event that he somehow missed Vanderlind and had to take the bags on to New York, he had left instructions with his Essex people to hit the son of a bitch. Vanderlind was still at the Marin County house; of that he was certain. He could tell by the tone of the Chink's voice when he had called earlier in the afternoon. And why shouldn't the clown be there? The stupid shit thought he was home free.

Novak lit a cigarette and wondered how he should waste Vanderlind. The last two times he had killed, he had neither the time nor Sutherland's blessings to be too creative. The priest in Chicago had been almost boring, and his anger had interfered with his pleasure in killing the Savitch woman. But with Vanderlind, he had nothing to sweat. He could put it all together any way he wanted. Novak's pulse quickened with the thought. He did not need a reason to kill, but this time he had a beauty. And whatever method he chose, one thing was certain. Vanderlind would hurt a great deal before he died.

He ground out his cigarette on the cabin sole and walked aft to see if it was safe to remove the bags. Sliding the hatch halfway back, he stood on the small ladder, peering outside; the Dacron canopy over the cockpit shielded him from the weather. Other than the drum of rain on the boat, everything was dark and quiet.

Satisfied with his inspection, Novak turned to go below again and collect the bags. Then he heard it. The sound of someone running along the dock. He looked in the direction of the sound, and at the same instant the automatic dock lights came on. Novak stared for a moment, then slammed the hatch to. Jesus Christ! The man who was running toward the boat was Phillip Vanderlind!

For a second, Novak stood motionless. Then he hurried quickly back to the forward compartment and locked himself in the head. Instead of the .45 tucked neatly in his waistband, he chose the knife he carried in the pocket of his slacks. He cursed silently and waited.

*   *   *

Phillip stopped running before he reached the *Spellbound*. He stood on the dock for a moment looking at her glistening wetly in the faint glow of the single overhead light. Nothing appeared out of order. He went on again and, clambering aboard amidships, made his way aft to the cockpit. Ducking under the canopy, he looked quickly around and reached for the hatch lock. He froze. There was no lock.

He fell to one side of the cockpit, simultaneously jerking the Walther from his belt. He lay there for a moment panting, his mind almost numb with fear. No sound came from below. The automatic suddenly felt omnipotent in his hand. The anger returned. He had no choice.

He took a moment to position himself, then rammed the hatch forward and dropped over into the cabin. Crouching in the gloom, he looked wildly about. But only the sound of rain and the water lapping the hull filled the cabin.

The bags. They had to be gone. He crept slowly toward the door to the forward compartment, eased it open, and hit the light switch. No. They were still there. But the open hatch! Whoever was coming for the bags had to have been aboard. Why had they left? Were they still somewhere close by, perhaps in one of the cars parked at the end of the dock? The thought sent another wave of fear through him. Snapping off the light, he slammed the forward compartment door shut, slid home the bolt, and ran aft to the hatch.

Nothing outside moved. And he could see no one in any of the cars parked close to the boat. But that meant nothing. They could be lying down in the seats. He had to move and move fast. He couldn't stop now.

Reaching quickly to his right, he turned the ignition switch, and the engine came instantly to life. He slipped the automatic into his jacket pocket, climbed topside, and raced forward to cast off the bow lines, his eyes darting over the cars in the parking area. He saw nothing. A few seconds more, dear God, he prayed.

As the last stern line plopped into the water, Phillip hit the reverse gear and was backing into the basin. Just a few feet more. Now! He cut the power, shifted to forward gear, spun the wheel hard to starboard, and slammed the throttle full open. He had made it. Thank God, he had made it!

The rain was coming down in wind-driven sheets now; the waters of the basin were choppy. It was going to be a hell of a rough night, Phillip thought. But he had no alternative, no place else to go. Before he reached the end of the breakwater, he stripped the cover from the mainsail, undid the stops, and raised it. It would suffice until he could set a headsail. Then as soon as he was free of the basin he sheeted in the big sail until it was drawing properly, shut down the engine, and headed off on a port tack toward the lights of the Golden Gate Bridge.

*   *   *

When he heard the engine start, Emile Novak almost panicked. But there was nothing he could do. He couldn't risk an encounter in the middle of a yacht club. Then moments later, as the boat heeled sharply to its right side and the engine stopped, he realized that Vanderlind was sailing somewhere. Goddamn boats! He hated them. They made him sick.

He was suffocating in the small enclosure of the head. He had to get out of there. He had heard the door of the compartment close and knew it was safe—at least for the moment. He opened the door to the head and peered out. Suddenly the boat rolled heavily in the water and he lurched out into the cramped passageway. He felt sick, but once he was back on his feet and leaning across the two bags on the forward bunks, he felt better. Goddamn fucking boats!

Then he turned his attention to Vanderlind and realized he had a problem. He couldn't waste the son of a bitch right here. If he killed him, how the hell was he going to get back to shore? But there was a way, there had to be a way. He knew he could work the engine and steer the goddamned boat. It was only the sails he was worried about, especially in weather like this. He would hold Vanderlind at gunpoint until he was sure he knew how everything worked. Then it would be a simple case of a man falling overboard at night.

Damn, he was going to puke!

He thought he would feel better after he got it all up, but he didn't. The boat's motion had intensified, and the darkness of the cabin only lent to his discomfort. He groped for a light switch and finally found it. But being able to see didn't help much. He had to get out of the damn stinking hole and take care of Vanderlind. He slipped off his jacket, pulled the .45 from his belt, and reached for the doorknob. The son of a bitch wouldn't open. That lousy bastard had locked it from the outside!

Then real fear struck him. What if the damn boat began to sink? He couldn't get out! He looked frantically about the small space. He could shoot the goddamn lock off the door if he had to. Then he saw it. The hatch above his head.

*   *   *

A few more minutes, Phillip thought, and he would have to go on a starboard tack. He had just passed under the bridge and was beginning for the first time to relax enough to feel the cold. Once he was safely on the other course, he would heave to and go below for some warm clothes.

Off to his left, he again measured the distance and bearing of the huge aircraft carrier steaming in from sea. He had been watching her for the past fifteen minutes, carefully gauging his progress across her bow. He would be safe with room to spare.

The wind slackened for a moment, and the boat eased to a more upright position. Then Phillip saw something on the waves. It was a light; there was a light coming from his boat. He had left no lights on below. That was crazy! He had searched the boat. No one was . . . The head. Goddamnit, he hadn't checked the head. Someone was aboard the boat!

Suddenly the bow lit up like a bright beacon; the forward hatch had opened. Someone was struggling out on deck. Phillip tore at his jacket pocket for the gun. The man was standing up now and coming toward him. Phillip couldn't get the gun free; the hammer was snagged in his pocket. He let go of the wheel and pulled at the gun with both hands. The boat cocked into the wind; her bow, slamming head on into the seas, suddenly pitched high and away.

The man on the foredeck teetered for a moment, then reached for the shroud lines. He missed and toppled overboard. Instinctively, Phillip grabbed the wheel and put the helm over hard. The bow swung off and the sail began drawing again. As the boat gathered way, the man's head popped to the surface just as the stern of the *Spellbound* slid by. And Phillip stared into the horror-stricken face of Emile Novak.

*   *   *

As he surfaced, Novak reached in vain for the passing boat. Then it was gone, its running lights disappearing in the darkness. He kicked off his shoes and began to tread water. Then he saw other lights in the blackness that engulfed him, and he began swimming toward them.

After a few moments he looked at the lights again. They were much closer than he thought. The water was achingly cold, and his clothes dragged heavily. He put his head down and began stroking again. The movement warmed him slightly.

The next time he raised his head to look, he had almost reached the lights. But they were so high. And then he was moving faster and faster in the water. And then deeper. And just before the wave closed over his head, he heard a noise, the deep throb of heavy turbines.

*   *   *

No one aboard the aircraft carrier heard anything. No one felt anything. Not even the gauges in the engine room registered the slightest difference as Emile Novak was sucked through the massive brass screws and the dismembered pieces of his body spewed out into the foaming wake of the great ship.

CHAPTER 17

Averal Sutherland fidgeted and looked at his watch. It was almost 10:00 P.M.—7:00 P.M. Pacific time. He should be hearing from Emile Novak soon.

He put aside the book he had been trying to read and went into the kitchen. The couple who served as his cook and butler were on a brief vacation. The house was quiet and empty. He made himself a sandwich with food that he found in the refrigerator. Then he took the plate into the library and made himself a drink.

As he ate, his thoughts turned again to Vanderlind. How could he have misjudged the man so completely? He was convinced that he had successfully made the passage all of them had had to make: acceptance of reality and the putting away of childish notions about right and wrong. Vanderlind had done so originally, he was certain of it. But something had happened to change his mind. If he had just been able to persuade Vanderlind to tell him what it was, it might have proved useful in recruiting the future members of Beta.

But Averal Sutherland was not a man to berate himself unduly. What else could he have done? Every possible precaution had been taken in the selection of Vanderlind; his every move had been closely monitored from the first moment the existence of Beta was divulged to him until after he had successfully completed the test run. Perhaps that was where he had made his mistake. Obviously, the second run should have been monitored, too. It had not been necessary with the other members of Beta. But he would instruct Novak to take that additional precaution in the future. As for Vanderlind . . . well, it was obviously unnecessary to waste any more time and money on him.

Sutherland glanced again at his watch. Why hadn't Novak called?

* * *

More than once during the next half hour Phillip's hand hesitated on the wheel. A man was overboard. The sailor's instinct was to put about and find him. The man whom he might have killed said let Novak drown.

He drove the boat hard to seaward through the rapidly dissipating storm, and when he was two miles off shore a full moon broke through the clouds, bathing the confused sea in a cold, blue light. Despite the danger of the shipping lanes, Phillip heaved to and went below. Chilled to the bone, he stripped, toweled himself vigorously, then struggled into dry woolen sea clothes. Grabbing a package of crackers, some potted meat, and a bottle of scotch, he went topside, and minutes later he was underway again. His course was southwesterly, his destination Half Moon Bay, some thirty-odd sea miles as he would sail.

For the moment he was safe. But there was little comfort in the thought. More than ever now he knew that Sutherland would want him dead, and his mind, numbed almost to the point of disbelief by the nightmarish events of the past few hours, labored to analyze and comprehend his predicament. It seemed almost hopeless. To go to the police was unthinkable. There was nothing he could prove about Sutherland, and only *he* would be guilty of smuggling. And he was no longer naïve enough to think that Sutherland would keep any promise he made, which precluded the possibility of trying to bargain for his life with the heroin. Only as long as he held onto the stuff would he be safe. But that was as unrealistic as it was insane: Novak was almost certainly dead, but there would be others. And he couldn't run or hide forever. He would never be safe from Averal Sutherland unless . . . What if he went at Sutherland? Not away from the man but *at* him? If you couldn't change something, you either learned to live with it . . . or you eliminated it.

Kill Sutherland? People committed murder every day and got away with it. It couldn't be that difficult. But no, he didn't think he could take a life—at least not with premeditation. Damn it—there had to be another alternative.

The wind had lightened. It was time to set a headsail. From the sail locker he selected a working jib, slacked the main, and let the boat wallow in the three-foot sea while he went forward to set the sail. Back in the cockpit, he watched the faint reddish glow of the binnacle and tried to fight off sleep. He was beginning to doze when suddenly he sat bolt upright, his eyes wide with the realization of discovery: he had *forced* Sutherland to try to kill him! Those goddamn tapes. He had left the man no choice.

"I have done you no harm. Should you, for any reason, attempt to harm me, I would employ whatever means were necessary to stop you."

Son of a bitch! How could he have been so stupid?

But if he was right, why couldn't he still strike a deal? All he had to do was persuade Sutherland that he no longer represented a threat to him. Still, how could Phillip be sure he would be safe? Somehow, he had to take the initiative and remain in control. And that meant he had to come face to face with Sutherland. The transfer of the merchandise would have to be between the two of them. If he could effect that, two possibilities would be open to him: the opportunity to, in some way, implicate Sutherland personally and irrefutably with Beta, and second . . .

"Nor is it difficult to kill when one's own life is in danger."

Sutherland had proved his willingness to act upon that philosophy. And if the man left him absolutely no alternative, a face-to-face meeting would give Phillip a chance to kill Averal Sutherland.

It was 4:00 A.M. when Phillip powered into the small public marina at Half Moon Bay through a light fog. Laying easily alongside the gas dock, he went ashore, awakened the manager, and arranged for berthing. Back on board, the two suitcases of heroin were his most immediate concern. If they were found in his possession, it would be all over for him. But what in hell could he do with them?

He dropped below and unlocked the forward compartment. The stench that swarmed out of the small enclosure made him gag. Christ, Novak must have been seasick, he thought. As he held his breath and stepped inside to open the overhead hatch, something cracked under his foot. He was standing on a coat. He picked it up and retreated quickly from the fetid cabin into the cockpit. It was Novak's coat. And in the right-hand pocket were two partially shattered plastic boxes containing cassette tapes. *His* tapes. He had been right: somehow Novak had been able to get them out of his safety-deposit box. Dear God, he wondered, was nothing out of Sutherland's reach?

His first inclination was to destroy the tapes. Then he realized they still had value. Trading value. He would offer them to Sutherland as proof of his willingness to keep quiet if Sutherland also kept his end of the bargain.

But where to hide the heroin? The more he thought about it, the more it seemed he would be a fool to take it ashore. If it had to be found, he wanted it to be aboard Averal Sutherland's boat. In any case, he couldn't just leave the stuff lying around in the cabin. But where in hell can you hide two large suitcases on a small boat? He dropped below again to look, but in seconds he was back at the main hatch staring up at the loosely done-up mainsail. Thirty minutes later, forty kilos of heroin lay snugly along the boom in a smartly furled sail. Perfect. To find it now, someone would have to work like hell or steal the boat.

When he finished, it was just after 5:00—8:00 A.M. New York time. Taking a final tug on the last sea-tie, Phillip stepped ashore and began walking quickly through the thickening fog toward the phone booth at the corner of the marina office.

*   *   *

Averal Sutherland had been drifting in and out of sleep for almost an hour, barely differentiating between fantasy and reality, when the phone by his bed began to ring. Even as he groped for it in the drape-darkened room, he wasn't quite certain which of his thoughts were dreams.

"It didn't work, Averal."

Sutherland recoiled from the receiver. Instantly awake now, he put the phone back to his ear. "Vanderlind?" he asked incredulously.

"That's just the first surprise, Averal. There are others. I still have the merchandise *and* the tapes, and I'm one hell of a lot smarter than I was a few hours ago. But it took a boat ride with a friend of yours to open my eyes."

"Where is Novak?" Sutherland said.

"I honestly don't know, Averal."

"Have you killed him?"

"I didn't lay a hand on him. But now that he's out of the way, I'm going to try and deal with you one more time. But this go-round, it's going to be face to face, Averal. No more telephones—or intermediaries. You will come to San Francisco today. I'll call you at the Sea Cliff house tomorrow morning. And I'll set the time and place, and the conditions, under which we meet."

Sutherland's mind raced. Without Novak he suddenly felt very vulnerable. Somehow he had to regain the initiative. "All right, Phillip. Something suitable to both of us can, I am sure, be arranged. But you'll have to come to New York and bring the merchandise and the tapes with you."

"Damn it, I want you here!" Phillip snapped.

"That is out of the question. If you wish to pursue an amicable settlement of this matter, come to New York."

For a long moment there was silence on the line. Then Phillip said, "All right, I'll come there. And I'll bring the tapes. But the merchandise stays right where it is."

"Have it your own way." Sutherland desperately needed that shipment of heroin. But more than anything now, he needed Vanderlind out of the way. And suddenly it all seemed so ridiculously simple that he had to restrain himself from agreeing too quickly. "Very well," he said grudgingly. "I will expect your call sometime this evening after you arrive."

"I'll be there," Vanderlind said tersely. Then he hung up.

Smiling to himself, Sutherland gently replaced the instrument in its cradle and began making a quick mental list of things to be done: Essex had to be alerted and briefed, the Lear jet made ready, the people in Boston updated, his Kaufman schedule for the first of the week rearranged. There was so much to do and so little time. He regretted that Novak had failed in his mission. No man is infallible, he supposed. And he would miss Novak. Now he would have to deal with some of the more unsavory aspects of the operation himself. But he did not doubt, in time, that he would be able to find a replacement.

He rang for his breakfast and then remembered that his servants were not in the house. He got out of bed and was putting on his robe when the phone rang again.

"Yes?"

"This is Stewart Cross, Mr. Sutherland. Leslie's friend."

Of all the things Sutherland couldn't be bothered with now, Leslie Parrish was one. "Yes, Mr. Cross?" His voice was strained.

"Mr. Sutherland, Leslie was quite upset about the last evening you spent together. I'd like to come over and talk with you about it."

"I'm terribly sorry, Mr. Cross, but I'm afraid that would be impossible. Perhaps you could call me tomorrow?"

"I don't like to be rude, Mr. Sutherland. But I insist you see me this morning." The voice was courteous but firm.

"I've told you tomorrow, Mr. Cross. Now, please be good enough—"

"Would you rather I saw the police?"

"What do you mean?"

"It's either you or the police. Take your choice. I'm not going to waste further words on the phone."

Extortion, thought Sutherland; Leslie and that faggot were going to try and blackmail him. He should have expected it. Well, for the moment at least, with Novak's services no longer available to him, he would just have to meet whatever demands they made. "All right, Mr. Cross. When shall I expect you?"

"One hour, Mr. Sutherland."

Despite his more pressing problems with Vanderlind, Sutherland was remarkably relaxed and confident as he bathed and dressed. That was the real gift of his wealth and power: those he couldn't persuade, he bought. And when all else failed, he simply eliminated. In the end, Averal Sutherland always got what he wanted.

*   *   *

Stewart Cross had nearly gone wild when he saw Leslie with his ear lobe sliced and a dark, heavy bruise on his cheek. That scum-sucking pig Sutherland. If it had not been for Leslie's pleas and repeated promises that he was once and for all through with Sutherland, Cross would have gone over and killed the man that same night. But toward morning his anger had finally cooled. And at least one good thing had come from Sutherland's abuse: Leslie had finally agreed to move back to San Francisco with him.

Still, the longer Cross dwelled on the incident between Leslie and Sutherland, the more he understood the true significance of his initial anger. Somehow, Averal Sutherland seemed to personify what Cross felt was an almost calculated ignorance and intolerance of the gay world that had cost him so much in his life. Then, too, there was something about Averal Sutherland that made Cross intensely curious.

*   *   *

Sutherland was compelled to open the door himself when the buzzer sounded signaling the arrival of Stewart Cross. Neither man spoke as Sutherland led the way up the staircase and opened the door to the library. Without waiting for Cross to enter, he walked to the center of the room, then turned and glowered. "Well?"

Cross stopped, spread his hands and smiled. "Aren't you going to offer me a chair?"

"You are not here as an invited guest, Mr. Cross. Just state your business."

"My business is you, Mr. Sutherland."

"How much?"

Cross cocked his head inquisitively.

"How much money do you want?" Sutherland snapped. "I will not haggle with you."

Cross laughed easily. "Well, of course, that's what you'd think. But you're wrong. I haven't come for money." He took off the leather coat he was wearing and laid it across a chair. "I've come to give, not take, Averal. And you *do* have time to receive."

Sutherland was startled by the use of his first name. And what could Cross give him that he did not already have? His words were spoken softly, but there was a hint of intimidation. Was he capable of violence? His face was smooth and clean-shaven, a babyish face. But he was tall and his shoulders were broad. Sutherland looked at him more closely and felt an emotion that was totally new to him. He turned away quickly and sat down. "Very well, Mr. Cross, what am I to receive?"

"Surely," Cross said, "a man of your intellect and sophistication can guess." And even before he had finished the sentence, he was pulling his dark turtle-neck sweater off over his head. "Take off your clothes, Averal."

A sort of Victorian indignation was the only emotion of which Sutherland was immediately capable. "Get out," he blustered. "Get out of this house!"

"It *is* going to happen, Averal. And once you make up your mind to it, you can relax . . . and enjoy . . . and discover."

The sight of Cross taking off his slacks brought Sutherland to his feet, shaking with rage. "Do you hear me?" he screamed. "Put your clothes on and get out or I will call the . . ." But before he could move, Cross was standing next to him, his muscular chest pressing against his body, his face inches from his face.

Sutherland tried to push him away, but Cross caught his

wrists and held them firmly. "Averal, Averal," he said soothing-ly. "I only want to make love to you. Don't you understand? I don't want to *abuse* you as you did Leslie. I'm turning the other cheek. You hurt someone I love, now I'm going to love you."

Sutherland choked and slumped back on the couch; he knew it was hopeless to struggle against the younger, vastly stronger man. His only hope lay in persuasion. "Cross, please. I beg you not to do this. It will accomplish nothing for either of us. I will pay you, pay you anything you want. Please."

"Begging? The omnipotent Averal Sutherland begging?" Cross laughed as he stepped out of his shorts. "Begging doesn't become you, Averal. Now, I'm undressed, shall I help you? Here, let me help you."

Cross was standing in front of him now, naked, his arms outstretched. Sutherland saw his opportunity. Moving quickly, he thrust Cross aside and struggled to his feet. If he could only reach the switch by the library door that triggered the security alarm system, within three minutes at least two Essex men would be there to help him—if he could only reach the switch. But he lurched forward and fell. His head struck the corner of a table and bright lights exploded in his brain. Then darkness slipped over him and he was unconscious.

When Sutherland's eyes fluttered open, what he slowly recognized as the ceiling of his bedroom oozed into focus. And then he was aware of his nakedness on the cool satin sheets of his bed. Raising his head slightly, he saw Cross's head between his legs, then felt the moist warmth of the man's mouth on him. "Oh, God," he choked, wrenching violently upward, only to fall back under the onslaught of an excruciating pain that tore through his head.

Cross turned and smiled back over his shoulder. He said something, but Sutherland couldn't hear the words. Only the hiss of silence filled his ears. He saw Cross's head undulating over his body, and then he was suddenly aware of another physical sensation: he was climaxing.

For the fleeting part of a second he allowed himself to believe it was all over. But as Cross brutally heaved him over onto his stomach, Sutherland knew it had only begun. And he surrendered. From somewhere in the distance he heard Cross commanding him to raise his hips, and then he felt the searing pain of penetration. "Don't. Please don't," he moaned. "Dear God, you're taking me."

"Yes, Averal, I'm taking you," Cross panted. "And you like it, don't you? Admit you like it, Averal. Tell me you like it!"

Sutherland buried his face in the pillow beneath his head. He couldn't speak. But suddenly he was thrusting in concert with Cross's surges, and the agony of moments before became an excruciating pleasure. Then he knew. Perhaps he had always known.

The pain in his head raged again, hung for a moment, then was gone. Somehow it seemed worse than before. Then, without warning, it stormed back. But mercifully this time he fainted.

When he opened his eyes again, Sutherland felt terribly fatigued. There was a slight discomfort at the base of his skull, and the knot on his forehead still ached. It was barely ten o'clock. What he needed was another hour of sleep. Just another hour, he thought, and then he would set everything in motion for Phillip Vanderlind.

As Sutherland pulled up the covers of the rumpled bed, he only dimly remembered what had just happened to him. He looked around the room with burning eyes and realized that Stewart Cross was gone. A wave of nausea suddenly swept over him, and he threw back the covers, dragging in deep breaths of air until the queasiness began to subside.

And then he saw a vision of Leslie. Beautiful Leslie, wearing a flowing pink gown and high-heeled slippers. She whirled in a cloud of pink before his eyes. But then the vision began to darken. Leslie slowly dissolved into the reddening haze, and in his confused mind he saw poised above him the strong, muscular body of Stewart Cross.

*   *   *

The commander of the U.S. Coast Guard Station on Yerba Buena Island looked across at Cyril Kennedy and shook his head. "No, sir, the only casualties of last night's weather that we know about, at least, were a couple of private fishing boats. Actually, Mr. Kennedy, if the man you're looking for was any kind of sailor, he wouldn't have had too much trouble going anywhere he wanted last night, especially with the boat you say he had."

Kennedy nodded and looked past the officer at the gray shroud of fog that choked down the Bay Area. "How long do you think before you'll be able to mount a sea-air search, Captain?"

"This one's a bitch, sir. Could be as late as this time tomorrow, maybe even longer. Stuff extends some twelve miles out to sea. But my guess is your man didn't go too far offshore last night. More than likely, he turned around and put in somewhere around the bays here. There are hundreds of coves and several small marinas."

"Okay, that's as good a place to start as any I can think of. Can you provide me with a list of some of these places that are accessible by car?"

"Matter of fact, Mr. Kennedy, I had our people start on that just after you called earlier this morning. If you'll excuse me for a moment, I'll see what they've come up with."

After the Coast Guardsman left, Kennedy got up and walked over to the window and stared at the opaque nothingness outside. Vanderlind had caught him with his pants down last night. He hadn't been quick enough with his order to apprehend, and the agent in pursuit had stood helplessly on the dock watching Vanderlind sail away into the storm.

The bags *had* to be aboard that boat. Any way Kennedy figured it, that was the answer he came up with; everything pointed to it. They were not in the house or in the Mercedes. And they weren't in the man's offices that had been searched two hours ago. The boat was the *only* place that made sense.

And now this frigging fog. Vanderlind could still be at sea, but Kennedy thought the captain was probably right. If Vanderlind had made it back to shore before the fog socked in, he—and those goddamn bags—could be a hundred miles away from San Francisco by this time.

*　　*　　*

As the 747 broke out on top of the massive bank of fog lying over the entire sweep of the Bay Area, the captain congratulated the passengers on being aboard the last flight permitted to leave San Francisco International Airport that day. Phillip leaned back in his seat and lit a cigarette. Averal Sutherland was only five hours away.

At seven-thirty New York time, he checked into a small hotel near Gramercy Park in Manhattan, quickly showered, and at eight o'clock picked up the phone and dialed Sutherland's number. There was no answer. Three hours later, after innumerable attempts to reach him, Phillip lay back on the bed, stared blankly at the ceiling, and tried to imagine why Sutherland was not at home. Where the hell was the man? Frustrated and angry, he finally fell into an exhausted sleep.

At midmorning the next day he started calling again. It was odd, he thought, that not even a servant answered the phone. But then it was Sunday. Perhaps Sutherland's help had the day off. But where was Sutherland? Goddamnit, it didn't make any sense—unless Sutherland was trying to set him up again.

At noon Phillip took a cab from the hotel to the corner of Madison and East 77th Street. He walked toward Central Park on the opposite side of the street from Sutherland's townhouse, turned and walked back to Madison. He didn't know what he was looking for—some sign of activity, a sign that someone was in the house. There was nothing. Goddamnit, where was Sutherland? He had to find him. But how? In New York, on a Sunday afternoon?

He hailed another cab, and on the way back to Gramercy Park he realized he knew absolutely nothing about Averal Sutherland. With the exception of Novak, Brock Chase, and the two men who had interviewed him at Kaufman, he had never met anyone who knew him. Who else was there? No one.

Then suddenly it hit him. Yes, damn it, there was someone else. The woman. What the hell was her name? The woman who had called to warn him about Novak. Leslie. Leslie Parrish— that was it!

He ran into the lobby of the hotel and found a phone book. Please, dear God, let her be in the phone book. Yes, there it was. She lived on East 84th Street.

He went back to his room, and for the next hour and a half he alternately dialed Sutherland's number, then the Parrish woman's. It was after four when Leslie Parrish finally answered. It was the same husky, sensual voice he had heard when she called him in San Francisco. After her second "hello" he hung up, grabbed his coat, and five minutes later was in a cab headed uptown. When he asked the doorman for Leslie Parrish, he pointed to the intercom. Phillip picked up the receiver and pushed Leslie Parrish's bell.

"Who is it?"

"It's Phillip Vanderlind, Miss Parrish—from San Francisco. I have to talk to you. May I come up? Please."

There was a long pause before the woman answered. "I . . . I don't know what to say."

"Look, I understand. I know it's a shock, suddenly hearing from me. But I promise you, it's all right. I just want to talk to you. I *have* to talk to you. Just for a few minutes. Okay?"

Again there was silence. For a moment he thought she had cut him off. Then the door buzzer sounded, he crossed the small lobby, and the elevator man took him to the twentieth floor.

Until he saw the woman standing in the open door of her apartment, dressed in a flaring silk robe, her dark, curly hair pulled back and tied with a scarf, Phillip realized he had never before thought of Averal Sutherland in terms of women. And Leslie Parrish was a beautiful woman.

"Hello, Miss Parrish."

Leslie stepped back from the door, and he entered the apartment. The place was in chaos. The shelves were empty, and newspapers and packing boxes littered the floor. "I'm sorry about the way everything looks," Leslie said. "I'm getting ready to move."

"Thank you for letting me come up," Phillip said.

"Well, as a matter of fact, I've thought about you a thousand times. I mean, I wondered, you know, what happened. If Averal really . . ." Her voice trailed off.

"They tried," Phillip said, and his stomach tightened with the sudden memory of Novak careening toward him on the deck of the storm-whipped boat. "And I think they would have succeeded if you hadn't called me. I wish there were better words than just 'thank you.'"

Leslie smiled and shrugged. "To tell you the truth," she said, "I was thinking about me. Because if they did what Averal had told them to do, and I knew about it, I was afraid they'd do something to me."

Suddenly Leslie stopped talking and the complacent smile vanished. "But that's not the end of it, is it? I mean, Averal will try again, won't he?"

"I came to New York to prevent that, Miss Parrish. Sutherland and I were going to talk, to try to resolve our differences. But I can't find him. There's no answer at his house. That's why I wanted to see you. I hoped you could tell me where he is."

"But I don't know where he is. And I don't care. I never want to see Averal Sutherland again. That's why I'm moving."

"When was the last time you saw him?"

"The night he beat me up."

"And you haven't seen him since?"

"No. But if he's not here in New York, maybe he's in San Francisco."

Phillip's skin tingled. That thought had vaguely crossed his mind earlier, but, for some reason, he had rejected it. Now it seemed to be the only thing that made sense: Sutherland had decoyed him to New York while he searched for the heroin in San Francisco! "That son of a bitch," he snarled. "He's trying to double-cross me again! Look, I'm sorry to have to say this, Miss Parrish, but my life is still in danger, and so is yours. The quicker you can leave New York, the better."

Leslie's eyes widened with fear. "My God, why? What's going on between you and Averal? I'm involved. I have a right to know!"

She was right. "Okay," he said gently, trying not to intensify her alarm. "Averal Sutherland and I were partners in something illegal. I decided I wanted out, and he wanted me to stay in.

Then I threatened to expose him if he tried to keep me in. And, well, you know the rest. Look, I'm sorry you're involved in all this. And I'm sorry to come here and upset you and then leave. But I've got to get back to San Francisco. You see, I've got something out there that Sutherland wants, something I've been trying to use to bargain my way out of this thing."

"You mean you're trying to blackmail him?"

"I guess blackmail is as good a word as any," Phillip said. "One last thing, Miss Parrish. If you don't hear from me within, say, thirty-six hours, I think you ought to get yourself some protection. I can't go to the police, but you can. Just go in and ask for protective custody."

"And tell them what? What can I *prove?* You don't know the police very well, do you? Five minutes after I'm through telling them some farfetched story about one of the most important men in the country, I'd be right back on the street. Besides, there are other reasons why it wouldn't be, shall I say, fruitful for me to go to the police. No, nothing's changed since I called you. The best way for me to survive is for *you* to survive."

"Okay, it's your decision," Phillip said. "But I think it's dumb as hell not to at least *try* to help yourself."

"Who said anything about not helping myself? As a matter of fact, if it's blackmail you're looking for, I might be able to help you, too." Then she smiled provocatively. "Well, I've been saving this for the right time—if I ever needed it. And I guess now we both need it."

Puzzled, Phillip watched as Leslie Parrish began walking slowly toward him, the long silk robe rippling around her body. When she had come within three feet of him, she stopped, tossed her head defiantly, and opened the robe. "What do you think we can do with *this?*"

So unexpected was the sight of male genitals pressed tightly to the body by the sheer panty hose that Phillip simply stared, frozen for a moment in time. Then he drew back a step. "God almighty!" he breathed incredulously. "You're a . . ." His voice failed him.

"That's right," Leslie said, pulling the robe to. "I'm a man.

And Averal Sutherland knows it. Just what do you think he would be willing to do to keep the whole straight world from seeing what you've just seen?"

*　　*　　*

Six hours later, somewhere over the Midwest at 38,000 feet, Phillip shifted to a more comfortable position in his seat, a smile twitching at the corners of his mouth. No longer was he faced with the possibility of having to incriminate himself to deal with Sutherland. Going to the police or being caught in possession of the heroin were both irrelevant now. And, thank God, so was the possibility he might have been forced to kill Averal Sutherland.

As Phillip analyzed it, just the specter of homosexuality hanging over the head of a man like Averal Sutherland was a near perfect solution. Maybe it was too much to expect anyone to believe Averal Sutherland capable of trafficking in narcotics, but, ironically, homosexuality was something people were all too ready to believe. And while the public—or even the shareholders of his company—might not care about a man's sexual preference, the prudish power of the Kaufman Family Foundation would, in Phillip's judgment, dump Sutherland instantly. Confronted with that prospect, the man would be easy to deal with. No one knew better than Averal Sutherland that without the respectability and power of his corporate façade, the rest of his rotten empire would collapse, leaving him with nothing.

Leslie had agreed to cooperate fully and had given Phillip a written account of his relationship with Sutherland together with the names of others who knew about it. He would simply disappear for a while, Leslie had said, but he gave Phillip an address in Los Angeles through which he could be reached, when and if Phillip needed him. In this case there would be plenty of evidence to damn Sutherland. And there were other advantages to the strategy. Unlike the two bags of heroin, Phillip would always be in possession of the proof of what he would hold over Sutherland's head. Then, too, he could now destroy the drugs. And he believed that Sutherland would be much easier to deal with once he learned the drugs were gone.

"Would you like anything, sir?"

Phillip turned away from the window and looked up at the stewardess. "Do you think the captain might have a recent weather update of the Bay Area? Tell him it's for an old sailor who's anxious to get out on the bay early in the morning."

Five minutes later the stewardess was back. The fog had dissipated significantly but still covered the coast, three to five miles inland, she said. But maybe it would clear out by noon.

Phillip swore under his breath. He *had* to get back to the boat. And the fog rolling up over the bluffs along the old coastal highway might permit just enough visibility to creep along if he was patient and careful. He would have to try it. He had to reach the *Spellbound*, destroy a fortune in heroin—and then find a madman before he found him.

CHAPTER 18

A t the small motel, fifty minutes south of San Francisco, a man left his room and walked to the light-green Oldsmobile parked just outside the door. He picked up the mobile phone concealed beneath the dash. "It's Al, Bobby. I'm just checking out a dump called the Starlight Motel, and I'm on my way to Half Moon. Any sign of Vanderlind where you are?"

"Nothing's moving at the yacht club. But what makes you think he's way the hell down there?"

"Look, he's got to put in somewhere, and if he sailed south out of the bay like he usually does, Half Moon's the only place. He might even be there now if he isn't still sailing around in this frigging fog."

"You heard from Novak?"

"No. Nobody has."

"I don't like this, Al. Where the hell is he?"

"What the hell difference does it make? We got our orders. Novak says hit somebody, we hit him. You stick around the yacht club and I'll let you know what I find when I get to Half Moon."

*   *   *

The white powder floated on the gentle swells of the Pacific for a moment, then vanished. One by one forty kilos of pure heroin found their way into the chemistry of the ocean.

Slumping down in the cockpit of the *Spellbound*, Phillip closed his eyes and heaved a sigh of relief. It was gone. The goddamn stuff was finally gone. He thought of Polly. He knew he wasn't responsible for her addiction. But how many other lives would have been destroyed if those forty kilos had gotten onto the street? No, there was no longer any way to rationalize his actions. He *had* been insane. And Sutherland had been right about his conscience.

But as he rose wearily and went forward to restart the engine to power the mile and half back to Half Moon Bay, he wondered what Sutherland's reaction would be when he found out the merchandise was gone. He didn't know, but at least he had destroyed the evidence that would link him directly to a smuggling operation. And how would Sutherland react to the threat of exposure from Leslie Parrish? Would he accede to Phillip's demands, or would it be just one more reason to kill him—and Leslie Parrish? He didn't know that either. But now it was the only chance he had. Still, nothing would change until he could confront Sutherland. And to do that he had to find him.

Running the boat at hull speed through the quartering land swells, Phillip made his way back to the marina at Half Moon Bay as the last remnants of fog were rapidly yielding to the midmorning sun. After the boat was secured he went quickly below and dug out the Walther automatic. Wrapping the pistol loosely in the few remaining clean clothes he had aboard, he locked the boat and hurried ashore to the rented Camaro parked behind the marina office. He started backing out when something caught his eye across the yacht basin. A Coast Guard launch was just entering the harbor. He watched the small white cruiser with her bold red bow slash running easily through the water. Then he saw that it was bearing out of the channel and heading directly toward the Bermuda 40. As he watched with mounting horror and disbelief, the craft backed its engines, nosed gently up to the stern of the *Spellbound*, and three armed men in business suits scrambled aboard.

Nearly paralyzed with shock, Phillip eased out of the parking lot, and seconds later he was driving as fast as he dared away from Half Moon Bay. His heart was pounding, his mouth bone-dry. Somehow, someway, the United States government was now involved.

Rather than going north in the light traffic on the narrow two-lane coast highway, he cut back south, then jogged eastward toward heavily traveled U.S. 101. If the Coast Guard had helicopters up, he wanted as much traffic around him as possible. But by the time he reached the four-lane highway and turned north toward San Francisco, the feeling of almost total panic had left him. Perhaps it was because everything that he could conceive happening to him now had. He didn't doubt that Sutherland was still trying to trap him, and now the police were looking for him, too. What the hell was he going to do?

His first impulse was to run, to drive and just keep driving until he was as far away from San Francisco as he could get. Then he realized he would spend the rest of his life running unless he could confront Sutherland. But he had to hide. And what better place to hide than in the heart of a crowded city? San Francisco's "Tenderloin" district was filled with old hotels and anonymous people.

* * *

"I got him, Bobby. I was right about the marina at Half Moon. The son of a bitch was just pulling out when I drove in. He's headed toward the city and I'm right on his tail."

The driver of the light-green Oldsmobile kept the red Camaro in sight as it dropped off the freeway into downtown San Francisco and turned left toward the Tenderloin. He saw it brake and swing into a parking lot, but by the time the Olds glided into the curb abreast of the lot, the driver's eyes searching, his hand cradling a long-barreled pistol by his leg, the Camaro was empty.

The man picked up his mobile phone again. "Okay, Bobby. I lost the son of a bitch. Too many people on the streets."

"Christ, man, you should have taken him out on the road."

"A moving hit on a state highway by myself? Get off my ass, Bobby."

"Well, what the hell you going to do now?"

The man squinted at the Camaro through the windshield of the Olds. "I'm hanging around here for a while. He just may be ditching the car. But I've got a feeling he's coming back. There's a flophouse that backs up to this parking lot where I can stay. And if I can get a room where I want it, man, I got the cleanest shot you ever saw."

*   *   *

The room looked and smelled its age, but it was clean, had a dial telephone, a battered but serviceable television set, and a bath. Satisfied, Phillip unpacked the small bag he had carried in from the car, slipped the Walther under the mattress, and then sat down on the bed. He was in one hell of a situation. But what confused and bothered him the most was how law-enforcement agencies had become involved. He was absolutely convinced that he had done nothing to arouse suspicion over the last few weeks. That had to mean only one thing: they had come at him through Sutherland. Either they had been onto the overall operation long before he became involved or—and this was the possibility that held the greatest danger for Phillip—Sutherland had somehow managed to rig a story that laid everything off on him. In fact, the longer Phillip thought about it, the more probable that seemed—except for one factor. Could Sutherland really afford to take that kind of risk? Phillip thought he probably could.

The way he figured it, then, he had three alternatives: he could follow through with his original plan to contact Sutherland, he could immediately turn himself into the police, or he could assume he was facing the combined threats of Sutherland and the authorities and run. Because if *both* Sutherland and the government were after him, there would be no place to turn, no possible way to deal with either side.

But despite all the confusion and conjecture of the moment, Phillip did know one thing with utter certainty: he would do nothing, not even so much as open the door to his room, until he had *facts*. Never again would he let panic, born of fear and masquerading as instinct, guide his decisions or actions. It was panic that had induced him to join Beta in the first place and panic that had compelled him to flee New York with two suitcases full of heroin. If he was to save himself now, everything he did had to be based on fact. He had to be certain he knew or certain he couldn't find out; either way, fact would be served. And the man with the facts was Averal Sutherland.

It took less than five minutes to complete his first calls. But Sutherland was not, nor was he expected, at either the house in Sea Cliff or the Kaufman offices in New York, and there was still no answer at the townhouse. The effect on Phillip was to heighten his concern that Sutherland *had* gone to the authorities and thus had no intention of taking phone calls from a fugitive. But he left the message with both the housekeeper in Sea Cliff and Sutherland's secretary in New York that he would call back at noon, Pacific time, tomorrow. And now there was nothing to do but wait. He stretched out on the bed, took several deep breaths to ease his tension, and never knew when sleep overtook him.

Three hours later the chill of early evening through the open window made him stir, and he remembered another call he had to make. With the police now involved, he could wind up on the front page of a lot of newspapers across the country, and it was time to prepare Jessica for that possibility. He lit a cigarette and placed a call to Vail.

"Phillip, where are you? I've been so worried," Jessica said when she heard his voice.

"In San Francisco," he said.

"Oh, Phillip. I'd hoped you'd be able to stop here on your way back. When will I see you again?"

"That's why I'm calling, Jessica. I'm not sure what my plans are going to be. Things are pretty confused at the moment. But I've got to tell you something and I want your promise that you'll trust me and not ask questions. Will you do that?"

"Darling, what is it? You sound so . . ."

"Jessica, will you trust me?"

"Of course I trust you. I love you, Phillip."

God, this was difficult. He didn't know how to begin. "Look, the deal simply is, I may well find myself in some legal difficulty over a business matter. But I promise you there's nothing to worry about. The only reason I'm saying anything to you at all is, the thing *could* get in the papers. And, well . . . obviously I wanted to warn you beforehand."

"Is there something I can do?" Jessica asked quietly.

"Yes, you can tell me what you've been up to the last couple of weeks."

"I want to know one thing, Phillip. Are you all right?"

He laughed. "I'm fine. And I'm going to stay that way. Now, before I have to go, let's talk about you. What's going on with the shop?"

"It's all so exciting," Jessica said. "I'm planning to open in another couple of weeks. I hope you can be here."

"I do too, Jessica."

"And I've even thought of a name. P.J.'s. How does that sound?"

"It sounds fine."

"You don't mind?"

"All I mind in this world is being away from you, Jessica." He had never meant anything more in his life. But the moment he said it he also realized how ludicrous it was. He might never see Jessica again. "I've got to go now, darling. I promise I'll call you as soon as I can."

"Phillip," Jessica said softly, "keep this with you. I think I've sensed that something has been troubling you. But I know you'd never do anything wrong. I love you, Phillip. Nothing will ever change that. Good night, my love. Call me soon."

When he hung up, Phillip knew he wouldn't have to worry about Jessica. She wasn't all ribbons and bows on her sixteenth birthday, someone to be pedestaled away from reality. She was a woman and she would be able to take care of herself, no matter what might happen to him.

He looked at his watch. It was after seven now, and he realized he was hungry. He hadn't had anything to eat since morning. He left the hotel, bought a paper, and found a restaurant that didn't look too bad. He was sitting in a back booth, sipping a scotch and waiting for the steak sandwich he had ordered, when a small headline in the paper caught his eye.

HOUSTON SOCIALITE DEAD

Mrs. Pauline Savitch, 39, former wife of Houston oilman Charles Savitch, was found dead in her New York apartment, the apparent victim of an overdose of narcotics. Discovered by her maid Monday morning, Mrs. Savitch lay sprawled . . .

"Oh God," Phillip breathed. Suddenly he was cold and his hands trembled. He downed the rest of his scotch and ordered another when the waitress brought his sandwich. He ate it, even though his appetite was gone.

Back in his hotel room, he couldn't get Polly out of his mind. For an hour or so he tried to lose himself in an old movie on television, but then he turned it off and tried to fall asleep.

It was after ten o'clock when he woke up the next morning. At twelve o'clock precisely, he thought, he would know which courses of action were open to him, what immediate direction his life was going to take. Averal Sutherland would have to talk to him now. But what the hell was he going to say to the man? And what would Sutherland say to him? He might very well counter the threat of blackmail with threats of his own. And of the two of them, Phillip had no doubt that it was Sutherland who had the greater power to carry out his threat.

At noon Phillip took a deep breath and picked up the phone.

At 12:15 he stood at the small, single window of his room overlooking the squalor of the Tenderloin, wondering if the rest of his life would be spent in back alleys like that. No one answered at the townhouse, and Sutherland had not been at either the Kaufman offices in New York or his house in Sea Cliff. Nor had he left any word for Phillip. Obviously the man refused to speak to him. It seemed a fact then that Sutherland had somehow conspired to turn him over to the authorities. "Damn it!" he swore viciously at himself. Sutherland would not bargain with him, and his alternatives had narrowed to two: surrender himself to the federal government, or run.

Why not give himself up? Phillip thought. But finally that seemed to make little sense. If Sutherland felt confident enough to turn him over to the police, that clearly indicated the man had absolutely no fear that Phillip could implicate him—or extricate himself. Surrender then meant certain prosecution and conviction. Sutherland had not been able to kill him, but he had found an equally effective means to get him out of the way. Phillip knew now that he would have to pay for what he had done—but not, he vowed, with his life to Sutherland, or locked away in some gray-rock federal prison.

So he would run. But where? How? He needed money, and the $500 in cash and traveler's checks he had in his pocket wouldn't get him very far. There was $6,000 in the bank in Marin County. But if federal agents had searched his boat, it was not illogical to assume that they had been to his bank, frozen his account, and were simply waiting for him to show up. The question then became, was trying for the money worth the risk of capture? Phillip quickly decided that freedom and $500 were by far the wiser choice. And if he was going to run, it was time to get started.

He began cramming his possessions into his bag. God, he wished he knew for a fact that federal agents were looking for him. Then, abruptly, he stopped. The Omni offices. Anne Elkman. If federal agents *were* involved, surely they would have been to his office. He grabbed for the phone.

"Oh, Mr. Vanderlind. Where in heaven's name are you?"

"Now, Anne, please. I'm back in San Francisco. I'll be in in the morning. I just wanted to check to see if everything's all right."

"Everything is just terrible. I wish I didn't have to tell you, but the people at Hospital Associates called last week. There's been some sort of litigation and they've canceled the lease. I'm so sorry."

"Damn," said Phillip, trying to sound concerned. "And all that work. Well, that's that, I guess. Anything else?"

"Yes. The building manager came by this morning to see you. He said some agents from the federal government were here on Saturday morning with a warrant to search our offices. I can't imagine what . . ."

Phillip depressed the button, then slowly replaced the receiver. There was no doubt in his mind now. Federal authorities *were* looking for him. And as a final irony, even Omni's deal with Hospital Associates had fallen through. Jesus Christ, he thought, shaking his head as he picked up his bag and walked to the door. He opened it, but then hestitated for a second and quickly closed it again, his heart pounding wildly. "Dear God in heaven," he muttered to himself. "If I'm right . . ."

He went to the phone and dialed the number of Omni's bank in San Francisco. If the federal government was less than completely thorough, there was a chance. An outside chance, but this time the risk was more than worth it.

A secretary answered. "Hello, Mr. Vanderlind. We've been wondering if we'd hear from you today," she said pleasantly. "How was your trip?"

Phillip chatted briefly with the secretary until he was as convinced as it was possible to be that she, at least, was unaware of any contact by the authorities. Then he asked when she expected her boss.

"Oh, I'm sorry, Mr. Vanderlind. He's playing golf with a customer this afternoon. Is there something I might help you with?"

He breathed a sigh of relief. A secretary would be far less apt to ask questions. "As a matter of fact there is," he said, trying to sound casual. "And you probably know more about what I need to have the bank do anyway."

"I shall certainly be happy to try," the secretary said, with just a trace of flattered smugness in her voice.

"But first I'd better ask you if the funds in the Hospital Associates deal have already been released from escrow."

"Oh, yes, sir. Last Friday. As soon as we were notified by the other two parties, the escrow terminated. I have your duplicate deposit slip in my outgoing mail right here in front of me."

"Fine," Phillip said. Then, in as matter-of-fact a voice as he could manage, he continued. "Now, I need your advice. We have a deal about to close in Argentina. How's the best way to get that five million down there so I'll have it available when we're ready for it?"

"No problem at all, Mr. Vanderlind. You just tell me which bank you prefer and we can wire the funds today. All I'll need is a letter of authorization from you for the transfer. Then it's simply a matter of you presenting proper identification to the bank down there."

"That's excellent. You've solved the problem. That will work perfectly. Let's use the Banco de Nacional of Buenos Aires, all right? And if you'll do me a big favor and type up whatever it is I have to sign, I'll drop by in about an hour on my way back from the yacht club. Can you do that?"

"I'll be happy to, Mr. Vanderlind," the secretary said cheerfully.

"And I'll also need some cash to take with me on the trip—say, one thousand dollars in fifty-dollar bills and another ten thousand dollars in traveler's checks. Can you have that ready for me, too?"

"Indeed I can, Mr. Vanderlind. Anything else?"

"No, I think that's everything. Except you might hold on to that deposit slip and I'll just pick it up with the money when I get there. And thanks a lot. I'll see you in about an hour."

Phillip was shaking so badly when he hung up he could barely get the receiver back on the hook. He had been right, all the way down the line. The escrow did have automatic termination provisions; the $5,000,000 was back in the Omni operating account on which *he* was the sole signatory. And you could have funds wired to a foreign bank where you had no regular account. It hardly seemed believable—but it was true. In less than forty-eight hours he would be in South America with

$5,000,000! "Now, Sutherland, you son of a bitch," he said, slamming a fist onto the palm of his hand, "let's see who wants to find who!"

He could almost hear the explosion that would occur when Averal Sutherland discovered he had left the country with the $5,000,000. If there was anything on earth Sutherland understood, Phillip knew, it was money. And with that kind of money he would have the power to fight back. For $5,000,000 and Leslie Parrish's silence, Sutherland would *have* to deal. And that would include undoing whatever it was he had done with the federal authorities. If Sutherland could put them on his trail, he could take them off.

But what if he were wrong? What if, for some insane reason, Sutherland *still* refused to make a bargain with him and his alternatives were once again reduced to running? If that happened, then at least he would be sitting in a foreign country with $5,000,000—out of reach of Averal Sutherland *and* the U.S. government.

He was sure it would work. But then he had another thought. His passport. He would need a passport. Where the hell was it? He opened his bag and started going through the sheaf of papers he had crammed into it when he left the house in Marin County. Yes, thank God, it was there. And now all he had to do was go to the bank, pick up his money, and then drive to Los Angeles, where it would probably be safe to board a commercial flight to South America.

Phillip glanced at his watch; it was time to get moving. And then he remembered the pistol. He retrieved it from beneath the mattress, wiped it clean, went into the bathroom, and placed the weapon gently at the bottom of the toilet tank. With the police after him, the last thing he wanted was to be caught with a gun in his possession. And he sure as hell couldn't take it aboard a commercial aircraft.

He didn't want to be caught with the tapes either. He found them in his bag, wrapped them in a piece of paper, and addressed the package to himself in care of the old Cocatlon post-office box in Houston. Then he quickly repacked his bag, took one final glance around the room, and ten minutes later, after checking out of the hotel, he stopped at a drugstore, bought scotch tape and stamps, completed wrapping the package, and dropped the tapes in a mailbox, a block from the parking lot where he had left his car.

* * *

In a second-floor back room of the Peabody Hotel, the bleary-eyed occupant idly checked the time, stretched, and casually resumed his surveillance of the street below. He blinked, leaned closer to the window, then stiffened. Reaching for the long-barreled automatic on the bed beside him, he dropped quickly to his knees and brought the gun up to the window with both hands. Using the sill for a rest, he trial-sighted the weapon just above the windshield of the maroon Camaro less than thirty yards away. Then he lowered the pistol, quickly rechecked the mechanism, and looked back out the window as Phillip Vanderlind walked up to the pay booth of the parking lot.

The gun came back up to sill height, and the man's pulse began to surge as he tracked his target across the lot. But he wanted Vanderlind beside the car. He wanted a still shot. And that would occur at the precise instant when Vanderlind bent over to unlock the door.

* * *

As Phillip approached the Camaro, he dropped his bag to the pavement on the driver's side and reached into his pocket for the keys. As he inserted the key in the lock, he stooped slightly to retrieve the bag. The turning lock made a strange snapping noise, he thought, as he straightened and withdrew the key. Then he wondered why he had never noticed the small, perfectly round hole in the edge of the roof just above the driver's seat.

Suddenly a terrible force slammed into him, and he felt awkward and embarrassed to be lying with his head on the filthy pavement, his face flush against the tread of an automobile tire. And when the pain that screamed up through his body became too great to bear, he closed his eyes and felt nothing.

CHAPTER 19

Harry Kane was pacing restlessly back and forth across his office. "All right, Cyril, I'll admit I was wrong. It sure looks like this guy Vanderlind is tied up with some kind of smuggling operation. But Averal Sutherland? The man is chairman of the board of one of the biggest multinational conglomerates in this country, for Christ's sake. He must pull down half a million a year. Why the hell would a man like that fool around with dope?"

"Look, Harry, we know that Sutherland found Vanderlind when he was flat on his back. We know there is some kind of a business connection between them. And Vanderlind was clean before that. But suddenly a respectable business executive begins to act very much like he's smuggling dope. Why? Everything points to the association with Sutherland, Harry."

"Then you believe Vanderlind? You believe the semiconscious ravings of a guy who's been shot?"

"I do. And he wasn't just shot, Harry, he was hit. Vanderlind knows something and somebody wanted him dead. He says it was Averal Sutherland and I believe him."

"And you're going to sit there and tell Averal Sutherland he's been accused of running narcotics *and* attempted murder by a man who might not even live to testify against him?"

"Sutherland doesn't have to know that, Harry."

Kane sucked on his pipe and exhaled a cloud of smoke. "And what happens if Vanderlind dies and Sutherland realizes we were trying to set him up?"

Kennedy shrugged. "I'll apologize."

"No, Harry, you'll be out on your ass. And I will be, too."

"It's the only way that makes any sense," Kennedy persisted.

"Okay, Cyril, okay. You've already got an appointment to talk to Sutherland. But for Christ's sake, get an update on Vanderlind's condition before you see the man. And we'll both hope the poor bastard's still alive.

*   *   *

Sitting in the hushed opulence of Averal Sutherland's anteroom at Kaufman Industries, Kennedy battled with his emotions. The longer he stared at the large oil portrait of the chairman of the board, hanging thirty feet away on the opposite wall, the less inclined he was to believe the distinguished figure that stared back at him could possibly be involved in narcotics, let alone murder. What evidence did he have? Just his connection with Vanderlind, which could be perfectly legitimate, two suitcases found aboard a boat owned by Sutherland and used by Vanderlind—two *empty* suitcases—and the accusations of a man delirious with pain. Harry Kane was right. This was one hell of a shot in the dark.

Kennedy looked at his watch again and wondered how much longer he would have to wait. He hadn't slept at all in almost forty-eight hours, not since he had been notified that a man identified as Phillip Vanderlind had been shot and was en route to a hospital. He and two other agents had arrived at the emergency room only minutes after the ambulance. Vanderlind was still partially lucid, but seeing the man lying there in his own blood, Kennedy had shuddered. It hadn't been that long since he had been shot himself and had to fight for his life.

Despite strenuous protests from the trauma-team doctors, he had gotten Vanderlind to talk to him—after a fashion. But while the man seemed to know where he was and what was happening to him, he had been incapable of responding to questions. All he said, over and over again, was "Don't believe Sutherland . . . Sutherland after me . . . Sutherland . . . heroin . . ." until he finally lost consciousness.

The official post-operative report said that a single bullet had struck Vanderlind in the upper right shoulder and ranged downward, exiting the body high on the right front side. Luckily for him, no vital organs or arteries had been damaged; shock would be the thing that killed him, if he died. An hour ago Vanderlind was still critical. But thank God, Kennedy thought, the man is still alive.

He was startled by the voice of a secretary. "Will you come this way, please, Mr. Kennedy?"

He rose and followed the woman through the massive twin teak doors of Averal Sutherland's private office. But the man who came forward to meet him was not the man whose likeness he had been looking at in the reception room.

"Mr. Kennedy, I'm Hugh Crowell, president of Kaufman Industries. Sorry you had to wait. Won't you sit down?"

Kennedy shook the man's hand and took the chair he was offered.

"I know this will seem rather rude, Mr. Kennedy," Crowell began, "but Mr. Sutherland is indisposed at the moment. May I help you?"

"Indisposed. Why?"

Crowell ignored the question. "As president of the company, Mr. Kennedy, I have the same security clearance as Mr. Sutherland. And in his absence I quite often—"

"Excuse me, Mr. Crowell, but I'm not here to see Mr. Sutherland on *company* business."

Crowell tilted his head inquisitively. "I see. Well, if it has something to do with his personal business, I might be able to help you there, too. Mr. Sutherland and I are quite close, and I'm very familiar with most of his affairs."

"I'm sorry, Mr. Crowell, but I must speak to Mr. Sutherland personally. Is he available?"

"At the moment I'm afraid he isn't, Mr. Kennedy."

"May I ask when he will be?"

"I can't tell you that, Mr. Kennedy."

"I see. Then you will force me to go through other channels." Kennedy rose. "Thank you for your time, Mr. Crowell."

He had almost reached the doors when Crowell called to him. "Mr. Kennedy, just a moment, please."

"Yes?"

"Averal Sutherland has had a stroke."

Kennedy tried to conceal his surprise.

"It was a cerebral hemorrhage," Crowell continued. "What caused it, we don't know. Until this happened, the man was in perfect health. Now, well . . . his doctors say he will never recover. He is being kept alive by machines."

"When did it happen?" Kennedy asked.

"His servants discovered him Sunday evening when they returned from a vacation."

"Then why all this . . ."

"Secrecy? There are business reasons, Mr. Kennedy. You see, when something happens to a man of Averal Sutherland's position and importance, things can become, well . . . rather chaotic—things like pending contracts, acquisitions, mergers, and the like. Our competitors are not above taking advantage of such a situation. Then, too, there's the stock market. Our executive committee met in emergency session this morning and agreed—in the best interests of the stockholders, I might add—to withhold the news of Averal Sutherland's condition until after the market closes this Friday afternoon."

"Is he capable of answering questions or making written replies?"

"Mr. Kennedy, Averal Sutherland is a human vegetable."

       *   *   *

In the early evening of the following day, Cyril Kennedy sat alone in the heavy dusk of the library in Averal Sutherland's townhouse with a portable tape recorder, dictating his preliminary report. After a thorough investigation at Kaufman Industries, nothing had been found in his files and papers that did not pertain strictly to company business. And not one staff member professed to know anything more about Averal Sutherland. Teams of agents in San Francisco, Aspen, and Martha's Vineyard had conducted thorough searches of his various residences, and they, too, had found absolutely nothing to suggest that Sutherland was in any way involved in anything illegal.

Kennedy's own team had spent over twelve hours combing through everything in the townhouse. Nothing that Sutherland owned had escaped being examined. Even the records in his vast music library had been spot-played for actual content. And not one thing remotely suspicious had been discovered.

Then, just a few hours ago, a first tiny break had come. Under interrogation, Sutherland's chauffeur had revealed two unsuspected aspects of his employer's life. Sutherland had a liaison with a young woman named Leslie Parrish, and when Kennedy inquired at her apartment house he discovered that she had moved suddenly, leaving no forwarding address. It seemed more than mere coincidence that she would disappear at the same time that Sutherland suffered a stroke. She would be found eventually, but Kennedy was less interested in the man's sex life than he was in the other piece of information he obtained from the chauffeur: the existence of a suite of private offices used quite regularly, he said, by his employer.

Kennedy had visited the office suite himself and found no one working there. Nor did he find anything in the files that gave a specific indication of what Sutherland had used the offices for. But the mere existence of a paper shredder and stacks of what were quickly determined to be coded computer runs were *prima facie* evidence to Kennedy that Averal Sutherland had had something to hide.

It would take time to break the code, and even then whatever information was revealed might prove to be inconclusive. Still, Kennedy had been encouraged. Finally, something had surfaced that gave credence to Vanderlind's confused accusations and his own increasing certainty that Averal Sutherland was—or had been—more than anyone ever dreamed.

But it was what he now held in the palm of his hand—something that he himself had found just a few moments ago—that brought it all together for Cyril Kennedy. Idly searching the corners of the ornate desk in Sutherland's library where he was still sitting, he had discovered a small package, apparently left in a drawer and forgotten. It was addressed, oddly, to a Mr. Averal *Gregg*. And inside was the small silver crucifix that Kennedy now held in his hand and a note:

My Dear Averal,
I send you this simple token of love and esteem, blessed by His Holiness, the Pope, whom I was able to meet in a brief audience this week because of your kind and generous heart.

In the name of Christ,
Leonard Kody

It was difficult even for Kennedy to believe the staggering coincidence. The note from a murdered parish priest suddenly shifted the possibility of Averal Sutherland's involvement in a drug operation to a distinct probability. But of all the evidence he had so far collected that suggested that, Kennedy knew there was only one realistic hope of proving it. Phillip Vanderlind was his only chance.

*   *   *

Phillip tensed and felt the wound in his shoulder throb. He knew how lucky he had been. A few inches to the left and the bullet would have penetrated his brain. Was Novak still alive? Or had Sutherland hired someone else to try to kill him? And how the hell had the man found him? It was almost a relief to be in the hospital. For the time being, at least, he hoped he was out of Averal Sutherland's reach. But the federal authorities had finally caught up with him.

Phillip lit a cigarette and watched the smoke twist lazily toward the ceiling. He knew he had to talk to the agent who was coming in to see him. It was time he began to deal with reality again. He wondered briefly if he should have an attorney, then thought better of it. If he kept his head, dealt only with facts and kept his mouth shut, he believed he would be all right initially. But he still didn't know why or how the federal authorities were involved.

An hour or so later, just as the attendant was leaving with Phillip's luncheon tray, Cyril Kennedy entered the room. "My credentials, Mr. Vanderlind," he said. "I'd like to ask you a few questions, if I may."

Phillip glanced at the identification and nodded toward a chair. "All right, Mr. Kennedy. Care to sit down?"

"Thank you." Kennedy drew a chair up to the side of the bed. "I presume you know why I'm here."

"I presumed you'd tell me."

Kennedy smiled thinly. He had known it wouldn't be easy. "Then I'll come straight to the point, Mr. Vanderlind. I want to ask you some questions about your activities in recent weeks. Specifically, do you have any knowledge of drugs—heroin to be exact—being brought into this country from England?"

Phillip tried to look puzzled, hoping his reaction wouldn't appear contrived. "What kind of absurd conclusion is that to draw from the fact that I was shot?" he asked.

"The conclusion we drew was not from your accident, Mr. Vanderlind, but from Averal Sutherland. I believe you travel under a special passport arranged for you by Sutherland."

"I assume he arranged it, yes."

"Well, of course then, he would have reason to be concerned if he felt you were misusing it, wouldn't he? And to protect himself, the only prudent thing to do would be to request an investigation."

"Am I to understand you're accusing me of smuggling narcotics on the strength of something Averal Sutherland said?"

"You surprise me, Mr. Vanderlind. I had hoped, in view of what I believe we both know, we could dispense with all this fencing. You were under surveillance during your recent trip from London to New York."

Phillip felt his pulse quicken. Just how much did this man Kennedy already know?

"On that trip," Kennedy continued, "you carried two large bags through customs and took a cab into New York. But you turned around almost immediately, chartered a jet to San Francisco, and took the bags with you."

Phillip's inner tension began to subside. He knew now that Sutherland could not possibly be the reason the federal authorities had kept him under surveillance. Sutherland could not have known he was going to cause trouble until *after* he had failed to call him in New York. No, Kennedy had been following him for some other reason, and now he was obviously on a fishing expedition.

"What was your original destination that day, Mr. Vanderlind?"

"New York, of course."

"What changed your mind?"

Phillip was silent for a moment. "Yes, something did change my mind, as a matter of fact. I stopped to see a friend, and when I found that she was ill, I was upset and wanted to get home."

"Do you especially like sailing in storms at night, Mr. Vanderlind?"

Phillip was startled. "What kind of a question is that?"

"I'm suggesting that a man would have to have a strong motive to sail off into a storm on a treacherous bay the way you did. And I'm suggesting that your motive could have been the delivery of two suitcases of drugs."

Phillip turned slightly in the bed and groaned as his shoulder burned with the movement. Then he managed a slight laugh. "Mr. Kennedy, I suggest your imagination is working overtime."

"Maybe so, Mr. Vanderlind." Kennedy saw now that he wasn't going to be able to finesse Vanderlind into making a confession by pretending it was Averal Sutherland who had aroused the suspicion of the authorities. He shifted his position in the chair before he spoke again. "Do you know what kind of information is contained in the coded computer runs in Sutherland's private suite of offices in New York?"

"What computer runs? What offices are you talking about?"

"You were never in those offices? You don't know the code system used?"

"I don't know what the hell you're talking about."

"I think you do, Mr. Vanderlind. You see, we've already discovered the thing I believe you're trying so hard to conceal: Averal Sutherland himself is running a large and very profitable narcotics operation, right from the chair of a major corporation. And, in time, we'll be able to prove it. Why are you defending the man when it's obviously his intention to make you the scapegoat? If you keep it up, you'll go down the tube alone."

Phillip reached for a package of cigarettes on the table by his bed. Should he take the opportunity Kennedy was offering him? he wondered. He decided to wait. Something in the man's effort to play him off against Sutherland didn't hang together. "I have no reason to think I'm going down the tube, as you put it, Mr. Kennedy. Would you care to tell me why you think so?"

"Then you still say you don't know anything about Sutherland being involved in a drug-smuggling operation?"

"That's *your* contention, Mr. Kennedy."

Kennedy picked up the lighter on the bedside table and lit Phillip's cigarette. "Then how is it, Mr. Vanderlind, that all you could say the afternoon they brought you into the emergency room was, and I quote, 'Don't believe Sutherland . . . Sutherland after me . . . Sutherland . . . heroin.' You repeated those words over and over. There were at least a half-dozen witnesses."

Phillip's mouth went dry and he reached for the glass of water on the table. Again Kennedy moved to help him, but this time he tried to ignore him. "Are you suggesting," he said after he sipped the water, "that the few words I may have muttered when I was delirious from pain and shock could be used as evidence against me?"

"I am merely suggesting that those words would be very difficult to explain to a grand jury."

Phillip sank back in the pillows on his bed and dragged deeply on his cigarette. "All right," he said wearily. "I guess there's no point in playing games with you. In fact, you can't imagine how relieved I am finally to be able to talk about Averal Sutherland. Besides, as you may have guessed, I'm not a very good liar."

For the next half hour or so, Kennedy sat and listened closely as Phillip told him about his relationship with Averal Sutherland: how he had been recruited, how he had been set up in the leasing company, given all manner of material things, and then propositioned to participate in a smuggling operation as a means of retaining what he had already received as well as making himself rich. It was all true. But Phillip veered from the truth when he said, "I rejected the proposal, Mr. Kennedy. And Averal Sutherland threatened to kill me."

"That's quite a story, Mr. Vanderlind. And it sounds plausible. But if, as you say, you were in no way involved in the operation, why didn't you immediately seek the protection of the police?"

"It's easy now to realize that's what I should have done. But at the time I didn't believe he'd actually try to kill me. Besides, what evidence did I have against the man? Then I suddenly recalled he *was* going to have me killed. That's why I went busting off into that storm. I was running, trying to hide from the bastard until I could figure out just what to do."

"Why didn't you come to the police then?" Kennedy said.

"Look, I was convinced—and I still am for that matter—that Sutherland is powerful and influential enough either to kill me or go to the police himself with some kind of story to make me look guilty without incriminating himself."

"How did you know that Sutherland wanted to kill you? Did he ever threaten you directly?"

"No, not directly. But . . ." Novak. Phillip remembered the night Novak came at him on the boat. He couldn't tell Kennedy about Emile Novak or he might find himself accused of murder, too. There was Leslie Parrish. He had overheard Sutherland instruct Novak to kill him. But how credible a witness would

Leslie Parrish be? "Mr. Kennedy," he said, feigning exasperation, "I was gunned down in a parking lot by a man who fired a
high-powered weapon from a hotel window and then disappeared without a trace. Does that sound like random target
practice to you?"

"No," Kennedy said. "I'll have to admit it doesn't. But there
are one or two things that still trouble me, Mr. Vanderlind. If, as
you say, Averal Sutherland hired someone to kill you, that
would seem to imply that you knew a great deal about his
operation and he had a good reason to want you dead. Yet you
tell me you refused to participate from the very beginning."

"That's right," Phillip said.

"Then I still don't understand why you didn't come to the
police. Unless, of course, you had something to hide yourself—
like the two bags of heroin you brought back from England. Do
you deny that, Mr. Vanderlind?"

"You're goddamn right I deny it," Phillip said angrily. "I saw
your men aboard my boat, Kennedy. Maybe you'd like to tell me
what the hell they found?"

"We found the bags."

"And what was in them?"

"They were empty, Mr. Vanderlind."

"In other words, you have no evidence against me?"

Kennedy nodded.

"Then may I suggest, Mr. Kennedy, you get the hell out of
here? I've told you everything I know about Averal Sutherland.
And I've told you he tried to kill me. Why don't you question
him? If you want to ask *me* any more questions, you'll have to see
my lawyer."

"Mr. Vanderlind," Kennedy said quietly, "Averal Sutherland
suffered a massive stroke last weekend. You'll read about it in the
papers tomorrow. He's alive, but that's about all. When he dies
his secrets will die with him."

Phillip's eyes closed and he dug his nails into the palms of his
hands. Last weekend! That's why he hadn't been able to find
Sutherland. All that fear and conspiring and chasing from one
end of the country to the other—all for nothing. He was safe
from Averal Sutherland. And he was safe from Cyril Kennedy.

Thank God he had destroyed the heroin. Thank God he hadn't let Kennedy whipsaw him into making a confession. He turned his head and looked Kennedy directly in the eye for the first time since he had entered the room and muttered, "You son of a bitch."

"Yes, I suppose I am," Kennedy said. "Personally I think you're guilty as hell. And I'll have to admit I enjoyed seeing you sweat. But I can't prove a thing against you that isn't circumstantial. You're home free, Vanderlind. And now that I've told you that, I want to ask you a favor."

For a second, Phillip couldn't believe what he had just heard. "You want what?" he asked indignantly. "You want me to help you? After you tried to trick me in every conceivable way into admitting something you think you knew but couldn't prove?"

"That's right, and I think I know that Averal Sutherland was responsible for some kind of elaborate drug operation, but I can't prove that either. That's what I'm really after, Vanderlind. That's what I'm asking you to help me with. We can forget Sutherland. He's paying for his crimes. But what about the rest of his organization? You were smart enough to get out. But there must be others who are still involved. So far we've been unable to find records or evidence of any kind we can use to get at that organization. You're the only hope we have of understanding how the operation works and who else is selling, smuggling, and buying narcotics."

"What happens if I refuse to cooperate?"

"Nothing—to you. But a lot of other people's lives will be destroyed. And I think you have a conscience, Vanderlind."

"I never met anyone else involved in the operation," Phillip said. "All I can tell you is what Sutherland told me."

"That's all I'm asking," Kennedy said.

Forty-five minutes later, Cyril Kennedy closed the small notebook in his lap and returned his pen to his pocket. "So that's it."

"That's all I can remember Sutherland ever telling me about the way the operation worked. And when you get right down to it, he really didn't tell me anything, did he?"

"I'm not surprised," Kennedy said. "It fits. I mean the pattern of intentional obscurity. It's almost as if Averal Sutherland didn't exist."

Both men were silent for a time, then Phillip said quietly, "I don't think he did exist. In retrospect, I think Averal Sutherland was a very frightened man. Everything in his life was defensively structured. He always had to be in control. I think he was afraid that if someone broke through all the defenses he built up around himself, he wouldn't find anything there."

"A lot of men are like that," Kennedy said. "They don't know who they are or where they're going. But thank God there aren't very many who are willing to destroy others to keep from finding out."

*   *   *

That afternoon, when Cyril Kennedy had left, Phillip lay back on the bed and began to collect his thoughts. He couldn't believe what had happened to him. Sutherland was no longer a threat. The federal authorities had no evidence against him. Was his nightmare really over?

And he thought of Jessica. He called her that evening but said only that he had had an accident and was in the hospital. Alarmed, she wanted to see him, to be with him. But he had asked her not to come. He would be out of the hospital soon, he said, and then he would come to Vail to rest and regain his strength. He didn't tell her he had decided to leave the leasing business and had no idea what he was going to do. Those things he tried to say in a letter he began to write to her after they hung up. And he tried to tell her how much he loved her—more than anything in his life. But when he realized the simplest way to say what he felt was to ask her to marry him, he stopped writing and brooded until he fell asleep.

He awoke the next morning, his mind clearer than it had been for weeks. He reached for the pad on the bedside table and began to read what he had written to Jessica the evening before. But suddenly his eyes widened as something he had absent-mindedly scratched in the lower margin of the page seemed to jump off the paper at him: $5,000,000.

Five million dollars. It was true. It was his. His mind reeled with the thought. There would be absolutely no way to trace a connection between Omni Leasing, Inc., and the Beta Group, no way to prove that any financial relationship existed between Phillip Vanderlind and Averal Sutherland. Cyril Kennedy had confirmed that the $5,000,000 in Omni's bank account was legally *his*! All of it, every cent, was his to spend as he liked. He could have everything he had ever wanted. He could marry Jessica, they could live wherever they chose, do whatever they wanted. He couldn't believe it.

He got out of bed and walked slowly to the window to look out at the gray skyline of San Francisco and the sea beyond. The pain in his shoulder radiated through his body. Take the money, a part of him said. But there was another part that reminded him he could never forget where that money had come from. He could never forget Polly Savitch. He could never forget the other countless thousands of people who were destroyed by drugs because of men like Averal Sutherland—and, God help him, by men like Phillip Vanderlind. No, he couldn't take the money and spend it, not a penny of it, on himself.

And Jessica? He couldn't have her any more than he could have the money. At least not now. He knew that love, like money, can become a refuge, and he could not hope that Jessica's love alone would be enough to give an identity and purpose to his life. Who was he? Where the hell was he going? Only when he found the answers to those questions could he and Jessica . . .

Suddenly he shuddered and leaned heavily against the wall. What was he thinking of? Lost or found, Phillip Vanderlind was a felon! No less guilty than Novak or Sutherland, he had knowingly and willfully been the vital link that put forty kilos of heroin on the streets of this country. The suitcases that Cyril Kennedy had found aboard the *Spellbound* were empty. But the suitcases he had smuggled through customs and left in a hotel room in New York were not. And those two suitcases would be with him for the rest of his life.

He picked up the pad of paper, ripped off the top sheet, wadded it up and threw it in the wastebasket. Then he sat down and began another letter to Jessica.

EPILOGUE

Summer was ending in the mountains, and so was Jessica Westbrook's time there.

It had been exactly twenty-six months since Phillip Vanderlind had written her to say that he could not come to Colorado, and almost a year had passed from time she moved to Aspen with the first expansion of P.J.'s.

In a matter of days, Jessica would be traveling through Europe. How long she would remain was uncertain. Perhaps six months, a year—even longer if she chose. She was financially independent now and had no reason to clutter her life with schedules.

It was late afternoon, and looking around the living room of the pretty little Victorian house that would be rented in her absence, Jessica felt her eyes sting as she thought again about what she was leaving. She loved the mountains, but it was time to say goodbye. And, in a way, she felt she was saying goodbye to Phillip, too. Colorado was where they had happened.

Because she half expected it, Jessica had not been completely heartbroken over Phillip's decision not to come to Vail when he got out of the hospital. Believing, as he had written, that he would return to her when he felt he could, she had let the press of her new business occupy her time and thoughts. But her heart had remained empty.

Although there had been no contact between them these last two years and she didn't know where he was, Jessica had heard what Phillip was doing. Working for a private foundation involved in drug rehabilitation and combating the abuse of narcotics, he moved about the country organizing and teaching. There was a rumor that he had funded the foundation himself. She had thought so many times of trying to find him but had always decided against it. Then, less than a week ago, she had received a newspaper clipping from Frances Marsh: Phillip's foundation had recently established its headquarters in Houston in an old building on lower San Jacinto Street. The urge to contact him had been almost overwhelming the past few days. But nothing had changed: only when he was free from whatever drove him would anything be possible between them.

After a light supper that evening, Jessica took a bottle of wine and a thick file folder into the living room and began a final review of the documents for purchase and sale of P.J.'s. Phillip's brain child had prospered beyond anything she had ever imagined; there were now seven locations in as many ski resorts, and prospects were excellent for still others. Yet, when a large hotel chain had offered $1.5 million for the little company, Jessica knew it was time to sell. P.J.'s had outgrown her interest and, she felt, her ability to manage.

Final closing of the sale would occur, for tax purposes, in thirty days, but the new owners had already assumed operating responsibility. The hotel people had been pleasant to deal with. The only trouble she and her attorneys had was in persuading them to issue two checks for the purchase price: one to Jessica for $750,000 and the other to Phillip A. Vanderlind for the same amount. The fact that all of the stock was in her name had nothing to do with equitable ownership as far as Jessica was concerned. It had been Phillip's idea, Phillip's business plan, and almost half Phillip's money. On her desk was a memorandum to her attorney instructing him to forward Phillip's check, in care of the foundation, the day of the closing. Now, she was doubly glad about her trip: she didn't want the money to be the reason he called her. And by the time she returned, there would be, she hoped, other reasons for him to call.

Jessica closed the file and rested her head on her arms. The effect of reading Phillip's name over and over in the documents only reminded her of how much she still loved him. But then she raised her head. "No," she said softly to herself. She would not let something she couldn't control spoil what she had planned for herself.

Her eyes fell on the two suitcases that stood in the corner of the living room, waiting to go into storage along with her things. Both full of Phillip's clothing, they had been forwarded to her from the Omni offices in San Francisco by Phillip's former secretary, who apparently thought he was in Colorado. Well, Jessica decided as she got up and started back to the kitchen, she might as well ship them to Houston now that she knew where Phillip was. She would do it in the morning.

At the door of the kitchen she hestitated, thought for a moment, then turned and walked back to her cluttered desk. From an assortment of papers in one of the drawers she pulled out an envelope and placed it with the memorandum to the attorney for forwarding to Phillip along with the check. It was a letter from some federal official named Cyril Kennedy who explained that he was releasing from custody the two suitcases he had picked up at the Sherry-Netherland Hotel in New York.

It all seemed very odd to Jessica. But then that was Phillip's business.